A Graduate's Guide to Espionage

A satirical spy novel of questionable intelligence

Samuel Ollie

This book is dedicated to my wife and daughter for their indulgence and encouragement.

It is also for all the young people starting out in their careers. I wish you the best of luck and ask you don't be too hard on yourselves. As my father once told me: at the beginning of your career, don't stress about any task you have. If it was really important, they wouldn't have given it to you.

PROLOGUE

CONSPIRACIES AND SCREW-UPS GO HAND IN HAND.

One often leads to the other, and they are regularly confused. Correctly identifying or picking them apart when entangled, is challenging. Especially in the murky world of intelligence.

Such a problem was about to hit Andrew, a young man inside Australia's Government Intelligence Headquarters. Unaware of approaching disaster, he was, for reasons we'll get to later, waiting outside the toilets trying to think of something smart to say.

Unfortunately, nothing good was forthcoming. He was distracted – running a loop of the day's low points in his mind. This was not what he'd wanted from the very first day of what should become a shining career in government intelligence.

All his expectations had been totally upended by the bizarre and relentlessly procedural induction process. It was more bureaucracy than black ops. Not how he thought it was supposed to go at all.

And that was when one of the greatest national security threats of the modern age ran straight into him.

In intelligence work, the biggest crises often occur when you don't know what you don't know, and mistakenly assume the little you do know is everything that could possibly be.

For example, Andrew thought the morning's mix of professional embarrassment and unfulfilled expectations were the worst that could happen. However, he didn't know how bad it could actually get. Or what a modern, national security threat could look like until well after one ran into him. So that he was unaware that such things could happen – especially outside the toilets in HQ, meant he was totally unprepared when it did.

So, through a mix of naivete, misguided helpfulness and bad luck, Andrew helped a young woman called Lisa escape headquarters with stolen, classified data.

She came running out of the stairwell, right next to where he stood. He didn't have a chance of getting out of her way. She was going at the kind of speed used to commit a crime or escape one, and they collided awkwardly but without injury. Lisa took the worst of it, dropping her things and falling completely out of her heels. Andrew, terrified of another embarrassment, picked up her bag containing stolen national security information and passed it back to her. She snatched it as he attempted introductions and small talk. Fortunately for her, Andrew unthinkingly suggested something that, in her haste, she hadn't considered.

At that moment, the security alarms went off. She seized the opportunity Andrew had flagged and fled through the fire exit, triggering even more alarms and leaving him standing there – an unwitting accessory to a national security breach. She left so quickly she abandoned her heels, leaving them discarded on the floor as though she'd been suddenly pulled skyward by the rapture. Andrew frowned as he looked down at them, creeping fear and doubt slowly entering his mind as he considered the possibilities. Those abandoned shoes, and concerns about the alarms he'd thought were a drill started to break down his confidence.

The alarms summoned people from everywhere. They poured into the hallway, confused or angry, making demands or asking questions. Andrew had no idea what was going on, but was increasingly anxious that he could be involved. What's worse, he'd completely forgotten about coming up with something smart to say.

So, when the one he wanted to impress finally emerged from the toilets and into the chaos, Andrew said something monumentally stupid.

ONE

Several hours earlier

IT WAS FEBRUARY IN CANBERRA, AUSTRALIA'S MODEST AND leafy capital city – a time of resurgence. Canberra is a government town. It typically shuts down from mid-December, as summer and Christmas combine to paralyse government productivity more effectively than government ever has. The roads out to Melbourne or the East Coast clog with holiday-makers and those left behind shrug and light the barbecue. But come February, the government cycle starts anew. By this time, highway fatalities, heatwaves and the celebrations, protests and combined hangovers of Australia Day are a memory. Back to work.

Sluggish, but with an inevitable momentum, the federal machinery rumbles back into life. The city fills with bureau-crats, politicians and lobbyists. Not to mention other practitioners of the dark arts like intelligence officers, journalists and wave upon wave of consultants. Each one keen to help or hinder the current government to their advantage.

Hence, the city thronged with commuters this February morning, all trying to pass each other like rally cars. Unless physically restrained, Canberra drivers attempt speed records at every opportunity. This morning was no exception, and cars flew along arterial roads, darted through suburban shortcuts and came to a screeching dawdle at the traditional traffic jam entering the National Security Precinct. This area, outside the CBD and on the edge of Canberra's central lake, housed DAS – the Department of Australian Security – headquarters, and the greater compound. DAS – an organisation formed by Parliament by amalgamating several agencies – was the nerve centre of Australian national security. The precinct comprised several buildings, the headquarters having pride of place. Each building was surrounded by security fencing, and could only be accessed through official gates and gatehouses.

Outside the main precinct gate, Andrew Stanton clambered out of a taxi, almost catching his cheap suit jacket in the door as he shut it. He looked over the taxi's roof with a near manic grin on his face as he viewed DAS Headquarters.

It was so damn beautiful.

The sun, still low but rising into a cloudless sky, gave off a warm, comforting glow as it began peeking out above the precinct's various buildings. Jewels of dew sparkled on the barbed wire and security cameras hummed like springtime bees as they turned from side to side.

Andrew paused to enjoy the moment. The morning breeze blew cooler than he was used to back in Perth. Despite this, a trickle of sweat ran from his brow. His shirt collar was too stiff and chafed against his freshly shaved skin. The tie was an unfamiliar restriction, and he didn't wear his suit so much as stand in it. His backpack slouched over his shoulder like a passed-out toddler. It clashed with the suit. He hadn't realised until he'd looked at himself in the hotel mirror. New suit, old backpack. Although they had cost almost the same.

Too late now; he'd get something more appropriate later.

Andrew drew a deep, savouring breath, but what he inhaled was exhaust from the departing taxi. As he coughed, he wondered if it was a mistake to say where he was going. He had a secret new life, after all. That's why he hadn't used a ride-share app. Or did not using one make him look more suspicious?

Fresh from university, Andrew had been accepted into the DAS Intelligence Graduate Program. He'd listened to a speech at a careers fair by a man with no surname, representing the intelligence community. Andrew barely moved as the man spoke of purpose and mission. A career most would dream of. When it was over, the applause hadn't even died away as Andrew started his application process on his phone. Almost a year later, just in time for graduation, his phone shook in his hand as he read the official offer. Full of congratulations and warnings in equal measure, it said he had been accepted into the 'Analyst Stream'. He wouldn't be a field officer – no James Bond or Jason Bourne – but something else. He was going to be an intelligence *analyst*. Like, um … he tried to think of a famous analyst. They were probably too secret for that. Was that what Q did? No, he was gadgets.

No matter, this opportunity came with new and worrying security requirements. The employment offer warned him not to discuss his new employment with anyone, save close family. There was only his mum, but even she thought he was going to be doing some vaguely defined 'policy work' for the federal government. No sense worrying her after what his teen years had been like. Nothing that resulted in a permanent conviction, but far more than she ever deserved to deal with. Especially as she'd lost as much as him.

Andrew wondered if giving the taxi driver the HQ address counted as discussing his employment. Should he have walked? But what if he'd been followed? How did you pick up a tail? Is that what they called it?

These questions settled into the ordinary background noise of his mind. His heart thumped as he headed towards the gate. This was it: a short walk to career greatness. His mind wandered as he stared into the future, an excited shiver bouncing up and down his spine. His eyes watered as he looked into the reflective glow of DAS HQ's top floor windows, wondering which office window would one day be his.

'You all right?'

Andrew blinked and refocused. The swirling images in his head – career glory, matters of state, spy games – vanished. They were replaced by a security guard. His face looked about fifty, his body closer to sixty-five. His stare held eternal scepticism.

'Oh, yes!' Andrew said to the unimpressed guard. 'I'm starting my career here today. Part of the graduate intake. I'm selected for …'

He paused, unsure of what he should, or was allowed, to say. This man was definitely not family.

'Wonderful,' said the guard flatly. His name tag read simply 'Jim'. 'Wait with the others behind the yellow line in the gate-house. Someone will be along to collect you lot eventually.'

Andrew entered the gatehouse. In reality, it was a small building serving as a gateway through the outer security fence and into the open space and complexes beyond. It housed a few security guards, a waiting area, and a series of security gates to let people in and out. As he walked in, Andrew was mildly appalled that he wasn't the first to arrive. His movie-based fantasies popped with less fanfare than a soap bubble. How long was this going to take? Whatever happened to sweeping into a building in identical vans with black-tinted windows? Instead, the other graduates were off to the left, several young people sitting behind an airport-style queue divider. It was an anxious yellow, as though they were suspicious packages, isolated as a precaution. Another guard sat in a security booth on the other side, staring down at a row of monitors. Andrew mumbled hello to the group as he sat in the only free spot left. The replies were similarly awkward, except for one young man.

'Good morning,' he said, with loud, over-caffeinated confidence. His suit, garish enough for a career in real estate, also made him stand out. But small talk wasn't needed. Official greeting delivered, his eyes darted back to his phone like everyone else.

The security gates were a row of glass panels that slid in and out of steel dividers, just like at a train station. As people entered, they showed their pass to another guard, who gave a quick nod or thanks, then swiped it on a reader before the glass. The gates beeped and swooped aside to let them continue. People had to be quick. The gates snapped back just as people got through, lest a conga-line of foreign spies tried to follow. The doors led to the outside area and other buildings. The light became dazzling as the rising sun shone straight through the entrance from the open courtyard beyond. Without his sunglasses, Andrew watched people vanish into the haze as though they were boarding an alien spaceship.

A clipboard-wielding woman emerged from the glare. She had a kind face, but a harried expression, and waved at them all.

'Grads? Sorry, graduate intake?'

Andrew leaped to his feet, thinking it was black-tinted van time.

'Yes! My name is—'

'Wonderful,' she said, cutting him off and addressing the group. 'I'm Pam, here to get you sorted, and we're in a rush! Get your ID ready and give all your details to the guard over there to get your temporary entry passes and lanyards.'

The group stared at the guard who, with a resigned sigh,

slapped a slab of forms and several pens on the counter. Then he pulled a melon-sized tangle of lanyards with rectangular passes, embossed with a 'V', out of a drawer. Both the lanyards and passes were an alarming red.

Andrew sighed. Maybe the guard was family after all.

Wonderful.

Two

On the other side of the compound and several stories up, the early sun shone through the windows of Intelligence Coordination and Response Management. The morning rays beamed on to Lisa's screen, making it unreadable. This happened daily at this time of year.

Lisa breathed out like a weightlifter. Not that she'd ever be likely to compete. She was skinny with long black hair, an Irish complexion lightly dusted with freckles, and an intense stare for one so young.

All right, now or never. She looked around. Just her, plus Darren on the other side of the room. The others would wander in after nine, coffee in hand. Darren, on the other hand, was always in so early they'd surreptitiously searched his desk for a sleeping bag. IT Support also ran on a relaxed schedule and would be a skeleton crew right now. Her stomach churned. She looked down and focused on unclenching her hands.

Show time. She was about to risk a lifetime in jail, or worse. First step was the easy part; break the computer.

Anyone who has worked in an office knows that IT failures

are common and ill-timed. But what Lisa needed was a specific failure at a specific time. She needed her whole account to go down. Right now.

It was simple enough to break a program or two, but to cripple her whole user account was surprisingly tricky. As all IT administrators believe, the most dangerous part of a computer setup is the fleshy thing in the chair. If you don't do your best to user-proof your system, they'll wreck it clicking some stupid link or deleting a vital system file. The answer is to tighten permissions, reduce access and make it as hard as possible for users to delete, change or grant access to anything. If literally left to their own devices, users are unintentional saboteurs.

Except for Lisa. She was the intentional kind.

She'd studied the IT. From the operating system to the hardware, to the programs they ran and how often patches were deployed. Fortunately for her, this was a government network and therefore only properly upgraded every third or fourth election. In fact, the previous year's graduate intake had to be retrained because no one that young knew how to use the ancient version of windows still loaded. It was the computer equivalent of asking someone to use a medieval forge or cotton-spinner.

So, to come up with a convincing outage, Lisa researched weaknesses and flaws she could exploit by digging through IT Support blogs and videos. This wasn't hacking, it was troubleshooting in reverse. By discovering the mistakes people made that caused issues, she could, in theory, now cause one whenever she wanted.

Her research had been successful, and her planned approach was simple enough. She'd found a weakness that involved moving a few key files, plus a few other shifty manoeuvres that should result in a corrupted system when restarted. The perfect thing to make an IT professional rebuild the account rather than try to fix it.

Lisa did as planned, then held her breath as she rebooted the PC. She'd tried doing this the week before and it had worked then. She'd had to go down to IT Support so they could rebuild her account and that was exactly what she needed now. Hopefully, they hadn't fixed the system's weakness since then.

She was in luck and smiled in relief when rewarded with a garbled error message that vanished to a black screen featuring just a blinking cursor.

Nailed it. It would have been far easier to throw a coffee over the PC tower, but she couldn't be that obvious and didn't need to start a fire.

For the next step, she smashed out a short staccato of key tapping before giving a loud, annoyed groan. She stopped the feigned typing and leaned back in her chair.

'Dammit!' she yelled.

'Geez,' Darren called out. 'What's the story?'

Lisa stood up, rolling her eyes.

'I can't believe it. My entire account corrupted again!'

'Again?' asked Darren.

'Totally.'

'Didn't you sort that last week?' he asked, unthinkingly referring to Lisa's rehearsal.

'Yes!' Lisa snapped back at him. She wondered if that was too much. Darren just grinned. He was ex-army after all. He always enjoyed playfully stoking someone's annoyance and tended not to hear much below a scream.

'So, what has to happen?' he asked.

'Got to rebuild my account. They can't do it from here. I'll have to go down to IT Support.'

'Hah! Good luck.'

Lisa's smile vanished as Darren turned away. She leaned down under her desk and pulled out an opaque Tupperware box. Her knuckles were almost the same white as the plastic.

'If anyone asks, back soon.'

Darren waved without turning around. 'I'm not your boss.'

Lisa walked down the corridor and took the lift down to sub-basement one. Down here, the fluorescent lights were cheap and harsh, yellowing the otherwise cream-painted halls.

Making sure she was alone, Lisa paused. Shifting the box as needed, she wiped her damp hands on her top. She felt her heart drumming as she flicked her hair out of her eyes and resumed heading down the corridor. A sign on the wall stated the IT Service Centre was a swipe-access door off to the left.

Inside was a waiting room and service counter you could look over to the cubicle farm beyond. The few people currently in were deeply focused on their screens. Joke posters and memes plastered the walls. One caught Lisa's eye: 'You have been exposed to classified material. Destroy yourself immediately'. On the far side of the counter sat a fake grenade, a jaunty red '#1' label hanging off the pin. A sign below it said: 'Please take a number!'

Instead, Lisa pressed the buzzer on the counter labelled 'service'. A doorbell chime sang out and a red light flickered in the centre of the ceiling.

'Oh, hi Lisa,' said a guy looking up from his screen. His eyes twinkled as he stood up and walked over. 'What have you broken now?'

'I broke nothing, Sunil. Your crappy system corrupted itself again. I need to rebuild my account.'

'Account rebuild? Ooh, that's—'

'Jason's problem. Yes, I remember. Can I go in and see him?'

'Logged a job in the system yet?'

Lisa tapped the top of the package.

'I can't wait for all that. I've logged a bunch of brownies. Baked last night. Please take some or I'll eat them all and hate myself.'

'Well …' he said. 'Just to help you. Go on.'

Lisa walked through the door next to the counter. Jason was further back, also lost in his screen. She waved at him until he surfaced and explained her issue. He rolled his eyes but opened the account management system and began tapping away, all with the typical cultish muttering and sighs that IT experts use to invoke 'The Fixing'. He paused and frowned as he found her account in the system.

'Wow,' he said. 'Something's really screwed up there.'

'Oh yeah,' said Lisa. 'Total rebuild needed.' She followed that up with a few lies and pled general ignorance on how it happened. 'Just gremlins in the machine, probably.'

'All right, I'll just run the rebuild,' grumbled Jason.

Lisa nodded sympathetically as he resumed muttering. On the screen, windows and commands flashed up and away as Jason flicked them around like a croupier dealing at a casino.

'Right,' he said eventually. 'Rebuild almost done. Just need to set your permissions and password.'

His chair gave a plastic creak as he got up and gestured to the keyboard.

'Set a new password, please.'

Lisa sat down and paused.

'Sorry,' she said, 'do you mind?'

'Oh! Of course not,' said Jason, looking away.

Lisa drummed her fingers on the desk. 'I hate coming up with new passwords. I'm sorry, could you give me a sec to think? Tell you what – I left brownies out the front. Have as many as you want.'

He looked unsure, so Lisa upped the ante. 'Sunil was scoffing them all. Better be quick.' Her eyes flicked to his desk, littered with online gaming figurines. 'Plus,' she gambled, 'he was talking about thrashing you in some game.'

'Oh, was he?' said Jason, eyes narrowing. 'Think I need a sugar hit to sort him out.'

Once alone, Lisa focused on the screen. This was the core software for creating and managing accounts. IT help are like cleaners – they have keys to everything. She navigated to the permissions tab of her account:

User: Chapman, Lisa, ID#61115
Permissions: L4-coord.
Data Transfer Rights: Nil.

This was the default. For obvious reasons, people in DAS weren't allowed to transfer data off-system willy-nilly. Lisa's heart beat faster. She heard Jason and Sunil bickering with the low-intensity endurance of a married couple settling in for the evening.

She switched 'Nil' to 'All Systems', then checked a long list of security access types. She probably needed them all to get what she was after. A fresh pop-up appeared:

DATA TRANSFER AND SECURITY RIGHTS ARE RESTRICTED.

ENTER ADMIN PASSWORD TO CONTINUE.

Lisa silently cursed. She hadn't thought of this.

Her eyes flicked up. Jason stepped away from his conversation and began heading back. Her stomach flipped. Sunil, smiling, called something out to him. Jason spun on his heel and sprayed crumbs in response.

Lisa forced her eyes back down again. Don't waste time watching them! She looked around. This place wasn't glamorous. Most of the team were filling in time until they got a better job. Lots of turnover. Which could make people sloppy with passwords. She chewed her lip and tried to ignore her twisting stomach.

Slow as a texting grandparent, she typed:

A-D-M-I-N

Accepted.

Yes! She breathed out and her stomach loosened just a notch.

'Oi!' yelled Jason. 'You done yet?'

'Just about!'

Lisa typed in the same password she already had (plus a '1' for variety), just as Jason waved her over. She flicked the main screen back up again and bounced out of the chair.

'Thanks guys,' she said, snagging the box as she passed Jason and Sunil. '*Such* a big help. Have an extra brownie.'

THREE

Outside, Pam led Andrew and the other grads through the main gate and towards the central and largest building. Their unfamiliar passes bounced around their necks, signalling their low status. The communist shading meant they were visitors and couldn't be trusted. Reds weren't allowed to walk around without an official escort in this high-security environment; they had to be under the watchful eye of a fully inducted employee. Their passes shone with a background of Australian gold.

At the headquarters, two large sliding doors eased apart and exposed the main DAS foyer.

There were more train station–style gates to the right, only these had extra features. People placed their palm on a glass panel, tapped a number on a keypad and looked into a scanner. A digital voice would then say 'access granted' and the doors would swing open. If anything wasn't done properly, the voice gave a robotic apology and refused to open the gates.

Pam led them to yet another security desk.

'Attention, everyone!' she called out. 'Please go to the desk for further security screening.'

Another guard regarded them with professional but bored eyes. He pinched his nose and sighed. In his right hand, he raised a laminated poster. It had simple icon-style pictures. Phones, cameras and USBs were most prominently displayed and covered with forbidding red slashes. There was even a black, circular bomb with a lit fuse, the sort of thing used by a cartoon coyote.

The guard interrupted Andrew's thoughts with a prepared speech. He delivered it in the monotone of one who'd given it thousands of times.

'Please pay attention – this information is for your safety and others. This facility is the property of the Australian government. Due to the classified nature of the building, the following items are forbidden inside.'

The guard took a deep breath. The sign wobbled in his grip. Andrew and the rest of the grads leaned back as the guard ran through the endless list of forbidden items. All electronic, someone had started the list in the 1960s and added to it as technology evolved. It started with cameras, then pagers, and moved on to every recording or transmitting device ever invented. Andrew and the grads felt the technology timeline wash over them. Phones, Furbies (whatever they were), Fitbits, all forbidden. No devices. Got it. The message was clear: the twenty-first century was to remain outside.

As the list came to a droning finish, the guard paused. Andrew hoped it wasn't for applause. This wasn't the adrenaline pumping entrance he'd been expecting.

'Do you have any of these items?' asked the guard.

There were various clunks and fumbling as people produced phones, smart watches, plus one wallet with integrated USB and a hairbrush with a GPS tracker.

The guard sighed and waved them towards the wall where rows of tiny white numbered lockers stood. Each was twenty centimetres high and ten across. There must have been a hundred of them in total. The majority were already occupied.

'Please place all phones, USBs or other electronic devices in the lockers provided. You may be subject to random personal searches when inside.'

Andrew looked at the unhappy faces around him as they were forced to part with their beloved devices.

He experienced at least three stages of grief as he put both his watch and phone in the locker.

'Sorry,' Pam told the group. 'But every modern convenience is a security threat.'

Satisfied they'd been stripped of threatening conveniences, the guard pressed a hidden button and a wide glass gate opened. The grads followed Pam through and down a bland hallway that opened up into a grand space. It was similar to a corporate foyer Andrew had seen when he was a child visiting his father at work. He'd worked at an aeronautics company, with an old jet engine on display in reception. But here there were bits of intelligence memorabilia encased behind perspex on custom-built stands. Typed top-secret messages alerting the government to developments in World War II. A German Enigma machine; a listening device in a packet of cigarettes; black-and-white surveillance photos of serious-looking men meeting without looking at each other. There were also notices and security posters saying things like: 'Insider Threat: Don't Turn Your Back. Report It' and 'Presentation Nominations Now Open for the Intelligence Futures Conference! Show How Your Area Is Defining the Future of Intelligence!'

They were escorted to large double wooden doors marked 'Main Auditorium'. At the press of a button, they opened with smooth, pneumatic confidence. Andrew and his fellow graduates shuffled in, exchanging silent glances and nervous smiles. Pam waved them in, but remained outside.

'Take the seats down the front. Brian will be along shortly,' she called out.

Once inside, the grads gawked like pilgrims at the Vatican. The empty auditorium stretched away, silent and clean. The only breaks in the minimalist style were a projector and a lighting rig jutting from the otherwise blank ceiling.

Andrew's pulse quickened. He was warm in his polyester suit. He selected a seat three rows from the front. It was a dull blue with a foldable bottom that sprang back up when empty. It *thunk*ed as he lowered it and settled down.

While the others made hesitant small talk, Andrew studied the stage. The room curved and dipped towards it. A wooden lectern with the crest of the Commonwealth was centre stage. Four Australian flags stood either side.

Who decided four? wondered Andrew.

A man entering the room snapped him out of his reverie. With a grey suit and an occupied expression, he didn't acknowledge anyone as he headed towards the stage. Instead, he walked with measured and unhurried steps, like an aloof sort of priest entering the church. He was here to do God's work while staring down from the pulpit.

Because of his careful approach, most of the chattering grads didn't notice him until he got up onto the stage. Silence spread like a spilled drink as he approached the lectern.

'Good morning everyone and congratulations on being selected for the Department of Australian Security, the multi-disciplinary hub for Australia's Defence, intelligence and law enforcement efforts.'

His tone was flat and businesslike. Andrew mentally tagged him as Intro-bot. He suspected he had only said good morning because it was in his notes.

'Any questions?'

A forest of hands went up.

'Good, please keep them until notified otherwise. I would

like to open with the safety aspect of the talk. This to ensure your well-being and the protection of government property in an emergency.'

He frowned and re-examined his notes.

'Apologies. *Unlikely* emergency. This is the alert you must respond to.'

Two shrill horn blasts rang out, followed by a recorded voice. Andrew recognised it from fire drills at uni. The tone of voice always struck him as disturbingly upbeat, as though it was announcing the winner of a game show.

'Attention! Attention! This is an evacuation signal! Please leave the building in an orderly manner!'

'If this occurs,' resumed Intro-bot, 'please secure all classified materials. This includes locking computers, collecting printed material, notes or media and locking them in a fire-resistant, class C safe. Then leave immediately via the nearest exit.'

Intro-bot cleared his throat.

'Civilian fire-fighting authorities are not security-cleared to enter this facility and cannot render assistance.'

At this, people shifted in their seats. Snatches of whispering broke out: 'They can't *what*?'.

'So, if we hear that, we have to evacuate?' Andrew called out, defying the ban on questions.

'Certainly. The building may be on fire.'

'But we have to lock up all computers, notes and media stuff first?'

'Certainly. The building may *not* be on fire. We must never forget information security. Left unguarded, anyone in here could see it.'

* * *

Back upstairs in Intelligence Coordination and Response, Lisa resumed her seat and took a deep breath. As she breathed out, she willed her heart rate to ease. Despite the chill of the ever-present air conditioning, sweat beaded on her forehead.

She opened her computer and logged into the usual systems. No need to raise any flags with unusual activity. Yet. To be honest, she had no idea how quickly they could pick up on things, but it paid to be careful. She got her chance when the morning caffeine craving kicked in and emptied the room. Regular as clockwork.

'Want me to grab you one?' called Darren as he picked up his keep cup.

'No, I'm fine, thanks.'

'Your loss.'

'All good,' she called after him.

Alone at last, Lisa mentally shook herself and opened her bottom drawer. Inside a hollowed-out lipstick was a USB stick.

She inserted it into the one permitted port on her terminal. Her heart froze as a warning sign flickered into life – 'FOR-BIDDEN DEVICE DETECTED' – but it flickered out. Her heart started again and sped to a whir. The admin privileges worked. But that would be useless if someone asked about the USB stick in her computer. She stuck a decorative Pokémon plushie in front of it. Perpetually messy, her desk didn't look any different to the casual observer, and now her crime-in-progress was hidden.

She shook her hands out and began searching for the data she was after. It had extra layers of security and was hidden away deeper in the bowels of the system. But, thanks to her research and some supplied information, she knew where to go. She found it and started the exfiltration.

'DECRYPTION AND TRANSFER BEGINNING' flashed up onscreen, along with an hourglass icon that rotated with glacial slowness.

Typical. Why did she have to have the slowest computer in the building? She hadn't realised it was a two-stage process, decrypting the information and then copying it. But having the information was no good if she couldn't read it, she'd have to wait. But that gave her extra time for a side project.

It was too late to worry about digital fingerprints now. It would all be out soon. She opened the main intelligence database and began typing.

The office was quiet as she searched. Her frown deepened as she worked.

Lisa, a habitual chewer, raised an already savaged pen to her mouth. The gnawed end of the cap fell from her mouth and bounced, unnoticed, off the keyboard and onto the floor.

'What the fuck?' she muttered.

Four

'ANY QUESTIONS?'

At the induction, Andrew shifted in his seat. He blinked as he tried to refocus on the stage. The auditorium was pleasantly warm and the speeches surprisingly dull. The grads had sat through a couple of speakers so far, all with a clear license to bore. One truism Andrew was already learning about intelligence work was there was a lot of paperwork. His eyes watered with the effort of fighting a rising yawn. In an act of mercy, the latest speaker on stage closed their presentation. On the screen behind them, a PowerPoint slide titled 'Legislation: Know Your Limits' winked out.

Intro-bot was sitting by the stage as though he'd been left plugged in to recharge. He rose with unnerving smoothness and made his way up onto the stage.

'Thank you very much,' he said. 'An important and timely introduction to the legal constraints under which we work. And now, our next speaker.'

He gestured stiffly to a man who was now standing by the edge of the stage. Andrew leaned forward. He hadn't seen or heard him come in and could have entered via an air duct for all he knew. The man was old by Andrew's standards – at least fifty. He had snow-white hair, glasses and a moderate frame that hinted at an ongoing war between the competing loves of rich food and cycling.

But unlike the earlier guests, who smiled and beamed positivity, he looked dour and unimpressed. He was like a young boy stuffed into a suit for church when he wanted to be in shorts, jumping in puddles or riding his bike somewhere dangerous. He climbed the stairs as slowly as someone accepting an award on behalf of a hated rival.

'Peter has had a very long and distinguished career in intelligence,' commented Intro-bot. 'We are all very lucky that he is here today.'

Andrew paused for a moment. There was something about that sentence that hinted at a threat, but he couldn't be sure.

On stage, Intro-bot continued with the passive-aggressive introduction. 'Despite his busy analytical schedule,' he said, 'he will be the main coordinator for graduate activities. He will facilitate your work area placements and assist with your ongoing learning and development projects. I strongly encourage you to heed his example.'

Again, Andrew wondered if he was listening to unthinking word choice, or carefully considered hostility.

Peter, still walking as if against a hurricane, arrived at the lectern, and Intro-bot paced off to a chair at the side of the stage. Peter looked around for a few seconds, just longer than necessary. He regarded the crowd critically, almost daring them to speak first.

'Who are you?' he said at last to the room at large.

Andrew scanned the crowd and noted others doing the same. He straightened up in his seat.

'The plain fact is you don't know, but you will. You will be intelligence analysts – like me.'

He let this sink in for a few seconds.

'It is your job to take all available information, classified or public knowledge, and objectively analyse it to present assessments or recommendations to decision makers. Intelligence is not what handlers bring in from their sources. It isn't what is intercepted by billion-dollar satellites. All that is information. You make it intelligence by taking that information and providing the value of human insight. You tell people what it *means*.'

Peter stepped out from behind the lectern and leaned on its edge. The microphone gave a metallic creak as he twisted it around so he could still be heard.

'Someone makes a phone call saying they are going to blow up Parliament. Is that intelligence?'

A few hands went up with varied enthusiasm. Andrew saw another grad three rows down sitting bolt upright in his seat, vibrating hand straining to the ceiling. It was the extrovert he'd met in the guardhouse – the one who looked like a dodgy real estate agent who'd charge you extra for asbestos.

However, lounging like a chat show host, Peter ignored him and the other raised hands.

Andrew cleared his throat, louder than intended.

'Uh, no?' he called out. 'You don't know much about them?'

'Correct! We know very little. Will this actually happen? Are they reliable? Who are they? Do they regularly blow up Parliament? So many other questions to ask first.'

Andrew's face reddened as people looked at him. The keen guy three rows down slowly lowered his hand.

'We are not spies,' continued Peter. 'They lie for a living. We are analysts – we tell the truth. We must give our best assessments of what is happening and what will happen – no matter how ugly or inconvenient. We face many challenges including new, disruptive technology and evolving networks of overlapping terrorism, criminality and espionage.'

He paused and ran a hand along his brow.

'Our major enemy, however, is complexity. It is your job to evaluate an increasingly complex world with less and less certainty. You will make judgements that impact on government resources, our reputation and even people's lives.'

'And don't worry about being wrong,' he added. 'You will be. Thank you.'

He gave a tradesman's smile signifying a job done and nodded. Without waiting for applause, he turned and walked off-stage.

The crowd looked around at each other. Real Estate Guy began clapping even before Intro-bot, although Intro-bot appeared less enthused and clapped like a dying toy. Peter shot him a dark look as he walked past and straight to the exit.

Intro-bot seemed to ignore him, but stopped clapping once Peter was out of sight. Continuing his oddly precise lines, he got up and walked to the lectern.

'Many thanks,' he said. 'Truly an expert on the pitfalls of intelligence.'

Andrew felt the barb in that last remark and wondered if he only said it because Peter was safely out of the room by then. But it was interesting to see a glimmer of personality at last. Perhaps there was hope for the robot after all.

He was snapped out of his daydream by an 'Ahem!' from the lectern.

'We have one more guest before morning tea,' said Intro-bot, primly hinting at luxuries others had only dreamed of.

Andrew craned around to look for the next speaker. They'd come in the same double doors up the back the grads had used. He saw a late middle-aged man with salt and pepper hair and a minor entourage, waiting in the aisle just down from the doors. They must have arrived during Peter's stilted applause. Andrew couldn't remember hearing the door.

He stared at the closest new arrival. His dress code was

expensive casual – the exquisitely informal look a successful male entrepreneur uses to show off his 'common man' credentials: A standard package of jeans (designer – $600), brown leather shoes (designer – $1,200), a plain white shirt (tailored – $400) and a relaxed dark sports jacket (also tailored – $3,000).

Next to him was a powerfully built woman of a similar age, standing as close as a bodyguard. She was dressed in a corporate and sensible grey dress, with her hair wrapped back in a sensible and immaculate bun. She held a leather folio against her stomach with both hands, a look of permanent impatience on her face. You could definitely see the athlete the man had been when he was younger, but this woman was still in the prime of her strength and could probably launch Andrew into space with an underarm throw. Next to them, and far more relaxed, was a suit-wearing man at least ten years their junior. He was leaning across a chair in a pose ready for the cover of a magazine. He too had an aura of expense and looked ready to bound over to tell you just how much money you'll save listening to his great offer. The kind of person known to commit finger guns in everyday conversation. He sat with one leg crossed over the other, displaying a trendy Italian loafer and no visible sock so that he flashed his ankle to the world like some eighteenth-century whore.

Each individual wore a security pass on an emerald green lanyard. This colour marked them not as DAS employees, but as outsiders. Albeit ones that had been welcomed in without the need to be followed at all times.

'We have here today,' said Intro-bot, making a beckoning motion, 'Roman Vortan, CEO of CMND.' He spelled out 'CMND' like a clunky AI, pausing for a beat between each letter.

As the classroom-style applause started up again, the man Andrew had been observing walked up to the stage while his entourage stayed where they were. The woman remained standing with her eyes focused on her departing boss. The younger man eased further into his chair and looked to be painfully missing his phone.

'Roman represents one of our major private sector partners helping us to develop new capabilities. He will explain how the private sector works with DAS and we are very happy to have him here today,' Intro-bot intoned.

Roman, all smiles, strode up onto the stage and gave Intro-bot a firm, double-handed handshake before taking the lectern.

'Thanks for that Brian,' he said, apparently briefed on Intro-bot's name. 'It's a real honour to be here today.'

He spoke with a pleasant American accent and all the confidence that went with it.

'So, as you just heard, I'm an arms dealer,' he said brightly.

There were a few double-takes and blinks in the room as the grads digested that. Up the back, the flashy suit noisily cleared his throat, trying to dislodge a poor choice of words.

Up on stage, Roman grinned and apologetically shrugged.

'Sorry,' he said. 'Michael – my head of sales up the back there – hates it when I go off-script. He and Talia, my executive officer, try to keep me in line. Feel free to introduce yourself to them.'

Roman pointed knife-hand style to his entourage at the back of the room. He had his palm side on, all four fingers extended, and the thumb crooked on top. As people twisted in their seats to stare, Michael waved, as if doing so from a neigh-bouring yacht. Talia, on the other hand, broke one hand away from the leather binder and stiffly displayed a broad palm.

'Truth is' continued Roman, 'my company works with government and private sector clients to develop cyber and information operation capabilities, while also securing our own infrastructure and narrative priorities. Is that better?' he said, addressing the last part to the back of the room. Michael the head of sales, again pleased to be the focus of the room's attention, smiled for an invisible camera and gave an exaggerated thumbs-up. There were a few light chuckles at this improvised bit of pantomime and Roman kept going.

'Or more succinctly,' he said, 'my company, and many others working with DAS and allied partners, are fighting what people call the information contest. But contest is just another word for war.'

Andrew could have sworn he heard another minor coughing fit from the back of the room, but Roman carried on regardless.

'New technology, changed communication models and sheer availability of data has utterly re-shaped the information environment,' he said.

An excited chill ran down Andrew's spine as he imagined the powerful shifts Roman spoke of. The rest of the room appeared equally rapt. Except for Intro-bot. As for each presentation, he was seated back off to the side with a neutral 'update in progress' expression.

'But this is just the beginning,' said Roman.

He let that sink in for a few seconds. No one said anything.

'At the start it was like World War Two air power – only if every country in Europe had an air force with millions of planes. Imagine all of them on the internet! Bot bombers droning back and forth to drop their narrative payloads. So, what's next? Where are the smart missiles? The space-based weapons and the asymmetric tactics that will rule the information space? Thanks to AI, scale and mass effort aren't special anymore. Anyone can spin up a hundred thousand bots to praise someone or cancel someone else. Especially as AI lets anyone generate almost any content they want. So, in my not so humble opinion, the future will belong to those who can bring finesse and tactics to a bot and AI battlefield where soldiers die by the second and are replaced by the thousand. It's about nuance and knowing your outcomes.'

Andrew had seen plenty of arguments and online fights in his time, but he'd never imagined a war. He'd come back to group chats that had melted down while he'd been working. Formerly friendly spaces now filled with destroyed relationships, strewn emotional wreckage and passive-aggressive final posts. But all that paled in comparison to what Roman was talking about. He imagined all this happening at the nation-state level. Probably lots of sarcastic back and forth like 'SORRY your elections collapsed', and 'Yeah? I'm SUPER HAPPY "someone's" supporting your violent revolutionaries. BTW here's a picture of your allies cheating on you.'

Meanwhile, Roman took on a more jovial persona as he headed into traditional cyber-territory.

'Then there's data,' he said, 'and we've never had more of it.'

Some definite nods in the crowd.

'Most people's browser knows more about them than DAS ever will,' said Roman. 'And even the people who are less public online are still spending more time online in total. They are still consuming, sharing and, most importantly, generating data.'

Roman stopped briefly and leaned on the lectern, as if to whisper some super-hot gossip to you alone. Andrew could have sworn he heard one or two seats lightly creak as others in the crowd leaned forward as well.

'Information.' said Roman flatly. 'Democracies want to debate it. Dictatorships want to control it. Corporations want to sell it, but smart people like you and I? We want to use it. For so many things people haven't even imagined yet. And that's what makes this space so exciting. That's why we are working with DAS, to bring our complementary skills and capabilities to this area. Any questions?'

A forest of hands shot up, Andrew's included.

Roman smiled at the enthusiastic response. 'I should point out,' he said, 'that we're a private company and aren't an option for the DAS graduate program work area rotations. But we look forward to working with at least some of you when further into your career.'

The forest of hands dropped.

Roman didn't get any further into questions as his slot must have been finished. Some internal timer triggered Intro-bot to power up and walk to the lectern while initiating the clap protocol.

Against the applause, noticeably stronger than for other speakers, Intro-bot endured another double-handshake and took the lectern.

'Thank you very much Roman,' he said, in a tone that sounded more memorised than warm. 'Here at DAS we strongly value our private sector relationships and all you bring. We appreciate the time taken from your busy schedule.'

Roman waved and headed off the stage. He swept past Andrew and the other grads to where the sentient suit and executive golem were waiting. They fell into formation behind him, and the trio strode out the door, leaving Andrew to wonder about how hard it would be to move into the private sector.

FIVE

THE EXCITEMENT GENERATED BY THE LAST TWO SPEAKERS was short-lived. By the time Andrew turned around, Intro-bot had resumed his post at the lectern.

Waiting until he had complete silence and watchful attention, Intro-bot spoke up.

'That is all for this session. Please head out into the foyer where morning tea has been provided.'

Andrew rolled his eyes at being forced to wait for the refreshments announcement, but got up with everyone else. Seats 'thunked' and bumped as people got up, stretched and headed into the aisles.

The grads filtered out of the door into the foyer. A table nearby held the traditional selection of carefully arranged drinks, sweets, fruit and mystery sandwiches that keep you guessing until the very end. To Andrew's young eyes it looked amazing until he tried to figure out what was actually in everything.

Andrew stood by the food and tried to look busy and efficient while holding a tiny oozing sandwich between finger and thumb. He looked around the room. At the other end of the table, he recognised a loud jacket, then the young man in it. Real Estate Man. He'd obviously gotten over being ignored by Peter and was chatting at a grad who had a slightly stunned expression. Suddenly he clapped them on the arm and looked away, right at Andrew.

Damn, thought Andrew. Overdressed turned his attention back to the guy he had trapped and made his goodbyes. Turning on his heel, he bore down on Andrew. He strode with purpose and held out his spare hand before even reaching him. The other one held a plate covered in fruit.

'Hi, I'm Liam. It's great to meet you,' he said. His enthusiasm shone through.

'Uh, I'm Andrew. How are you?'

'Wonderful, thanks for asking. It's pretty exciting, isn't it?'

Andrew nodded and took a bite of fish sandwich. Fish? Chicken, maybe. Or an outside chance it was some sort of flavoured tofu.

Liam took the opportunity to take a bite of watermelon, and they stood in silence for a few seconds. Andrew's mind spun as he tried to think of an opener, but Liam suddenly fired questions at him like a machine gun.

Where did Andrew come from? What was his background? Who did he know here? Both in the building and in town generally? Could anyone help them with connections? Did Andrew have good networks?

Andrew's stammered his mostly negative answers in the small windows Liam left before firing off a fresh question.

Apparently satisfied that Andrew had said all he could, Liam followed with his own credentials. He approached conversation like an ancient martial art – all sudden strikes in between formal greetings. His father was a 'very connected individual' and Liam was the same. He knew someone at the Minister's office already. Did Andrew? No problem! Always happy to help. On the fast track you know. He lectured

Andrew on his time at university and his influence in the student council. He had been on the board of several societies. Always keen for a development opportunity! Now he was a volunteer for two think tanks and considering a Masters to complement his Honours degree.

Andrew bobbed like a cork in rapids. He nodded and made affirming noises as he felt was appropriate.

'So that's the lot,' said Liam finally. 'Now to make sure I'm in.'

'Aren't you already in?'

'Yes, but not *in* in. That's how you go up.'

Liam leaned in conspiratorially.

'Then you could even move *on*. In a lucrative way, of course. Promotion. What's the point otherwise?'

Andrew, flailing, nodded at this. Promotion was important. He had thought he was keen and ready for the challenge, but this guy was an education in himself. He cleared his throat.

'But what about the job itself? Have you heard what we're actually going to be doing?'

'I'm more focused on overseeing expertise than providing it. Management approaches, that sort of thing.'

Andrew raised a finger, an unfortunate habit that told salespeople and lecturers they were about to be questioned. 'So, what about extracurricular?' said Liam to cut him off. 'Have you been on any boards or committees?'

Andrew's finger dropped as he searched for an example. 'I was the treasurer of my ultimate frisbee club for a semester? Don't really know anyone in a minister's office.'

Liam's smile set slightly.

'Got to keep networking, you know,' he said brightly. 'Really important to make sure people know you. Great to meet you!'

He patted Andrew on the arm and oiled over to a woman

agonising over her next snack. She leaned back as Liam leaned in with his hand outstretched.

Andrew enjoyed the solitude for a moment and took a deep breath. He let it out as he looked around. All the grads were energetically discussing something.

Confidence. That was the key. He considered Liam. His dad had warned him about guys like that years ago.

'Why do I have to worry about them?' he'd asked.

'Because you'll wind up working for them.'

No, he was not falling behind this early. Liam was too much, but the confidence didn't hurt.

He hadn't understood at the time, but had a better idea now. Or so he thought. It's an age-old rule of parenting that children will take away the wrong lesson. Andrew's father wanted to warn him about ruthless and untrustworthy corporate climbers. Andrew missed this and, thinking about his own status, merely learned those were the people who got promoted.

It was worth a shot. Time to make the most of his sudden education. He looked at the others. Groups of three to five, talking, or eating so they didn't have to talk. There were a few outliers. One of them was a young woman sitting with the air of an old guard in an art gallery. She was staring off into the distance, having perfected the art of boredom around everyone else's enthusiasm.

He finished his sandwich and headed over, hand outstretched.

'Hi,' he said. She shook her head and refocused, previously unaware of him. 'I'm Andrew. How are you finding it?'

'I'm Shanti,' she said, hesitantly shaking his hand. She had several bangles that clashed and sang as they shook. 'But I'm not—'

'Oh sure', he interrupted, borrowing from the Liam school of air-strike networking. 'It's a lot to take in, I know. But don't worry, you'll get the hang of it in no time. This is quite a' – he paused – 'uh, development opportunity.'

Shanti stared at him through narrowed brown eyes and a politely restrained expression that wouldn't last long.

Andrew looked at her properly for the first time. A few inches shorter than he, she stared up at him as if annoyed he couldn't do the homework she'd set. Her long hair was black but shaded to brown closer to the bottom. It was gathered into a wild ponytail that rested over her right shoulder. He fumbled for another Liam-ism.

'Do you know anyone in the Minister's office?'

'No,' she said simply.

'No problem,' he replied. 'I know someone if you need a contact. Well, I know someone who knows someone. You know how networking works.'

'Sure,' she said. 'But if you'll excuse me, I'm on next.'

With a sinking heart, Andrew realised what was missing: a visitors pass. She had the gold ID on her belt.

She looked around the room and waved an arm.

'Hello?' she called out. 'Sorry, but if everyone could head back in by half past, that would be great. I'll be leading you through the next session.'

SIX

ANDREW HUNCHED IN HIS SEAT THROUGHOUT SHANTI'S session. His arms stayed by his side as if stapled. On stage, she spoke of her experiences since joining DAS three years earlier. The presentation was titled 'A Day in the Life of an Intelligence Analyst'. Record keeping was paramount. It seemed to involve recording all your activity around reviewing other people's activity. That way, if questions were asked later, someone could review your activity to ensure you had reviewed other people's activity appropriately. Shanti hit the end of her prepared remarks, punctuated by the 'Questions?' slide behind her.

'One last, important thing,' she said, 'is integrity.'

Andrew tried not to roll his eyes – she'd probably spot him.

'We all want to prove ourselves,' said Shanti. 'But be humble. In our work, honesty is essential. If you don't know something, ask. If you're unsure, say so. If you don't think the boss wants to hear it, say it anyway. Don't get someone hurt because you didn't want to look stupid. People depend on us.'

'Yes, *thank you*, Shanti,' said Intro-bot loudly – she appeared to have gone beyond her time slot. He got to his feet and walked to the lectern, clapping like a teacher to get everyone in class started.

'I'd like to take this opportunity to thank Shanti for giving us her time,' he said to the crowd. 'She's one of our bright young stars who means so much to the organisation.'

Andrew, remembering himself, hurriedly joined in the smattering of applause. Liam clapped the loudest. Because of course he did, thought Andrew.

'Okay,' said Intro-bot. 'We need to escort you back to the front gate so you can go to lunch. Many apologies, but until you have permanent passes, we can't have you walking around the place with no control. We have security for a reason.'

* * *

Meanwhile, at her computer, Lisa raised the data transfer window, previously hidden behind a mind-numbing training course on cyber security.

Transfer 98% complete.

At bloody last.

Transfer 99% complete. 'Aw, come *on* you bloody thing!'

'What?' called Darren, who'd been absorbed in emails. 'You watching a race or something?'

'Sorry!' she called out. 'Just got something to work here.'

'Definitely a reason to celebrate.'

Transfer 100% complete. The data alert flashed blue and white with its confirmation.

Holy crap, she thought. This is it. I've done it.

With trembling fingers she reached out and moved the plushie she had sitting in front of her computer stack. The USB stuck slightly and had to be wiggled free. The scrape of plastic and metal seemed to echo around the room, but no one else seemed to notice. Time to finish it.

She stuffed the USB in her bag and stood up so fast the chair jumped up and skidded across the carpet.

'Seriously?' said Darren. 'You break something again?'

'Sorry,' she repeated. 'But I just remembered I've got to go. I'm going to be late.'

Fighting the urge to break into a sprint, she headed out of the room, slinging the bag over her shoulder.

After a minute or two, Darren wandered past Lisa's desk on a journey to the printer.

In government facilities, it's common security practice to lock your screen every time you walk away from your computer. It's seen as a way of stopping traitors or the terminally nosey.

If one were to come across an unattended, unlocked screen, it was previously tradition to craft loving or hateful emails to unsuspecting third parties. That was stamped out as it started too many feuds or affairs. Then a new calorific incentive was developed: Breach Cake. If one of your team saved you from a security breach, you owed the entire team a cake. It worked. Nothing makes colleagues watch each other like the potential of winning the professional high ground and some chocolate sponge.

Darren leaned on the desk as he looked at the screen. The flashing transfer notification reflected in his glasses.

* * *

Downstairs, Intro-bot intercepted Shanti as the grads packed up.

'Just before you go back, please escort this lot back to the front.'

'Me? But I've got a meeting to get to,' said Shanti.

'Wonderful, thanks,' said Intro-bot. 'You really are a leader.'

Shanti bit down on her response and glared as Intro-bot glided away with the joy of an annoying task well dodged. Andrew, overhearing this, watched him disappear out the door. Job done, he imagined Intro-bot being dismantled like a vacuum cleaner and stored in a cupboard somewhere. Shanti, meanwhile, resigned to her fate, waved the grads over to her.

'Listen up! It may take a while to sign you out, so how about we do bathroom breaks now?'

She led them out of the auditorium and along a corridor past the main stairs. Everyone went to the appropriate door as fast as dignity allowed. Shanti looked around.

'Look,' she said to Andrew, 'are you going in?'

He shook his head.

'Great. Can you just stay here please? When they come out, make sure they don't wander off. Understand? No one walks off!'

Andrew smiled and nodded. She turned in a ponytail swirl and vanished into the toilets.

After their first conversation, he was saying nothing to Shanti for fear of making things worse. Now he had a moment to craft something smart to say. But an alarm startled him out of this dream.

Whoop! Whoop!

Strange, he thought. That wasn't the fire alarm.

He turned to the sound of heels clattering on stonework. A young woman came flying around the last corner of the steps and, while trying to stop in time, fell almost directly into his arms. He caught her, barely keeping balance as she threatened to take them both down.

'Gotcha!'

She looked at him so ferociously he let go and backed away.

'I'm sorry, I didn't mean to scare you. It's just that I … *got* you. Caught you. You know, stopped you falling.'

'Right. Sorry,' she said, blinking.

'I'm Andrew,' he said. 'Andrew Stanton. I just started here today. Grad program.'

'Good for you, Andrew Stanton,' said Lisa, looking back up the stairwell. 'You know it's an evacuation. Gotta go.'

'Don't forget your bag,' said Andrew, holding up the one she'd dropped. She snatched it out of his hand, almost dislocating two of his fingers.

'There's a fire exit behind you,' continued Andrew, shaking his sore hand, 'but I don't think it's a fire drill—' It was too late. She had smashed the glass on the exit seal and vanished into the sunshine beyond.

An automated voice joined the alarms echoing through the hallway.

'Emergency! Emergency!'

'Now that's the fire alarm,' thought Andrew, remembering the induction. He walked towards the staircase. On separate steps were two modestly heeled women's office shoes. They lay forlorn, as though kicked off after a long day. Had she just run out barefoot?

Voices joined the alarms and commotion, pulling Andrew back to the corridor. Grads poured out of their respective toilets. Shanti emerged and called for calm in the hubbub.

Two security guards ran up to them. Their equipment bounced and clanged even as they stopped.

'Everybody stay where you are! We're looking for a young woman coming through here. We need to check ID.'

'Oh!' said Andrew, a chance for recognition appearing. 'I caught her! When she came off the stairs.'

The crowd turned as one to stare at Andrew. 'Which one is she?' a guard demanded, gesturing at the group as the other gabbled into his radio; *insiderinterceptednearfrontentrance* …

'None of them,' said Andrew. A pit opened up in his stomach. Under the weight of the combined stares, he found himself out of control of his tongue. He sat in the control room of his brain, mashing buttons and impotently watching as words march out unchecked. 'I caught her. Well, more helped her. Helped her with her bag. Anyway, I just showed her the exit. She's gone.'

'What?! You helped her get away?'

Andrew started mouthing like a goldfish. In his brain he'd finally found the mute button but was still working on stopping the jaw moving.

The other guard started saying something on his radio in even more of a frenzy. *Multiplesuspectspossibleaccomplice* ...

Questions and confusion filled the corridor again. Shanti stared at Andrew with her mouth open and disbelief all around her. Overhead, fresh alarms joined the banshee wail of security systems going berserk.

'Hi!' he said loudly, words returning as he caught her stare. 'Um, no grads walked away from the toilets. They're, uh, all here ...'

SEVEN

SHOUTING ORDERS ABOVE THE ALARMS, GUARDS ESCORTED the group back into the auditorium. The hallways filled with people going all directions, some leaving the building, some going back in as they remembered to lock their work away before leaving again. Every now and again, a volunteer fire warden in a coloured helmet would appear, supposedly to direct people to safety, but they had little impact.

Back in the auditorium, the grads milled around, leaned over chairs to exchange gossip or formed authoritative cliques. Excitement crackled from person to person, as in a classroom after an unexpected pet ferret escapes from someone's bag and runs around the room, setting everyone shrieking.

The chatter and excitement washed around the cold, motionless stone that was Andrew. He was only just aware of it. The commotion was far off, muffled as though by headphones. He waved off attempts to communicate. His mouth silently opened and shut as he thought. Someone with a stopwatch could have predicted his flinches as he mentally replayed letting a national security disaster run out the door.

Someone grabbed his arm – a small hand with a firm grip.

The grip switched to nails, and the world crashed back into Andrew's thoughts. It was Shanti. She mouthed something amidst the noise.

'What?' said Andrew. She looked at him. There was anger in her look, but also concern.

'What the fuck happened?'

Her face was red. Andrew guessed she didn't swear much.

'It's too late,' said Andrew. 'It's over.'

Shanti went white. The sharp grip turned to something more gentle.

'What is?'

Andrew shrugged and stared at the carpet.

'My career.'

Shanti's hold on his arm dropped. As did her jaw.

'It's just …' began Andrew. 'How is this going to look?'

Shanti's mouth snapped shut. She rolled her eyes so far back she may have glimpsed her own brain. Luckily for Andrew, she didn't have time to express herself. Fresh guards bellowed for everyone to head to a door on the far side of the auditorium.

Andrew stood, but a wall of uniform stepped in front of him. The guard was more fat than muscle, but he'd moved faster than Andrew had expected. Probably best not to test what kind of speeds he was capable of.

'Hang on,' said the guard. 'You're coming with us.'

Andrew nodded. Did he have to mention hanging?

They walked back to the main doors, where two more guards waited.

As Andrew followed his guard, the others fell in behind, forming a triangle with Andrew at the shadowed centre.

The front guard threw both doors open, and they headed into the hallway. Andrew shuffled at high speed to avoid stepping on the shiny black heels ahead or being run over from behind.

He could hear the jangle of their equipment and felt the occasional humid blast of breath, plus the unpleasantly masculine smell of someone who'd exercised, then substituted a shower with something canned and musky.

They went down a few floors. The hallways were wide and beige. There was no natural light this deep in the building. The setting became less friendly the further they went. Corporate artwork gave way to warning signs. The guard at the front opened a door, painted white to appear wooden, but it swung with a metallic finality. Andrew suspected trying to kick your way in would only send your shin out through your knee cap.

The front guard took one deft step sideways. The two behind grabbed Andrew with a shovel-sized hand under each arm and propelled him into the room.

The door clanged shut, leaving him alone in a glaringly white space. There was a single desk and two cheap plastic chairs – the sort used by demoralised school children. Andrew sat in the nearest one. His heart hammered in his chest. He shifted about in his seat as previously ignored sensations made themselves known. His stomach was churning, his throat was scratchy and dry. What was worse, he really regretted not using his toilet break back at the auditorium.

The door opened behind him. He twisted around as two people entered. The first, his lead guard, ignored the chairs and glared from a chosen spot in the rear corner.

The other man was older. Smaller than the guard, but this wasn't saying much. There were tax havens smaller than that guy. Beating Andrew in height, he was built like a middle-aged lumberjack, complete with beard and ham-hock forearms. On that neck, a tie would look like stray dental floss.

He consulted a manila folder. A tattoo, something with a Celtic curl, peeked out from the edge of his rolled-up sleeve.

Andrew kept his hands on the table and tried to resist the urge to wipe them on his jacket.

The lumberjack sat down on the far side of the desk, still staring at the folder. Andrew heard a uniform creak as the guard behind him shifted.

'Hi,' said Andrew, trying to fill the silence. 'I'm not sure—'

Still reading, the man held a bratwurst finger up for silence.

Andrew obediently hushed, then wiped his hands on his jacket before remembering himself. He took a deep breath of hot, stale air, crossing his arms.

'Can I—?' Again Andrew's voice dropped as the finger rose.

The ball of sandpaper in Andrew's throat bounced again. His shirt's top button felt just tight enough to impede circulation, jugular veins drumming his pulse against the collar's hard edge.

It was probably too late to loosen anything, Andrew thought. And would it make him look guilty?

He stared at the cracked plastic clock on the wall. The seconds dragged by.

Tick ... Tick ... Tick.

'Right,' snapped the man, making Andrew jump. He looked Andrew in the eye for the first time. His stare was interested but uncaring. He'd probably stared at lots of people that way. Through a rifle scope.

'My name is James Barnold, Assistant Director Internal Security.'

Andrew nodded. 'Hi, I'm—'

'I know.'

James closed the folder and pulled out a notebook.

'Run me through exactly what happened. Leave no detail out.'

He made an attempt at a friendly smile. It didn't suit him.

Andrew went through the events in the stairwell. He spoke like someone half-remembering a joke, desperately hoping the punchline is worth it. James scribbled the whole time, dragging a cheap biro across the paper hard enough to carve his notes into the desk below. He looked up occasionally, but his face was solid stone and impossible to read.

After what felt like an eternity, Andrew trailed off into silence. He'd said all he could remember.

James waited for a few seconds before speaking again.

'Before joining DAS,' he began, 'did you complete the mandatory security documentation, *including* the declaration confirming your loyalty to Australia and the government of the day?'

'Yes,' said Andrew, with no idea about specifics. The application forms had been denser than a Russian novel, covering his whole life. He couldn't remember what it all was, but he had bloody well filled out and signed everything he was supposed to. All of it. His history of drug use (limited), his love life (even more limited), travel, job history, family and more. After all that hellish admin, he'd felt nothing would ever be more likely to radicalise him against the government than getting a security clearance.

'So, what happened to your loyalty?' asked James.

'Nothing!' said Andrew.

'So why help her?' said James, looking straight at him.

'I didn't know what was going on!'

James's eyes narrowed. 'So, you admit to helping her?'

Andrew gaped like a fish. Sweat was building inside his jacket. He imagined that he might dissolve into water and splash across the office if he pulled it off. He couldn't tell if he or the post-exercise guard were responsible for the musky funk in the room.

James didn't seem to notice anything. He looked down again and began engraving fresh notes.

In a small voice, Andrew said, 'Am I fired?'

James stopped his writing to look up and give a genuine and disconcerting grin.

'You know most people ask "Am I being charged with something?"' he said, with wry amusement.

'Really?' said Andrew. 'I mean, *am* I being charged?'

'Oh, you've still got your job. Don't worry about that for now.'

James chiselled notes again as Andrew's shoulders sagged and he let out a heavy breath. His relief evaporated as he began to worry about being charged with something.

James, however, gave him something fresh to worry about.

'Why were you waiting in the hallway alone? Where was your escort?'

Dammit! thought Andrew. He'd forgotten about Shanti and his promise.

'She was there.'

'You said,' James flicked back a few pages, 'that you were alone.'

'I meant in the area, the proximity.'

Andrew wiped his hands on his jacket again. He shifted in his seat like a toddler, sweat running down his cheek.

'She was in the toilet with the others. I was on the other side of the door, like she asked.'

'This was her idea?'

'Well, she asked me to, but not like that!'

An image of Shanti flashed into Andrew's mind. He was never getting on her good side now. But she wasn't the one currently squirming in a chair.

'Look,' said Andrew, 'do you mind if I take this jacket off?'

'Why didn't you just remove it earlier?'

'Oh!' said Andrew and began wriggling out of his jacket.

James held up a hand. 'Stay as you are, please.'

Behind him, the guard shifted just enough for his uniform to creak again – like thin ice.

Andrew deflated back into his seat. His jacket, now out of alignment, the collar riding up to his ears, made him look like a retreating turtle. At least he hadn't dissolved as he'd earlier feared.

James leaned in. The chair and table both groaned under him as he moved.

'Let's be very clear,' he said. 'You are linked to a major security breach in one of the most secure buildings in the country. This is a national security matter.'

Andrew nodded, trying not to make it worse.

'You're not fired,' continued James. 'However, we *will* confirm your role in this – accidental or otherwise. In the meantime, you belong to us.'

James gestured, and the guard tapped on Andrew's shoulder. At least that's how he meant it, but his fingers dropped like rolling pins. Andrew wondered if he was going to need an X-ray.

'You are currently classified as a witness. But that classification can change in a heartbeat,' said James as Andrew rose. 'Come back tomorrow as planned and continue your induction. Make no mistake, though – if I find you had any willing role in this, or have left something out, you'll serve your prison sentence where sunshine and legal aid will never find you. We'll be watching.'

The guard escorted Andrew out of the room and eventually out of the building. They merged with a general, unhurried exodus of departing workers, making Andrew realise the entire afternoon had been consumed with the security fallout. Once outside he shivered with relief and fear in the evening air.

Not fired! But there was no way this was good for his career…

* * *

Two hours after Andrew left DAS, the building was still a kicked hive of activity. Emergency briefings, hurried reports and other desperate scraps of crisis response were passed higher up the chain as bosses upon bosses demanded answers. Now it had reached the top and all the DAS senior executives were assembled in a vast meeting room.

By coincidence, many of them had been in this room when the incident happened. They'd been attending a 'One Day Senior Executive Strategy and Play-Think Methodology Session'. It was led by a private consultant who promised to 'unlock their play-potential to enable effective engagement with strategic complexity'. Play-think was the latest corporate trend that encouraged childlike play to allegedly improve problem-solving skills – proving consultants can make money out of anything. This one had even brought his own props. However, once the alarms started, guards scooped up the colouring pencils, figurines and Lego sets and escorted the consultant to his electric Porsche. He was happy to go as there were no refunds.

Now, hours later, the meeting room crowded with senior executives fell silent as the Director-General – or DG – marched in and took his place at the top of the table. The head of DAS, he moved with all the military precision of his former career. With a shaved head and hard eyes, he was a man who knew where all the bodies were buried, both on the battlefield and from the politico-bureaucratic knife fights in Canberra's halls of power.

'What's the update?' said the DG. 'I want more than "We've had a theft".' His tone was curt. He wasn't a man to arrive shouting, but those who knew him heard the anger roiling below the surface. He steepled his fingers and stared down at the assembled executives, waiting for someone to begin.

The table collectively looked to a thin, middle-aged, blonde woman in minimal black wire-frame glasses called Angela. Seated three down from the DG, she was the head of Internal

Security. Angela was often described as a "shrewd operator" when she was nearby, and a "smiling assassin" when she wasn't. But that went with the turf when your job was protecting, monitoring, and investigating a workforce trained to break other people's rules. But she'd climbed high by accepting difficult or politically problematic roles – succeeding where others failed. If you handed her a poisoned chalice, she'd throw the contents back in your face and be left holding a trophy.

Angela cleared her throat to speak, but before she could say a word, someone else got in first.

'We have a press release ready to go and talking points so far,' they said. 'A full media crisis response is being put together to make sure we get the right message out when needed.'

Angela's shocked expression mirrored most of the table and people turned to look for the warbling source of this interruption.

'Who said that?' said the DG with narrowed eyes.

A young face, slightly chubby with brushed-back hair and a wiry moustache, leaned into view from the far end of the table.

'Simon Fitcham,' he called out by way of introduction. 'Senior Adviser from the office of the Minister for Law Enforcement and Security.'

'Simon Fitcham,' the DG repeated flatly. 'Adviser to *Minister Fitcham* was it?'

'Senior Adviser,' Simon cheerfully corrected as several of the executives shuddered and Angela rolled her eyes. 'Aunt Louise, I mean Minister Fitcham, is at an industry engagement event and asked me to attend and bring you all up to date on our planned crisis response.'

As various executives wondered which vineyard the industry engagement was at, the DG stared down the table at Simon.

'You can assure the Minister,' he said, 'that we will handle this and don't need your input at this time.'

'But what about optics?' said Simon. 'Media? Socials? What about rumours or leaks? I mean, more leaks? We've got to get ahead of the competition.'

'You mean the Opposition,' said a nearby executive.

'Nah, that's the other party,' said Simon. 'The *competition* is our party. This could look bad for the Minister, and before the next Cabinet meeting we need to show the PM we're ready for whatever the media could do.'

'Right now,' said the DG pointedly, 'we're more worried about *our* competitors – like the MSS, GRU or FSB,' he added, listing foreign intelligence agencies.

'Who are they?' asked Simon. 'Are those their handles? I can't check them now. Some idiot out the front took my phone–.'

'Enough!' snapped the DG. The executives all avoided eye contact and even Simon uncharacteristically sensed danger and leaned out of view again.

'Angela,' said the DG after a moment to gather his composure. 'Your report please.'

'We're still investigating,' began Angela, 'but the perpetrator has been confirmed as an insider threat.'

'A contractor?' asked the DG with a hint of hope.

'No sir,' replied Angela. 'She was apparently one of us.'

She paused for comment, continuing after nothing was said.

'The insider – Lisa Chapman,' she went on, 'reconfigured her IT account to enable C-level access. According to the logs, she didn't waste time. As soon as she had the new permissions, she took the lot. After which, she escaped by triggering an evacuation. She left the area via her car, which we later found abandoned. That's where the trail ends for now.'

'And,' said the DG, 'by "took the lot" you mean?'

Angela nodded. 'She took Central. Or at least a copy of it.'

Chairs and spines creaked as senior executives – some

senior in more ways than one – leaned forward. A few exchanged wide-eyed glances. One unthinkingly sucked air through his teeth as he considered. It was the same expensive noise a tradesman makes when he's doubling the bill in his head.

The DG merely stared into the distance and asked another question.

'How did she hack her own account to get higher access? That shouldn't be possible.'

Angela glanced at her notes. Internal security had already interviewed Sunil and Jason from IT – Lisa's unthinking dupes into getting her the access. She'd underlined and circled the word "brownies" from the transcript, along with several question marks.

'We're still getting the details sir,' she said, hoping she wouldn't have to air said details in this room. 'But I wouldn't call it a hack. More of a con.'

The DG frowned and said nothing. Angela knew better than to continue. The man was a master of aggressive silences, specialising in a most disquieting quiet. The kind of silence that dragged confessions and ill-timed statements from people desperate to fill the void. Angela considered it the corporate equivalent of being in a river when a nearby crocodile vanishes beneath the water. Someone was about to feel the jaws.

'Well,' began a male executive on the far side of the table, verbally walking into the proverbial water. 'At least that doesn't affect any ongoing ops—'.

'Really?' snapped the DG, making him shut up mid-word. Everyone stiffened.

'It could affect *every* ongoing operation,' the DG growled. His voice got even louder. 'This is Central we're talking about! Good God man! Think for once!'

Taking that last point, everyone at the table thought it would be good to let the DG finish.

'Any witnesses or leads?' he said after allowing everyone to simmer in another silence for a few seconds.

'We're tracking down everyone connected to Lisa in case she seeks help or makes a mistake,' said Angela. She looked down at her notes again and saw James' summary incident report and his interview with Andrew.

'We also have a witness or possible accomplice, too early to say which. But he was the last person to interact with Lisa as she escaped the building. It's possible he was helping her, but we're still investigating as it's an unusual situation.'

'Really?' said the DG, eyebrows lifting. 'Unusual how?'

'He's a grad sir – Andrew Stanton,' said Angela. 'Today was his first day. As such he's a relative unknown, but we're looking into him. We'll vet his background again and make sure—

'Vet him?' interrupted the DG, silencing Angela. His gaze swept the room. 'Does anyone know what all traitors have in common?'

Not wanting anther crocodile moment, no one answered.

'They all had a security clearance,' said the DG. He refocused on Angela.

'Look at his past, by all means,' he continued, 'but it's his present and future that concern me the most.'

'Absolutely,' said Angela. 'We'll make sure he isn't an ongoing threat.'

'What about Lisa Chapman and Central?'

'Cyber Division,' said Angela, nodding to a man called Matthew, the diminutive head of Cyber Division sitting opposite her, 'is monitoring for any mention on the dark or surface web. The good news is that we haven't seen any sign of it so far.'

She paused to allow Matthew a chance to speak. He was an elf of a man – if Santa's jolly helpers specialised in infiltrating or destroying global cyber networks. He certainly worked on a naughty list of sorts and was not to be underestimated. But rather than speak and endanger himself, he merely nodded to agree that his division was indeed doing something. He left Angela to continue with the scenario he was expecting, but didn't want to say.

'And the bad news?' asked the DG.

'Just because it hasn't leaked yet, doesn't mean it won't,' said Angela. 'We may also still get a ransom demand.'

'What kind of ransom?' asked the DG.

'At this stage,' Angela replied, 'we don't even know if it will be money. It may be something much harder to get and more costly.'

'High approval ratings?' said Simon, leaning into view from the far edge of the table again.

Angela ignored the comment and continued.

'If,' she said, 'Lisa is working with a hostile foreign power, they may want our overseas sources. Perhaps what we know about certain American operations, a demand that we remove collection assets or release some prisoners, who knows? If we don't comply or pay up, they publicly release Central or use it against us. They can do both easily enough. This potentially compromises us for years to come.'

'What if she's not working with a foreign power?' asked Simon.

As irritating as Simon was, the question was more important to answer than rebuking him, although Angela responded to the DG instead.

'It's almost certain,' she said, 'that when she has time and a phone with more than two bars, she'll dump it all on the internet for free.'

There was a moment's quiet as the DG and the rest of the executives digested this.

'So, if it goes public, we'll use the talking points?' asked Simon hopefully.

The assembled executives, Angela included, looked down as

though in prayer. This was like watching someone breakdance through a minefield, waiting for the inevitable boom when flaming sneakers and bodily debris come scything out of the smoke. But he was miraculously unscathed. You could almost see the benevolent protection of Aunt-Minister Fitcham shining down on him from Parliament Hill. Or whatever vineyard she was at.

The DG just glared at Simon until he got the message and leaned back to withdraw from sight once more.

'Angela,' he said. She snapped up to look at him. 'Use whatever resources you need for your investigation. Catch Lisa Chapman and confirm any threat from Andrew Stanton. It may be necessary to engage with our allies to let them know we're fine. They'll know something happened today, so reassure them.'

Angela nodded and scribbled a note for the look of the thing. She knew what she had to do.

'The Minister's office,' said the DG loudly, 'can do whatever they like as long as they don't tell anyone. Does anyone else have anything to add?'

The executives sat mute or shook their heads, waiting to be dismissed.

'All right,' said the DG, 'every division is to review security and cooperate with this investigation. Thank you.'

The room filled with chatter, creaking chairs and legs banging on furniture as the executives got up and out as fast as dignity allowed.

'Angela,' said the DG through the babble as a crush formed over by the door, 'if you have a moment.'

Angela, who'd been patiently waiting for the rush to abate, walked over and took the chair closest to him.

As she sat down, he leaned in. Immediately losing some of his command posture and deflating a little.

'Be careful,' he said, notes of concern and worry in his

voice. 'Something's not right. From what you've said, this feels more professional than we'd expect. There may be more at play.'

Angela nodded her agreement. They were alone in the room now and the DG leaned back again.

'I miss the old days,' he said. 'When we mostly just worried about our spies. Not our bloody IT and admin staff. What would a traitorous spy do? Trickle out reports a bit at a time. They knew the *value* of what they had. They betrayed you slowly and even if they did terrible damage, it was spaced across years. But not anymore. Now the lowest IT lackey can walk out with all your secrets stashed in their sock and splash it across the planet in seconds! They don't even understand what they steal! Traitors used to be recruited by known enemies. Now they're radicalised by who knows what.'

He irritably waved a hand as he tried to assemble his finishing thought.

'It's all so ... *American.*'

EIGHT

Four years earlier

'HEY,' CALLED A YOUNG, BLUE-HAIRED WOMAN. 'LOOKING to help?'

'Uh,' said Lisa. She shifted her weight as people pushed past her in the crowd. 'I'm not sure.'

'Let me tell you about us,' said the woman. 'Want some jellybeans?'

Lisa looked at the beaming speaker. She sat at a cheap plastic table inside a marquee identical to all the others filling the university courtyard. Except for the signs, of course. The one hanging off her table, in bright protest red, exclaimed 'Global Justice For All Now!'

The rest of the marquees said things like 'Ultimate Frisbee', 'Politics Society' or 'International Student Union'. People ebbed and flowed depending on the popularity of the stands. Off in the distance, a sign saying 'Welcome Week' hung in the branches of a purple-flowered tree. Rich, warm smells of food and coffee pop-ups wound through the young crowd, like a mealtime cat slinking around your legs. The food and coffee smells were occasionally drowned out by a cloud of acrid marijuana smoke as someone walked past, making no attempt to hide their habit.

Lisa shrugged, holding onto both backpack shoulder straps. The pose echoed her first day at school. That little girl had liked jellybeans too.

'Sure,' she answered.

'Great!' said her new companion, pulling out a couple of folders and pushing a plastic packet towards her. 'Grab a seat, I'm Jenny.'

'That's funny,' said Lisa. 'Me too.'

* * *

Present day

In Canberra, it's often said that everything is 'about twenty minutes away'. This is completely true as long as everyone doesn't try to go to the same place at once. And so, eighteen minutes from DAS, Lisa sat on the edge of a couch in a suburban house and took some long, soothing breaths. In through the nose, out through the mouth. A well-known-calming technique, it's one of the few areas where health professionals and social media influencers are often on the same page.

So when it didn't work, she tried screaming into a cushion.

Remembering she was still on the run and hiding in someone else's house, she stopped with a fast intake of breath. Unfortunately, this only triggered a coughing fit that made her eyes stream and head throb.

Luckily, both the homeowner and their neighbours were currently away. The house belonged to one of Lisa's colleagues.

A woman called Jane who had taken the family to the beach for a week. A nice woman, if a bit too chatty for Lisa's tastes. But keen to share enough details of her life for Lisa to put a comprehensive picture together. The walls held various pictures of a smiling family, which Lisa was quick to ignore. She didn't need that extra guilt on top of everything else.

The house was a temporary stop. Basic security, guaranteed empty. Plus, she didn't actually have to break in. The spare key was under a potted succulent on the back deck and there were no cameras. Pretty lax for someone who worked in a security organisation. But to be fair, Jane was in administration and policy.

Lisa had already taken a quick look around. There was probably cash and jewellery that could be useful in the long run, but it was better to leave no clues she'd been here.

It hadn't been Lisa's first choice, in fact, it was a mistake. This kind of irrational move was how you got caught. She'd followed the first steps to escape; multiple forms of transport, travelling into areas without CCTV, changes of clothing from the go-bag she had stashed in the car. She even had temporary accommodation ready, but she'd panicked enroute, and changed the plan. She thought back to DAS HQ, the last-minute searches she did and what they revealed. It made her stomach tighten and her head hurt even more.

Feeling ready to get up, she staggered into a nearby bathroom to recover. It was a small space, with some missing tiles and sink and cabinet that looked older than Lisa. But, in any case, the water still flowed, and that's all she needed. She splashed her face and leaned on the sink, her forehead resting on her arm. For a few seconds, she felt the cool water drip off her nose and lips. Then she looked up at the red-eyed wretch in the mirror.

'You really fucked up, didn't you?' she said.

No, she thought to herself. Someone else was to blame. But what to do about it?

She drummed her fingers on the sink, still staring at herself. Her options were hand herself in (not likely) or finish the mission (uncertain).

That was the unbearable part. Being uncertain. For longer than she could remember she'd been scared, exhilarated and wary, but never uncertain. She knew what she was doing, what she was preparing for, and why she was doing it. But now all that was gone. Great towers of belief had crumbled and left her in the ruins of her previous convictions. She burned with the shame and embarrassment of it all.

Then she thought of a third option. She reached into a pocket and pulled out the USB. She still had some leverage should DAS catch her. As long as they didn't catch it with her. At least she wasn't on the news yet. There were no mentions online. They might just be sitting on it, not willing to admit what they lost. That was fine as far as she was concerned, it was their little secret.

She twirled the USB in her fingers, taking a moment to consider what she had. It may be good for more than a bargaining chip. But if she was to go with the third option, what she needed was now inside one of the most heavily guarded buildings in Australia. A place where she was a known and hunted traitor. Plus, who could she trust? How far did this go? She needed someone who wasn't experienced, not involved in all the politics, and who could potentially be turned against the system. Everyone she knew would have the knowledge and experience to turn her in in a heartbeat. Or perhaps they were part of the greater problem already.

Lisa recalled the face of a young man, a couple of years younger – fluffy hair and earnest expression. The sort of face you'd let watch your laptop when you went to the cafe toilet.

It was as though the clouds had parted, finally letting the sun in.

The ground floor toilets! That was it. Lisa remembered him now. She looked at the USB.

A definite possibility.

NINE

As Andrew arrived at work, on the second day of his career, DAS Headquarters lacked the previous day's lustre in his imagination. His fears had kept him up all night. A threat to national security running into your arms before you direct them to the exit is a poor way to begin a career. This morning, there were no jewels of dew on the barbed wire, no morning glow, and the hum of the moving cameras was no longer springtime bees. Now it just sounded like the judgemental 'hmming' of an elderly female relative who just heard you're still single.

Andrew's shoes scraped on the ground as he dragged himself across the road to the main gate. His ego and self-worth sagged along behind him like a dying balloon, long after the party.

Just inside the waiting room next to the main gate, the graduate group sat around, talking excitedly. They buzzed like cicadas. That is until one spotted Andrew walking in and coughed. The buzzing stopped instantly. Andrew remembered previous summers being almost deafened by the damn insects.

But sometimes, when you got close, they shut up, leaving a silence that was worse, as he felt millions of little eyes on him.

His face twisted into a smile and he waved.

'Hi, everyone …'

The others looked at him. A couple of weak waves in return. One woman whispered to the person on her left. Actually whispered!

Andrew's smile vanished. He stared at the whisperer. She reddened and bent over her phone, thumbing with frantic professionalism. The phone of the woman next to her buzzed. They both giggled.

Andrew decided to ignore them as much as possible, but still ruin their fun.

He walked over and made sure he was standing in the absolute middle of the group. This led to a frosty but convenient truce. Even Liam, super-networker, was suddenly more concerned with his book – a biography of some retired politician who'd had the PR smarts to die recently.

Andrew and the other grads waited as employees flowed into the gatehouse and through the turnstiles. The atmosphere had shifted from the 'factory worker' vibe it had had before. Yesterday, the guard had been behind a desk, risking only boredom. Today there were two extra on duty by the entrance gates. The gates themselves were flanked by two signs: 'PASS ID MAY BE INSPECTED' and RANDOM BAG SEARCHES ARE BEING CONDUCTED'.

So far, people seemed to go through easily. No one was being spear-tackled or tasered. Just the usual 'Thankyah!' from the guards as they waved an ID going through the gate.

After a few awkward minutes wait, Shanti entered to collect them, coffee and banana bread in her hands. One bag under her arm, another two under her eyes.

Had she been interrogated as well? Andrew looked to see if her clothes were the same as yesterday, then realised he had no idea what she'd been wearing yesterday. She gave a half-hearted good morning and motioned for them to follow her. She needed a hand free for the security gate panel. Having to choose between holding coffee or banana bread, she stuffed breakfast into her handbag.

The group did their duckling chain, following Shanti through the gates. Andrew, at the end, halted as a guard politely but firmly stepped in and eclipsed the view beyond.

'Excuse me, sir,' he said, staring down at Andrew. 'Please present your pass ID for inspection.'

Andrew tried looking over the guard's shoulder, but he didn't have the height. Hoping Shanti was waiting on the other side, he held his ID up at head height. The guard bent down and stared for a full ten seconds, as if waiting for a surprise 3D image. If one appeared, Andrew would never know. The guard gave a curt 'Thankyah!' and stepped aside. The eclipse over, Andrew was dazzled by the sudden flood of sunlight from the other side of the barrier. He scurried through, eyes watering, and almost crashed into the group waiting beyond.

Andrew hurried towards Shanti. He wanted a private word but found that wasn't a problem. The grads were giving him a two-metre bubble. Once they all started walking, they slid away like water downhill.

'So …' he began.

'I don't want to hear it,' she said, staring ahead. 'Whatever bullshit apology or explanation, you can save it. I'm now stuck babysitting you lot.'

'Why?' asked Andrew.

She stopped and spun around, skewering him with her expression.

'Because you let a huge security breach walk out the door and I was supposed to be watching you! Now I'm in the shit as well!'

Andrew shrank back so much his tie loosened.

'Sorry?'

The rest of the group had pulled up at a safe distance and were watching with a mix of amusement and judgement.

Shanti drew a breath for another blast, then her shoulders dropped, and she seemed to change her mind.

'All right, everyone,' she called out. 'Let's get into the main foyer quickly. It may take longer today.'

Her eyes flicked to Andrew and back to the group.

'They've upped security for some reason,' she added sourly.

Inside the complex, just beyond the main entrance, was another security guard.

'Excuse me,' the guard said. He stared through several people to look at Andrew. 'Random search. Could I see your bag, sir?'

The group turned as one. Andrew sighed and handed it over.

Everyone now got a brief presentation on the random rubbish he hadn't gotten around to cleaning out. He remembered an old incident when he had bought condoms at the supermarket and tripped over. He had seen the packet go spinning across the polished floor, right into the sensible puce shoes of an elderly woman who lived opposite his parents. Looking up at her, he would have preferred condemnation, but her *grin* made him want to dig down to the Earth's molten core. Now, his face burned just as badly as it had that day.

Search over, Andrew tried to close his bag with a vengeful yank of its zipper. But it got stuck halfway, which spoiled the effect. No one else was searched and Shanti led them back into the auditorium.

Inside, Intro-bot stood centre stage at the lectern as before. Peter, the old analyst, sat in the back row, as though to maximise the space between them.

The grads trickled past him and took their front row seats. Intro-bot seemed to scan them as they settled in. His head turned back and forth as precisely as a laughing clown in a carnival ball game, only with a far more solemn expression.

'If I could have your attention, please,' he said. 'Your area assignments have been decided. Each of you will be assigned to a different area in the organisation, with your own mentor.' He appeared to pause for thunderous applause or a spontaneous rendition of the national anthem. Neither was forthcoming.

Unperturbed, Intro-bot tapped a hidden control. The screen behind him switched to a jolly image of a smiley face over a 'Thank you' in cursive.

'Welcome to your careers in the Department of Australian Security. Peter will now take you to your placements, where you will continue your probation.'

The grads turned to see Peter, sitting rock-still with arms crossed, his expression familiar to anyone who'd tried to ruin a family photo. A side door banged shut, indicating Intro-bot's departure while everyone was distracted. Peter shook his head and waved for everyone to come over. Once surrounded, he got to his feet with only minimal middle-aged noises and waved a fistful of lanyards at them – their official IDs had arrived.

They all eagerly looped the little rectangles over their heads. Andrew looked at the photo he'd had taken by security yesterday. ID photos generally aren't good. They range all the way from 'tired' to 'drunk' to 'Police Hope This Person Can Help Them with Their Enquiries'. Andrew was pleased his was mid-range, the kind of expression a drunk uses to convey sobriety to the police.

Peter consulted a piece of crumpled paper, muttering as though checking a list of chores

'All right, you lot,' he said, folding the paper. 'Let's do the Graceland tour.'

It must have been a reference to something, because he waited a moment, rolled his eyes, and began walking.

Andrew exchanged excited glances with the other grads. This was it!

Until now, their world had been the front security desk, the cafe and the short journey to the auditorium. Now the smell of coffee and toasted sandwiches dropped away as they headed further into the complex.

The excitement picked up as the natural light dropped away. Windows were fewer the further in you got. Andrew and the other grads couldn't help but exchange excited grins. Andrew pictured what might lie beyond the next door: great big screens with live satellite feeds. Grainy green night vision footage from some special ops head cam. People intercepting phone calls, grim profile photos of known spies and terrorists on every computer, and cyber-attacks being visualised on stadium-size screens in real time. This was it!

Peter approached a solid-looking door. On the front was an officially laminated sign: 'Intelligence Operations and Support – Entry Highly Restricted to Authorised Personnel Only'. An A4 sheet of paper was sticky taped beneath it using a party invite template from MS Word: 'Social Club Drinks Thursdays by the Cafe – All welcome!'. There were smiling cartoon balloons on either side of the text.

Peter swiped his card and placed his hand on a silver plate angled out of the wall. It had a helpful outline of a hand and a row of lights that flashed green after a few seconds. He grabbed the handle and pulled. The grads watched his shoulders tense and veins bulge in his neck as he levered the door open. From this angle, Andrew could see that the door was several inches thick.

'Right!' said Peter, breathing heavily. 'Swipe your ID and palm please, then head in.'

Inside, the space opened up into a central foyer that split off into different corridors. Everything had a sensible, almost dull corporate façade, only slightly disturbed by the different doors spaced evenly throughout each corridor. Some were frosted glass and looked like they would slide aside spaceship-style. Others were plain wood, and one or two hinted at the heaviness of painted steel. Apparently, it was all to do with each area's level of security sensitivity. Or the budget they had when renovating.

While the group excitement stayed high, it was diluted by a trickle of confusion and surprise. There was none of the stuff Andrew had imagined. It was so ... normal. Some differences, though. It wasn't open plan, for a start. The building was like an ant's nest, each area a different chamber hidden around a corner or behind a door. Every now and again, a fresh door blocked the corridor. You had to swipe your pass again to get through.

'Stops people wandering around if they get loose,' said Peter vaguely, when a grad asked about it.

Once inside, though, each area was a mix of open space or cubicle farms like in any office building.

Except for the decorations. Each section was draped with various gag signs or thematic props – typically of the groups, countries, or issues they were analysing. Analysts apparently couldn't resist collecting bits and pieces. But there were also the family photos, pictures of pets, awards from hobbies, and chocolate-based fundraisers.

Acronyms were everywhere. They were stuck to the front of every door, swinging on signs hanging by small chains like a bat colony, and peering out from every document and piece of paper in sight. SEA CT, MER OP DISC, CECY, CEPSY.

Peter made tour guide announcements as they walked, ignoring the curious looks from passing co-workers. 'Our work is split into several themed areas,' he said. 'Although in reality it's all mixed. Make sure you stay in contact with each other. Always good to know people in other areas.'

They turned left, then right, and went through a door into

another den of cubicles. Police logos and merchandise were scattered about on desks. Old newspaper clippings about 'colourful' characters were posted on walls, with red marker gleefully bragging 'arrested' on them. On a table in the centre of the room was half a birthday cake.

'Listen up,' said Peter. 'This is HTC or High Threat Crime. They work with state and federal police forces to counter the more serious organised crime. Especially the ones who cross over into terrorism or espionage. Dodgy networks will support anything.'

He consulted his piece of paper as a middle-aged woman emerged from a nearby office to meet them.

'Patrick, Elise, Isabella. This is your stop,' said Peter.

He threw a mock salute at the woman, who returned it with far less snap.

'Hello, Peter,' she said. 'I see they've got you on deliveries now?'

'For my sins,' he replied. 'Enjoy your grads, no backsies.'

He led the remaining grads through the building and into another area. Nazi, militia and far right imagery rubbed shoulders with ISIS, Hezbollah and the New Levant Defence Front. This time, there were several leftover cupcakes of different shades and frostings. Empty plates and crumbs showed the grand pile that must have been there.

'Counter Terrorism,' announced Peter. 'Political violence of all kinds. Knife attacks, mass shootings, and bombings. Kim, Akeem, Pushpa – enjoy.'

'Hey, Peter!' one of the local analysts called out. 'Presenting at the Intelligence Futures show 'n' brag this year?'

'Nope,' said Peter, 'too busy defending democracy.'

Next stop was Counter Espionage – via an airlock arrangement of secured doors. It was decorated with various national flags, dictator caricatures and propaganda posters. Beneath a poster of Putin someone had written 'In Russia, intelligence does YOU!'. John, Kim and Toni were dropped off to start their careers with some chocolate Breach Cake, compliments of a glowering analyst who had left a safe open, putting the nation in peril.

Each new section had dazzling possibilities, new subject matter, and baked goods. But Andrew worried he was on a train getting further and further beyond the ritzy suburbs. What if he missed all the good assignments?

Peter rushed them through the next area – Strategic Intelligence. He practically hurled the chosen grads in without breaking stride. 'They talk for hours if you let them,' he explained afterwards. 'Political wonks going on about macroeconomic this and geopolitical that. They take great pride in knowing their reports go to the PM's office. No one has time to read them of course. But they feel there's a lot of prestige in being ignored by such important people. Haven't figured out the difference between reach and influence.'

Liam's stricken expression told Andrew how sorry he was to be leaving that particular station. Speaking waffle to power sounded perfect for him. Instead, he was called out next at Cyber Command – home to defensive and offensive cyber capabilities, information operations and critical infrastructure security. They didn't get a glimpse of the food on offer. No one was allowed in, and Peter had to speak through an intercom, as though he was delivering lunch.

'They're very special,' said Peter gravely, as they waited at the vault-style door. Andrew sensed sarcasm.

'Right,' said Peter when the door clanged shut on Liam's worried expression. 'Most of you that are left go to Warheads On Foreheads.'

This was the nickname for Military Support, or MS; counterinsurgency, foreign military capabilities, and a mysterious catch-all called 'operational actions'. It was a joint military–civilian effort, designed to get more flexibility on one side and more focus on the other. Andrew watched a pair of wide-eyed grads – Ahmed and Sonya – walk off with officers from the army, navy and air force, all of whom argued over who got these new resources.

'Enjoy it,' Peter had told the two grads. 'Most in there are the friendliest and most dedicated you'll ever meet. But if someone calls you "champ", that's an insult. Best to throat-punch them to avoid looking weak.'

As the door shut, Andrew looked around, despite knowing it was just him and Peter.

'Well now, Charlie Bucket,' said Peter, with what Andrew had recognised as his trademark dryness. 'You're with me. Lucky us.'

The journey to Peter's area wasn't far, but involved going down too many steps. Peter ushered Andrew in through an unmarked door into an area with no windows.

'This,' said Peter, 'is Operational Support for Threats, Research and Analysis, or "OSTRA" for short.'

Andrew looked around. The room had an assortment of people slumped at ancient computers. Their chairs and desks looked like they'd been thrown away at least once already. Above the entrance, an overhead fluorescent light flickered dire morse code. Andrew's eye twitched in sympathy, but no one else seemed to notice it. Or they had gotten used to it.

'And, uh, what do we do here?' asked Andrew.

Peter tilted his head from side to side in a moment of quiet contemplation.

'We're a support team. We do research for other areas.'

'Research?' repeated Andrew. 'So, we don't investigate things here?'

Peter waggled one hand in a so-so motion.

'We sift through spreadsheets or data. Sometimes read manifestos or foreign military manuals for anything interesting. Things other areas may not have time to do. It's rarely exciting work, but it's … thorough. Computers can only do so much. Some things need a human—'

'Eye?' guessed Andrew.

'I was going to say "brain",' replied Peter. 'Right, you lot! Meet the new guy!'

Chairs rattled as people got up to join them.

Andrew nodded and smiled mutely as Peter introduced him. He shook hands with the brave and exchanged affirmative nods with the more cautious. It was a small team of varied ages. There was Michael, of dapper hair and empty expression. Sarah, who radiated keen but nervous energy. Greg, who'd either just had a nap or was about to. Al, who wore a wool vest and had glasses that were too large. Then Heather, who seemed to have forgotten to retire.

'And, of course, you know Shanti,' said Peter, with only the most distant hint of amusement. A forensics team would have struggled to find a smirk, but Andrew had a hunch it was there. After meeting people whose smile never reached their eyes, here was someone where it started in the eyes, but never reached his mouth.

As the shock drained away, Andrew took in more details. The OSTRA offices were shades of corporate blue, from the carpet to the plastic mouse pads. The decorations here didn't have a central theme. This was a crossroads, a mix of cultures. A clash of terrorism, espionage, and criminal motifs adorned the walls. Someone had even mocked up an OSTRA poster. A muscular cartoon ostrich flexed a bicep at the watcher under an OSTRA banner in heavy, gothic script. Some joker with a pen had scribbled a name for the ostrich: Ozzie.

Each desk was decorated to various levels of mania. Photos were in vogue – sticky taped or pinned to the fabric-covered cubicle walls. This, Al later explained to Andrew, was because no phones meant everyone had to go back to old-school prints and frames.

Some people had human children, with one or two photos to prove it. Fur babies, on the other hand, were everywhere. Those people slathered their cubicles with as many dog or cat photos as the walls could hold, a montage of animal inbreeding stuffed into silly outfits.

Andrew found himself staring at a framed picture of a pug in a clown outfit, its expression wheezily pleading for escape. He blinked and saw himself in the glass, wearing the same expression.

'Welcome to OSTRA,' said Peter. 'Like it or leave it.'

'I can leave?' said Andrew incredulously.

'No.'

* * *

Over the next few weeks, Andrew settled into his role like an old man trying to make himself comfortable on a concrete floor.

Each morning, he arrived at DAS and headed straight for the tiny lockers by the entrance. There he locked away his phone, smart watch and headphones. It was ironic, on reflection, that this meant only in intelligence headquarters was he not being tracked, monitored, or secretly listened to – for commercial purposes, anyway.

Beyond the first set of gates was Jim, a security guard assigned to randomly search people in case they had someone from the People's Liberation Army of China hidden in their backpack. Jim had a fighter's stare above a badly broken nose, but was a genial soul. He smelled of cheap deodorant and cigarettes from long ago. It wasn't that he was a smoker; there was something second-hand about the smell. Andrew imagined him as a barrel-chested younger man, wading through last century's smoke-filled nightclubs long enough for it to leave a permanent mark, like the way an ice sheet stores pollutants across millennia.

Then the ground floor lifts took him down to his level. Every couple of days, a second guard would be posted in the corridor outside the lifts – again, to 'randomly' search people, but somehow Andrew always got picked. Sometimes he didn't zip up his bag after Jim, in anticipation.

In a moment of relative lightness, Shanti had assured Andrew that everyone got searched from time to time, and nobody cared, but he wasn't convinced. Each time someone went past him laughing, he flushed crimson from the cheeks down. He had no idea what they were laughing at, but it was probably him. His role in the breach had spread through DAS like wildfire.

Once in OSTRA, he began his day, dredging through information. 'Data cleaning' was the worst part. Excel spreadsheets, CSV files, Word documents that had to be put into another database. In each case, he had to go through the entire thing and make sure everything was formatted properly. If it wasn't, the programs that were supposed to move the data threw a fit and either didn't finish the job or transferred garbled nonsense. A single extra character or space could throw the whole thing into disarray. It even made him more enthusiastic about reading intercepted technical manuals. A particular standout was the Chinese military's new XT-17 Mk3 'Hell's Gourd' in-theatre management system. After wading through the ultra-dense translation, he figured out it was a portable toilet.

When he complained to Peter, he just shrugged.

'Classified doesn't always equal interesting,' he said. 'Some agencies would declare a blue sky top-secret, just because it's in their records.'

Regardless of where they were posted, the grads' days were broken up by regular 'Tradecraft and Organisational Awareness

Training Sessions'. They ran at ten-thirty each morning in a training room littered with the colourful corporate scat of used post-it notes. 'Consultant droppings' Peter called them, when kicking off the first training session. He ran most of the sessions, introducing the guest instructor if he wasn't doing it himself. As declared by Intro-bot, he was involved in everything to do with the grads. Not that he seemed to enjoy it. Andrew decided Peter was naturally grumpy and weirdly enjoyed not enjoying it – like someone hate-watching a show for all the details they get wrong, because they get all their cardio from outrage.

'Intelligence analysis,' Peter started one day, 'must be timely, relevant and concise. Perfect reporting delivered late is useless.'

Formalities over, he settled into a more conversational flow.

'So, to be timely, we have to accept one truth: *You will never have all the information you need, so make the call as best you can.*'

He snatched a marker off the whiteboard, pointing it at the group like a torch.

'*If* you think you have all the information, you're being lied to. Or lying to yourself.'

'But,' said Isabella, one of the grads, 'what if we're wrong?'

'Often nothing happens,' said Peter matter-of-factly. 'Or people may die, resources are wasted, threats evade justice, whatever. It varies.'

Isabella, now regretting the question, nodded, wide-eyed.

'Don't feel bad,' said Peter. 'It's like doctors. They can't discuss their patients, have their own coded language and get people killed despite good intent. But we don't condemn their profession – we hold it to a high standard. Just like us.'

He lowered the marker and let a rare smile emerge. 'Practice good tradecraft and you will always make the best call,' he said.

Around the room, people collectively breathed out, looking reassured.

'It just won't always be the correct one,' added Peter.

* * *

But Peter was good for more than booby-trapped pep talks. Despite his black belt in grumpy, he was generous enough to take Andrew around to other areas and introduce him. Andrew found that his infamy preceded him. The reaction to his name – 'Oh, you're *that* guy' – became so regular he began sitting mute in meetings, unwilling to introduce himself.

He also couldn't escape the mockery from the other grads. Being young and newly salaried, there were weekly after-work drinks at a nearby bar. They couldn't uninvite him, but there was always an underlying tension when he was around. Andrew had a suspicion there were more grad events he didn't even know about. He could tell because of the way they'd start talking about some place and then abruptly shut up as the others stared pointedly. So instead of relaxation and levity, the other grads were always … careful around him. The official joke was that he had been OSTRA-cised. People were hesitant to appear too close to someone who'd damaged national security. Then he overheard a conversation in the toilets about how 'that guy' memes were trending in grad chat groups he wasn't part of. He sagged against the cubicle wall and wondered how he had come to be a hashtag.

Then there was the problem of finding somewhere to live. In Canberra, by February, the property market became a brutal Hobbesian battle for survival. It is a career and university town and every year swarms of academics, graduates, military and other government personnel flooded in. Sooner or later, they flooded out again, but this transient workforce made renting almost impossible. DAS gave all grads a few weeks accommodation for free, but that was running out fast, with no other options having presented themselves.

He was ready to give up when he mentioned this to the grad group.

'Brilliant!' said Liam.

After some initial caution, he'd taken a curious shine to Andrew. Andrew's guess was that notoriety was better than obscurity and Liam was using it to his advantage. Knowing the guy who fumbled the biggest breach in decades must be great for office banter. But Andrew was just grateful for someone to talk to, even if they creepily hung around like they were preparing material for a tell-all book.

'Why didn't you say so sooner?' Liam said. 'There's a spot in my flat – I mean, townhouse.'

Liam went on to point out that he had found the place through someone he knew. A contact made at a party. Andrew wondered if this contact worked at the Minister's office. His mind spun as he tried to think of an excuse, but common sense won out. 'Sounds great,' he heard himself say. 'Give me the details.'

The flat was indeed a three-bedroom townhouse. It sat in a complex of similar apartments –three large buildings built alongside each other. When he pressed it, the bell gave an arch trilling ring, guaranteed to notify and irritate.

Liam opened the door and met him like he was greeting a camera crew.

'Welcome!' he cried out, sweeping an arm out behind him.

Andrew nodded, grimacing as he hauled his overstuffed bags up the steps.

In the hall, he met Pascal, the only other tenant, and it was all Andrew could not to stare. Pascal looked nothing like Andrew's imagined idea of someone Liam would live with.

'Good to meet ya,' said Pascal. He was shirtless and wearing a pair of faded cream shorts, having seemingly stepped out of a rum commercial shoot in the Caribbean. Andrew nodded. 'Yup, you too.'

Andrew could see why he was shirtless. He had the cocky confidence of one who knew he could get away with it. He was like a fashion model they kept in a cryogenic chamber until it was warm enough each summer to thaw him out and let him out-glow everyone. The shorts were ragged around the edges and looked like they were from an op shop. Or maybe they were 'distressed' and cost several hundred dollars from a designer. Couldn't be sure with this guy. But he wasn't perfect, not in Andrew's opinion. He imagined him coming from some celebrity family of handsome movie stars. Although in Andrew's jealous imagination, Pascal was the under-achieving younger brother of the main star, tops.

The house seemed to have been furnished by accident – it looked like a mess of leftovers and different tastes. The living room had a red three-seater couch with a peach fuzz fabric and a human imprint in the middle. Andrew guessed it to be Pascal-sized. The room smelt of laundry baskets and the remnants of a lost beer bottle still hiding somewhere. The room's other couch was a faded blue. It had comfy cushions that looked like they'd consume the unwary traveller – like if you sat down, you'd keep sinking in until your legs were over your head with your torso long since enveloped. The lamps were classic IKEA, as were the shelves. The only new thing in the place was the television. It was an 80-centimetre wonder. Samsung smart TV, all the trimmings. It sat on brackets in the wall, like the mirror of an evil Disney queen. Beneath were a few different gaming systems, their paraphernalia trailing cords into an old Amazon box.

'Well,' said Pascal. 'Good a time as any to go through the rules.'

Andrew was expecting stuff about dishes, et cetera, but that was sorted with 'Clean your crap.'

'You guys can debit the bills. I'll chuck my contribution in the jar in the kitchen for everything. But transfer the rent to me. I'll sort that out.'

Andrew nodded, wondering why he dealt in cash.

'Also,' said Pascal, 'girlfriends, boyfriends, whatever floats your boat. No judgement, all allies here. Just don't let them become a problem. We have to live together.'

Andrew suspected he wouldn't have much of a problem with that. He would later learn that Pascal had a steady stream of girlfriends coming and going. Typical.

'Guess I'll leave you Dashists to it,' said Pascal, using a common insult for DAS employees, and wandered off into the kitchen.

'He's kind of loose,' said Liam.

'I bet,' said Andrew. 'How exactly did you meet him?'

'Never mind,' said Liam. 'Just make sure you don't discuss anything …'

'Anything?'

'You know …' Liam waggled his eyebrows.

'About partners?' said Andrew.

'No! Classified secrets.'

'Gotcha.'

Andrew stifled a sigh, feeling less than delighted about getting security lectures at home as well.

'We have a duty to prevent leaks,' insisted Liam. 'You never know.'

'Oi!' Pascal called out from the kitchen. 'Sound really carries here. I've got a secret mystery – who left the milk out?'

Andrew pinched the bridge of his nose and wished he were someone else.

TEN

THE SUMMER SUN GLARED DOWN ON VICTORIA'S Parliament House and the motley group gathering on its stone steps. Rain was predicted later on, mostly because it was Melbourne. The typically randomised mix of sun, rain, hail, monsoon or biblical plagues on any given day meant all weather predictions were right eventually.

Dave took his hat off and rubbed the back of his shaved head. His chest and biceps strained against a grey t-shirt as he stretched. Although he was more average than large, with a lean frame that was a gift of youth. Also, as a veteran musician of an underground rock scene, he did the equivalent of a half marathon with every performance.

Sweat ran down his cheek and he fanned himself with his hat for a few seconds. He looked around at their anti-mosque protest. It was small, but growing as more showed up. Australian flags were being waved or worn. Black balaclavas or face-covering scarves were in for some. Others, like Dave, didn't bother as they didn't care who knew their allegiances.

The signs were better this time. At the last protest, they had been barely legible. But now swastikas and slogans like 'Muslims Out!', 'Ban The Mosque!', and 'No Sahara Law!' stood out bold against white cardboard. Probably too late to do anything about the last one, but still not a bad effort.

The megaphone was familiar, but uncomfortable against his hip. Just in case the stage microphone failed. Plus, it completed the look.

At the centre of the protest, three young men worked on a makeshift stage. A banner straddled the front – Extreme Far Riot. That was his band. They'd been stuck with nowhere pubs and Cold Chisel covers until they'd started writing their own alt-right anthems. Political music was huge. Protest songs, all that shit. All about how the white man was in danger of being swept away.

Dave, band leader and ever the entrepreneur, at first made them simply play at white supremacist events, but now they streamed them too. It was brilliant for the brand. Right at the front line sort of stuff. They'd built a strong following in Australia and, for some reason, Norway.

That's the internet for you.

But Dave wasn't arguing, and this was the big one. Earlier he'd set up cameras on the three-lamp antiquarian streetlights outside parliament – they gave the best front and wide shots. There were also mini-cameras on the microphone stands for the gritty, screamy bits that went well with close-up teeth and nostrils. The live stream, now running, had the wide shot. The rest were recording for the final film clip they'd drop in Neo-Nazi forums.

Dave admired their handiwork, how far they'd come. It'd been quite a journey since seeing his first alt-right music video clip. A younger Dave had nothing special in his life except music. He loved classic rock, punk, all the flavours of metal and whatever else his mate's dads raved about after a few beers. One winter's night at a party, after a romantic rejection he put down to feminism, Dave had left the house to sulk in the backyard. Instead of solitude, there was a group of young men gathered around an oil barrel filled with burning wood. Despite the cold they were wildly animated – head banging and air drumming to the music video one held up on his phone. Dave approached and found them welcoming - making space around the barrel and giving him a beer.

That night Dave found his path to extremism. Through a booming far right online music scene, more catchy, widespread and appealing than Goebbels himself could ever hope. The music was intense; rocket fuel compared to the mainstream. These weren't just songs, they were manifestos. Wild, political summonses to a new and exciting scene. One where Dave could be part of not just a great movement, but a great race.

He didn't think of it as a hate movement, like the lamestream media called it. It was about pride (but not the gay kind). It was being proud of who you were, knowing you weren't alone, and committing to a cause. A righteous fire had ignited inside Dave, pushing him to reinvent the band as a full nationalist outfit. Ironically, the other members had been in the movement long before him. But they weren't committed, just social Nazis. Dave however, knew they were on to something. They'd follow the music. He wasn't a fighter or a politician. He was an artist and would do what they always did – raise awareness.

Dave's timing couldn't be better – the online reaction to their music had been amazing. Only a year later they were here: headlining an anti-Islam protest in Melbourne's CBD. It was supposed to take their group – and the movement, of course – to the next level. The rocket fuel of alt-right music was going to launch them globally. Finally, they'd tour the US and Europe, Norway, in particular – gotta repay the early fans.

Dave smiled at the notoriety and fame that was coming his way; Extreme Far Riot was going viral. He wouldn't just be part of something huge, He'd *be* something huge.

There was a cheer as a fresh group of face-scarf and bucket-hat enthusiasts joined the protest, pulling Dave back to the present.

Right, he thought. Once the crowd was big enough, the band would start revving them up. Then the mussies, communists, neo-anarchist, whatevers, would show up and shit would kick off. The video was gonna be great.

They still had to be careful to keep the odds on their side. Reinforcements were waiting in a few handy pubs. Because, once word got out they were here, Mohammad would call up his cousins and hundreds of fucking jihadis would be all over you. That's why the cops were already setting up nearby. Dave watched another police truck stop and offload a fresh lot of riot police. Their armour made them look like troops of some alien emperor.

His phone went off from a lookout he knew about a few blocks away. It read: "Jihadis incoming from south". Ah, fuck it! They were early. Still, if they wanted a showdown, they'd get it. Maybe not from Dave, but he'd provide a hell of a soundtrack.

He headed over to the main organisers, an eclectic group of men and women united in their hatred of Islam – and plenty else. Some were full-on Neo-Nazis, tatts and all. Others were less outwardly committed, hiding their faces to protect whatever job or business they had. But at least they bought the merchandise and were here to protest.

'Yeah?' said Olaf – real name Tom. He had a shaved head except for a Viking-style ponytail that dropped halfway down his back. His beard was plaited the same way. A strange wavy symbol, claimed to be an ancient Viking sigil, was tattooed on his neck. In reality, it was meant to be a swastika, but halfway through the tattoo session, the drunk Olaf/Tom had pitched forward to vomit into a pot plant.

'Got a message. Company coming in, south side,' replied Dave.

'You better go fuckin' check it out then,' said Olaf/Tom. 'I'm not going off what some fuckwit staring through a beer glass thinks.'

Dave resented being treated like some nobody. He was a musician, after all. But it paid to show willing. He headed out of the crowd towards a group coalescing in the distance. Just in case, he also brought his bass player and drummer with him. They brought the kinds of protest signs you saw on a particular type of professional. The signs themselves were flimsy and small, but attached to an axe handle. The sort of heavy thing you could swing at someone and later claim to police you were just showing them the fine print.

Dave peered at the distant group's protest signs. As he got closer, he could see these weren't Lebs. Or Africans. What the—?

He stopped with his mouth open and tried to think.

Behind him, his drummer sniggered and pointed a sausage finger at the approaching crowd.

'Someone order a curry?'

Further down the road, Ajai Mehta walked ahead of a hundred members of the local chapter of the Hinduvta Action Alliance, an organisation infamous for riots, lynchings and ultra-nationalist mayhem across India. They wore a similar uniform of white, either a shirt or an entire outfit. This was offset by saffron flags and signs like 'No Islam' or great red slashes through Islam's star and crescent. Chants and songs filled the air, all of which were lost on the Neo-Nazis watching with their mouths open.

Ajai turned to yell and hold his arms up. They all came to a bumping halt.

'Watch yourselves,' muttered Dave as Ajai approached with some backup of his own.

'Who are you lot?' he demanded, when Ajai was within earshot.

Ajai drew himself up to his full height. 'We are patriots protecting our values from the threat of Islam.'

'Wait …' said Dave. 'You're not Muslims?'

'How dare you?' cried Ajai. 'We represent true and incorruptible Hindu values! Our organisation upholds this holy mission in India or anywhere else! We will not be overrun! What are you doing here?'

'This is our rally, mate. We're stopping the jihadis from taking over the Australian way of life!' Although some certainty drained from Dave's voice as he saw the similarity with what Ajai had said.

'What?' said Ajai. 'Oh no, this is our protest.'

'Bullshit! We're fighting Muslims just like the ANZACs and every digger since!'

'Oh, really?' said Ajai, raising an eyebrow. 'And how many wars have you fought against nuclear-armed Muslims? Hindus have shielded you from Pakistan!'

Dave cracked his knuckles and glared.

* * *

Two blocks away, confusion had spread to the Mobile Police Command tasked with keeping the peace. Constable Christos Nomikos ran a hand through his curly black hair and focused on the video hook-up in front of him.

The Commissioner filled the screen in an unfortunate close-up. His hard and jaded features went from edge to edge. His image appeared to strain at the glass, which looked unable to hold much longer.

'Extremist Hindus?' the Commissioner thundered. 'Mixing with Nazis? Do we split them up or contain them? Are these idiots going to fight or fuck?'

Constable Nomikos cleared his throat and reviewed his notes.

'Unknown, sir. For now, they seem as confused as we are. Leftist groups are also arriving. We're not sure who they're aligned with, but they mostly seem to be arguing amongst themselves. For example, the New Marxists have split off to occupy a bank foyer, the Social Justice, Gender Affirmation and Tolerance League want non-members banned from the head of the march, and the Anti-Fascist Peace Collective is just here to fight police.'

The Commissioner closed his eyes. Every pore and angry vein grew larger as he grimaced.

'Any appearance from the Muslim community?'

'Yes, sir, we've just had word they're approaching from the north and north-east sir.'

'Two groups? Let me guess – the Sunni and Shia thing again.'

'No, sir, both from the same group. It seems there was some sort of disagreement over the new mosque site. The local Imam, very helpful, visited us this morning to explain. Two prominent families have their own sites they want to donate for the new mosque. The argument over which site to use has divided the congregation. Lots of prestige and internal politics on the line, that kind of thing.'

A scarred and reddened hand briefly eclipsed the face on the screen.

'Are you telling me *Muslims* are coming here to protest the site of the new mosque?'

'Sort of, sir. Both groups want to petition the authorities to deny the other group planning permission.'

* * *

Back at the protest, Dave and the alt-right organisers were trying to figure it out as well. Huddled at the centre of their crowd, they draped an oversized Australian flag over their heads so no bastard could spy on them. At least Dave remembered to turn off the megaphone before they started speaking this time. Olaf/Tom was still staring daggers over that.

A skinhead wearing a Pepe the Frog t-shirt had the floor.

'So, whose side are the curries on? Don't we hate them too? Saw a bunch of them arguing with the hippies. Hindus, mussies, same difference.'

'Nah!' said Dave, missing the rhetorical question. 'It's like rugby. You know? League and union? They both kinda look the same, but they're different. See?'

There was a considered pause. An older guy with a swastika tattoo on his cheek pointed ominously at Dave.

'This is Victoria, mate,' he growled. 'It's AFL or fuck off.'

ELEVEN

LISA SAT HUNCHED OVER HER LAPTOP, FROWNING IN concentration. In espionage, as with dating, you should always do your online research before picking a partner.

Lisa was no stranger to online research. Although, she reflected bitterly, engaging in it a bit earlier could have saved her a lot of trouble. But now she had a different problem to solve.

This kind of research goes by various names; online investigation, net-sleuthing, Open-Source Intelligence – OSINT – but a common goal is discovery of information people often don't know they've made available.

Such as in one conflict, a proud young fighter uploaded a selfie he took in front of his local command post, promising death to his enemies and glory to his own forces. Within ten minutes, it had thousands of reactions and comments. Within thirty minutes, one of those reacting individuals, watching from a rival military, located that command post from background landmarks in the photo, and sent a guided missile that levelled the building. By the end of the day, the fighter was trending again – in memory of.

Lisa knew other applications for this kind of research. It would be vital to her plans.

Starting with basic searches and working up, she dived into the world of Andrew Stanton. There can be an amazing amount of information available to those who know how to get it. The first principle is understanding that the world of online information isn't a neat array of databases. It's a vibrant, changing ecosystem — a digital coral reef of towering, overlapping structures including open web, social media, news media and almost infinitely more. Most users float on the surface, looking down at this richness. From above, much is visible, but it isn't the whole picture. A skilled researcher can dive deep, look in cracks and under outcrops to find the things others miss or ignore.

'Andrew Stanton,' Lisa murmured as she typed. 'Let's see who you are.'

She had all the basics she needed. Name, age, some address information, plus she remembered what he looked like. But all that was just information – basic data. What she needed was some insight.

She started with his university days. There he was – treasurer of the Ultimate Frisbee Club. He had a head and shoulders photo in the organisational chart on the club's official website – which Lisa saved. As she did so, she dwelled on the picture. It was a good moment – his smile was broad, genuine, and the raised shoulder indicated they'd cropped out someone he had his arm around. Lisa felt a pang of sympathy, but only briefly. I guess lots of us were happier back then, she thought. Even if we didn't think it at the time.

She refocused and resumed her search. Going through the archived news and events section, she found an old contact sheet for members attending the annual finals event and barbeque. Aha, there was Andrew with his phone number and an email address she hadn't seen before.

Lisa copied and added them to the growing list of data points she had.

There wasn't much else useful for identification. There was a Robert Stanton linked to the same area Andrew grew up in. But he was killed in a hit and run by a driver later said to be 'well-known to authorities'. That was usually a polite press term for someone the pigs arrested every other week. The news story had a smiling picture of a middle-aged man. His hair and face shape were the same as Andrew's in the university photo, so Lisa dug deeper. She found the eulogy that praised a much-loved senior executive of some aeronautical company – husband of Jenny and father of Andrew. Usual 'great loss' etc. No more details.

Not immediately useful, but Lisa filed it away anyway.

Using the data collected so far, she tracked down Andrew's social media before opening each one in separate tabs.

Lisa frowned, her face scrunching up as she went through them. For the most part, they were locked down. Some basic things like his bio pages etc, but you couldn't see his posts and pictures unless you were already linked to him. Clever boy, he changed the security settings.

Okay then, no casual snooping here. He'd actually listened to the speech on online security when he joined DAS. They were picky about that, as most of the big platforms defaulted everything to 'publicly visible' and 'please give all my data to billionaire tyrants'. Given the potential for security breaches, DAS were pretty big for online security. Even if they lectured like an old Aunty warning of all the rapists and murderers 'looking at your googles'.

Lisa paused in the face of this dead end. A new approach was needed. As one of the old war-horses in DAS told her, 'you're only as secure as your network'.

She sat back, hands behind her head, and stared at the ceiling. What network did he even have? New to Canberra, so probably no friends. Might get some joy from local ultimate frisbee clubs… She thought back. One of the few visible things he recently posted was about the 'beginning of a new career! So excited! It'll be huge!'

'Career …' Lisa muttered. She looked back at her notes and grabbed a likely name from her list.

'Sonya,' she said, 'let's see what you have for us.'

Sonya was another grad in this year's DAS intake. Lisa tracked down her social media even faster than Andrew's. But best of all, it was open to the world.

Lisa 'hmmd' in a quietly judgemental way as she went through the feeds. Sonya was into fitness. That is, she spent a lot of time posing in active wear. Lisa tried to shake off her bias and get the bigger picture. She had to grudgingly admit that Sonya carried it off well. Going through the pics and video, it was clear Sonya was pretty high-energy. Regular gym routine, netball player – note to self, Lisa thought; bitch probably knows how to throw an elbow. But also active in the political science society, a couple of overseas trips, interned for a think tank, plus lots of women's rights and safety advocacy.

Good for you, thought Lisa, reconsidering her pre-emptive judgement. I just hope you took to the streets for it. That's all they respect.

She thought for a moment longer. Almost all, she added.

But she found what she was after next to #cocktails and #fridaydrinks.

The video was a few seconds long. The point of view swung around on a group of young professional-types in a bar before Sonya turned the phone around for a selfie with everyone behind.

Lisa hit pause.

'Hello grads,' she said, staring at the screen.

It was the entire intake. They seemed like any other table of new workmates, huddled together but still not entirely certain of each other.

Not completely huddled together, Lisa noted. Andrew was off to one side. Beer in hand, shoulders slumped, and his smile waxy and forced.

'Not having a good time?' she asked the screen.

Lisa scrolled further back. There was another group selfie – this time a photo – from a dinner at a restaurant the previous Wednesday. She looked through the group but saw no fluffy hair. In that or any of the other photos.

The pattern repeated. Andrew was present in the previous Friday drinks but no other grad outings.

'Guess you're not in the right group chat,' said Lisa. 'Probably harder to ditch you on Friday when everyone's out the door at the same time.'

So, he was isolated and clearly not enjoying himself. Lisa tried not to think about why. But he had access. That's all that mattered.

She logged in to an AI that could find locations from images and videos. It compared whatever you uploaded with who knows how much satellite and other data. Lisa uploaded a few screenshots from Sonya's videos of the bar. Some of the footage was from out on the balcony, overlooking a lake and buildings in the background. That was enough. Within a few seconds, she had the bar's name and location. Lisa also knew when they were usually there thanks to the timestamps on Sonya's posts. Not a bad place to find and follow him. Time for the next step.

TWELVE

Two weeks later

OSTRA HUMMED WITH QUIET ACTIVITY. IT WAS STILL early enough in the morning for caffeine-fuelled enthusiasm, and each workstation was a studious example of quiet efficiency.

Except for one empty one.

Andrew, fresh from his morning security rituals, hurried into the office. He flicked the computer on and dropped into his office chair like something landing in a skip.

'Sorry,' he called to Peter. 'Bag search ran overtime.'

Peter didn't shift from the report he was reading and gave a non-committal 'Hmm'.

Assuming it was safe to proceed, Andrew opened his emails. The first was marked 'URGENT – Research needed for Operation Perpendicular Frypan'.

He read it and groaned. Another manifesto to go through. He was sick of these. No one liked reading some extremist's stream of consciousness. Especially when they tended to lose track of their own points and rambled – for hundreds of pages.

But someone had to make sure there wasn't some specific threat or nugget of info that was useful. That's what all these operations used OSTRA for – the crap work.

'And why are the op names always so stupid?' said Andrew aloud.

'To protect ourselves,' said Peter. 'From one of the gravest ongoing threats to national security.'

'Hostile intelligence agencies?' said Andrew.

Peter shook his head. 'Hints,' he said.

'What?' said Andrew as the other analysts nodded in agreement.

'Hints,' said Peter grimly. 'Some intelligence personnel can't help themselves. Left alone, people always pick some name that's a sneaky hint. Or a pun. Look at the classics: Operations Good Boy, Mincemeat, Zigzag – all of them. Each of them reveals in some way what the operation is actually about. Sometimes people crack it and – disaster.'

'So, we use these crappy names instead?'

'Exactly,' said Peter. 'They're randomly assigned from smashing a few words together. Keeps us all honest and not trying to leave cryptic clues for people to follow.'

'Go for the boring ones too,' Heather called out.

'What do you mean?' asked Andrew.

'The interesting operations usually have boring names, and vice versa,' Peter explained. 'Look, career tip: operations with names like "Dragon Max Power Nuke" are just there to pull in the idiots. It's going to be working out how big an army is by how much toilet paper they order or something.'

Peter snorted to himself and turned back to his screen. He rested his hand on his chin in a way guaranteed to trigger an afternoon lecture on his bad back acting up again. Andrew turned back to his computer as well. He logged into CRYS-TALBALL, the main information database. Lots of databases and computer systems had names that made some classical or geeky reference. It was the insider humour typical of people whose jokes are protected from public ridicule by national security legislation.

He looked at his feed. There were several new reports from overnight. The first was marked 'SECRET – HUMAN-SOURCE INTELLIGENCE'. It related to an anti-government anarchist group trying to infiltrate a major political party. Several members started by joining a local branch before voting each other into positions of power on the executive committee, their ultimate plan being to use that access to recruit insiders, conduct an attack, or both. Fortunately, they'd been absorbed by the politics and had fallen out over a proposed property development. The whole thing had disintegrated into passive-aggressive emails and public audits of each other's travel expenses to trigger resignations.

Andrew chuckled to himself. 'Idiots,' he said.

'Find something good?' Al called out. Andrew relayed the report, including his derision of both the anarchist group and the supposedly professional political party.

'But how could they have not known they had extremists right in front of them?' asked Andrew. 'I'd have seen that coming a mile away.' He paused as the image of Lisa flashed into his mind.

Peter came to life, no longer a wax dummy of desk-based scoliosis. With a supervillain chair swivel, he turned to face Andrew. The seat's metal frame gave an incredulous squeak, almost singing '*Reeeeaally?*' He peered over the top of his glasses. 'And you would be immune to manipulation?' he said to Andrew. 'Being so sophisticated, of course.'

Andrew bristled. He stared at Peter as he heard other chairs subtly creak around the office as their owners shifted to listen. If each one had had a laser microphone, Andrew would have lit up like a Christmas tree.

'I'm not talking myself up,' he said. 'I'm just saying that *some* people aren't very smart and can be easily manipulated.'

Peter's face wrinkled up as a rare smile appeared. 'But others can't? A wager then? Care to bet?'

'Bet?' Andrew paused as eavesdroppers abandoned subtlety and paid attention. Shanti leaned back in her chair as though her favourite show was about to start.

Ignore the audience, he told himself. 'Sure. How much?'

Peter waved the suggestion away. 'Oh, we only ever bet coffees here. Keeps things low-key and unlikely to escalate. I bet I can manipulate you. Let's see ... By the end of the week, you will have given me a pen. If you haven't, coffee's on me. If you have, it's on you.'

Andrew's eyes narrowed as the surrounding grins widened. 'A pen? You're going to trick me into giving you a pen?'

'Trick? Oh no, I'm going to *manipulate* you.'

Andrew stood up and held out his hand to Peter. 'All right, boss man, but I play to win.'

Peter shook the outstretched hand, his expression bright.

'I'm not playing,' he said.

* * *

It started after lunch.

'I need a volunteer to empty the paper shredder,' Peter called out. 'Anyone who doesn't want to do it, please pass me a pen.'

Pens sailed across the office and clattered onto Peter's desk.

Without a word, Andrew headed out the door. A few minutes later, he walked back in, looking like he'd lost a confetti fight. Shredding, sometimes referred to as 'filing', was a big part of DAS life and the waist-high industrial machines were typically stuffed to exploding. Opening the door on one produced a paper blizzard. Andrew walked back to his desk, trailing ultra-fine slices of formerly classified documents. The room was quiet, except for Peter having a muttered conversation with Michael. He was another analyst, a couple of years older than Andrew, with a manga hair style and unsettling positivity.

Peter and Michael stopped talking and looked over at Andrew. Michael's smile was unmistakable.

So that's how it is, thought Andrew. Michael was just the sort of keen bean Peter would wrap around his finger.

'Can you chuck me a pen?' Michael called out.

Andrew looked over. Michael's desk was just beyond Peter's. Peter had sat down again, absorbed in his printouts, but for all he knew, Peter was ex-SAS who would leap like a border collie and snap the pen out of the air mid-flight.

'Can't help you, sorry.'

'C'mon on, Andrew!'

'Yeah,' added Heather. 'Do him a favour.'

'Not a good team attitude,' said Shanti. Andrew couldn't see her face, but knew she was smirking.

He stonily glared at his computer as mischievous calls bounced around him.

Andrew gritted his teeth. Enemies surrounded him, opposing pawns in Peter's stupid game. Nice try, he thought, but you're not winning this one.

'I see how it is,' he said to the room at large, scooping up all the pens on his desk and putting them in a drawer. 'I'll win on my own, then!'

'Listen up!' said Peter. 'Now I need someone to reformat all of last year's Counter Espionage reporting from docs into PDFs. Any pen-less volunteers?'

* * *

Several hours later, Andrew walked out of headquarters and into the evening, jacket in one hand and his battered backpack in the other. The sun was a way off from sinking behind the hills and Andrew blinked and squinted as he adjusted. It was the price of spending the day in the bowels of the building. The day's weight slid off him as he strolled to the bus stop.

Once home, he headed straight into his room. He had no interest in catching up with his flatmates tonight, if they were even home. Liam had made a point of mentioning how busy he was with networking events, and Pascal came and went erratically for work, errand or just getting lucky – who knew what he did with his time? When Andrew had asked about his work, he'd just shrugged and said 'IT'. For all he knew, Pascal could be shooting a porno somewhere, in between drug deals and arms dealing. But maybe his work was classified as well? The thought briefly sparked the nascent paranoia that Andrew was cultivating into a professional qualification.

Nah, he thought to himself. They'd never hire that reality TV reject.

After an hour of scrolling, he opened a stashed packet of double-choc Tim Tams and headed over to his computer. Andrew played games to relax. In particular, a massive online multiplayer role playing game set in a fantasy land. He started it up and settled back as it loaded. A familiar intro sequence appeared: armies of fantasy creatures rushing to battle before a dragon flies into view. The dragon blasted the screen with fire that died down to reveal the menu screen beneath a title in high fantasy font: Armies of Azeroth.

Andrew logged in and started playing. Not many in this area today. Only goblins and minor orcs. Good place for side quests.

He was only three Tim Tams in when his message alert went off. *Boo-raaaaahh!* It was an old Viking horn, suitable for the game but rendered slightly tinny by the cheap speakers.

He ignored it. He was in no mood for homophobic slurs from some spoilt shit of a twelve-year-old looking to troll.

The message alert went off again. And again.

Another player approached his Paladin. Their avatar was a thief. You could always tell by the hood. It always struck Andrew as flawed that the thieves always dressed to stereotype. Realistically, it should count against them. But it was just a game.

Boo-rah!

Andrew gave up and opened the chat window.

Hi Andrew

He paused. He didn't recognise the name. Andrew's game name was 'octoplural673'. How did they know who he was?

Andrew? I know ur there.

Who u? He typed.

It's me, Lisa. You helped me leave work.

Andrew recoiled, standing up and away from the computer. The chair slid backwards until it hit the bed. His hand went to his face, unconsciously rubbing chocolate across his cheek.

Andrew mentally listed all the players he knew who'd be enough of a smart arse to try this. Surely not many? He then combined that with a list of people who'd know about his interaction with Lisa.

No one. He didn't game with work people. No one wanted to play with him.

Cautiously, he sat back down again. Suspecting a possible prank by another grad, he typed: *Who really?*

The reply flicked up on the screen almost instantly.

Lisa, left without my shoes.

A Tim Tam slipped out of his hand, bounced off the keyboard and onto the floor. He remembered her heels lying forlorn on the ground as she vanished through the exit. Before the guards arrived, he'd thought she was just really into fire drills.

Right. What would Shanti and Peter do? What would an analyst do? Gather information!

Where are you?

Safe. For now.

Okay, he thought. That didn't help. Plus, he didn't care about *her* safety.

Why contact me? he asked.

You have bigger problems than me in DAS, she replied

You stole info, Andrew typed.

Forget that, she replied.

Andrew tried to mentally accept that, and failed.

Why contact me? he repeated.

Need help. I know about other threat activity. More going on.

What's your plan? Andrew typed.

Need more INFO. Andrew could almost hear the exasperation in the capitals. *Need to find the source of the threats.*

How? he typed.

Be in touch. Keep playing. Remember, we had a deal. Get me caught and I'll tell them about the real help you gave me. We're in this together.

'What?' Andrew yelled at the screen.

The hooded figure vanished from the screen.

THIEFNAME2134 has left the game.

What deal? Or real help? Her last message made no sense. Andrew paused for a moment, then groaned. Dammit. She had just created a conversation that looked like he knew more than he had told Internal Security. Not hard evidence, but enough in a world where suspicion was compelling, if not actual proof. A vision of James from Internal Security appeared in his head, opening a floor hatch to an oubliette Andrew would never return from.

Andrew sat at his desk, lost in confusion and adrenaline. He jumped as the front door crashed open. But rather than compliance-demanding shouts from the SWAT team of

Andrew's imagination, he heard Pascal's muttering and the clink of bottles in shopping bags. As Andrew's room was closest to the front door, he'd become accustomed to the opening and closing. He'd learned to ignore it.

There was a knock at the door.

'What?' yelled Andrew, his voice cracking slightly.

'It's me!' called Pascal through the wood. 'Two of us are gonna be having, you know, an evening out here. Could ya give us some space?'

Andrew rolled his eyes. His stomach turned at the thought of catching Pascal getting lucky on the couch. Netflix and fuck in your own room, he thought to himself.

'No worries, mate,' he called out instead. 'Got lots on.'

Andrew listened for the thanks, but it never came. All he heard was Pascal's footsteps hurrying down the hall.

Typical of the handsome bastard. He was a good enough housemate, but the dramas of having to evacuate rooms to simplify someone else's love life grated. Especially when he never got the chance to reciprocate.

Andrew looked back at the screen, his shoulders dropping. He'd found and lost the person who'd ruined his reputation. Perhaps his career.

But what if he found her again?

Outside, he heard someone give a shriek of delight and the groan of the sofa shifting on the wooden floor. With a resigned sigh, he reached for his noise-cancelling headphones.

Thirteen

The next morning, Andrew stifled a yawn as he sat alone in the office. He hadn't slept all night thinking about his incriminating game chat. Eventually, at an hour he'd normally curse, he crawled out of bed and went into the office. At least there was no one else around this early. It gave him time to think. What to do? Report the conversation or pretend it didn't happen? What if they used it as evidence he was working with Lisa? It was only in-game chat. If he deleted the game and stayed offline for a while, maybe it never happened?

His sense of peace shattered as the phone rang. He stared at it like it was a spider on a toilet seat, willing it to go away of its own accord. A message flashed up on his screen via the in-house chat system.

It was James. His interrogator.

Andrew? Answer the phone.

Andrew's hand shook as he reached out to the receiver. His mind ran at breakneck speed. He had a story ready, one he'd worked on all night. The second security called he'd be ready. He didn't know why she called him. He didn't know how she found him. He didn't tell her anything, and he definitely didn't help her steal from DAS.

'H-hello?' His voice hadn't cracked like that since he was thirteen.

'Andrew?' James's voice was as gruff as ever.

Andrew launched into his alibi. 'Yeah, look what happen—'

'Come to Internal Security,' interrupted James.

The phone clicked as he hung up.

Another message flashed up on his screen.

Now.

Andrew scrambled out of his chair with adrenal shock and spent a few sweaty minutes powerwalking to the Internal Security wing. As he got to the door, it snapped open and James sprang out. No trap-door spider had ever snared its prey more efficiently.

Andrew didn't even have time to say hello. He half expected that hulking frame to keep coming at him. He braced, preparing to be smashed to the carpet with his arms twisted up behind him.

Instead, James took him by the arm and spun him around but didn't slow down.

'We're in here,' he said, half guiding, half dragging him to a larger office on the other side.

Andrew squirmed uselessly in James's calloused hand as he was dragged across the hall. Seriously, he thought, he works in an office! What does he do with his spare time to get that kind of grip?

James gave a quick double-tap knock, opened the door, handed Andrew in like he was passing the salt, and remained outside. For all his previous roughness, the door shut with barely a click.

'Good morning, Andrew. Nice to see you in so early.'

Andrew blinked. He was in a room with so many pot

plants it looked like a garden nursery. But there was a desk, partially visible amongst the vegetation at the other end.

A woman rose out of the greenery. She stood behind the desk with an arm extended, inviting Andrew to sit in the chair on the edge of the forest. She wasn't Peter old, but at least forty. She was, Andrew thought generously, looking good despite this. His eyes caught hers and he coughed and moved to the indicated seat.

'My name is Angela,' she said. 'Do you know what it is I do?'

'Uhh,' said Andrew. 'You're James's boss? Sort of security thing?'

There was a moment's pause as this response went down.

'I've been called worse,' she said. 'Yes, a *security thing* is not inaccurate.'

Andrew smiled, hoping this was the right reaction. This was like talking to Shanti all over again. He would just get things wrong and make everything worse. Be complimentary instead.

'Your name has "angel" in it,' he said. 'That's nice.'

Angela stared for a few seconds, or several thousand years. Andrew couldn't be sure.

'I called you here today,' she said finally, 'to offer you a development opportunity.'

At this point, Andrew showed how early he was in his career by not running out of the room screaming. Every jaded white-collar veteran will tell you; development opportunities precede career suicide, soul-destroying drudge work, or both. Only novices or the self-deluded think development opportunities are a good thing.

'Sounds good,' said Andrew. 'How can I help?'

'Help us find Lisa Chapman,' she said, rubbing her hands together.

'Don't you have floors of people doing that? Peter says—'

'Peter,' interrupted Angela, 'is highly experienced but

narrow-minded. I recognise the need for multiple viewpoints. Outside talent.'

Andrew nodded, feeling like he was being sold something, but no idea what.

'It's just that with the, umm …'

'Oh, I'm well aware of your role in The Breach.'

Great, thought Andrew miserably. He could hear the capitalisation. *The Breach.* The single biggest one. One that he had unwittingly abetted.

'Frankly,' continued Angela, 'this is going on longer than we'd hoped already. The pressure is enormous and the reward to those who find her will be great.'

In that moment, it was like a gong was gently sounded in a Zen Garden somewhere and the rest of the universe fell away. Angela's words bounced back and forth in his head: *The reward to those who find her will be great.*

What if he found her? Aside from the panic, that same thought had been occupying him since last night as well. Within two minutes, Lisa had wrecked his reputation, but what if he brought her in?

'Andrew?'

The universe snapped back into being, with Angela staring at him.

'Absolutely,' he said. He had been paying just enough attention to know no questions had come his way, a habit that had driven at least one girlfriend to dump him. But Angela's stare was different. This wasn't rage, it was a curious, disaffected interest. He was a baby turtle, waggling his legs, as she gently turned him around in her hands.

'Also, as you said, there is an element of angel about me. What is it angels do, Andrew? They help. I want to help you make up some ground. Do you feel like that could be a good thing? For your future career, perhaps?'

Andrew grinned like a lotto winner. Angela had taken on a definite glow in his mind.

Angela, sensing his sudden enthusiasm, warmed to her topic.

'I'm sure this could be a great opportunity for you. This is the pointy end of the spear, where we need smart, dedicated people like you.'

Andrew leaned forward and put both hands on her desk. A fern lightly brushed his forehead as he leaned in.

'Whatever I can do to help, Angela,' he said.

'Perfect,' said Angela. 'Report all findings directly to me or James. You'll be sent tasks shortly. Stay at your current desk. You're an outside talent, so you won't be sitting with the team.'

Andrew was pondering what outside talent actually was as she stood up, perfectly framed by the towering greenery on either side, and waved an arm at the door.

Andrew took the hint and stood, thanking her profusely.

'Andrew?' she called as he placed a hand on the doorknob.

'Yes?'

'Is there anything you want to tell me?'

Andrew's outstretched hand slid off the door handle, almost costing him his balance, but he rallied well.

'No,' he said, pleased he had kept the squeak out of his voice. Lisa's message played in his mind, but he was already guilty by association. If she got caught by someone else, it'd be the end for him. It needed to be him. Nothing else would prove his loyalty to DAS and everyone in it. Angela would be grateful once he could give her Lisa's location, or a way to find her.

Angela walked across the carpet to pat him companionably on the arm.

'You've been part of a very serious event,' she said. 'I've found that where it happens once, it can happen again. Report anything even remotely strange and be wary of random contacts. Don't let us down.'

He nodded and tried the door handle again.

'Andrew,' she said as he turned to leave. 'Know what else angels do? They destroy the unrighteous. Remember that.'

* * *

By the time Andrew got back to the office, word had gotten there ahead of him. There are various forms of intelligence: SIGINT (signals intelligence), IMINT (imagery intelligence) – the list goes on. But they all take a back seat to the speed and reach of RUMINT (rumour and gossip intelligence).

As he entered, Peter raised an eyebrow like an annoyed spouse who'd caught their partner coming home late.

'Well, well,' he said. 'Look who's back from Insecurity and in on the big investigation.'

'How'd you know that?' asked Andrew.

'A good analyst always has sources,' said Peter. 'But thanks for confirming.'

'Whatever,' said Andrew. 'It's a great—'

'Development opportunity?' finished Peter, raising an eyebrow again.

Andrew tried to collect his thoughts. Peter was typically amused by things that only he could see.

'I'm sure you'll be vital to their efforts,' Peter added wryly.

Andrew bristled at this. He *would* be vital. Not Peter, not even Angela, knew just how important he would become. What was it with these boomers and their attitudes to his generation? Always telling them they were lazy and expected too much – like affordable housing on a liveable planet.

'I'll catch her, just wait and see,' said Andrew.

Peter snorted, his reply cut short as the computer pinged and he swivelled back around to his computer. 'Ah!' he said, staring at his email. 'So good of Angela to let me know she's stealing you. But you'll still be based in this office with me.'

Andrew shrugged his concern about that.

Tapping the screen with the end of his pen, Peter continued, 'Looks like she assigned you social media and open-source information. There's a bunch of groups here who may know something about her. Anarchists, anti-government movements, etc. Just check their stuff, you know.' Peter waved a hand, an ancient rite to summon unfamiliar things; 'You know, Insta … Tok … Chat. Or whatever.'

As annoyed as he was not being given anything secret, Andrew paused, and an incredulous grin spread over his face.

'Seriously? Instatokchat? Wow. All I have is wow.'

Peter rolled his eyes.

'But before you check the instachats,' he said, 'I need you to sign a few things.' He picked up a fat pile of forms from his desk and handed them to Andrew, who sighed.

That was another joy of government: the paperwork. Every bit of admin needed to be printed, filled out, and signed several times. The department head – who was Peter's age – had heard of digital signatures and wanted none of it. Everything had to be printed. Otherwise, what were shredders for?

Andrew paused. He hadn't carried a pen in days. Just in case.

'Use mine,' said Peter, reading his thoughts. A blue office special stuck out of his fingers. No obvious poison barbs or teeth marks on the lid.

'I'm still allowed to give *you* pens,' he said.

Andrew snatched the pen out of Peter's hand, leaning on his desk to scribble through the pile with the speed of someone agreeing to online terms and conditions. The worst part was initialling all twenty-three pages of the updated confidentiality agreement.

'Done!' he snapped, as the last illegible scrawl hit a dotted line.

'That's great,' said Peter, 'thanks.'

What infuriated Andrew later on was that Peter didn't actually ask. He just held out his spare hand as he scooped up the forms. Andrew unthinkingly passed the pen across. Time slowed as his mind scrabbled to catch up to his body. Horror surged through his body as he watched the pen tumble out of his grip towards Peter's outstretched hand.

'No!' he yelled. Instinct kicked in and he flicked the pen across the room with his fingertips.

'Well,' said Peter mildly, 'I hope you're nicer to your better half. Or isn't there one?'

'It's hard to meet people when everyone associates you with betrayal,' grumbled Andrew.

'Don't worry,' said Peter. 'I know lots of spies who'd love to set you up.'

* * *

The hours ground on as Andrew quietly worked through Lisa's social media. AI had already scanned for extremist content – nil – but Angela's email insisted he go through it the old-fashioned way. Read every comment, look at every picture, list every like, comment and emoji. Andrew vaguely wondered if Peter had somehow arranged this, reducing his brain to mush just to get his hands on a bloody pen. Sources indeed.

He made notes as he went, but they were chaotic and not in the required style. He knew this was going to cost him double the time when he had to write everything up formally. Served him right for not listening to Peter's lecture on the language of written intelligence analysis.

But that's what lecture handouts and style guides were for – his personal saviour. He opened a PDF: 'Estimative Language:

A guide to conveying likelihood with corresponding analytical confidence in intelligence products'.

That was another thing. They didn't do reports or documents, they did products. Always *products*. He'd heard other analysts talking about good or bad product coming from whatever team. They'd sounded like some hackneyed movie about cocaine kingpins. Ironic, since that may be who the products in question might be about. He heaved a teenaged sigh and continued.

When assessing event likelihood, use the following terms to convey confidence in your assessment:

X is <u>*highly likely*</u> *(greater than 90% probability event will occur).*
X is <u>*likely*</u> *(greater than 60% probability event will occur).*
X is <u>*unlikely*</u> *(less than 45% probability event will occur).*
X is <u>*highly unlikely*</u> *(less than 20% probability event will occur).*

'For fuck's sake,' muttered Andrew. He stood up and looked across the room. Most people were in meetings or protected by headphones. Shanti's desk faced his, but all but the top of her head was hidden by her computer screen. No headphones that he could see.

'Shanti?' Andrew called out.

Her head dipped slightly.

'Yes?' she said warily, without looking up.

Attention secured, he hurried over to her desk. No need to shout his issues across the office.

'I have a style guide question and—'

'Then read the guides!' she snapped. 'It's what they're for.'

She stayed focused on her screen the entire time, apparently engrossed in an Excel spreadsheet.

After a few moments, Andrew mumbled 'Thanks' and headed back to his computer. No need to get between her and a pivot table.

He had only just unlocked his computer when she appeared at his desk.

'Look,' she said, hands clasped in front of her. 'I'm sorry, that wasn't necessary. You know how tense the people at Internal Security can make you.'

Andrew wanted to give the old stink eye to an Excel sheet of his own. But, to his surprise, he blinked and accepted her apology.

'That's all right,' he said. 'I'm spending far too much time with them too.'

'So, what's the problem?' she asked, hands unwinding.

'Estimative language,' he said. 'What do we say when we don't know if something will happen? What if it's a fifty/fifty chance?'

'Possibly, maybe, could,' she said. 'But honestly, that's frowned upon. Look at the evidence and make a call. Peter always says, "You won't find greatness on the fence".'

'Thanks,' he said.

'No problem,' said Shanti. She turned back towards her desk.

'Shanti?' Andrew said, and she turned back.

'I'm sorry about The Breach and dumping you in it,' he said. 'But I'm doing everything I can to fix things.'

Shanti shrugged. 'Thank you for the thought, but move on. I'd call fixing all that *highly unlikely*.'

Nevertheless, she gave him a conciliatory smile before she went back to her desk.

Andrew faced the screen, but his attention went inward to an image of Lisa, captured at last.

Highly likely, he thought to himself.

* * *

That evening, Andrew hummed as he swept through his front door. With a burst of speed, he jumped on the old, threadbare hallway rug and rode it along the wooden floor like a modern-day Aladdin. Right to his bedroom door. Back in the game, baby! Oh yeah, it was going to be sweet to be on the Lisa investigation.

He couldn't believe his luck. He could use this. A guy with a direct connection to Lisa on the investigation? The second she let something slip, he could use DAS's resources to track her down or lure her somewhere. Speaking of trickery, an image of Peter and the pen popped into Andrew's mind. Close call there. He would have to stay on top of that one.

With barely conscious thought, he kicked off his shoes, threw his jacket on the bed and switched his computer on. The chair groaned in protest as he plonked down and spun like someone on an inflatable pool toy.

Andrew logged in and clapped his hands together. Time for the next move, as soon as he knew what that was. But for now, time for some rest and relaxation, side quests and—.

Boo-rah! The Viking horn of his in-game messenger went off.

Andrew?

Lisa again. The notification flashed in the screen's corner, spiking his blood pressure. Even seeing her thief avatar filled his stomach with centipedes.

Andrew slapped his forehead. How could he have forgotten that his game was the way she contacted him? Habit was as powerful as it was forgettable. It's all right, he told himself. Gotta stay prepared. Just get her to meet you somewhere. If she makes a mistake sooner, all the better.

His hands prickled with sweat as he typed. He tried not to think about what Angela and James would do if they knew about this, lest he dampen his underwear as well.

I'm here, he wrote. *Haven't got long. We should meet.*

NO. She replied so quickly the keys probably burned.

So much for the dance, he thought to himself. Too abrupt. He'd done the same thing on dating apps.

He was formulating another approach when she took charge of the conversation.

I want all materials and information about Koil.

Andrew leaned back in his chair. Despite being alone in the room, he looked over his shoulder before typing his reply.

What's Koil? he typed.

WHO. She responded, before adding an eye roll emoji.

Andrew bristled at this. Just who did she think she was?

He began typing a sentence with sarcasm ladled on. He paused mid-sentence and cocked an ear as the sound of approaching footsteps sent paranoid shivers up his spine. Several people at least …

Crap! With visions of masked commandos about to crash through his bedroom door, Andrew flicked off the screen and leaped away from the computer. Destroy the evidence! He snatched an old can of Red Bull and shook it over the PC tower. A single drop of sugary caffeine flicked out and lightly stained the plastic.

Reality crept in. The footsteps weren't the synchronised steps of some synced-up death squad. They turned into the babble of a group of people coming in, Liam's voice in front.

'Ah yes, come on in. Plenty of space for everyone.'

Andrew cursed himself. Each Wednesday Liam hosted a meeting for some think tank's youth league. Full, no doubt, of people from the Minister's office.

He'd heard them spend entire meetings arguing about the politics of what snacks to bring, coming up with options that included gluten-free, dairy-free, vegan and fair trade and avoided cultural appropriation. When they would work up to geopolitics was anyone's guess.

Andrew was considering putting a chair up against the door

when he heard Pascal's door slam. Good to know his evening was ruined as well.

The weekly argument moved further into the living room. Before the living room door clicked closed, Andrew heard someone suggest a food delivery, only to be shouted down with 'Do you even know what they pay their drivers?'

He looked at the screen. Lisa was gone. So much for meeting. He thought about what she'd asked for. Koil? Well, at least he knew it was a who.

Could he pretend to know about Koil and get her to meet him? Maybe not. Seeing how careful she was, he'd need some sort of proof. She'd know if he didn't have something legit.

No, the best course now was to get a little something on Koil and use it to lure her out, organise a meeting. And the rest of DAS would be coming with him. With appropriate credit given to his tip-off, of course.

Fourteen

Two days later, the morning cafe rush hour was in full swing. People queued up for their coffee, tea, breakfast rolls and whatever sugary snacks were claimed as necessary to get through morning meetings.

This was the cafe inside DAS Headquarters. To enjoy a drink or snack there, you just had to get past the external fencing, guardhouses, and several layers of electronic and physical security inside the building. It may seem unusual to have a coffee space in a high-security building, complete with vetted baristas, but it was seen as a vital national security measure. Much of the world's law enforcement, intelligence and military organisations run on an unhealthy amount of caffeine and sugar. Having an in-house cafe was convenient and reduced the number of people wandering off to a place where someone could spy on them. It was considered far safer to let them sip and gossip inside – where the right people could keep an eye on them.

It was a pleasant enough and functional space. Made slightly more homely by the tongue-in-cheek sign that welcomed people to 'Cafe Redacted'. A crowd of four-seat tables was set up off to one side, separated from the queuing space by another airport-style divider. This line was designed so that customers walked past the sweets cabinet and hot food before they could order at the register. It was a visual and aromatic feast that preyed on human weakness, turning people against whatever health kick they were on. The service wasn't particularly fast, and it was speculated this was to ensure people had maximum time standing in front of temptation. It was a compact, efficient and brutally effective study of human motivation and exploitation. So much so that even seasoned human-source recruitment professionals found themselves nodding in respect when they walked away, now holding the treat they hadn't planned on buying.

Andrew stood at the register and ordered a mocha, plus a brownie for some reason. The woman who took payment didn't try any of the chatty banter you sometimes got from other staff. No, she was a lifetime hospitality veteran and had the stare to prove it. She directed him to wait on the far side where all the other grads had already gathered. The grads, now scattered to different departments, synchronised their morning coffee run so they could meet in the cafe and catch up. Even Andrew got an invite to this ritual, but mostly because he had stumbled across it by accident sometime prior, and now it was too awkward to exclude him.

The tables were full, and the human overflow was scattered around the cafe. The noise and chatter was immense as everyone caught up, complained or gossiped. Every now and again, a name and drink order was shouted out from behind an industrial coffee machine at the end of the counter, and someone would hurry up to grab it before it was accidentally taken by some other fatigued addict. Fortunately, the shouter sounded like he'd had a previous life scaring people on military parade grounds, so was more than capable of making himself heard above the hubbub and announced each coffee like he was closing an auction.

'Elise! **CHAI!**' he bellowed.

Elise broke out of the grad group to fetch her coffee. Unable to get a table, the group stood in an awkward clump just beyond the cafe seating, but still within screaming range as they waited for their orders. The chatter dropped as Andrew arrived from the counter, brownie in hand. People suddenly became preoccupied with their coffee or something in the distance.

'How's Military Support going Sonya?' said Andrew, as an attempt to revive the conversation.

'Pretty good,' she said. 'But can't say much. It's the need to know.'

Andrew nodded. He understood, but felt Sonya was just using that as an excuse not to tell him anything. 'Need To Know' was a forceful concept in intelligence and part of the lectures they'd sat through. It meant you shouldn't share information with anyone, even if they had the correct security clearance, unless they had a specific need to know that exact information. Like many initially sensible ideas, it often backfired, and in this case, made people as ready to share as a kleptomaniac who'd locked themselves in a bank vault. However, RUMINT, gossip and whispered conversations in hallways occasionally helped bridge the gaps between teams and organisations.

Unfortunately for Andrew, the grads weren't ready to gossip about their own areas with him. All enquires just got variations of 'pretty good', and 'got stuff going on you know' – just in case he gave whatever they said to another traitor fleeing the building. Whatever, he told himself. They won't be so cagey when he's known as the one who caught her.

'Kim! **LATTE!**'

Kim headed off, one of the few grads who didn't have their order yet.

'Oh!' said Sonya in the tone of one remembering something juicy. 'Did you hear more about the, uh,' – her eyes flicked to Andrew – 'the Breacher?'

Everyone leaned in, while Andrew reddened, feeling like had Sonya heard his thoughts. Immediately theories and snatches of gossip began sailing back and forth. The Breach, as it was now known, was a hot topic in DAS. The only thing DAS had admitted to publicly was a 'security incident' but gave no other details citing national security. Naturally in Canberra, this kicked off a storm of speculation and gossip. The story possibilities of a national security incident drove the political opinion columns crazy. Not to mention the online gossip and conspiracy theories. This spurred journalists to try scaling the walls of secrecy, but with no sources and endless 'no comment' from the government, they had eventually given up. Inside DAS, people knew someone in Information Coordination and Response was involved, and a few even knew her first name. They also knew this person took something huge, and that Andrew helped her escape. Possibly on purpose. The people who knew more had been on the receiving end of Angela and James' investigation. They were either tight-lipped or had decided to use a lot of that leave that had been accruing.

'I heard she's in China,' said Sonya. 'Hitched a ride on a private jet run owned by a CCP billionaire.'

'Nah,' said Kim, 'Russia, for sure.'

'Does anyone know why they haven't released who it is?' asked Isabella. 'Surely we'd be telling everyone in the world to catch them.'

That triggered a flurry of comments around operational priorities, strategies and other corporate fertiliser used to fill the gaps when you don't know something. Andrew would never admit it, but knowing he knew more than the gossiping hordes gave him an excited shiver. He knew Lisa believed there was more going on, something connected to someone called Koil. A piece of information he could use to eventually catch her. Plus, if it revealed other threats to DAS, that would just make his catch all the more impressive. His initial searches on Koil hadn't turned up anything, but he hadn't pressed too hard in case it triggered some alert somewhere. But he was still troubled by one mystery Lisa had.

'What did she even take?' said Andrew loudly.

The grads went quiet.

'Could be a list of all our human sources and where they are,' said Sonya after a few seconds.

'I heard it was some new US technology,' said Kim. 'Like a new satellite-killer or something.'

'Or the name of a source somewhere vital,' said Isabella.

'I said that!' snapped Sonya. 'Whatever it is, it's part of some massive operation.'

'Really?' said Andrew. 'If she was in Coordination and Response, she was in an admin role. They just organise all the internal information. You know, everyone in DAS talking to everyone else in DAS. From what Peter told me, they don't actually see what people do, they're just the central point for requests. Then they pass it on to whatever branch needs to know and they take it from there. She may have seen the occasional target or operation name but wouldn't know much else.'

'Unless,' said Sonya, 'she was working with someone on the inside who told her.'

Everyone looked at Andrew again.

'Oh, come on!' he said, temper flaring. 'It was my first day! I had no idea!'

'Oh absolutely,' said Sonya. To Andrew, her tone oozed disbelieving condescension. But it might have just been the mood he was now in.

'Akeem! **ALMOND CAP!**' barked the barista.

'I think that's all our orders,' said Kim firmly, ending the game before tables were flipped. 'We probably shouldn't keep blocking the area, time to head back.'

'Hang on,' said Andrew, as people turned and began heading their own ways. 'I still haven't got mine.'

But he was ignored and the grads, waving and calling their goodbyes, headed off to their respective areas. Andrew bit down on saying something that would get him sent to HR as they left. That was absolutely typical of them. He took a bite out of his brownie like was a predator trying to mortally wound it.

'That looks good,' said someone from off to one side. 'I'm starting to wish I'd got a brownie too,'

Andrew turned to see Roman Vortan, the CEO of CMND, standing there. Today he was sporting a suit with a subtle pattern and a white shirt, but no tie. With his dedication to white shirts, Andrew started to wonder if he had ever spilled anything in his life. He came across as too controlled for that. Probably explained how he'd withstood the temptations of the sweet cabinet.

Andrew's eyes widened as he desperately chewed. He'd bitten off a boulder of brownie and now his cheeks bulged as he desperately tried to break it down to give a response.

Roman chuckled in a good-natured way as Andrew struggled.

'Take your time,' he said. 'It's Andrew? Isn't it?'

Andrew nodded as he finally swallowed.

'I recognise you from, uh–' said Roman.

'The Breach?' finished Andrew, unable to help himself.

Roman shrugged in a 'maybe' kind of way. 'I was going to say the induction,' he said. 'But I keep my ear to the ground and know about that too. Sorry if it's a sensitive subject.'

'I don't care,' lied Andrew, 'really.'

'In that case,' said Roman conspiratorially, taking a step

closer. 'We can talk about it. I'm guessing you know more than most.'

Andrew threw his shoulders back and lifted his chin. 'I'm on the taskforce,' he said with a hint of grandeur. 'But mostly going through old files plus the open-source stuff. Right now, I'm trying to find what she wants.'

Roman cocked his head to one side. He had a curious expression with a slight smile, but he stared with piercing blue intensity.

'Didn't she already take what she wanted?' said Roman. 'That's why everyone's in such a damn mess.'

Andrew paused, feeling his heart speed up. He madly played back what he just said in his head. As he was doing one investigation for DAS and another for Lisa, he'd made the verbal mistake of conflating the two.

'I meant …' he said slowly, to buy time. 'I'm trying to understand her motivation. Whatever's driving her. That's what Peter's been teaching us.'

Roman nodded thoughtfully, eyes still locked on Andrew.

'Smart,' he said at last. 'But is that Peter running OSTRA? I've heard of him too. Be careful what you share with that one.'

Andrew's brow wrinkled at that.

'Why?' he asked. 'What have you heard—'

'Say!' said Roman, interrupting him. 'Speaking of what she took, any sign of that yet?'

Andrew blinked. 'No,' he said bluntly. 'But I don't even know what it was.'

Roman looked around. There were people everywhere, but they were all lost in their own gossip.

He dropped a firm but gentle hand on Andrew's shoulder and leaned in close.

'*Central,*' he whispered and leaned out again.

Andrew was wide-eyed, feeling like he'd just been passed some massive state secret. If only he knew what it was.

'But what's—' he began before Roman cut him off.

'Shhh!' said Roman with quiet urgency. 'That was 'cos we're such good pals now, but I can't go into it.'

Andrew nodded his acceptance of this, but his mind buzzed with a chorus of questions.

'Don't feel too bad about The Breach,' said Roman, changing tack. 'You were all alone and had no guidance, although being unescorted is a problem as well,' he said with a knowing grin.

'Shanti was … nearby,' said Andrew. 'She got in trouble too. Although no one blames her constantly.'

'Shanti Banerjee?' said Roman, as though peering at some file in his mind. Andrew mumbled yes and had another bite of brownie.

Roman refocused. 'Listen to me,' he said, not unkindly. 'Take it from someone who's worked in influence operations. You're not going to stop what everyone in the building is talking about. Manipulating groups of people is possible, but the trick is to change the individual who will have the biggest impact on your situation.'

'How do I figure out who they are?' asked Andrew.

'Andrew! **MOCHA!**' boomed the barista as though it were a call to arms. 'Roman! **LONG BLACK!**'

'It's been great talking,' said Roman, giving him a suitably manly pat on the arm. With that, he headed off to the counter, grabbed his coffee and vanished into the crowd.

Fifteen

In government, IT upgrades take time. In the 1970s, the United States government built SACCS; the Strategic Automated Command and Control System. These cabinet-sized computers, dumber than modern watches and using floppy disks, controlled nuclear weapons until 2019.

In government circles, this kind of delay isn't unusual. Security and bureaucracy stagnate technological change. How can you change something when not enough technically skilled people have a security clearance? What's the point when the system will be out of date by the time the purchase order is approved?

Years of delayed changes, patch jobs and misapplied new systems make for a clusterfuck; an IT network closer to a sprawling coral reef, many parts forgotten and unmaintained. Consultants and IT companies make a fortune building so-called solutions to this problem: data lakes, fusion centres, universal search tools to unify all your systems! They sound good, but once installed, fail to deliver. And so, another block is added to the Jenga tower of IT systems just as another one is removed below as legacy systems fall into obsolescence.

DAS typified this – much to Andrew's annoyance the next day, as his search for Koil failed again and again. When no alerts had been triggered, Andrew had abandoned his initial hesitancy. Now he searched with increasing frustration. He tried different spellings, wildcard searches, everything, to no avail. He thumped the desk, making an empty takeaway coffee cup dance off the edge. This was harder than he thought. For all the induction speeches and documentation DAS delivered, there was no graduate's guide to espionage. At least not in his area. Certainly, it was expected that any espionage was done outside the building.

Taking a steadying breath, he glared at the screen. But it wasn't impressed. Searches for 'KOIL' returned nil results, or randomly said *ADDITIONAL CLEARANCE REQUIRED* – standard DAS parlance for you needing a higher – or more specific – security clearance.

'Hey there.'

Andrew's eyes flicked up from his screen. Shanti, fresh from some meeting or other, was wandering over. He locked the screen with porn-concealing speed as she arrived.

'Hi,' he said, a picture of failed nonchalance.

'Still going?' she said, raising an eyebrow. 'You were scowling at the screen hours ago.'

'Oh, it's just uh …' Andrew paused and thought desperately. To his horror, honesty came bursting out of his mouth. 'I just can't get the information I'm after.'

To his surprise, Shanti laughed.

'Of course not!' she said with a genuine smile. 'You're in intelligence.'

She pulled a chair over and sat down.

'Come on,' she said. 'You'll never get the information you need. Hasn't Peter given you that lecture yet? It's one of his favourites.'

Andrew thought back. The lack of information was a

common theme. Information never arrived in one, complete piece. It was a stew of gossip, inference, assumptions, and shaky evidence. Data was either absent, or arrived as a tidal wave and overwhelmed you. Chatting suspects, on the phone or internet, often lied, both to themselves and others, but it was the same result for analysts. Unclear information was unfair. James Bond never had to sort the fact from fiction or work a fucking Excel spreadsheet that killed the ancient computer you were using. But then he was, as Peter had pityingly said, not an analyst.

Shanti watched the thoughts cross Andrew's face like weather over a landscape. Taking pity, she said firmly, 'Time for a break. Let's grab a coffee, always helps.'

She tapped the top of the monitor for emphasis and turned to the door. Andrew's neck crackled like someone twisting a handful of bubble wrap as he turned. He was only mildly distracted from the neck pain by the pins and needles exploding in his arm. She was right, he'd been still for too long. He hurried after her, moving his limbs like someone shaking off a sudden spider. Fortunately, she was walking ahead and didn't notice.

Coffee, thought Andrew as he caught up, was the lifeblood of DAS, as well as a social nexus, a political tool and a currency. People were always headed to the cafe housed within DAS HQ. It was the organisation's biggest unofficial meeting room. People could take a break, or actually get something done without the distractions of work. It was most useful for those little chats that make things happen and keep the world turning. Cafes were where decisions were made. Official meetings just happened later, so they could be officially recorded in the minutes.

Shanti and Andrew wandered across the white tiled flooring to the airport-style rope barrier that kept the queue in order. Today's barista was a young man suffering from a near terminal level of caffeine-fuelled-enthusiasm. Andrew and

Shanti marvelled at their good timing. The only other people in were a few senior executives deciding next year's budgets, and an investigations team hogging a table while trying to untangle whose source was whose.

Shanti exchanged pleasantries with today's barista as he knocked out their orders. It was always a good idea to be nice to people preparing your food and drink. She playfully rebuffed his admiration of her top and insisted she would be back tomorrow. The barista assured her he would remain heart-broken and forlorn until her return.

They were only a few steps away when someone else came in. The barista's period of mourning instantly ended, and he practically screamed, 'Oh, hi!'

They settled into an isolated table in the corner.

'What's up?' said Shanti once they were comfortable. 'Maybe I can help?'

Andrew thought for a moment, assembling his phrasing with care.

'I've been given a target,' he began slowly, 'and I can't figure out who they are or what they're involved with.'

'No direct reporting?' she asked.

'Nothing I could see,' he hedged.

Shanti frowned into the distance. 'No problem,' she said, seeing something. 'Look at the gaps and find the links.'

'What?' said Andrew. He didn't need a fortune cookie.

'If you can't find anything on the person directly, find what they may be linked to. Don't just look up the person in a list of people. Get their emails, phone numbers, friends. See what *those* are connected to. It's not just the person you look for, it's everything around them. Like, their mobile, or someone they speak to might be in the Counter Terrorism database or some-thing. Then, at least you have some context.'

Andrew's eyes widened as somewhere, deep in his brain an idea flared into life. Connections? That might work.

'Oh, and don't rely on the universal search,' continued Shanti, referencing an internal and highly inferior google clone that searched top-secret systems. 'Go into all the databases separately.'

Andrew, who had thought Big Brother knew all, frowned.

'Are you saying the universal search might miss something?'

Shanti smiled. 'I'm saying the information might be there. But what you want to see, are allowed to see, and get to see, are usually three different things.'

Andrew felt he was back in fortune cookie territory.

'Interesting tip,' he said, 'but where were you all morning?'

Shanti brightened and clapped her hands together.

'Didn't you hear?' she said. 'I'm moving! Got my next assignment in IOE! That's Information Operations and Effects. I was up there meeting a few people and getting organised.'

'Information Operations and Defects?' said Andrew.

'Effects,' corrected Shanti. 'The whole area is like an experiment. It's what they call fusion. There's staff from all over DAS, but it's also got the private sector. All developing new things in information warfare. Very cool stuff.'

'Like what?' asked Andrew.

'Well, I don't know much yet,' admitted Shanti. Andrew just nodded and drank his coffee.

'It's a skunkworks, you know?' she said. Andrew shook his head. Shanti waved her hands for emphasis. 'Like a lab trying to dream up the future,' she said.

Andrew still wasn't getting it.

'So,' she said, holding up a sugar sachet, 'the government has all these new technological threats, right?'

Andrew nodded.

'We know how crap they are with tech – they need outside help. So, a private company teams up with the intelligence community,' said Shanti. 'Helps them develop some new capability or technology for cheap, well, during the initial phase anyway'

'Why?' asked Andrew.

'Because they get access to things no one else sees. They're first in line to get a whole bunch of fat government contracts if they get something right. Plus, whatever they develop can be sold as a product or service to other countries. Get it right here and you can sell it to the big markets.'

Andrew digested this as Shanti drank her coffee.

'So, a good opportunity?' he asked.

'Absolutely,' she said. 'Why do you think I did my time in OSTRA? I wasn't going to do other people's research forever. This was my hardship post – always helps your transfer chances when you're coming from a bad assignment you did well on. I thought my transfer application died when you, uh, when The Breach happened. It wasn't just your prospects that got hit. But late yesterday, IOE contacted me and said it was all going through! Finally, I'm getting somewhere!'

Andrew smiled weakly, glad *someone* was getting somewhere.

'What about you?' said Shanti, reading his internal angst. 'Where do you want to go?'

Andrew drained his coffee, shrugged and gave a partial answer.

'Up,' he said. Out of this hole, he thought to himself.

Before long, Shanti tactfully pointed out she had another coffee date. She was getting some more gossip on her new work area. Andrew took the hint and headed back to OSTRA, leaving her to make contact. Back at his desk, he faced his problems with a new outlook and caffeine buzzing in his veins.

Shanti was right. Time to go into the databases separately. Technically, the universal search looked at everything and brought back information that you were cleared to see. However, its retrieval was about as reliable as a concussed

Labrador. But he'd been thinking about this all wrong! In his previous searches, nil found meant that there was nothing to find. But if it asked for clearance, well that was confirmation there was *something* – even if he had no idea what it was. But various databases were linked to different themes. Things like country-specific espionage. If he got a nil result for that, then no links to that country's espionage activity. But if it denied him access? Boom, that's what Koil was mixed up in.

So, what was Koil linked to? If he couldn't find which people Koil was linked to in the real world, he could find out what topics they were linked to in the databases. Chinese spies? Russian? Neo-Nazis? Maybe religious extremists? Cyber mercenaries?

By searching each team's part of the master database, he could figure out what had zero results and what had results he wasn't allowed to see.

Andrew cracked his knuckles and hunkered down.

He started with the Counter-Chinese Espionage database.

Zero results.

All right, he thought to himself. A negative is still an answer: nothing there.

Counter-Russian Espionage database.

Zero results.

He chewed on his lip, resisting an obscene outburst.

Counter Terrorism database.

The search icon spun for several seconds before *ADDI-TIONAL CLEARANCE REQUIRED* flashed up.

Yes! He grinned from ear to ear. So, there was *something* there, but he wasn't able to see it. Yet.

Cyber Warfare database.

ADDITIONAL CLEARANCE REQUIRED.

He leaned back, hands clasped behind his head, and basked in the warmth of that warning message that was now an unwitting confirmation. It was amazing he'd thought that was a dead end before!

Andrew pulled a small notebook out and rested it next to him on the desk. It was dark blue and small enough to fit in a top suit pocket, behind the polyester handkerchief. The sort of place that is rarely searched. Despite the writhing snakes in his stomach, he grinned. This was like falling off a cliff but enjoying the most amazing scenery on the way down. It was a lead, but now he needed to play it cool. He assumed the attitude of someone quietly working through something important, but dull. Every so often, he'd throw a fresh query in. Just enough to check all the team databases and maybe narrow things down even further.

People came and went around him. Andrew forced himself not to panic or shut his computer down when someone called his name or his phone rang. Hide in plain sight, that was the idea. He even left the blue notebook lying there like an invitation to question him. No one did. Scribbling notes was fine. It was being caught leaving with them that could be a problem.

No, he told himself. What I'm doing is completely normal and fine. They spend their entire days looking up suspect activity, prying, looking at who called who. His invasions of privacy were no different to anyone else's.

No different at all.

A pity his body didn't believe him. His mouth was bone dry, and he sweated profusely. Andrew wondered if he was going to dry out like an old sandcastle, collapsing into individual grains all over the desk.

That's enough, he thought to himself after a while. That will do for Lisa, but now to see if there's anything else to learn from her.

He checked his emails and saw another with directions from Angela. Peter, as his mentor, had been cc'd. He was to go through her social media. Uncover any links to people/groups of interest and see if there was any information to reveal her likely location or support networks.

Three hours later, Andrew approached Peter's desk.

'Find anything, Zuckerberg?' said Peter, without looking up.

'Stop the Facebook references,' said Andrew. 'You boomers are the only ones on there. Also, how did you know it was me?'

'Your deodorant,' said Peter. 'You need to upgrade. It smells like someone shat a pine tree.'

Andrew cleared his throat. He had put extra deodorant on from his gym bag after sweating so much while checking for Koil. He'd also gone to the bathroom enough times to make a colleague wonder if he had irritable bowel syndrome.

'Anyway,' said Andrew, moving on, 'I've been through Lisa's social media, like you asked.'

'What's the pattern? Any particular friends? Favourite locations?'

'Sure,' said Andrew. 'I've got a pile of them and they're in the report, but here's the weird thing – there are almost no photos of her.'

'So? We tell everyone to stop with the 'selfies' every second of the day.' Peter even did the quotation marks with his fingers.

'I've checked out her social media,' Andrew said, 'and the change is weird.'

'Change?'

'What?'

'You said change,' said Peter, swivelling to face him. 'Believe me, the biggest indicator of something being wrong is change. People lead very predictable lives. Change is what you always look for.'

'Well,' said Andrew, gratified he had some attention, 'when she started with DAS, she began using her social media more. Or appearing in the things for the first time. Isn't it usually the opposite way around?'

'Not necessarily. We warn people not to get carried away, but not being on social media is a giveaway itself these days.'

'Right! People get more cautious, but she got less. Is that likely?' asked Andrew.

'Show me.'

They hunched over Andrew's computer as he carefully scrolled through the feeds of Lisa's various social media exploits. He suppressed his frustration when he had to explain slang, emojis or memes to Peter. But that wasn't as bad as when Peter reached over his shoulder and hesitantly two-finger-typed his own search terms.

But there was no denying it. All the photos or videos of Lisa appeared after she joined DAS. Before that it was videos and photos of food, sunsets, buildings, parties, full nightclubs. Each one had enough hashtags to give the average user carpal tunnel syndrome, but no Lisa. No besties. No boyfriends. No girlfriends.

Peter, with typical restraint, grunted to admit Andrew had something.

'But what are you saying?' Peter asked him. 'Why's that important?'

Andrew steeled himself.

'I don't think it's her social media. I think she's someone else and took the account over when she joined DAS. This is just what she told us.'

'So, who is she?'

Andrew shrugged.

'These accounts go back ages,' he said. 'They've been updated for a long time. Pretty generic stuff mostly, but I think this is something bot-generated.'

Peter leaned back with the thoughtful expression of someone who no longer understands what is being said.

'Meaning?'

'Meaning,' said Andrew, 'that it's possible the rest of her identity is fake as well.'

Peter pulled his glasses off with one hand and dragged the other down his face. He stared down as if praying to the Carpet Gods for better news.

'First thing tomorrow,' he said, replacing his glasses and looking back at Andrew, 'I want a full summary of your findings and linked assessments. Do it right. Go through everything to make sure we're on the right path with this and we'll pass it on to Insecurity.'

'No worries,' said Andrew, wondering if they knew Peter called them that. 'Some insider threat, huh?'

Peter leaned forward in his chair, his eyes focused on Andrew.

'Actually,' he said. 'This person was never one of us.'

SIXTEEN

In outer Melbourne, hundreds of kilometres from Canberra, the glass doors of the Greenhill Club and Bistro hissed open as Dave, aspiring revolutionary, approached. A curtain of chilled air from a ceiling vent gave sweet relief as he walked in. The doors hissed closed again and Dave took a moment to savour the cool. The Greenhill Club and Bistro occupied a new and unusually upmarket building on the far edge of Melbourne. Unlike the humbler local businesses that sat meekly within brick two-storey shopfronts that had been in place for decades, this was a newly built castle of money and influence. Its shiny façade dominated the main drag, pulling all the people – and their money – in for miles around. What else was there to do this far out? Dave recognised this kind of place. He'd only ever gotten as far as one gig in corporate suck-holes like this. They didn't like real music. The day crowd usually got some hot and clueless blonde doing nineties indies covers, with some man-bun-wearing idiot on guitar. Then the night crowd would be treated to whatever band could play the softest rock from the same era. Dave's band usually got the lights and sound pulled the second they tried their own material – before they'd gone fully into the alt-right scene. Security had walked them out of a similar place when they'd tried their single, 'wake up yuppy fuck-face'.

The club's hallways stretched off, presumably to dining areas, bars and a kids' playground. There'd also be the function rooms with foldable walls that opened up or compacted down, depending on how much space you needed. But no matter where you went, the discordant song of the pokies and gambling room was always on the edge of hearing. Did they pipe that shit everywhere?

A sing-song voice snapped Dave out of his thoughts.

'Hello, can I help you?'

The voice belonged to a woman standing behind a blindingly white reception desk. She was middle-aged, with perfectly parted hair and a dark complexion that could be from a thousand different backgrounds, but what Dave mentally catalogued as 'them'. One of two categories he typically used. Her uniform shirt was white and had the club logo in a queasy green next to a name tag that said, 'Service Specialist'. Off to the side of the desk were several machines for scanning licences or membership cards. Dave never liked that stuff. Too much surveillance, he thought, his eyes flicking to the dark-domed cameras dotted on different vantage points around the entrance. The receptionist waited patiently, a professional but secretly insincere smile on her face.

Dave took his cap off and held it in both hands, an unconscious nervous habit. He no longer had a completely shaved head – didn't have to. Instead, he sported a new, but severe, hairdo: high and tight with no more than a centimetre on top – like a US Marine. The receptionist's nose wrinkled as he approached.

'I'm here for the Freedom Ricky Tour,' he said, uncomfortable with how it sounded out loud.

'Ah,' she said, without adding, 'of course you are.'

Instead, she followed with 'Reserved ticket or buying one?'

Dave paused. He needed a ticket. The cash in his back pocket got heavier as he thought of his beloved guitar, sitting in a pawn shop since this morning. He could always go back and get it. But what would he do with it? He hadn't played a note since everything went wrong with the movement.

The thought flashed Dave back to the riot and its immediate aftermath. It was bad enough seeing the extremist Hindus, marching away like someone had taken his group and bloody coloured them in. Then his own side showed just how pathetic they were. No one knew what to do. It was just sit around and piss and moan about bullshit. It was all so … small. Between his group, crazy Hindus, idiot-lefty race traitors and everyone else – it showed his movement was just one amongst so many. All squabbling as bigger things happened elsewhere. Then the cops rolled in and broke everything up without breaking a sweat. He'd tried rallying people but changed his mind in the face of a line of shield-thumping riot police advancing in lock-step. After all, he was an artist, not a front-line fighter.

However, the worst was yet to come from the alt-right forums. Seeing all the extremist Hindus join in via the livestream killed the band's credibility. Not to mention the easy way the cops rolled the small alt-right crowd up like a carpet in front of the cameras. It was like watching your favourite team lose entirely on own goals.

So, faced with failure, the anonymous online hordes turned on Dave and his band as well. Cancelling them like some bunch of left-wing losers. #ExtremeFarRaceTraitor was slapped on all their posts and the legion of memes were plain cruel. They were called posers and traitors, losers and failures. One of the stupidest comments was from someone who said he'd achieve more with his van than they ever could with a bloody sing-song. Whatever that meant.

Dave burned with the perceived injustice of it all. How dare they turn on him like that? Kick him out when he was so close to glory? He was the one doing something, not them. Maybe not direct action, but he would have done more for the movement than any meme-poster ever had.

Dave's self-righteous anger dwindled to self-pity and depression. Even his music left him, and he found he couldn't play a note, let alone write one. It didn't matter, he told himself. Those songs had just been for idiots anyway. His internal fire faded to an ember. But it was still enough to know he burned for … something.

And so, in search of that something, he'd retreated even further online. Eventually, while scrolling, the algorithms recommended an online activist and general troublemaker – Freedom Ricky. A performer and truth-teller – also known as a conspiracy theorist – with a knack for stunts and raising awareness. He'd shot to fame by tricking a major US news network to interview him as the 'Australian Minister for Information'. Ricky claimed this was the product of months of special preparation and planning. Although, in truth, he'd just given it a go with a fake but official-looking email. Fortunately for Ricky, both people responsible for vetting interviews were distracted when he sent his email in. One was busy with a divorce, and the other with a lot of cocaine. So, when the guest list was low, they jumped at the chance to get a senior politician – even an Australian one – to dial in. It didn't take long for the studio to realise something was horribly wrong. Not only because Ricky was at least twenty years too young to be a senior politician, but because once the remote interview started he switched his virtual backdrop to an image of several old men in collars and skin-tight leather catsuits being led around on a leash. All their faces were covered with crude labels for the various political parties. Except for the leash holder – her label was 'The Rich'. Overriding his interviewer's confused questions, Ricky said it was the last meeting of Cabinet where they'd decided to float the Australian government on the New York Stock Exchange. They cut the feed just as Ricky ripped his shirt open, revealing a temporary tattoo of a wolf in a UN Peacekeeper's helmet.

While Ricky wasn't on TV anymore, it hardly mattered. He was already blowing up on the internet. A couple off-camera friends streamed the entire thing – and it trended almost straight away. His chaotic but rebellious message was picked up by algorithms on multiple platforms and scattered to people all over the internet. To people who had never heard of him and would never have had the idea to search for him. People like Dave.

After that, Freedom Ricky spun his viral fame into an online following for his stunts or short speaking clips. The two things were separate extremes. He'd do a loud stunt, like the time he dressed up as a syringe and screamed an oath of loyalty at Australia's Chief Medical Officer during his press conference. As per usual, this stunt was going to finish with Ricky being led off by security. Only this time they didn't realise his costume was two halves held together by Velcro. As soon as they grabbed him by the fabric – *riiiiiip* – he was off and running around the room totally naked with a tattoo above his butt that said, "consent this!". A couple of prepared friends recorded and streamed the whole thing again. He defended subsequent charges in court by claiming he was 'forcibly de-clothed by the deep state' and demanded an apology. He got a fine instead – easily paid for by his monetised social media platforms.

But his speaking clips were far more gentle. Almost conspiracy mindfulness. It suited him with his bright blue eyes and the kind of long hair many women would kill for. But his major attraction was confidence and the ability to make the crazy sound totally reasonable. He never referred to the millions watching as a crowd, but as individuals. Ricky would look directly into the camera and speak like he was on one end of a personal conversation. A call direct to you – warmly talking like an earnest friend giving you the boost you needed. You weren't in the wrong. *They were.* It was more comforting and intriguing than the violent and overtly savage forums Dave was used to. People came for the stunts but stayed for the speaking posts. Delivered smoothly, they had all the confidence and authority of a papal decree – even when claiming the Vatican was pulling the strings on global markets. Dave hadn't been so sure about that one. As if the Jews would ever let go, he'd thought to himself. But he went along with the rest of it, often agreeing with Ricky's questions, if not always his answers.

However, each speech was a trojan horse of lies, built with misrepresented truths, emotional appeals and the formidable power of a comfortable and compelling delivery – a reliable means to get inside people's thoughts and warp them – but his followers were oblivious to this. At the end of each talk, when viewers like Dave were nodding along, Ricky ended it by with the same verbal sign-off: 'Don't you wanna do something?'

His last video promised 'The Next Stage' for Freedom Ricky. He was kicking off a tour and promised some 'big actions' to come. Get your early bird tickets at a discount or miss out! And that was why Dave was on this journey. Why he pawned his beloved guitar to raise funds, and why he was now outside the first show of the tour: He wanted to do something.

'I'm sorry, but there are people waiting,' said the receptionist, a high note of impatience in her voice. Dave blinked a few times, unaware he'd been so far away. Hopefully, it had only been a few seconds.

He put his hand in his back pocket and produced his wallet. For a moment, he weighed the options between his pawned guitar or the promise of Freedom Ricky. The receptionist opened her mouth to ask him to wait to one side, but he spoke up.

'One ticket,' he said firmly, slapping crumpled notes down on the reception desk.

Seventeen

The Freedom Ricky Tour was in conference room two as a local flat-Earth society had booked conference room one. The door was partially ajar as Dave went past and he snuck a look. Inside, an elderly man with a brown suit and a gentle voice was pouring a glass of water over his own head. As water poured down his cheeks and off his chin, he triumphantly pointed out the idea of a globe as ridiculous, seeing as water would not remain on a round object. Dave snorted with derision and kept on walking. What a bunch of nutcases, he thought as he walked on to listen to a man who once publicly declared all birds were drone technology.

At the double doors to conference room two, Dave gave his ticket to a young guy in a Freedom Ricky t-shirt and headed in. The organisers had clearly planned for a big crowd. They'd folded an internal wall away and included conference room three in the same space. No-frills plastic beige chairs filled the room. The kind designed for easy deployment and packing, not comfort. They were arranged in neat rows with an aisle down the middle and were, as Dave was running late, mostly occupied. A temporary stage draped in black, with three steps on either side, was at the top of the room. Behind it, and probably the same size as the stage, was a smart screen of some kind. It was currently in standby mode, with Freedom Ricky's logo gently bouncing around. The stage itself was empty except for a wooden lectern that had a microphone off to one side and a mobile phone in a holder at the centre.

Dave surveyed the crowd. Compared to his social experience, they were from every demographic you could imagine. Both old and young, men and women, white and … everyone else. Faced with a surprisingly multicultural turnout with a white component who didn't care, Dave wasn't sure what to do. They were not his people. He felt out of place, or worse – exposed.

However, on the right of the room, down near the front, three whites caught his attention. They all had shaved heads and the skinny one in the middle wore a singlet and had tattoos that were not so much sleeves as a jacket. They snaked up his arms and met across the shoulders, pooling at the neck.

Dave set off. At least he could do this amongst friends.

He decided the casual approach was best. He turned into the correct row at the last moment, mostly watching the stage as if trying to remember where he'd seen it before.

He gently eased into the seat next to them and murmured 'White power', as an in-the-know greeting.

'Excuse me?' said the person next to him loudly. The other two turned to look at Dave as well.

He looked at them from the front for the first time, lost for words. They were all …women.

'No, nothing,' he stammered, feeling like he'd landed on some other planet.

The closest two stared with deep suspicion, but the third gave Dave the kind of hungry smile that makes introverts shudder. It was an expression that foreshadows a highly chatty disposition. The sort of person who assumes they'll be best friends with anyone they meet, sharing mutual opinions on the poisons of the modern world – like fluoride and medical science.

She leaned across the tattooed woman in the middle and gave a little wave.

'I'm Karina,' she said. 'Lovely to meet you.'

Dave was still struggling for something to say, so Karina continued with the introductions.

'He's Rob,' she said, giving a masculine pronoun to the tattooed individual in the middle who, to Dave's eyes, was clearly a woman. Dave shifted in his seat as deep discomfort swept through him. Rob didn't seem to care about it though.

'And they're Astra,' Karina finished, pointing to the woman next to Dave. Astra nodded, but continued to stare with narrowed eyes and pursed lips.

'Glad to see such a good turnout,' said Karina, in the absence of anyone else wanting to speak up. 'As practitioners of natural healing, we're disgusted with the health apartheid and mass experimentation. And why? Who knows how many killed and it wrecked the economy. Now people can't afford the basics and things are only getting worse. So sad, no one is allowed to choose their destiny anymore.'

For a moment, she sagged and looked dejected. Rob and Astra, clearly used to this, patted her on the shoulder or murmured sympathetically.

'But,' said Karina, brightening up again, 'you can't stop people who really want to do something right?'

Dave's face tightened and he nodded, secretly glad that none of his tattoos were visible. An unseen MC's voice boomed out of the speakers, saving him from further small talk.

'WELCOME EVERYBODY! TO ALL THOSE WHO WANT TO BE FREE, YOU KNOW WHO TO LISTEN TO!'

The unseen MC paused as people in Freedom Ricky t-shirts

started clapping and cheering to get the crowd started. The voice thundered in again over the rising applause, as though it were welcoming a champion boxer to the ring.

'IIIIT'S FREEDOM RICKY!'

The crowd, Dave included, cheered and hollered for Ricky.

He's here! Ricky! Over here! Ricky!

Swaggering hip-hop blared over the speakers as Ricky entered via the rear door, igniting the crowd into wild excitement. He wore jeans, a white shirt and a bright orange jacket. He was followed by two guys about the same age who were recording and streaming the event from a few different angles. They both had cameras strapped to their head and chest, as well as phones in their hands. Ricky worked the crowd, stopping for selfies, hugging people and giving high fives amongst the cheers.

Awesome, thought Dave, grinning to himself. The carnival atmosphere was heady stuff.

Ricky got to the front of the room and, ignoring the three steps off to the side, jumped straight onto the stage. The crowd roared their delight.

Up on stage, Ricky waved and made thanks gestures. As the applause dimmed, he walked to the lectern and pulled a microphone from his inside jacket pocket.

'Thank you!' he said. 'For that amazing welcome.'

Dave tilted his head as a thought hit. Ricky sounded a lot like the unseen MC.

Ricky swept his hair back with his spare hand and cleared his throat.

'Thank you,' he said, directly to the phone on top of the lectern. 'It's so wonderful to be here with you.'

One of Ricky's colleagues came on stage and stood behind him to capture the shots of the crowd with Ricky in the foreground.

Ricky looked up beyond the phone and around the room.

There were a few nervous coughs as he lingered, letting the suspense build.

'We are here today,' he said finally, 'because we care about children.'

The crowd rippled like a disturbed pond as people nodded. Trying to protect children from cruel and terrible fates was a common theme in Ricky's conspiracies. As well as an iron-clad way of ensuring a wide audience.

'As you know,' he said, 'there is a secret cabal of thirty-two, I say again, *thirty-two* paedophiles who have powerful positions in the government and in the economy. Protected by wealth, privilege, a complicit mainstream media and the shadowy forces of the deep state, they take what little we have, day by day.'

The crowd muttered and hissed. Dave cracked his knuckles.

'First,' continued Ricky, 'we lost the right to protest as they did a global medical experiment. Millions died. Then they launched wars of control to train the same armies that will subjugate us all. Now our voices are repeatedly silenced on social media that is again controlled by these same forces.'

Meanwhile, Ricky's online feed – running on three different platforms – flashed up links to his other five channels.

'Their ultimate goal,' continued Ricky, 'is control. The cabal of thirty-two wants a total surveillance state! No rights, no consent, no freedom.'

Slowly, and for the camera, a confident and knowing smile spread across his face.

'But we won't let them,' he said slyly. 'Let me ask you: *don't you want to do something?*'

Dave shouted 'yes!' along with everyone else. The resounding applause crashed around the room, making Ricky run up and down the stage, giving thumbs ups and thanks to individuals in the front row.

'Fantastic!' he said to the crowd at large, 'No to the thirty-two! No to the surveillance state!'

People clapped for this as well. Online the ecstatic emojis and comments flowed.

Ricky paused, raising an index finger as he suddenly remembered something.

'And for those here in person,' he said, 'please sign our petition. It'd be great if you could include name, email, phone number and address.'

Around the room, Ricky's merchandise-wearing underlings walked about with clipboards, complete with forms and the obligatory pens hanging by a string. They stood at the end of the chair rows and began enthusiastically offering them for people to pass down. Dave frowned for the first time since Ricky had arrived. What's this about? he thought to himself. His slightly irritated confusion was shared by others in the crowd. Even Karina looked unsure. Beside her, Rob glared over crossed arms and Astra was all raised eyebrows.

Aware of the crowd's dropping temperature, Ricky struck a pose and threw out some fresh drama.

'Remember that we're here today for some big announcements!'

'Like what?' someone in the crowd shouted above the conversational buzz.

Ricky placed both hands on the lectern and looked solemnly into the camera.

'As you know,' he said, 'the deep state is in an ongoing operation to ban cash. They want to remove it from society to give them complete control over commerce.'

Ricky looked thoughtful and ran a hand across his mouth, as though the next part was possibly too secret to be told. 'To stay independent,' he said, 'I've created a new source of wealth! FreeRicky coin!'

Behind him, the screen flashed up with a slowly spinning

image of Free Ricky on a coin, along with a QR code and a website.

'This decentralised digital currency is our base and wealth!' said Ricky as the crowd quietly rumbled various opinions. He ignored them and ploughed on.

'It is how we stay free from the World Economic Forum and the machinations of the global deep state. Don't you want to break free of the control of the one percent?' he said.

People murmured in a broadly affirmative but unsure way. Snatches of conversation broke out in different corners of the room. While some were still nodding along, the general mood had shifted. No more dramatically than for Dave. His face screwed up with confusion. He'd come here for purpose, not money. He was already in debt to come here as it was.

'So, it's crypto-currency?' called someone in the crowd.

'Called it,' said Astra. Rob nodded while Karina just looked ashen.

'Decentralised digital currency,' corrected Ricky, before turning to the camera in front of him. 'And unlike the markets that are pegged to mere gold,' he said, a hint of choking emotion entering his voice, 'this is pegged to freedom itself.'

The crowd considered this. Eventually, someone else called out: 'So …it's free?'

Ricky's face dropped. 'Well, no,' he admitted, with an uncharacteristic ruffle. 'Freedom isn't free, remember. But Ricky-Coin is supported by those who love freedom, it'll explode in value as we grow. Early buyers will be rich!'

He looked into the camera on the lectern again, his face draped in solemnity. 'So, buy now,' he gently urged, 'and stay free. For low cost.'

The crowd's rumblings kicked into a higher gear. Aware he was losing them, Ricky made some soothing motions and stepped away from the lectern. His camera-strapped assistants stayed on either side.

'But that is just one part of my plan!' he shouted. 'There's more! *Don't you want to do something?*'

This time, the catchphrase had less impact. There was the occasional half-hearted 'yes' from the crowd.

'Oh, come on!' shouted Ricky, a showman's grin on his face. 'I said, *don't you want to DO something*!?'

A chunk of the crowd shouted out a yes like a game show audience, but one that was getting tired.

'Well,' said Ricky, throwing an arm to the screen behind him. 'This is what you can do!'

The image of the rotating coin vanished, replaced with a checkbox with a big blue tick in it. Next to the box was the message: 'Vote One FR Party'.

'What the hell?' said Dave.

Ricky was back at the lectern now, staring deep into the camera.

'I'm delighted to announce that I'm running for local election – stop the rot people! At each tour event, people can fill out the petition and we'll have enough signatures to register as a political party!'

This announcement hit the earth harder than the FreeRicky crypto coins. Online a flame war broke out in the comments as various fans, trolls and combination of the two hurled insults at each other.

'So, you're giving our information to the deep state?' someone asked.

'No, I'd never do that!' said Ricky, safe in the knowledge his audience had ignored many contradictions before.

'Isn't the political system rigged?' shouted another voice. Everyone in the room rhubarbed and rumbled their agreement.

'Of course!' said Freedom Ricky. 'But once elected, I promise to de-rig it!'

A couple of boos were yelled across the room. More soon joined them.

'The government isn't real!' a voice cried out.

'Totally illegitimate,' agreed Ricky. 'That's why it's ripe for us to take charge!'

'He's a deep state plant!' someone else shouted. With that, the rumbling and chaos reached new heights. Nothing like a crowd of conspiracy theorists to grab hold of a juicy new angle.

Ricky held up his hands and tried to regain control.

'Listen to me!' he shouted. 'I will name and shame the paedophiles controlling our government. I will push for the everyday use of digital currencies, and I will ban anyone who ever tried to silence us!'

Boos and catcalls rang out, now joined by the plastic clunks of chairs colliding as people pushed out of their seats to leave. But at least a few on the fence voters shouted out questions. Like his stance on chem-trails and whether, in a hung contest, he'd consider power-sharing arrangements with the illuminati.

Dave had all he could take. He got up and made his way to the rear door. As he approached, it opened from the other side and four police officers stood there, blocking his way. Three of them were in uniform and one wore the kind of cheap suit that lets you look vaguely respectable while still having the freedom to tackle someone. Dave froze, fearing they'd finally tracked him down after the riot.

'Out of the way,' growled the one in the suit, although he barely waited, pushing past Dave with impatience as the other three trailed behind him. Dave turned to watch. As he clearly wasn't the target here, he stayed for the show.

'Richard Daggs!' called the detective. The crowd fell quietened down except for a few muttered comments about fascists and them not consenting to this invasion.

Dave looked at Ricky – AKA Richard Daggs. He'd gone white and stared with horror at the detective, who was clearly enjoying this. He had the swagger of a cop who knows the evidence brief is an inch thick and bullet-proof.

'You are under arrest and will be taken back to Brisbane,' the detective announced, still approaching Ricky. 'You're wanted in connection with two fraudulent financial schemes, plus an online charity to pay for the treatment of your' – the detective checked a tiny notebook – 'so-called "back cancer". Good to see you're feeling better. Nice new look by the way.'

Ricky, after eyeing off the rear door where one of the uniformed police had wisely remained, looked around wildly at any other options.

'It's the deep state!' he shouted at the crowd. 'Get them!'

But no one seemed in a mood to get them. Ricky's former-acolytes burst into open revolt, shouting things like 'imposter' and 'false flagger'. Dave turned to leave, hearing a crash as Ricky pushed the wooden lectern over to make a pointless barricade. From the hallway outside conference room two, Ricky's shouts of protest got distinctly muffled as he was arrested.

Hope they bounce him down some steps, thought Dave as he left. Red-faced and muttering, he kept walking until he left the cool air of the club and stood back in the noisy street where rush hour still hadn't died down. Amid the smell of exhaust, occasional honking and passing conversation of passers-by, Dave tried to focus. He stared at his hands, unconsciously balled into fists, and thought about things. He saw his guitar sitting in the pawn shop where he'd never probably get it now. Then there was all the time wasted with Freedom Ricky and the acute embarrassment and shame from being genuinely excited about something that was a total mirage.

Uncurling his hands, he took out his phone and opened a few apps, looking for some of the more violent forums he'd been on the edges of. There were a few good people in there. Some of them had been starting to make real sense to Dave. They got him.

Karina, Rob and Astra swept past on their way to find a pub nearby.

'Just don't,' Karina was saying. 'Not one word from either of you.'

'Bloody politicians,' muttered Rob as he went past. 'Told her to stick with QAnon.'

Dave didn't notice them, he was too busy posting.

Anyone ready 2 fight for real?

Eighteen

Unless there's been a regional terrorist attack, coup, cyber attack or nuclear missile test, Friday mornings are fairly relaxed in DAS. They are a time when people are typically happy to spend time lurking in the cafe, gossiping in hallways, or leaning back in chairs idly discussing the upcoming weekend in their team areas. Safe in the knowledge the boss won't object because they've joined in. However, there was no such relaxation for Andrew and Peter. They'd been summoned to Angela's office in Internal Security. Only that morning, Peter had sent Andrew's now polished findings about Lisa's social media off to the task force trying to catch her. Within fifteen minutes, Angela emailed back to politely, but firmly pointing out they should have a meeting about this. Now. She didn't bother saying where, safe in the knowledge they knew to come to her.

So now Andrew stood before her desk. He wasn't sure if it was sweat or the humidifier working away that made his collar damp. As soon as they'd walked in, Angela had, without tearing her eyes away from her screen, waved them both to the one seat that Peter promptly took. Andrew stayed standing with a kind of bored teenager hunch. He looked off to the side. Sure enough, James lurked like a bouncer waiting for the word to throw everyone out into the street.

Andrew shifted on his feet and enjoyed the moment. They could pull the silent treatment, but no one could deny he'd found something. Him! He smiled at the thought. He had picked up on something several floors of people missed. So much for AI searches as well.

'Right then,' said Angela, looking away from whatever vital thing that had occupied her.

Andrew's neck cracked as it whipped back around. He thought he heard a corresponding snap from James.

'So you see?' said Andrew. 'Her identity is fake.'

'No,' replied Angela. 'It's real. She was the fake one.'

Andrew's internal mental struggle must have registered on his face.

'I mean, there is a Lisa Chapman in the system. We've already confirmed that. One who has an address, birth records, education. She's a real person, but not the one we're looking for. She's a victim of identity theft. That's why we haven't gone public on this – we'd be crucifying the wrong person with the information we have. Not to mention if we just released 'Lisa's' face, people would ask why we don't know her name. It's a very neat trap. Instead of trying to create someone from scratch, they found a likely candidate, took her identity, and used it to enter DAS.'

She paused and leaned back against a fern. Andrew could have sworn something jumped off a branch.

'*They*,' she said. 'Know what that means?'

'Non-gendered pronoun?' said Andrew. His tone felt around like someone looking for a dropped contact lens.

Angela closed her eyes and rubbed her temples. Andrew heard a floorboard creak as James moved ever so slightly.

'It means plural,' said Angela. 'She had help. This isn't easy to do.'

She crossed her arms and looked at Peter and Andrew with a grave expression.

'This is serious,' she said. 'We can't rule out more and similar threats, sponsored by some hostile nation-state or extremist group. This whole investigation has been one surprise after another.'

Andrew hoped his panicked expression wasn't too obvious. Angela continued regardless.

'See if her social media connects to anyone else inside DAS,' she said. 'Then go through everything and see if you can find similar activity in any other accounts of personnel that I will send to you.'

'People inside DAS?' said Andrew.

Angela leaned in.

'Lisa knew our systems far too well and has achieved far too much,' she said, staring him down. 'I am now operating on the assumption that she had more internal help than we initially assessed.'

'I see,' said Andrew, as his chest tightened.

'Anyone helping her is our next best target. We get them, we get her, and figure out how far this goes.'

Andrew's pulse kicked into overdrive.

'*Anyone* helping her?' he said.

'Of course,' said Angela. 'They're going to be in a world of hurt and I want your help to find them. And don't even think of mentioning this in the cafe. I will find out.'

Nineteen

A world of hurt, Angela had said. Andrew's mind raced with the implication as he and Peter walked back down to the OSTRA offices. What had he done? Now that Angela was hunting Lisa's associates, Andrew realised she already had one in the building – him. But Lisa had also warned him about others. Who was he stuck between? Internal Security hunting him, Lisa blackmailing him, and some other foreign spy group watching him?

Peter was saying something, but Andrew was focused inwards, staring unseeingly ahead as he watched being fired, or even arrested, play out in his head. Trying to catch Lisa himself was getting too risky. What had he been thinking? It was only game chat, and he could always claim he thought someone was playing a prank on him. Yup, that would check out. He hadn't reported it because he thought it was a prank and played along to figure out which one of the grads it was. He'd pull the same chat trick on her, make a paper trail. Next time she contacted him, he'd pretend to guess or ask about the prank before pulling the plug. Then maybe, just maybe, he could safely report the conversation to Angela and James.

He glanced at Peter, who was still talking and gesticulating. He loved to lecture so much he didn't need an audience – he just assumed it was there. But Andrew couldn't hear a word. His ears were filled with the imagined shouts and jeers from everyone when they found out he'd helped Lisa a second time. But it wasn't too late to get out. He reached a decision.

'Well?' said Peter.

Andrew gave a start, aware of Peter's direct attention.

'I'll get right on it?' he guessed.

'See that you do,' replied Peter. 'Review all of Lisa's online connections to see if the same pattern appears. Doubt you'll find anything but write up your results for Angela by the end of the day, cc me.'

* * *

Andrew spent the rest of the day engrossed in his work. He started by searching Lisa's accounts for connections to DAS personnel, but found nothing. Although he still went about writing it up as professionally as possible. He needed to build his credibility with Angela as a good and loyal analyst. Getting on her good side was essential in case Lisa's messages surfaced. His fingers stabbed at the keyboard as though each keystroke pushed Lisa further away. He was tempted to just burn his account now and be done with it, but that could be too hasty. He wanted her to feel safe, so she didn't pull any more tricks. The next time she made contact, he'd be ready. If she organised a meeting, he could agree, give an anonymous tip and deny everything once they caught her. If he didn't hear from her in a few days, or she had more requests, he'd buy time, delete his game account and pretend nothing happened.

As the afternoon wound down, Andrew completed his report to Angela. There were no extra ties to Lisa to point to who her other associates might be.

'How's it going with the report?' asked Peter, appearing behind him.

'Sending it to you and Angela now,' said Andrew, clicking send and hearing the 'whoosh' of an ancient email program. He felt it carry some of the stress away with it. Clean start.

'Aaand I'm out!' said Andrew, shutting down the computer. He stood up and smiled with relief at Peter, who gave a genial nod. Lavish praise by his standards.

Andrew's smile widened as he remembered something that had escaped him. He had to go, but not just yet.

'The week's over,' said Andrew, standing up. 'And no pen.'

'The week's not over yet,' replied Peter, 'not for you.'

Peter darted to his desk with a speed that belied his age. He returned at a sedate and confident pace, a single sheet of white paper swinging back and forth in his hand. Andrew would only have felt greater foreboding if Peter had walked towards him putting on a medical rubber glove.

'Remember signing all that paperwork?' said Peter. 'You didn't notice this in the middle of the other forms. Scribbling out of habit by then, I guess. Attention to detail is very important in our work.'

Andrew felt a familiar shrinking feeling in his stomach as he looked. 'Oh, you're kidding!'

'We all make our moves,' said Peter.

The paper, with Andrew's inadvertent signature on the bottom, read: *I, Andrew Stanton, agree to work late on Friday afternoon and complete Peter's admin for him while he catches up on his book. OR I will give him a pen.*

Andrew stared into Peter's eyes. He pulled a pen out of his pocket and held it up. Then, with Peter's full attention, dropped it in a bin.

The defiant effect was spoiled a few seconds later when fished the pen out of the bin again.

'My only one,' he mumbled.

'Thanks so much,' said Peter. 'I've sent you a link. Go through that folder and make sure all those phone intercept requests are correct and properly recorded. One has a small mistake somewhere.'

He headed back to his desk without waiting for a reply. He gave an elderly 'Aaahh' as he settled into his chair and pulled a novel out of a drawer.

As Andrew watched Peter recline, a dull pounding started behind his eyes. He didn't have time for this. Right, he thought. Gotta take charge. Time to end Peter's games.

Andrew followed the link. True to his word, Peter had a pile of phone intercept requests. Andrew worked his way through them as quickly as possible. Each one was a maddening mash of bureaucratic legalese, incomprehensible to the average person but defensible in court. He checked each for spelling or other errors, made sure the legal justifications were in place and that all the references were properly recorded.

But he knew this was only delaying the inevitable. Peter would have something else in mind. He had more tricks than a magicians' convention. As he said, we all make our moves. So, what was his countermove? As Andrew finished the last phone intercept request, an idea blossomed.

The phone. That's it!

'How are you going with those forms?' Peter called out from his reading nook.

'About halfway,' said Andrew, buying time. 'Didn't we have a reference booklet for the intercept legislation?'

'Try Sarah's desk,' said Peter, giving a vague wave without looking up from his book.

Andrew walked over to Sarah's desk. He peeked at Peter – still absorbed in his airport thriller – took Sarah's phone off its hook, loudly turning the pages of the reference booklet as he placed the handset on the desk. Then he dialled his own desk phone.

Peter's head snapped up as it rang.

'That's mine!' called Andrew. 'I'll get it!'

He ran back over to his desk and picked up the phone.

'Hello?' said Andrew to no one. Peter put the bookmark in and frowned at him. It was late for a call. Andrew nodded and said 'Hmm' a few times. Then, when Peter seemed about to get out of his chair, said, 'Oh? He's still here. I'll let him know. Thanks, he's on his way.'

He hung up as Peter stood up, the novel slapping onto his desk.

'Well?' he said.

'That was Alerts and Monitoring,' said Andrew. 'There's some live situation and they want your input. Said it's your area of expertise?'

Peter cursed and hurried out. Andrew giggled as the door shut. He scrambled to gather his things and left a post-it note on Peter's desk.

P,

We all make our moves.

I won. See you in the cafe Monday morning for payment.

8.30.

Andrew signed the note with relish. One down, one to go.

TWENTY

TODAY DAS HAD, QUITE UNUSUALLY FOR A MONDAY morning, quite a glow in Andrew's eyes. The anxiety he'd left with on Friday hadn't gone, but he had a way out. Finally, there was a light at the end of the tunnel, and it was neither a fire nor an oncoming train. After work on Friday, giddy with the thrill of tricking Peter, he'd considered his Lisa problem. He started by avoiding home so he couldn't turn on the computer out of habit and make contact with her. Instead, he'd wandered the city centre, discovering an alley-way eatery that served a fusion of Polish and Cambodian street food. It was a combination that was as pleasing as it was confusing. As he ate, his options began to become clear. He couldn't risk playing any more of Lisa's games. At her next contact, whenever that was, he was going to write something accusing her of being a prank, sign out and delete his account. It was time they went their separate ways. Ghosting her wasn't an option until he gave himself some shred of deniability.

Having that knowledge lifted his spirits almost as much as his victory over Peter. As such, Saturday was spent playing a new online game and then he even followed Liam to a house-party in the evening – Pascal stayed at home to noisily 'entertain' again. Sunday was a write-off, but survivable thanks to the miracle of greasy food delivery.

Now, on Monday morning, refreshed and ready to gloat, Andrew grinned as he spotted Peter in the cafe. He sat at a table half obscured by a potted plant.

He was scribbling in a notebook, seemingly oblivious to the world around him. Andrew suspected that wasn't the case. As he got closer, Peter snapped the notebook shut and looked up at him.

'Good morning,' he said, curiously upbeat.

'Good morning to you!' said Andrew, high on victory and the rich smell of roasted coffee.

Peter gestured to the empty seat. Andrew took it with gusto. The screech of the chair moving back was lost in the general hubbub of the early morning coffee rush.

'So,' said Andrew. 'I'm here to collect!'

Peter raised his eyebrows. 'Of course. But first let me know how you think you're a winner.'

Andrew looked at the two cups on the table. One had a tea bag in it. That was Peter's. The other was a large takeaway cup that towered over its tea-filled brother and was embossed with an 'M' for mocha, Andrew's poison of choice.

Andrew began counting his points off on his fingers.

'One, you bet you could manipulate me. Two, that manipulation would be you tricking me into giving you a pen. And now, you failed and sit there with no pen. Please bring the caffeine!'

Peter nodded amiably and slid the takeaway cup towards him. Steam escaped the cup's mouth hole, making it seem like an old steam train puffing across the table. Andrew grabbed it and took a cautious taste.

'Ah,' he breathed. 'Tastes like victory!'

Peter sipped his tea. Reaching into a pocket, he produced a

couple of shortbread biscuits wrapped in plastic. The wrapping crinkled in his hands as he took one out and placed the other, still in its wrapping, on the table.

'You won the coffee,' he said, dipping a biscuit. 'But not the bet.'

'What?'

Andrew raised his coffee and waved it in front of him. 'Coffee equals victory. Know how a bet works?'

'You bet I couldn't manipulate you.'

Peter bit into his biscuit, savouring it like an old lady at high tea. Andrew stared as doubt edged in. Peter was too confident.

'Think about the week,' Peter continued, the first biscuit consumed. 'It's true, you did not give me a pen. But what *did* you do?'

Peter unwrapped the remaining biscuit. Andrew let go of his coffee and sat back as his mind raced. Had he made a mistake? Did he *technically* pass all the components of a pen or something?

Peter chuckled, not unkindly, at the confusion in Andrew's face.

'You abandoned your colleagues, believing them enemies. Then, amongst other shit jobs, you did my admin and repeatedly cleaned the shredder. You revealed personal information, like your desired but missing love life, your need for validation, and so much more.'

Peter dunked his biscuit as Andrew sat in confused silence.

'You spent the week focused on some stupid pen you didn't care about before I said anything. I appealed to your pride and competitiveness.'

He took a genteel bite of biscuit.

'In short,' he said, spilling crumbs, 'you spent the week doing things you didn't want to do and everything I wanted you to do. Your price was cheap. All I had to do was give you a focus and buy you a coffee.'

'But that doesn't matter!' cried Andrew. 'I won! That wasn't the bet! You just … just …'

'Manipulated you,' finished Peter. 'Why should I tell the truth? Since when do manipulators have an honesty only policy? The bet was nothing more than the lever to flick you open. Sure, you can tell everyone you won. You got the coffee. There it is, piping hot in your hands. But was it worth it?'

Andrew's teeth ground together as he looked away from Peter and stared at the coffee.

'I won, according to the rules.'

'What rules?' said Peter, looking amused. 'I had no rules, just goals. You're upset about *your* rules that only *you* decided to follow.'

Andrew glared at his coffee. He silently sulked and hated himself for it. It was so juvenile, but every time he made a move, Peter changed the game. It was like playing chess with someone who abruptly revealed it was tennis. The moment you made a check, they served a tennis ball into your forehead.

'So, what's the lesson? I should assume everyone's manipulating me because I'm an idiot?'

'Goodness, no. You're not an idiot, but everyone has weak spots. You're intelligent and curious, but inexperienced. You work hard, but not always smart, and most of all, you try to do too much by yourself.'

Andrew felt the heat in his face as Peter kept throwing truths at him in a clinically cool and measured tone. It was the brutally honest assessment of an experienced analyst.

'You should still trust people,' said Peter, 'but use your judgement. Remember, everyone measures victory differently.'

Andrew sipped his coffee. Despite the barista getting the chocolate mix just right, it was a different kind of bitter. He made a decision, looked Peter in the eye, and held out his hand.

'Should I congratulate you for manipulating me?' he asked.

'No,' said Peter, smiling as he shook the outstretched hand. 'You should wonder if I've stopped.'

* * *

That evening, Andrew slunk through his front door, sullen and sore from an unexpectedly long walk in cheap office shoes. On the bus home, he'd been so absorbed in his sulk that he'd missed his stop, along with the next two. The walk back was uphill, undeserved, and a fitting metaphor for his time at DAS.

He kicked the door closed behind him. It slammed with enough force to echo back from the hallway. Hoping it hadn't left a mark he'd have to pay for, Andrew headed into his room to nurse his battered ego.

The backpack hit the wall and slid down onto the bed. His jacket joined it moments later.

Andrew settled into the desk chair and stared at his reflection in the computer's black and silent screen.

'Fucking pen,' he said to himself. He remembered Peter's words about working hard but not smart and trying to do too much himself. Speaking of manipulation, it was time to part ways with Lisa and he finally felt strong enough to do so.

Andrew powered up his computer and settled in. He took a deep breath and opened up the game. There was no guarantee she'd contact him, but at least he'd be ready. He spawned in his usual spot and explored. He idly wandered the digital landscape, killing minor enemies and time. He didn't have to wait long.

THEIFNAME2134 HAS ENTERED THE GAME

Andrew's pulse quickened as Lisa's avatar come over to him. Just make it quick, he told himself.

You alone? she typed.

Yes, he replied.

Three little dots appeared above her avatar – she was typing.

Right, he thought. Time for you to go. Tell her you're done. She's just some prankster or something.

Plan has changed, she typed. Then added, *We need to meet.*

Andrew's mouth dropped open and his hands paused over the keyboard. Did she have to agree to a plan he'd already changed?

Andrew's fingers stumbled across the keys. *No,* he typed. *Not funny.*

Her response flashed up: *We have to. If I get caught, bad for you.*

Andrew drummed his fingers on the table. Was that true? Or was it just what she wanted him to think? Who did she think she was anyway? Constantly putting him off-balance and making threats. She deserved a taste of her own medicine, and this was his last chance to get her. He rubbed his forehead and typed:

Where and when?

Lisa's avatar idly swung its arms back and forth, then checked their daggers. It was the standard waiting pose for this character type.

Tell you soon

Andrew leaned back, dropping his hands on his head. What did that even mean? Okay, never mind that. What had he done? He wasn't out, he was still playing games with her. He suddenly felt like he'd woken up next to the person he'd been planning to dump. He leaned far back in his chair, groaning at his own foolishness.

Andrew's wallowing was interrupted by a knock at the door. The shock of it caught him mid-lean. He waved his arms desperately to prevent himself from going over backwards. His flailing knee hit the desk and made this morning's abandoned cereal bowl dance and spill what little milk was left. Something twinged in his neck. He regained his balance, looked at Lisa's incriminating message, then back at the door.

His pulse jumped higher as the knock came again, more insistently this time.

'Oi!' called Pascal through the wood. 'I'm doing a beer and food run. You want anything?'

'No, thanks!' Andrew called out with relief.

'Suit yourself!'

Pascal's footsteps padded back down the hallway.

Blip!

Andrew turned around. Not a message from Lisa, a game notification.

THIEFNAME2134 has left the game

Andrew rubbed his eyes and stood up. The chair groaned its appreciation. He looked at the milk slopped across the desk.

He was normally fine with a messy deskbut drew the line at curdling milk. He wandered into the kitchen in search of paper towels. Both Pascal and Liam were out, but he could see a peak of vivid hair sticking out over one edge of the couch and socked feet on the other side. Another one of Pascal's girl-friends. He recognised the hair. It was electric red from a presumably radioactive dye. It blazed like an astronomical corona. Looking at it left sunspots in Andrew's vision. He'd seen it, and presumably her, a few times now, typically vanishing into Pascal's bedroom after furtive fridge-raiding or bathroom-hogging missions.

'You back already, babe?' she called out from behind the couch.

'No, sorry,' said Andrew. 'I'm Andrew, Pascal's housemate.'

'Great,' she said.

A laptop snapped shut. She sat up and leaned over the edge of the couch to face him.

'Hi, Andrew,' she said to his astonished face. 'I'm Lisa, remember me?'

Andrew's high-pitched 'WHAT?!' echoed through the house, cracking with adolescent awkwardness.

Lisa sat up and leaned over the back of the couch. She held up both hands in a conciliatory fashion.

'Take it easy,' she said. 'I'm sorry to surprise you, but I couldn't resist. Be chill.'

Andrew gaped at her for a few seconds before sarcasm took the wheel.

'Says the fucking criminal hiding out in the living room of two DAS analysts?'

'That's a long story we don't have time for right now. We have to help each other.'

Andrew leaned over and placed his head on the kitchen bench. The cool faux marble cooled his forehead as the room moved around him.

'You're the most wanted person in the country and you've been staying at my place?'

'Uh huh,' she said. 'Even got a few selfies with you when you and Liam were on the PlayStation a few nights ago.'

Andrew looked up and stared at her, still unable to fully comprehend she was in front of him.

'That and a few other things are just part of an insurance package for me,' Lisa continued. 'Now look, it's really important that—'

'And Pascal?' said Andrew, trying not to think of what else she'd got up to. 'How long have you two been working together?'

'Pascal?' Lisa's face scrunched up in a slightly embarrassed smile. 'He doesn't know a thing. He's ... fun, let's put it that way. Not really into current events. I needed somewhere to crash, and he was open to it. Come on, I can't be the first one to do that? He's a major fuckboy.'

Andrew watched as his personal and professional lives crashed into each other. He could smell the office coffee and dusty air conditioning. He expected to see the hallway writhe and break out in glass security doors and security cameras.

'Maybe you should sit down?' said Lisa. She cocked her head to one side, her embarrassed smile changing to an expression of apparent concern.

Andrew pulled a kitchen stool close. Lisa winced as it screamed across the tiles.

Once he sat down, she came out from around the couch. She was wearing one of Pascals t-shirts and some jeans, fashionably distressed.

'What do you think?' she said, twirling a lock of hair between her long fingers. 'Part of my new look. Everyone has to make some changes when they go on the run. I went extreme. I literally cried when I first saw it, but now I think it works. Like it?'

'No,' said Andrew. 'I mean sure. Whatever.'

He took a deep breath.

'What the fuck are you doing in my house?'

'Koil,' she said. 'Any progress?'

'Hey' growled Andrew. 'I don't take orders from you.'

'Look.' Lisa paused, her eyes closed as though reading calming mantras on the back of her eyelids. 'We don't have much time,' she said, opening her eyes. 'Pascal will be back soon, and we don't know each other, okay?'

Andrew opened his mouth to object, but she waved in his face.

'Koil? He's a way bigger threat than me. Get me the info and say goodbye to me forever.'

Andrew just stared at her, goggle-eyed. In his mind, he was standing on a tiny island in a raging river, big enough for just one foot. As he balanced, she gave him a nod.

They both flinched as they heard the front door bang.

'Oi!' called Pascal. 'Beer and food's here!'

'Coming!' shouted Lisa. She ran into the hallway to intercept him. Andrew listened to them murmuring in the hallway, then they both came in. Pascal walked ahead and slapped the beer and a couple of takeaway bags on the kitchen counter.

'So Andy, you in?' said Pascal.

'What?' snapped Andrew.

'Want a beer?' he said, pointing to the ones he was ripping from cardboard and putting in the fridge.

'Can't say no,' sighed Andrew, looking at Lisa.

Twenty-One

Two years earlier

Lisa uncrossed her legs and stretched. Muscles twitched as blood flowed back, triggering pins and needles. She shambled to her feet and admired her handiwork.

'Free her now!'

The words were black against a white background. Nearby, an empty frame of splashed black paint on the dying grass showed where she'd done the first coat. It blended into the general chaos of a true share house backyard. Aside from the standard rubbish and stolen garden chairs, it had a barbecue, an oil drum for fires and three dilapidated couches. The lawn only survived at the edges, near the fence line and shade. Some years ago, some creeping bush had consumed all three wooden fences, creating a high green wall. Everyone preferred it this way, neighbours included.

A shadow crossed the drying sign.

'Aren't you done yet?'

Lisa smiled more broadly than she was aware of.

'Hi, Blake,' she said. 'Ready to go if you are.'

'And everyone else,' he reminded her. 'They're still getting ready.'

'Take a seat, then,' she said, patting the patch of dust next to her.

Blake dropped onto the parched earth. You could learn a lot about people from the way they approached sitting on the ground. Self-conscious? Precious? Unfit? Many were aghast at the idea. Some looked around first, or had to check what they were wearing. Blake slid down with athletic grace, his legs folding under him like designer furniture. At first glance, he looked pretty casual – just some old jeans and a black t-shirt – but any outfit looked good on him. Some guys could slip on a new suit and instantly look like they'd slept in it. Not Blake. He was the opposite. Things smoothed out or took on that laundry commercial glow.

But that same outfit on repeat so often? Lisa wrinkled her nose. She found it strangely irritating. Especially when seeing the repetition in photos. Not that there were many. He hated having his picture taken. What a waste. Lisa had gone through a few unique looks over the years, but Blake was always in jeans and a black t-shirt in all but the hottest summers. It meant you could look at two photos of him and not be sure if they were taken a day or a year apart.

His hair was northern Sydney beaches blond. Probably the same place he got his cheekbones. He never talked about his family, but gave the impression he was doing everything he could to piss off some rich parent.

But he wasn't some rich kid tourist. Blake's presence made you concentrate on where he was now, not where he came from.

Lisa was just thinking of something to say when his phone buzzed. He scrambled for it at once. So typical. Everyone needed their phone, but he would swoop on it with every notification. Lisa remembered a story from a woman at a party.

She was just some random. A bourbon-breathing dragon, two sips from hammered. All outside voice, waving arms and mid-sentence pauses to remember where she was up to. Lisa gave it ten minutes max before this creature was puking, crying, making out with someone or a weird combination of all three. *Any*way. The dragon claimed, from alleged experience, that Blake stopped mid-fuck if his phone buzzed. Lisa, watching with narrowed eyes and pursed lips, doubted anything had ever happened between them. Although, if she was screwing this woman, she'd stop to check her feeds as well.

Lisa smiled as she imagined the woman's head on a dragon's body. Blake would probably look good in a suit of armour, sticking a sword in her and nothing else. She snapped back to reality. Blake was still tapping away. She waved a hand in his field of vision.

'Just levelling up,' he said, staring at his phone.

'You're *always* playing those games,' complained Lisa.

He shrugged and tapped the screen a few more times. Lisa leaned in, allegedly to look at the phone. A magical warrior was being overwhelmed by enemy orcs. Blake groaned as the screen turned dark and the death message appeared, red and dripping with blood.

Koil has died

'Better luck next time,' said Lisa.

TWENTY-TWO

Present day

ANDREW LAY ON HIS BED AND STARED AT THE CEILING. OR at least where the ceiling would be. He couldn't see much with the light off. He wore over-ear headphones, hands clamped down on top of his head. His brain was whirring away so fast he felt it might fly off if he didn't hold on.

He'd wanted to know where Lisa was. Now he did. In the room across the hall with his housemate. They were both definitely in there, and that's why he was still wearing noise-cancelling headphones. At least this wasn't a night Liam got lucky as well. With his room in the middle, Andrew would blast his headphones as competing sexcapade noises came through both walls like duelling banjos.

He ground his teeth and cursed his choices. It was too late to call in Angela. He wasn't just in contact with Lisa, he was living with her! He had to get her out of the house and away. Tipping off the authorities wouldn't help him now. He'd never work again. Hell, if she talked, he could go to prison. She'd outsmarted him twice so far. He just had to stay alert.

His bedroom door swung open, and the light came on. Andrew yelped and covered his face as acid-trip spots and squiggles exploded in his vision. He'd been staring right at the bloody light bulb. Served him right for not buying a cover for it. His headphones flew off and hit the floor with a warranty-voiding crack.

'Sorry,' someone said. 'I was knocking for ages.'

The door clicked shut.

He sat up, lowered his hands and squinted at Lisa's blurred form, now sitting on the end of the bed.

'What do you want?' he groaned.

'Koil,' she said. 'Keep your voice down. Or do you want Pascal to wake up and wonder what we're up to?'

Andrew paused. That scenario didn't need to play out.

With an 'I'm-only-doing-this-because-I-choose-to' expression, he ran Lisa through what he had learned; Koil was connected to multiple extremist groups and shady cyber activity. Most of the info was old, but it linked him to another operation. Something to do with 'cyber effects'. But it was locked down tight. He couldn't get any details about it. Each time he tried to go further, he hit a curt message about needing the proper clearance.

'So, have you tried?' asked Lisa.

'Tried what?'

'Getting clearance,' she replied. 'Either get it yourself or convince someone who's got the access.'

'I can't!' exclaimed Andrew, aghast. 'I'll be caught and then you will be too. I'm jeopardising myself and now you want me to recruit other people? Did you ever meet Internal Security? Well, I have! They're happy for now, but I can't jeopardise that.'

Andrew fell back onto the bed. He considered himself far too tough to call it a flounce, but that's what it was.

Lisa stared at or through him as she thought.

'What about Secret Truth?' she said.

'What?'

'My group,' she muttered.

Andrew opened his eyes and sat up again.

'No,' he said. 'I've been through all your stuff and I didn't see that one.'

He tried not to grin. This was amazing! A group she was part of? Another lead. Perfect. Angela was going to love this. Well, she would if he could tell her.

'Look them up,' Lisa said. 'You won't find anything.'

'Why not?'

Lisa glanced at the door and listened for a moment. All was quiet. The cheap floorboards would creak and groan if anyone walked up the hall.

'They were my group,' she said. 'At least I thought they were. They helped me plan.'

Andrew waited silently as Lisa seemed to gather her thoughts. After a moment, not looking at Andrew, she began.

She had been recruited by someone she would only call Koil. He had introduced her to a group of fellow recruits who met online. Everyone was anonymous. All chat encrypted. It was the safest way. They knew her mission. They were there to support it. Each one had some different expertise. They could help with security interviews, knowing what to say during psychological assessments. Another passed along the social media accounts she claimed as hers. Documents and contacts, a history. They built up the façade of a life for her, one that screened her real life and public political activity. Others schooled her in operational security, developing networks and how to influence and coerce people on the inside. But most of all, they gave her encouragement and justifications for extreme actions, even violence, in the face of creeping tyranny.

They were all kind, encouraging and constructive, in equal measure. Lisa did not know where the name came from, but they referred to themselves as Secret Truth. They were one cell, and there were others in each major city, each working on their own projects. The more time she spent with them, the more she withdrew from everyone and everything she'd previously known. She still couldn't pinpoint exactly when she'd lost everything except these wheedling voices online. It was only after betraying and escaping from DAS that she started to realise how long she'd been alone. Lisa stopped talking and turned to Andrew.

'I was part of something big, you know?' she said to him. 'Do you know what that's like? Joining something bigger than yourself and wondering where it will take you?'

Andrew thought back to the morning he started at DAS, standing outside, dreaming of career glory.

Lisa continued, 'I had a major role in a direct campaign. Real action! But I knew others were working in secret as well. Others got arrested, or otherwise noticed. Or so I was told. I had to keep my head down.'

Andrew nodded cautiously.

'I kept it under control,' continued Lisa. 'I knew that once I entered DAS, there was no going back.'

Her voice trailed off, resulting in a pregnant pause that felt long enough to almost go full term.

'So, what happened?' Andrew asked, breaking the silence. 'I mean, it looks like you did what they wanted you to do. I don't know why you're here or why you think something else is going on.'

She turned to face him on the bed, sitting cross-legged like someone gossiping at a sleepover.

'I broke the rules,' she said.

'No shit,' said Andrew.

'No!' she exclaimed. 'Koil's rules!' She stopped and glanced over her shoulder again. There was still nothing but the closed door and Andrew's nail-pocked wall. 'He told me the group was being watched, at least parts of it. We had to be careful.

Once inside, I wasn't to get any information on what they knew about us. I had … a different target. I was to sit tight until I got the signal to go.'

'So, what happened?' said Andrew.

'I saw something as I was … leaving.' Here she had the decency to look slightly embarrassed. 'It was Koil. His code name was on a document – mentions of foreign influence operations and who knows what else. He was someone's spy, not an activist, and I was working with him.'

She paused for a moment, looking down as she scratched the back of her neck. Her incandescent fringe fell in front of her face. Andrew shook his head in an attempt to focus as she looked to the side and brushed it away.

'I didn't have much time. It was just a couple of references, but I suddenly thought – I've been tricked.'

Perhaps manipulated, thought Andrew, remembering Peter.

There was another pause. Lisa leaned in just a little. So did Andrew.

'I was already committed to the action,' said Lisa. 'I'm only talking to you because something worse is coming. I want to get back at the people who got me into this and if I'm working for the Chinese, Russians or whoever the fuck else, I want to know.'

'What about Secret Truth?' asked Andrew. 'Are more of you, I mean them, in DAS too?'

Lisa reddened, her mouth tightened to a thin line.

'I looked them up straight after I saw Koil's real status. With my new system privileges, I searched everything I could, but nothing. No mention.'

This close, Lisa's eyes were even brighter. Andrew tried not to be distracted by her perfume. What was it, though? Jasmine? Something summery.

'What does that mean?' he said, letting his lean pull him in a little closer.

'I don't think they exist. I'd been told they'd had close calls with the authorities, needed to stay low. But how could that be if they were nowhere in the system? The group I thought I was a part of didn't exist. It was all just Koil, or Blake, as I first knew him. One person with many different accounts. He played me. But I don't know why he, or someone in DAS, wanted it to happen.'

Lisa sat up a little straighter. Her eyes flicked down to the blanket and back up to Andrew, who swallowed. The noise this made was uncomfortably loud.

'Look,' he said, 'I agree something's going on and maybe we can help each other.'

Lisa gave a small smile at this.

'Do you know what it's like?' she said. 'One minute having a cause, something you've given years of your life to? Then discovering it's all bullshit? I still believe in what I did, but now I'm not sure how much was me and how much was him.'

Lisa's hand slid along the blanket, closer to his.

'Lisa?' said Andrew.

'Yes?' she said. Was it his imagination, or was there a slight flush in her cheeks?

'I need you to leave,' he said.

'Excuse me?' Lisa recoiled as though Andrew was electrified.

He panicked.

'Not the room, not right now, anyway. I meant the house!'

Her expression did not improve.

'What?' Lisa's tone carried across the sleeping building.

'You don't understand the risk! My career's over if you're caught here!'

Lisa's mouth formed a perfect 'O' for outrage as a perfect storm gathered on her face. Andrew's shoulder blades bumped against his bedroom wall before he even realised he'd been shuffling backwards on the bed. The way she was leaning towards him reminded him of big cat documentaries – the way they would lower their head and narrow their eyes before pouncing.

'I'm going nowhere,' she hissed. 'We're in this together, remember? Something much bigger than your fucking baby career's going on.'

Andrew felt the wall stud behind him creak as he pressed harder.

'Look,' he blurted. 'You can keep contacting me in the game, but I need you out of here. The odds of getting caught here are too high.'

'Let's make this clear,' she said, enunciating every word like a gangster taking deportment lessons. 'I'm. Going. Nowhere.'

Out in the hallway, the light flicked on, spilling under Andrew's bedroom door. It might as well have been a cartoon light bulb of inspiration, or a heavenly sign, for Andrew found The Way. Or at least A Way to get Lisa out.

She was too focused on him to hear the creaking floorboards as someone walked up the hall.

Andrew shot forward, close enough to smell Lisa's perfume again, and put his hands on her waist. She slapped a hand on his chest and stuck a finger in his face.

'Whoa!' she said. 'You need to back off.'

'Uh huh!' he yelled, like some mid-chorus rock star. 'Yeah, baby! I love it, do it again!'

Before Lisa could reply, Andrew's bedroom door burst open. Pascal stood framed in the doorway, in nothing but a singlet and his underwear.

'What the hell?' he said, rubbing the sleep out of an eye. 'Fuck's going on?'

Lisa's mouth turned into an 'O' of horror.

'Listen, babe,' she said. 'It's not what it—' but she was cut off by Andrew pushing past her to Pascal.

'Oh, mate!' he cried. 'I'm so sorry! She came in here, and

you know, it just happened. It was just a quickie, it meant nothing! We're sorry!'

Pascal blinked a few times, then focused on Lisa. Caught off-guard, she stared unseeingly as she whirred through options in her mind. In the awkward silence, Pascal cleared his throat.

'Seriously?' he said, his tone dropping to a near growl. 'I know we're not exclusive, but my housemate when I'm asleep? Damn … I think you should just go.'

Andrew turned to Lisa and revelled in her shocked expression. Her face reddened to match her hair – especially when he winked at her. With a smug smile and victory assured, Andrew turned back to Pascal.

Just in time to be punched in the face.

* * *

The next evening, Andrew sat on the living room couch, as still and solitary as Rodin's thinker. The cinema-esque TV that dominated the opposing wall sat quiet for once. It often stayed on for weeks at a time, endlessly streaming something because everyone assumed someone had to be halfway through watching it. Andrew had turned it off after slinking into the living room. He stabbed at the power button so savagely the remote flipped off the table. Plinks and pings broke the silence as the electronics cooled and the plastic frame popped back into shape. They should turn it off more often.

Andrew's stomach growled, reminding him how late it was getting. He ignored it. Didn't matter. Least of his problems right now. He looked at the dormant TV and found his morose reflection pathetic.

He thought back to the previous day. Lisa had stayed on this very couch in the end, refusing to leave until daylight. She hissed 'Talk soon' to Andrew as she departed, tottering under a tall backpack. He watched her go. Her hair poking over the top of her backpack made it look like it had ignited. How could she stay under the radar looking like that? Although, come to think of it, the hair had distracted him before he knew who she was.

After she left, he grabbed another pack of frozen veg for his throbbing eye. Fortunately, they were a staple in the house. A young man's minimum to keep the scurvy at bay. Pascal's hit had spun him around and onto the floor. The room had kept spinning even after he stopped. He hadn't slept all night, fearful of round two with Pascal or, worse, Lisa.

Pascal had gruffly asked about Andrew's condition the next morning. He seemed pleased with the improvement. In some ways, Pascal was an old-school kind of guy. Challenges were issued, duels fought to right wrongs. Now honour was restored, and life could continue. Although Andrew wasn't sure about how honourable it was. He would have liked more warning for a start, if only to stand a better chance of running away.

He'd spent the day gathering his thoughts in various sulks around the house. Now, for the next part. Lisa was out of the building, but not his life. Her words echoed in his ears: 'Get the clearance or convince someone who has it.' But maybe he didn't have to keep following her lead? He could come clean to DAS, hope they didn't drop him in a deep hole somewhere. But the worst thing about Lisa was that she was right. Something was going on. For all he knew, if the wrong person knew he'd met her, it could make him a target for a more traditional hole, six feet deep and rectangular.

Liam's door opened with a bang that echoed up the hall. *Right*, thought Andrew. Time to decide.

'Good evening,' said Liam, sweeping into the living room. He was always so formal with his greetings. He'd been born a hundred years too late in a country without a formal aristocracy. He always behaved like he was wearing a tuxedo only he could see.

'Andrew?'

Andrew's mind had wandered. Now he blinked and looked at Liam properly for the first time.

'I said I'm off to meet with the Brenton Institute Youth League,' said Liam. It was always so important to him that other people knew his plans. Andrew had wondered if this was a good idea in their work.

'Lots of influential people there,' he continued. 'And of course, great—'

'Networking, yes,' finished Andrew. He paused as an unexpected pang of sympathy welled up. Not long ago, he'd heard one side of a phone conversation Liam had been having. He'd been giving an update. It had sounded quite official, and he sounded keen to impress – lots of 'promising developments' and 'doing his absolute best'. Almost as if he was briefing the Minister. Once he hung up, Andrew plonked his glass on the table. Liam had spun around ashen-faced, as though caught in a lie.

'The office?' asked Andrew, wondering if they were being called in for something.

'Uh, no,' said Liam. 'Father.'

Father, thought Andrew, unsure what to do as Liam kept his guilty pose. Most people have dads.

'He's a senior diplomat,' said Liam, unasked. '*Very* senior.'

Andrew left it at that, merely nodding and smiling. What he did understand in that moment was that there was more. More to Liam, that is. He didn't know what it was, but he knew there was something he was missing.

Andrew mentally shook himself as the memory was pushed aside by his current woes. He cleared his throat and went for it before Liam could leave.

'Hey,' he said. 'You mentioned you have 'Spectre' clearance, right?'

Andrew just assumed this. Liam had said no such thing.

Spectre was the security clearance sub-type given to people in Cyber Command. It was another geeky in-joke that typified an insular and pun-indulgent culture. But having Spectre clearance meant you could see the inner workings of Cyber Command and their broad remit.

This was another thing Andrew had learned at DAS. Security clearances weren't just vertical concepts, going from unclassified to top-secret. Each level had specialised sub-parts, labelled with a codeword. If you got access to a particular codeword, you could see all the linked information that related to a specific work area or subject. As in any corporate entity, just because you work in Testing doesn't mean you get to see what's going on in Finance. In the movies, people would rush into high-security rooms saying, 'I have top-secret clearance!'. In DAS that would get a cool look and 'So does the cleaner, but do you actually work in this area? No? Fuck off then.'

In theory, this prevented malicious insiders – except Lisa, apparently – from accessing vast amounts of information they had no legitimate right to. It also prevented normal employees from sharing or cooperating with each other, as well as inspiring a high school clique mentality. Even Peter and Shanti weren't immune to it, rolling their eyes whenever someone mentioned an area they weren't a part of.

'Yeah,' said Liam. 'Spectre and others,' he added. 'That codeword is used to hide a very special source.'

Andrew raised his eyebrows. 'Nice,' he said. 'It's just that for my new role, tracking Lisa Chapman down, I got Merlin clearance. I wish you could see some of this stuff. It's incredible.'

Andrew suddenly wished he'd taken the time to think through what his made up codeword let him see.

Fortunately, Liam was too competitive to be inquisitive.

'Oh, I've got pretty extensive compartments. I can see most

things,' he said, rounding on Andrew, all thought of the youth league forgotten.

Right, thought Andrew. Target acquired. Time to strike.

'Are you sure?' he said. 'The Minister's office is all over this, so they're keeping it pretty tight.'

Liam blanched at the mention of the Minister's office. Those were fighting words.

'I know about the Minister's interest!' he snapped. 'My clearance gets me everything! You'd be the one shocked by what I can get into! Cyber Command gets to see everything because we're involved in so many projects!'

Andrew leaned back out of the spray – Liam was a spitter when upset. He held his hands up placatingly.

'Okay,' he said. 'Maybe you're right, but care to wager?'

Liam paused and colour returned to his cheeks. He was only willing to fight to the metaphorical death. He needed a non-violent way out of this shouting match without losing face.

'We can't gamble for money,' said Liam. 'We'd both have to declare it at our next security review.'

Andrew fought not to roll his eyes. A vision of Peter to him. 'Oh, don't worry,' he said. 'How about a coffee? I'll bring you the name of one of my targets in the Lisa Chapman investigation. If you can bring up all the same stuff I've seen on my system, which I doubt, coffee's on me.'

'Well …' said Liam, his caution cracked but not broken. Andrew pushed on.

'All right,' he said, throwing his hands in the air. 'I wasn't going to say anything, but someone in Strategic Intelligence was looking to swap,' he lied. 'You wanted in there, right? I'll ask around. But only if you win.'

Liam broke into a grin and threw his hand out.

'Done!' he said. 'Come into Cyber Command tomorrow! You'll see *my* clearance is beyond anything they'd give *you*!'

'We'll see,' said Andrew.

Tomorrow, he added to himself, I'm finding Koil.

Twenty-Three

Eighteen months earlier

THE STUDENT BAR DOZED. A COUPLE PLAYED POOL ON A nearby table, as several others went unused. Their shots echoed around the room. At the front a band, on a black foot-high stage, were setting up for the evening. A drum thumped a few times as the guitar scratched a brief warm-up riff. The stylishly dishevelled musicians wore matching sunglasses, not for effect, but necessity. The afternoon sun flooded in through the glass frontage that led to the beer garden. The bar taps lit up in the glare and the hanging glasses sent refracted light dancing around the room.

It was the lull between the day and night drinking, when the few students who straddle both are still hanging around, but the crowds have drifted away. The carpet was sticky with last night's beer. Plus, this morning's beer. And this afternoon's beer.

Lisa sat behind one of the brutalist concrete pillars that held the ceiling up. She was enjoying her beer in a bit of shade, trying to ignore the visual pyrotechnics.

'Hey, stranger.'

Lisa looked up in alarm before softening again. It was Blake. Typical stealthy entrance. He might as well have slipped out of an air duct.

'Oh hi,' she said. 'Was wondering when you'd turn up.'

Blake gave a dismissive wave as he pulled a chair in and sat down.

'Oh, you know me. Busy, busy.'

'Yeah, but with what? Or aren't I allowed to know about her?'

Blake smiled and drummed his fingers on the table.

'Any fallout from the hotel?' he said, changing the subject.

That was Blake, thought Lisa. Non-committal as ever on what else he got up to. She let him get away with it again. One of her friends called him 'Captain Teflon'. Nothing ever stuck.

'No,' said Lisa. 'Cops have no idea. You could shout it on the concourse and they wouldn't know.'

'Don't get cocky,' he warned her. 'There aren't many willing to throw a grenade into an annual shareholders' dinner. We need people like you.'

'Smoke grenade,' she corrected, taking a long pull from the schooner.

As she put the glass down, she felt a shiver that had nothing to do with the cold beer. She'd done it! All those corporate sociopaths living it up after what they'd done? No one had been hurt, but it had sure filled all those big boy pants.

She looked into Blake's eyes.

'Do you really need me?'

She was pushing her luck. They'd talked about this. Nothing stuck to Captain Teflon.

He looked back at her with a gentle smile.

'Of course I do!'

Lisa blinked. 'Really?'

'There's important work to be done,' he said.

Lisa shut her mouth, unaware it had been open. She took another drink, emptying the glass.

'Okay, then,' she snapped. 'Got another smoke grenade?'

Blake leaned forward. The afternoon light reflected in his eyes.

'Ever considered government work?'

* * *

Present day

Liam's beaten-up old Mazda trundled into the DAS open-air car park. It was an immense series of bitumen fields with thousands of white rectangles. As a small city, Canberra could still afford that kind of spatial extravagance. The car park still had plenty of spots. Most people were still at home, wrapped around their coffee. Liam and Andrew snagged a coveted spot close to the main gates. They got out of the car and headed towards the entrance. Liam, bursting with tetchy bravado, strode ahead. Partially out of injured pride, but also wanting to get it over and done with. He had insisted on an early start. Just, you know, so no one got the wrong idea about what they were up to. Andrew, poker-faced, had agreed.

DAS headquarters loomed ahead like an approaching iceberg. Andrew shook himself and steamed ahead.

Inside, shift change hadn't happened yet. The guards were the remnants of night shift – all yawns and cranky stares. But at least they didn't recognise Andrew. Despite his thumping heart, he enjoyed entering without being 'randomly searched' for once.

Liam walked briskly ahead. He gave curt and important nods to a couple of other early arrivals and one departing cleaner as he passed. Most seemed surprised or confused, but enough nodded back out of unthinking habit it to make it work. That was Liam, though. Always networking, and when it didn't work, he just moved on.

They crossed out of the main atrium and through the cafe, eerily silent at this hour. Then they went into a stairwell and dropped three levels, slipping out into a corridor that ended with a door that wouldn't be out of place in a gold reserve.

This entrance strongly suggested 'No Entrance'. Andrew remembered it from when Peter casually dropped him off. All steel, standing at least a foot taller than most doors. Bolts thick as a man's arm sat back in their recesses, ready to emerge when the lock was engaged. A matching doormat would have been made with land mines, stitched together with barbed wire.

'Okay,' said Liam, 'here we are.'

Liam swiped his pass, keyed in a code, and pressed his palm to the reader on the wall. Nothing happened for a few seconds. Then the door inched open, beeping like a reversing truck to prevent you being flattened against the wall.

As they walked forward, Andrew gasped. To the left, the hallway dropped away into an open space teeming with activity. The contrast to the rest of the building could not have been greater. It was like walking through the empty halls of an abandoned cruise liner, nothing but silence and forlorn items scattered on the ground, then discovering Mardi Gras was in full swing in a side ballroom.

It was a cathedral for cyber threats, full of the traditional prayers of those who work in IT like, 'Please, God, let rebooting work.' A football field filled with rows and rows of desks, computers and activity. Each desk's occupant worked with quiet but ferocious focus. At least one monitor on each desk had a light on top, that occasionally lit up. Then, a harried individual would come over, glare at the screen muttering orders, or grab one of the red-striped phones. Otherwise, most people stared at their screens or at one of the huge ones dominating the far end of the room. There were four in total. Several clocks sat beneath, showing different time zones. Each screen showed something different. One was a map of the world, with glowing lines linking China and the rest of the world along cyber super-highways. The others were harder to decipher. One reeled constantly, refreshing information in a list format. Another two scrolled text from websites monitoring worldwide outages and data breaches.

The air had a curiously mixed feel as air conditioning fought with local conditions to a standstill, overhead vents blasting bitingly cold air at the resilient male-dominated funk of sweat, pizza and cheap deodorant.

Liam nudged Andrew out of his reverie. He blinked and turned away from the massed rows of terminals.

Liam pointed at the nearby metal sign fixed to the wall: 'Cyber Threat – China Division'.

'Not my area,' he explained. 'We have to keep going.'

They headed towards the other end of the hallway. Further along, next to a battered door with peeling laminate, hung another sign: 'Cyber Threat – Rest of World'.

The scanner accepted Liam's pass with another cheery beep, but the wooden door was swollen and old. Liam threw his shoulder into it to get it open.

Andrew's expression fell like an old apple. If the previous room had been a cathedral, this was barely a confessional. It struggled to fit the limited furniture. Everything was packed in so tightly it resembled storage more than an office.

A long, thin table, pockmarked and leaning slightly, served as a room divider, necessary to avoid bloodshed in such a small space. It sat between two chairs facing away from each other to their own tiny desks and computers. Andrew recognised Liam's precision on one of them. The other was less pristine. Aside from the computer, it was covered in dust, old computer journals and printouts from the 1980s onwards. Old terminals and hard drives were stacked underneath, with a gap exactly wide enough for two feet.

'Oh,' said Liam, following Andrew's gaze. 'That's Roger. He's been here since World War II or something. Nice guy, but not very … connected.'

Andrew wondered what Liam meant by that. Certainly, looking at his desk, there were connections everywhere. Possibly he meant the social type.

Andrew took Roger's chair, sliding around in the fossilised cushion indentation. All the fluff at the end of the left armrest had been picked off by a compulsive fidgeter. Liam sat at his desk and switched on the computer.

'Actually,' said Liam as the computer powered up, 'Roger had some interesting things to say about Peter.'

'Like what?'

Liam leaned in. 'Peter,' he said, '*is a double agent.*'

'What?' said Andrew. 'Then how does he still work here?'

'All right,' Liam conceded. 'It's not proven, but he's been investigated. He was in some task force that had been infiltrated. Someone was giving everything to the other side. Internal Security went all through it and nailed a few people, but he got away with it. They didn't have enough evidence to get rid of him. That's why he's in OSTRA – he's not really trusted with much else.'

'I dunno,' said Andrew. 'He's … Well, he's sneaky and clever enough, I guess. But he seems okay.'

'Seems,' said Liam. 'Just get out of OSTRA as quick as you can. Someone with your … backstory doesn't need any more security scandals.'

The computer finished loading and the main login screen appeared.

'Here we go,' said Liam.

'Wait …' said Andrew. Security scandals? He was already in several! But this was new territory. He had manipulated someone and was about to illegally access classified material on behalf of a declared enemy of the state. He was suffering the anxiety people got when chasing their losses.

'What's the problem?' said Liam. 'You going to accept I win the bet already?'

'Sorry,' Andrew said. 'It doesn't matter. Be as quick as you can.'

Liam muttered as he entered in his account password, system password and program passwords, then pressed his thumb to the biometric scanner.

Andrew shifted impatiently in Roger's bum imprint and stared at the towering piles around them. Possible death by a junk avalanche was not something he'd expected today. He also wasn't sure how long it was before Liam's cologne became lethal.

'And here we are,' said Liam, bringing his profile up on screen. 'All the accesses you have *and more*.' The profile screen listed all the compartments Liam had access to.

Andrew had five. His mouth dropped open as he read, much to Liam's satisfaction. This list had dozens.

'Hang on,' said Andrew, thinking of his own lack of access and attempts to find Koil. 'How come you can search everything?'

'You know how there's only me and Roger?'

'So?'

'So, with 'rest of world' it's far too much hassle to try to figure out exactly which security permissions we need, so we got them all.'

'Everything?' said Andrew. 'That's it? No restrictions at all?'

'I had to sign something to say I wouldn't abuse it. Also, Roger says they do random audits of all activity. You know, make sure you're not accessing anything inappropriate. But it's never mattered.'

'Why not?'

'Because, according to the computer, we had permission to look at everything we accessed – no problem.'

Andrew shook his head at the mix of logic and insanity he'd found here so often.

'So, who's the target?' asked Liam.

'Koil. K-O-I-L,' said Andrew.

'That's it?' complained Liam.

As Liam typed in his searches, Andrew lost himself in speculation. What if Koil was a Chinese spy? A Russian one? Some other hostile power that was trying to plant moles in DAS or incite chaos? What then? War? Is that kind of intelligence enough to buy his way out of this hole?

His fatalistic musings were interrupted by Liam letting out a yell of triumph.

'What have you got?' asked Andrew, his heart beating in his throat.

'Koil,' said Liam, without looking up from the screen. 'At least, I think so. There's something here linked.'

'Got his real name? Who he works for?'

Liam's eyes stayed fixed on the screen. He frowned as he read.

'Well?' said Andrew.

'Uh, I've got a list,' replied Liam. 'For starters …'

'What?' snapped Andrew.

'Well, that's weird,' said Liam.

'*What?*'

'The government he works for?'

'Yes?' said Andrew.

'It's ours.'

Twenty-Four

Andrew pushed past Liam, upsetting a pile of old computer manuals that hit the ground with a dust-raising crash. He scrolled as quickly as the mouse would allow. The results were a mess – they filled the screen, all linked to different people, operations, intelligence reports. It made no sense.

'He's a person!' Andrew shouted. 'I know it!'

'You said Koil is a person, right? Only if you give it a quick look,' said Liam, his car salesman's self-assurance bubbling back. 'If you have my access and experience, it's different.'

Andrew pushed back from the computer. The seat's wheels bucked on the old carpet like a four-wheel-drive churning mud. He finished up facing the wrong way and swivelled around to Liam, who had snapped up the prime keyboard position again.

Liam waved an arm at the computer.

'Okay,' he said, 'Koil is an online persona in certain closed-off forums. Probably infiltrating anti-government movements, but he, or rather *they*, are also linked to this other stuff.'

'They?' said Andrew. 'Please tell me you don't mean more than one person.'

'Absolutely,' said Liam. 'Not a fixed set, either.'

Andrew's blank expression sent Liam into a hand-waving explanation. 'What about this? None of these files seem to call out one person or group, but it's all linked to Koil. It's metadata! Koil is … is … a hashtag! Yeah. Or a method. Perhaps a category? Think of it like that. The Koil method. A bunch of different people doing different things under the same name. Maybe both online and real life.'

Andrew fought the urge to bring his legs up onto the seat cushion as the metaphorical ground dropped into the abyss around him. The Koil method? He wanted a person's name, not something that sounded like a diet fad or a tendon-snapping sexual position.

'Or the Minister's office,' said Liam, with a trace of bitterness. 'The Minister's always sending emails, letters or press releases, sending out orders or demanding things. But none of it is the actual minister. It's just different people under that banner acting with that authority.'

'What's it all connected to?' asked Andrew, wondering who the Minister for Koil was. 'There's got to be a common thread somewhere.'

Liam leaned in and clicked about for a few seconds.

'Hah!' he said in triumph. 'Operation Polarize Dunk. Something run out of Information Operations and Effects.'

Andrew nodded, mentally noting this all down.

Across the room, Liam's self-satisfied smile faded. He leaned forward in his chair.

'Hang on,' he said, all thoughts of victorious coffee forgotten. 'How come you didn't know that?'

In the silence that followed, you could almost hear the silverfish munching Roger's paper pile.

'Uh, I did,' said Andrew, trying the direct approach. 'Just making sure you knew. But you were right. Coffee's on me.'

Liam's face contracted in disturbed concentration, as though he was trying to figure out who stank in a crowded room and worried, on some level, that it was him.

'You do have the proper access? This isn't wrong, is it?' he asked, far too late under the circumstances.

'Nooo,' said Andrew in a tone that was not at all convincing.

'No to the access, or no it isn't wrong?' said Liam, at a similar pitch.

'This was something on the edge of the investigation,' said Andrew. 'I just needed some context before I followed the wrong clues.'

Liam's lips moved as he thought. His eyes widened, like someone realising a bitchy text accidentally went to the person they were complaining about.

'So, you tricked me?' said Liam, aghast.

I manipulated you, thought Andrew. But, unhappily, not as well as Peter.

'*No, don't!*' Andrew yelled as Liam stabbed the power button on his computer. The screen winked into blackness.

'I think you'd better go,' said Liam. He looked around in case someone had snuck into this glorified cupboard.

'I don't want any other part in whatever this is,' he said. 'Head back to your area.'

Andrew could see Liam wasn't to be convinced otherwise. He got out of Roger's chair, turned around, and grabbed the doorknob.

'Andrew?'

He turned, almost hitting his elbow on a pile of books.

'Yes?'

'You can catch the bus home,' said Liam.

* * *

Andrew spent the rest of the day trawling through possible active shooter alerts. The usual stuff, people posting online about how they were going to shoot up an office, place of worship or restaurant that doesn't redeem old coupons. They were automatically scraped from the web and reviewed. God, it was boring. It was a pointless task because the sheer volume was ridiculous. The amount of crazy threats was insane. The software – designed to pick up 'toxic or threatening sentiment' – was quickly overwhelmed. They'd reduced the volume overall by filtering out blogs relating to Hollywood casting and mother's groups, but still couldn't compete with the torrent.

Andrew clicked through like it was mandatory online training – skipping through to an end that wouldn't come. His mind was on other things. As much as it annoyed him, Liam was probably right about the Koil method. He needed to know more.

He was interrupted in his thoughts by Shanti walking through the door. Glad of the distraction, people called out various greetings.

'Well!' said Peter. 'About time we saw you again. Or have you forgotten us in your new glory?' he added sourly. Like all people with a distaste for office politics, he hated being beaten by it. Shanti was a good operator. Losing her to IOE rankled.

'Hi all,' said Shanti. 'Just grabbing a few things.'

At his desk, Andrew's eyes widened as an idea flared into existence. He stuck his head over the divider.

'Shanti!'

Shanti stopped collecting things and looked at Andrew, a favoured coffee mug hanging from her hand.

'Hi, Andrew' she said. 'What's up?'

'Actually,' he said, 'quite a bit. Can I talk to you about it sometime?'

'Grab a coffee tomorrow?' she replied.

'Sometime sooner?' he said. 'It's, um … a security thing.'

Shanti's expression plunged to absolute zero. She placed the coffee mug back on the desk with enough force to make the screen wobble.

'*What*,' she hissed, coming almost nose to nose over the divider, 'have you done now?'

'Um,' said Andrew. 'Got a second to chat? Somewhere private?'

Many walls in DAS had ears, or even eyes. Plus, there were a couple with noses for detecting explosives. For relative privacy, they sought refuge in an empty meeting room down the hall. It held a single conference table, and every spare space was stuffed with chairs. They surround the table like frenzied sharks around a whale carcass, crowds of unlucky onlookers waiting for their chance to feed. Andrew pushed several aside to get through the door. He looked around at the microphone in the centre of the table. It was for video calls, and the sullen red eye meant it was off. But then, that's just what they'd want you to think.

Shanti dropped into a chair and gestured for him to do the same. He pushed through and sat on the opposite side of the table, like in a job interview.

'Are … are we going to be overheard here?' asked Andrew.

'No,' said Shanti. 'This is a meeting room, no listening goes on here.'

Andrew couldn't tell whether or not she was serious.

'Now,' she said. 'What is it?'

'It's my Lisa Chapman investigation,' he said. 'I found a link to her, something about the Koil method.'

'The what?' said Shanti.

'It's someone she was meeting when she left that day. She said so,' said Andrew, hoping Shanti wasn't too good at reading him.

'You said it was a method,' said Shanti flatly. 'Not a person.'

'I think it's both,' said Andrew.

'We'll come back to that,' said Shanti. 'But why are you telling me this?'

'There's something big happening,' he said.

Shanti merely stared – a statue of annoyed scepticism.

'I'm serious,' said Andrew. He wished he'd turned the air conditioning on. There was nothing else to do but go for it.

'She was recruited to steal data from DAS by someone who works in this building,' he said.

'Who?' asked Shanti, aghast.

'I don't know!' said Andrew. 'But I found some links that point in-house.'

'And you're sure of this?'

'Yes,' he said. 'Maybe someone within IOE, but I haven't got much. I … heard her talk about a contact called Koil that she had to meet. You know, as she left.'

'Seems a strange thing to say,' Shanti said slowly.

'I did some research on Koil,' said Andrew, moving past this, 'and found it all linked to some operation call Polarize Dunk. It's run out of Information Operations and Effects. I don't have the clearance for it, but you do.'

'You want me to get classified information for you? Why not put in an official request?'

'I don't want to show what I know. I'm testing a theory and just need some—' he stopped himself from saying information. 'Context,' he finished.

'So,' she said, 'what is it we do now? I'm guessing you've told Internal Security?'

'I've been speaking to them,' he said, trying to keep his voice steady. 'But I just want to make sure before I go reporting anything officially. I need your help. If there's an internal leak, if Lisa Chapman has accomplices, I want to be sure before I pass it on.' He shifted in his seat, banging his elbow on one of the other chairs wedged against him and the table. 'All I need to know is the official rundown. What's Operation Polarize Dunk? Who runs it? That's it, I swear. No details. I just want to see if there's a connection I can show to Internal Security.'

Shanti drummed her fingers on the table. Her beloved bangles added some extra percussion.

'You trying to make yourself look good?' she said. 'Save your precious career?'

'No,' he replied, surprising himself. 'Trying to stop things from getting worse. For everyone. Maybe save some people? C'mon. If there's nothing there, you can tell Security yourself.'

After an age, she finally replied. 'All right, I'll do some digging for context. Nothing more. Deal?'

'Deal,' said Andrew. 'I promise it won't go any further – analyst's oath.'

Twenty-Five

Dave, former Neo-Nazi rock star, sat at home, alone. He lived with several others in a tired 1970s weatherboard write-off. It sat in an outer suburb that had missed gentrification but hit inflation. The people in this house lived together out of financial necessity, not a sense of community. Dave had the smallest room near the front door, meaning he was constantly woken up by people coming and going at all hours of the day. Inside, slivers of orange light were peeking through the window blinds. The source could have been sunrise, sunset or a gloomy midday. Or perhaps a midnight streetlight by the window. The dented plastic blinds were drawn too tightly to tell.

The room consisted of three main areas, all within arm's reach of each other in this cramped space. The first was the single bed that almost blocked the door. A keen observer, risking personal safety by getting close to the mattress, would notice it had a central dent in the doona that scattered clothing fell into. Next, Mount Laundry. Or rather, Mount Dirty Clothes. Calling it Laundry implied it would be cleaned eventually. The bottom of the pile was already forming into soft peat and couldn't be saved. At least the peak had impressive views of the next area: the computer. It was the only new thing in the room. A monitor and tower setup, the keyboard even had its own multi-colour lighting scheme. By contrast, the whole system sat on a basic desk that had literally fallen off the back of a truck.

Dave sat at the desk in a white plastic lawn chair, hunched over the keyboard with his chin resting in his hand. His sour expression dimly lit by the screen.

'C'mon,' he muttered, waiting for responses. He had several chats going at once. At last count, there were eleven tabs open in his browser, two dark web windows – that he'd finally learned to use – and an encrypted chat on his phone.

Dave leaned back, dragging his hands down over his face.

Initially, he'd gone back to the cheap sugar hit of some of his old forums. They were once his people. His tribe. But not anymore. Shit-posting and memeage had been fun once, but now he felt nothing. Especially as everyone piled on if they figured out who he was. He was still cancelled, after all. So much for a master race, or being a legendary musician, or … well, fucking anything.

But the internet is a multiverse of humanity, from its most divine to most vile forms. As such, Dave found new, tantalising worlds amongst the violent and paranoid. It was hardly difficult for someone who'd bathed in Neo-Nazi hatred for so long. But modern online extremism isn't a path, it's a buffet. A completely open selection of hatreds, conspiracies, and twisted ideologies with no sneeze guard, where everyone uses their hands. Cross-contamination is rife, creating new and virulent forms of extremism. You don't have to become fully fledged anything, you can pick and choose. Stack whatever you want on your ideological plate. Perhaps some Nazi racism, dollops of militia anti-government violence, a serve of woman-hating resentful entitlement, all topped off with a holy war from whichever religious extremism you'd care to choose. In fact, one open forum had white nationalists calling for jihad, albeit a militarised Christian version. They knew a good slogan, even if they didn't know about irony or the original meaning of jihad.

In short, from an already terrible place, Dave was diving down a deep, narrowing tunnel of paranoid violence and fear-driven hatred. His world was increasingly filled with sinister government-controlling organisations, secret death-camps and brutal experimentation and execution for those like Dave. Or so he believed. It was personal.

That's what made it different. The early extremist forums he frequented were like an ear-shredding metal concert. Calls for hatred and genocide blasting like a stereo for thousands of people. All playing in the hope that someone, anyone, would eventually go out and shoot up a place of worship just to get the song out of their head.

Now for Dave, his experience was like having the band take requests and play them for him alone. They made him feel like he was in the right again. Encouraged by different individuals, algorithms and trending topics that appealed to his darker instincts, Dave's internal fire blasted back into prominence. He needed to act. Before he was stopped permanently. He'd been convinced by the wheedling voices of the chats: This was about survival.

So tonight, as he scrolled, posted and chatted with anony-mous people who fanned his paranoia and self-importance, he saw a post about something called The Meet. A gathering of like-minded people somewhere secret. Those posting about it were into some pretty serious stuff. This was no anti-vax moth-er's group. It was a chance to act. This looked real.

Dave set about connecting with people who could let him

into the locked forum that had the location. He had enough contacts and referees in the dark corners of the internet now. You had to show your extremist bona fides with chat logs and trusted endorsements before they let you in, and this could be his big break.

Twenty-Six

In Canberra, DAS executives and private sector players had converged on Information Operations and Effects (or IOE). IOE occupied prime real estate in DAS HQ, a few floors up and towards the front of the building. Close enough to the executive to influence, far enough away to dodge their requests. Technically part of Cyber Command, it was a multi-disciplinary team carving out its own niche. It had embedded staff from different parts of DAS and the private sector. It's no secret that governments, particularly intelligence agencies, bring private companies in to build personal gadgets, collection capabilities, computer systems and to clean up and sell coffee. While governments take years to pay their bills, for those who can afford to wait, the profits are immense, reliable and long-term. Defence and intelligence contracts – known in the private sector as the Khaki Teat – are especially sought after. Firms all over the world fight like piglets to suckle and enjoy guaranteed shareholder returns.

Shanti had been surprised to see how involved some companies had become. It was fine for them to provide systems and capability, but something irked her about them doing actual analysis. Developing networks, identifying threats, providing briefs. Give analysts the tools and information, sure. But actually work it up as well? Unaware how much of Peter's intelligence puritanism had rubbed off on her, she felt uncomfortable. But if you left it all to government, the technology wouldn't move beyond the Microsoft Office Suite.

CMND – pronounced by their devotees as 'command – was an American firm occupying pride of place in IOE. They did so because Roman and his crew had beaten all their competitors by delivering advances in cyber and information warfare operations. Theirs was a reputation for AI, big data wrangling, open-source analysis, encryption, decryption and other highly valued dark arts. They didn't look like a major player on paper – but looks can be deceiving. A small company by US standards, they operated a 'non-linear network model'. People couldn't tell if this was a genuinely different business structure, or just the latest trick tech companies were pulling – like communal bean bags or free snacks for those who came into the office. It was hard to get much more on them. They didn't appear in magazines or trade shows, preferring to be known in other places where people would only speak in vague terms, before heading back to a secure site to make the arrangements.

Back at IOE, CMND's motto – 'Complexity? Simple!' – adorned corporate posters someone had slapped on the walls.

Like the rest of headquarters, IOE was full of strange professional touches. Propaganda posters, video stills from faked footage, conspiracy imagery. One eagle-eyed analyst had a poster detailing all the various makes of Rolex and other high-end watches – useful for outing 'poor' government officials who couldn't resist flashing some corrupt bling on foreign state media.

Rich afternoon sun streamed across a digital clock face on

the far wall: 8:02 am. Shanti frowned. Wrong clock. That was Moscow time. Three clocks along she got to AEST: 3:02 pm.

Both the time and her confusion now made sense. Three o'clock. The lazy hour, when fuzzy-minded office workers go in search of chocolate and gossip, save the few still stuck in meetings scheduled by some sadist who can exist without afternoon sugar.

Shanti stayed at her desk, her mind wandering instead. She pressed her tea mug to her chin, soaking in the gentle heat as she thought. Andrew was rattled. That much had been obvious. But what if there was something more? She'd brushed it off at first. He was a keen grad, like she'd been. Convinced people only slept safely thanks to their tireless reports and spreadsheets. She had believed there was more to it than that. Had to. In her first year, she'd been saddled with the crap job of combining gigabytes of 'legacy data' that had been sprayed all over the IT network. Names, phone numbers, emails of targets, scattered messages. They related to various investigations but were in personal drives from a time before the centralised databases. Some intelligence work that turned out to be. It was laborious; cutting and pasting Excel spreadsheets and Word docs into a single source – if you could find them. They were scattered across people's hard drives like leaves. She'd complained to Peter. With first class honours and three languages, was this the best use of her? He'd shrugged, stoic as a mountain that's watched empires rise and fall in the valley below.

'Who else?' he replied. 'This needs doing and the others are just putting PowerPoint slides together. Besides, this might help. In this job, you don't want to be someone who let something happen. If you get it right, they'll never know; if you get it wrong, they'll never forget.'

'They?'

'People, taxpayers, our suspicious public.'

Shanti didn't argue. She couldn't, really, as he'd walked away as soon as he finished his sentence. So, she'd swallowed her pride and got back to work. It took weeks of soul-draining effort, during which she developed a deep hatred of formatting. But it got done. The day after she finished, Peter showed up at her desk with a coffee and a chocolate muffin.

'Well done,' he said, with a twinkle in his usually stern eye. 'Nothing happened.'

'That's not because of me,' she said.

Peter put the coffee and the muffin down on the desk.

'You don't know that,' he said.

'Neither do you,' she replied.

He pushed the muffin over to her.

'It's an assessment,' he said.

Back in the present, she unconsciously tapped the mug's edge against her teeth as she thought. She didn't want to be the one to let something happen. The mug had been a farewell gift from her first team. It was white with childlike blue writing on it: '*I'm an ~~annolyst~~ ~~ananalist~~ spy!*'

She'd searched Polarize Dunk on her system. Being in the same broad area helped. She got further than Andrew, but not by much. Her result was still a denial, but at least it told her who to speak to.

All Results: Restricted Access – Contact CMND Fusion K Cell.

Hmmm … *tap, tap, tap* went her teeth against the mug – the kind of noise that drives a partner quietly mad at breakfast each morning. She didn't recognise the name and could only guess at what the 'fusion' and 'K' meant.

'Hello?'

Shanti snapped back to reality, suddenly aware she'd been chewing on porcelain. It was Michael, Roman's head of sales, half-perched on the end of her desk. His presence typically meant Roman was nearby, or someone with a big, fat procurement budget was. He parachuted in whenever deals were to be made or hyped. From initial scepticism, he could reassure and whip up enthusiasm from the grumpiest of clients – metaphorically tap-dancing through meetings while throwing handfuls of sales glitter to the delight of all.

Probably not all, thought Shanti. Peter had briefly come to visit once and, at one look, dismissed Michael as 'a parrot seeking a pirate'. But from what the buzz in the office was, Michael was extremely good at his job and Roman depended on him.

It was unusual that an American CEO was personally watching over the Australian arm of their operation. More so that he was staying in Canberra to do it. But when he wasn't around, Michael was Roman's warmth to others as required. Just as Talia, the heavyweight executive officer, was his wrath. It was joked that Michael was a genie that had been trapped in a mobile phone, now indentured to grant Roman's wishes. He was the very model of a modern slick sales executive, all bleached teeth and dyed hair. He was so smooth that Shanti imagined him coming out of a tube in a factory somewhere. Emerging like toothpaste in an ad, fully formed and with the little lick at the end that formed his brushed-back bouffant. But in his profession, it went with the territory.

'Hi,' she smiled. 'I'm fine, was just thinking about stuff.'

'Well, don't think too hard,' he said, with a roguish wink. 'We're not that kind of operation.'

She nodded amiably, but she knew his pattern. Step one: greeting. Step two: banter. Step three: favour.

'Real quick,' he said, 'but could you do me a solid and whip up an email for the team? Just to remind them about our upcoming workshops. We're putting a few presentations together for the Intelligence Futures do. After that, we're packing up for a while.'

'You're leaving?' asked Shanti?

'Weeell,' said Michael, drawing the word out like he'd just

accidentally let on what he'd bought for her birthday. 'We're presenting all the hard work we've done and then we're out of here for a few months while the bigwigs chew on it. Got other contracts to work.'

Shanti's brow furrowed as she took that in.

'Don't worry!' he said, mistaking her silence for concern. 'This is going to open up a whole pile of contracts – I mean, work. We'll be back and bigger than ever!'

Shanti smiled with her mouth alone.

'Of course you will,' she said.

'So … about that email?' he replied.

She prepared an acid-dipped response but thought again and gave an amiable 'Sure.'

'Thanks!'

Michael slapped his thigh in a 'it's-been-grand-but-I-gotta-go' kind of way and slid off the desk.

'Actually,' said Shanti, as he walked away, 'there's something you can do for me.'

He stopped mid-stride and smiled the smile of one who knows this conversation isn't chargeable, but still has to make nice.

'Certainly,' he said, forgetting he hadn't offered anything.

'What has CMND got on Operation Polarize Dunk?' she asked. 'I'm getting up to speed with the big operations and people say that's something Fusion K Cell is running. No one really knows much about it, and I was interested in reading up on it and seeing if I can help.'

Michael paused. While the sales smile stayed, his face stiffened and took on new lines, dimming the otherwise handsome glow.

'Or whatever else to learn about this area,' she said to his narrowing eyes. 'You know, on-boarding stuff, whatever.'

She kept her expression casual and keen as she stared back

at him. He tilted forward, forcing her to crane her neck back slightly to keep eye contact.

Shanti rethought her previous impression. He was smooth, yes. But like a snake. You didn't see the fangs until it was too late. She'd met men like this before. Utterly delightful until they didn't get their way, then watch out. Fortunately, whatever internal calculation he made went in her favour.

'Sure!' he said, his face brightening again as he leaned back. Shanti let go of the breath she'd been holding as gently as she could.

He gave her another wink. 'I'll dig something up for you, but first gotta ask the Big Man!'

'Who?' asked Shanti, without thinking.

'Roman himself!' he said.

'That's good,' said Shanti. But noting Michael's desire for praise, threw in a bright smile. 'Thanks,' she added, 'I really appreciate it.'

'Have you met him yet?' asked Michael.

Shanti quickly ran through her recent arrival at IOE. It had coincided with Roman being in the office, although Talia had custody of the CEO that day, not Michael. Roman had come over to her, knowing her name before they were introduced. But she supposed he would be across transfers and things, given his reputation for tight control over CMND's operations within DAS. He had salt and pepper hair and a deeply lined face, but she got the impression that this was not necessarily from age, but a price paid for something. His suit was immaculate, perfectly fitted with a confident, subtle style that said the only tag would be the master tailor's initials tastefully sewn in some discreet corner. He was also physically fit – or that suit was *really* good – without being unbalanced. Some middle-aged men went all massive biceps without losing the beer belly or cycled themselves into emaciated wrecks.

He was used to command, she could see that. The way he

stood and spoke, confident he wouldn't be interrupted. Despite that background, he'd been quite nice, asking questions and listening like he'd taken lessons. But Shanti couldn't help but notice no one else approached them. Normally, when a senior person walks in somewhere, juniors start buzzing around to get noticed and gain favour. But in this case, they were left alone, as if an invisible circle extended around Roman and crossing it meant death.

'Roman's a great guy, a genius even!' said Michael, sales-level enthusiasm sparkling.

'Dangerous tech bro,' muttered Cassie, from two desks away. She was another DAS analyst like Shanti, but had been there a few months. She'd been welcoming, but reserved. She didn't engage much and was usually fixated on her screen. Michael glanced over at her. She was staring at the monitor as per usual. This wasn't eavesdropping, not by DAS standards, where it's a professional habit. If you whispered your deepest desires in a darkened room next door, when you came back, people would suggest how to achieve them or ask probing questions.

'Oh, you don't mean that!' called Michael, with slightly more frivolity than was necessary. 'If you did, *you wouldn't say it.*'

He waited for a moment to see if she'd respond, but her focus was exclusively on her screen. Shanti wondered if Michael played more than one role for Roman. She hurriedly resumed her keen expression as he turned back to her.

'You're in luck,' said Michael. 'He's been in *that* meeting room with the senior executive. They're finishing any minute now. That's why I'm here.'

Shanti glanced over to the double doors to the conference room. They'd been closed when she came back in. She hadn't noticed, let alone been wildly excited by having a great Captain of Industry so close.

'Oh, great!' said Shanti, wondering if it was. She felt like she'd just poked one bear and was about to throw a stick at a bigger one. An American grizzly. This sounded like how Andrew spent his days. All she wanted was a rundown!

'So, tell me,' said Michael. 'Who's been telling you about—,'

But he got no further. The conference doors opened like an air lock on a spaceship, rapidly sucking up all the attention and oxygen. Michael slid over to them as though the building had tilted.

Various executives rushed out to attend other calls – no doubt 'of nature' given the length of the meeting. Shanti recognised Roman emerging out of the crush. He farewelled the executives and left without waiting for a response. Striding across the room, he passed a folder behind him without looking. Talia, who'd been quietly shadowing him the whole time, snapped it out of his hand. People sometimes mistook her for an executive assistant, not an executive officer. It wasn't a mistake they repeated. An executive assistant would only schedule brutality to someone, whereas an executive officer would dish it out. It's hard to say whether the audible creaks were coming from the floor or her suit pleats straining against muscle. In earlier life, she had probably trained for the Olympics by shot-putting professional rugby players.

'Hi, boss!' Michael called out. Shanti suddenly realised why he'd been hanging around her desk. It was the perfect midway spot between the meeting room and the exit. Good way to catch someone who doesn't deviate.

'Hello, Michael' said Roman pleasantly. Behind him, Talia eyed Michael off with a 'now what?' expression.

'Just a few quick things,' said Michael, 'but first, perfect timing, as always.'

He waved an arm behind him.

'Shanti here is curious about Polarize Dunk, plus whatever

else the Fusion K Cell get up to in their Cave of Wonders,' he said, referring to the separate work area that held CMND's most restricted work. 'Our good stuff is the talk of the town, apparently!'

Roman paused for a second, then broke out into a smile he must have kept in his jacket pocket for such an emergency.

'Of course!' he said. 'We'll organise something later on, but can I ask who's been recommending us?'

'Oh,' said Shanti, 'I can't actually remember. I think it's just got people excited.'

'Why's that?' said Roman.

This was feeling more like an interrogation by the second. She thought of Andrew.

'I guess it just may help with catching Lisa Chapman.'

That was the wrong thing to say. Roman's stare took on a new intensity. This was in a different gear to the ones Shanti had experienced so far. When someone is gushingly described as a 'visionary' and 'someone who gets things done', they forget both parts can have radically different personalities.

Shanti felt her pulse quicken as Roman stared at her with an unnerving focus.

'How so?' he asked softly, but with a hint of menace.

This was far too much attention from someone she'd expected to be brushed off by. Shanti had enough of being on the back foot. She'd briefed ministers, operational commanders and withstood interrogation about her personal life from four aunties and two grandmothers at every family event. She didn't need this.

'Well,' she said, standing up and looking Roman in the eye, 'aren't we in Information Operations and Effects? I heard CMND and the K cell are developing new digital capabilities. Isn't catching someone like Chapman what we're paid to do?'

Roman nodded.

'Absolutely,' he said, enunciating each syllable separately.

'You're right, but a target that knows it's being hunted is much harder. Excuse me, I have a meeting to go to.'

'Ah,' interjected Michael, 'on that. Damien's people called me. You sent the wrong presentation. It's the update they need.'

Roman's brow furrowed before some realisation hit.

'Of course,' he said. His face darkened and he said, 'I'll have to go back to my office to send it. Get onto the meeting and stall them until I'm there.'

Michael was still nodding when Shanti heard herself say, 'Wait, you can log in here if you like.'

Before Roman could reply she was bent at the keyboard, logging out of her system and jamming any interjections with a stream of chatter – 'It's no problem, it'll save you time', etc. She'd be gripped by a wild idea, spurned on by some instinct she couldn't put her finger on.

She stood away from her desk and yielded the terminal to Roman.

Roman considered things for a moment. 'Appreciate it,' he said, moving closer.

He bent over the keyboard and typed in his login name. He paused at the password prompt.

'Sorry,' he said to Shanti, gesturing for her to look away.

'Oh, of course!' she said. 'No problem.'

Roman had, Shanti reflected as she turned her back, an unusual way of saying sorry. While the overall tone appeared polite, it implied that *someone* and not necessarily him, was going to be sorry.

Shanti stepped away from her desk, but not too far away, as Roman went through his files.

Michael gave a tactful cough, covering his mouth in such a way as to show off his watch to the best effect. 'They're waiting, Roman.'

'Yes, yes,' muttered Roman, typing away. 'All right,' he said. They heard the whoosh of an email sent and Roman stood up.

'Let's go,' he said.

He stepped back from the computer. Shanti slid back into the seat as he walked away.

Right, she thought. Now to just—

'Wait!' he said behind her.

Shanti froze, staring at the screen. Roman swept over her like a storm cloud and grabbed the mouse.

'Excuse me,' he said. 'Forgot to log off.' Shanti swallowed. It was about the only movement she dared make as he loomed. She smelt his cologne, something woody with a hint of tobacco. Surprisingly pleasant, but unwelcome at this distance. However, it still struggled to compete with Michael's citrus bath of a cologne. Which, even a few metres away, was as subtle as a squirt of orange juice in the nostril.

Shanti twisted in her seat, creating some space from Roman.

'Got it,' he said, straightening up.

'No problem,' she said. In front of her, the computer began cancelling programs and starting the log out.

He gave a military turn and marched out, Michael and Talia in his wake.

Shanti turned almost as fast and mashed the keyboard. A warning sign flashed up:

System cannot start new programs. Abort log off?

Shanti clicked okay and ended the log off. Boom, she thought. She had Roman's account open, violating every rule. Her heartbeat climbed up from her chest to her throat. She didn't dare look around in case it aroused suspicion. Too late now.

Just breathe, she told herself, despite the lingering musk of the departing corporate alphas. She breathed slowly in, then out. Count of five for each.

She opened his email. Like any powerful executive, he

barely touched the stuff. His inbox was crammed with unread messages, urgent requests, and immediate invitations.

Okay, she thought. What he's getting isn't as important as what he's sending.

She opened 'sent items', starting with the last two emails. Sent one hour apart, both were titled 'CMND Fusion Cell – Monthly Status Update' and had the same attached file. They were your office variety PowerPoint presentation. Full of standard blather about 'goal achievement' and 'ongoing strategic alignment'. She moved to 'Project Summary'.

'Oh wow,' she said. 'You're kidding.'

She skimmed through and let the details settle into her memory. She could be interrupted at any moment. Beyond the astonishing content of these two emails, Shanti was struck by their similarity. Not just similarity, in fact: these presentations were identical. She had a ferocious eye for detail and didn't miss things. Especially as her father was an engineer who had overseen her homework and could spot a misaligned document table or icon from a mile away.

So why send two identical files if one was an update?

Shanti looked around. No one was paying her any extra attention. The office was still in the grip of the usual afternoon malaise. She dived back into the files. Content? The same. File name and type? Same.

Shanti bit her lip as she brought up the files' details side by side. There it was.

The latest file was much larger.

But how was that possible, given the content was the same? Unless it was only the visible content that was the same.

Of course! Steganography! Shanti hadn't heard of this until Peter told her about how previous targets swapped illicit material online. It was the art of encoding hidden information – either written or an image – inside another image. So, what looks like a photo of a wheat field is hiding a still from an execution video, or something worse. All you had to do was run it through the right program to get the hidden stuff underneath. Some operators thought it was flawless and hoped anyone intercepting the messages thought they just enjoyed boring stock photos. Context is everything.

A quick search gave Shanti the software she was after. With one last look over her shoulder, she submitted the file and waited.

It only took a few seconds. The result was one image and some written text. Shanti stared. There was no mistaking the smiling figure in the photo. It was Lisa Chapman. But younger, more of a university vibe judging by the band t-shirt and joking rude gesture. Not a selfie, some kind of couple or group shot. Judging by the white male arm hanging over her shoulder anyway. The rest of him wasn't visible; this was an edit to feature Lisa. The text below read:

Target still unaccounted for. Psychological profile and refreshed Course of Action analysis to follow. Highest priority.

She clicked 'forward'. The message and attachments popped up in a new instant message.

DO NOT REPLY, she typed with shaking hands. *U right. Tlk soon – S.*

She hit send, and the message vanished. Shanti felt her stomach drop away. The send-regret was worse than the time she'd sent a text intended for a secret boyfriend to her mother. At least that was just emojis her mother didn't understand. Plus, this time, she could cover her tracks. Her heart crashed around her chest as she selected the sent message and deleted it.

The whoosh of the automatic door cut through the afternoon hush and Shanti's concentration. She looked up to see Michael strutting in.

'Shanti!' he called out, approaching with the enthusiasm of an old friend who needs money. 'Did I leave my pen here? Mont Blanc Meisterstück?'

Shanti's heart climbed into her throat as he headed over. Her computer didn't face him, but that wouldn't mean much if he was right there. She stabbed at the power button and held it down. The computer winked off as he got to desk-leaning distance.

'Nope,' she croaked. But then her eye caught a small, glossy, black missile of a pen. It was on the desk, right where he'd been before. Strange that he still hadn't noticed it being so close. Had he left it there deliberately? To come back and finish his questions?

'Got it,' she said, grabbing it and standing up. As he thanked her, Shanti scooped up her bag and tucked her jacket under her arm.

'By the way,' he began, holding his hand out for the pen, 'I'd love to know–'

'Sorry!' she interrupted. 'Got a family emergency, got to go. But I'll catch you later.'

Shanti held out the pen but dropped it at the last moment, stepping by him as he bent to pick it up. By the time he stood up, she was out the door and Michael was left standing next to an empty desk.

'Sorry,' called Cassie insincerely from her desk. She was still staring at her screen as she'd done when disparaging Roman earlier.

'I guess no one likes sales,' she added.

Michael glared, but despite his frustration, said nothing. On the whole, he reflected, it was quite true.

Twenty-Seven

Mostly, being a DAS security guard had a pleasant monotony. Especially at this time of morning. Marko, the highest-ranked person in the security control room, didn't hide his yawn. The others ignored his fatigue-inspired yodel with casual ease. The only other sounds were mouse scrolling, conversational keyboard tapping, and the electronic hum of the server room next door. They'd had the morning rush of arrivals. Now it settled into the quiet zone when most staff had arrived, finished their coffee runs and couldn't escape meetings until lunch. With no VIP visits planned, there wasn't much to do.

Marko slid further into his chair and stared at the monitors. There were dozens, all snugly encased in the white wood of the desk. All were colour – one even showed the heat signature of everything outside the front office.

He heard the six beeps of someone punching in the code outside, and the door opened. 'Anything?' said Jim, another guard entering with a tray of cups. Steam curled gently from the tops as their awakening aroma filled the room.

'Nope,' replied Marko. 'Rosie searched that Andrew kid

going out on a coffee run. You can do him again on his way back in.'

Jim snorted. 'Next time, just give him our coffee order so I don't have to go out.'

* * *

Outside the gates and further down the road, Andrew and Shanti walked through the morning air. Andrew's eyes watered in the glare, and he cursed himself for leaving his sunglasses on his desk.

'It's just …' began Andrew, before a private bus trundled past. The exhaust's roar drowned out his sentence. Shanti grimaced at the black smoke left behind.

Andrew tried again. 'Why drag me out so far?' he asked. 'We could have gone to the DAS cafe.'

Shanti threw him a look that was a full data-burst of annoyance. She did this a lot, Andrew reflected, using looks to broadcast emotional and mental gigabytes of, of … something that was his fault, somehow. But he was ill-experienced in receiving and interpreting large information dumps – however deserved.

Another bus roared past, forcing Shanti to wait to respond.

'Because,' she said, once clear, 'while doing you a favour, I found your traitor.'

Andrew stopped dead. He said nothing, saving his breath to hurry after Shanti when she kept going. She was already halfway up the brutalist concrete front steps of the cafe as he caught up. The sign above the entrance said, in nostalgic type-writer font, 'Imontagu'. The sleek façade left Andrew in no doubt he was about to pay bougie prices. It was the kind of cafe you could start a panic in by yelling 'gluten!'.

Shanti went in and Andrew nipped in behind, letting the door thump closed after them. A third and fourth bus rumbled up the street towards DAS, banners and flags hanging out of windows.

* * *

Back in the control room, the radio squawked into life; 'Come in, Control.'

'Control room,' said Marko.

'We've got protesters,' came the reply. Marko recognised it as Eric, the cop on duty outside.

'Copy that, we're aware. Got it in the daily this morning.'

The daily was a report that was mandatory reading at the start of each shift. Updated at least every twelve hours, it gave a running report of all the predicted activity – from protests to spies to terrorists – likely to affect the building.

'Should be light,' said Marko. 'No worries.'

He glanced at the latest daily, still up on one of his screens:

Light Protest Activity possible – category: non-violent
Protests are ongoing against the MILMAX arms expo being held in the Canberra Central Business district. Additional protests targeting DAS facilities are possible, but likely minor (fewer than twenty individuals). Should they occur, previously observed tactics indicate likely non-violent protests or only minor property damage/graffiti.

Rob's reply cut into Marko's thoughts.

'Light? Mate, we've got heaps showing up here. Several bus loads and more appearing from fuck knows where. Patrol says they're also gathering in nearby parks. Got to assume they're getting ready to head over. We need some more bodies here.'

* * *

Inside Cafe Imontagu, office workers went elbow to elbow, craning around each other to see the menu and the baked goods display. Viewed from above, the cafe's layout was an awkward shape stolen from Tetris. It zigged and zagged in a space likely reserved for storage on the original floor plan. But it meant there were lots of corners to hide in. Chatter ricocheted off the industrial chic concrete walls, making a rolling ocean of noise. Shanti and Andrew snagged a table near the back, next to a pile of milk crates.

Not wanting to be interrupted, Shanti refused to speak seriously until her coffee for 'Sarah' arrived. Years ago, she'd adopted a different coffee name after being mistakenly called 'Sharty'.

Andrew, now wondering if coffee code names were part of standard procedure, stayed silent.

'Did you look at that email I sent?' she asked at last. 'From Roman's account?'

'No,' Andrew admitted. He turned his coffee in his hands as he spoke. 'I didn't think that was a good idea until I spoke to you. That warning in the subject heading freaked me out.'

'I found a direct link to Lisa Chapman,' she said.

Andrew sat bolt upright.

'That's right,' said Shanti. 'Your precious Breach.'

Pleased with Andrew's blanched expression, Shanti looked over her shoulder before getting closer.

'Roman was sending hidden messages, through the top-secret system I might add, that identified her as someone he was looking for. Like him, not DAS. This looked unofficial.'

'Really?' rasped Andrew. He tried swallowing a few times.

'It was hidden in boring corporate presentation rubbish. Stuff he was sending to CMND people embedded in DAS.'

They both paused. The cafe was packed tight. A man squeezed past their table like a parade balloon being forced through a check out.

'What else?' asked Andrew, once the man had gone, dragging at least one chair with him.

'Oh no!' said Shanti, waving a finger. 'This has been far too one-way. You need to tell me what's going on here.'

Andrew mentally thumbed through the betrayal, manipulation, and treason he'd both suffered and committed.

'I got a connection to Lisa Chapman,' he admitted. 'Something called Koil. I thought it was a person, but then I found out it was ... something else.'

'Like what?' asked Shanti.

'A bunch of online personas, maybe some operatives in the field. It was something wrapped up in the Cyber Warfare and Counter Terrorism departments – but working for us, not a target. Part of an operation called Polarize Dunk.'

Shanti closed her eyes as she massaged her temples.

'Let me get this straight,' she said. 'You found a connection between our biggest leak and an information warfare division in DAS? One largely run by a private corporation whose CEO I just caught secretly messaging others about said leaker?'

'Pretty much,' said Andrew grimly. He took a long, contemplative drink of his coffee.

'Why steal information and sabotage DAS? he asked. 'Isn't that killing the golden goose, if you're a company?'

Shanti cocked her head to one side and shrugged.

'It doesn't make sense,' she said. 'They could be a front for somebody else ... But it's time we went to Internal Security.'

'Angela?' said Andrew. He didn't relish the idea of trying to explain how he knew about Koil.

'Perhaps we should make sure we have all the facts ...' he said.

'All the facts?' Shanti spat the phrase. 'This is intelligence!' she hissed. 'We're never going to have all the facts, the full story or the fucking lowdown. This is what we do. We operate with limited information, assess as we can to try to prevent disaster.

We have evidence of a conspiracy right inside DAS! Let security sort the rest out. Who knows what's going to happen? People could die.'

Andrew leaned back from Shanti's vehemence. He had a vision of Peter shaking his head as he remembered that first speech.

Spies lie for a living. Analysts tell the truth.

'All right,' said Andrew, feeling a weight lift. 'We'll talk to Angela.'

Shanti was right; so was Lisa. This was more important than the career crap he'd been obsessing about. Whatever the professional consequences. Andrew smiled and felt freer than he had since his first day in DAS.

'Great,' said Shanti. 'Let's head back. We need to act.'

* * *

Back up the road, the crowd outside DAS swelled to hundreds as more sign-waving groups pooled together. A pool that was becoming a tsunami. The lakeside breeze carried approaching chants and ever more people flowed into the area. Orange flare smoke drifted across the main gate from those already there.

In the control room, Marko said 'Yes, sir' and slammed down a phone. The air was thick with worry and coffee fumes. The formerly silent phone bank was lit up and wailing. Marko's expression soured further as he glanced at the security monitors. One distant traffic camera screen blacked-out as someone spray-painted it, then the next view also vanished in sweeping black lines. Babble reigned as guards relayed updates to authorities and gate personnel.

'Lock it down,' said Marko.

All across DAS, in the centre of each room's ceiling, flowerpot shaped amber warning lights flickered on. This warning was used to alert staff when something was happening, but you didn't fully know what it was, ensuring a consistent level of worry across the building.

Ding, dong, ding! The three-tone precursor to an announcement chimed out of the PA system. In OSTRA, Peter paused, blowing on his tea. His raised eyebrows and pouted lips made him look like an exaggerated selfie.

'Please remain calm,' said the voice over the PA. 'There's a disturbance outside. For your protection, please remain inside until notified otherwise.'

Peter shrugged, accustomed to the occasional false alarm at protest activity or bomb threats.

'All right, everyone,' he said to the room at large. 'No evacuation order yet. Back to work.'

'We can't,' someone called out. 'Network's down.'

Peter turned to his computer, only to see applications throwing error messages and freezing. He tried fixing it the way his generation knew best. The monitor rocked from the impact of his hand, but didn't improve in any material way.

'What fresh bullshit is this?' he asked.

* * *

Several floors down was the dedicated Cyber Security Centre, or CSC. It ticked along as peacefully as Pearl Harbour before the Japanese Imperial Air Force arrived. The CSC protected all the computer systems in DAS. Powerful software scanned the comings and goings of the networks, checking no suspicious connections were made. This is because once inside, malware can spread anywhere. In an IT system, it can go from the internet to a laptop, a router or an air conditioning unit if it has the right connection and system. The digital cancer metastasises at breakneck speed.

But that's why DAS air-gapped their systems – no public internet connection to anything remotely secure. Each employee had access to one unclassified system with internet, but that was it. You'd have to be a maniac to connect intelligence databases to the World Wide Web. Sooner wear a swimsuit made of steaks to go swimming with sharks.

So, it came as an unpleasant surprise when something – a virus, worm, malware of some kind – ignited in the systems like an oil-well fire.

Alerts rang out across the floor as the malware swarmed the DAS mainframe. It was everywhere. Swear words rang through the CSC as servers stopped responding and systems self-encrypted or wiped themselves. Figurines and soft drink cans went flying as people spun back to their desks and tried to stop the spread.

It was too late.

'Oh, come on!' cried Peter, thumping the glitching computer again.

'Come on!' screamed a protester at the security fence.

'Come on!' screamed a techie in the CSC, as his computer screen locked up in error messages. As did the one next to him, then so on through the room. Across the building, entire networks seized up as malware bounded through like a ballet dancer throwing grenades over their shoulder. Screens gave brief error-descriptive epitaphs before freezing or blinking into darkness.

In the subterranean utilities area, a senior engineer used a fire axe to get into the locked power switches and slapped them down to save what was left of the network.

At the front gates, the protest was building momentum. In the security control room, Marko sweated profusely as he relayed information to the police outside.

'We've locked everyone down, but something's going on. I can't get into the computers and now we're … hello? Hello?'

He swore and slammed the telephone down. The lights flickered and died, and the emergency lighting dimly kicked in.

* * *

Outside their cafe, Andrew and Shanti watched the masses swarm past with all the paraphernalia of protest. The cafe door gave an emphatic thud as it closed behind them.

'Um, this is different,' said Andrew.

'Where did they come from?' asked Shanti.

'Look,' said Andrew, 'we should head back before even more arrive.'

'I'm not sure that's a good idea,' said Shanti.

'It's a big crowd,' said Andrew. 'We'll just cruise through.'

They cautiously approached the protest's edge. Both had had the sense to take off their business jackets. Now they looked like the march of the semi-formal. Off to the edge of the crowd, things had more of a carnival air. Slogans and issues bounced around as individuals competed for collective support. The chants formed a cacophony.

'No way to NOA!'

'Cancel racism!'

'Vaccinate against dictatorship!'

'End shark culling now!'

'No war with China!'

'Rights for true Australians!'

'Freedom from deep state!'

There were more issues here than on a magazine stand. Rather than being a coherent movement, this felt more chaotic. More scattered. More *emotional*. This was a mixed group of people united by feeling. Something was wrong, and they were galvanised to do something about it.

Andrew tried to read as many signs as possible. NOA, whatever that was, was a strong theme, but not a dominant one. There was also anti-government stuff, something about the PM not being real, save the kids, #endtheDAStapo. A woman walked past with a hand-printed t-shirt saying 'NOA, I do not consent!'. Underneath was the Australian coat of arms, but both mascots wore police uniforms either side of a biblical ark. This was the strangest mix of issues and people he'd ever seen. He'd heard of red, blue and green political protests, but this was a spinning kaleidoscope.

Shanti ignored the signs and looked at the people. She sensed something. An animal would have sniffed the air. The easy-going crowd had overtaken them. Now the mood was getting darker. These people weren't just shouting slogans into the air. They yelled as though the source of their frustration was right in front of them. Something, a sparkler maybe, spun through the air over everyone's heads.

Bang!

It was a firework. Some flinched; others cheered and hollered. Another firework launched up from the crowd, got stuck in a tree, and exploded. More cheers.

Shanti recoiled as a flare bloomed into life in a nearby man's hand. He hadn't shaved in days and gave her a leery wink. She coughed as acrid smoke, red in the flare-light, swept over her. The change in mood was a storm cloud rolling over a sunny day.

She remembered catching the train home from school. Some days, there was a group of boys hanging outside the station entrance. They were anywhere between fifteen and twenty-one, but that's not what concerned Shanti. The way they stared and called out to her made her walk that bit faster. She always looked at the ground as she passed them, one hand on her school bag's shoulder strap and the other holding her uniform's skirt down against her leg. One day they had smashed a bottle as she was passing, and she almost broke into a run.

She remembered the smell of their cigarette smoke as that feeling came over her again, via a shiver up her spine. Some primal instinct made her look around.

Through the crowd, a sign-less, middle-aged man with a receding hairline stopped scanning the protesters and stared at her. He wore cargo pants and the standard polo top they issue to men his age. His stare deepened from concentration to something worse.

Shanti turned back to Andrew, still gawking at signs.

'Andrew,' she said urgently.

'Hmm?' Andrew was scanning the crowd.

'I *really* don't think this is a good idea,' she said. 'Look!' She grabbed Andrew's arm and pulled him close. 'We're being watched!' she hissed in his ear.

Andrew paled as he looked. The man on the other side of the crowd pulled out his phone and looked at it, then at the two of them.

Then he turned on his heel and shoved his way through the crowd back to where they were coming from.

Shanti and Andrew were an uncertain island as the sea of protesters flowed around them.

'He's gone,' said Andrew. 'Nothing to worry about.'

They jumped as a protester behind them yelled: 'Oi! Move it on!'

Shanti began dodging her way out of the crowd. Andrew, a veteran of crowded pubs and football meets, pushed and ordered his way through until they reached the edge. Tone of voice was all it took. By the time the big bastard you ordered to shift had turned around, you were long gone. They emerged out of the main crowd body and took refuge under a eucalyptus.

Andrew leaned against the tree. Another firework went off somewhere.

'You see?' said Andrew. 'All good. We're fine.'

Shanti gave him another data-burst stare. Andrew didn't fully understand, but he knew it was worse than when he forgot his ex's birthday.

The middle-aged man from before emerged from the crowd. Andrew wanted to duck behind the tree, but it was too late. The man gave a shout of recognition and rushed towards Andrew and Shanti.

'Umm,' said Andrew. 'Maybe we should go.'

'Don't move!' screamed the man when he was several metres away. He still wasn't carrying a sign. But he now had something long wrapped in a jacket.

Andrew barely had time to move before the jacket slid to reveal the barrel of a shotgun.

BOOM!

Andrew felt leaves and scattered bark fall about him. His ears rang as he smelt the gunpowder in the air. The man had been too enthusiastic about raising the shotgun and fired high. Some nearby people looked around, but fireworks being thrown like wedding rice hid the noise.

'Run!' screamed Shanti.

But it was too late. The man cornered Andrew with the jacket-covered shotgun. The barrel shook as the man licked his lips and cleared his throat.

'It *is* you! I'll give you one chance,' he croaked. 'Let them go! Let them all go!'

'Who?' asked Andrew. He flinched as the man thrust the gun towards him.

'The kids!' he spat, sweat pouring down his face. 'The innocent children you and the rest of the dark servants kidnapped. They won't suffer for the shadow force anymore!'

Andrew gaped as he tried to make sense of this illuminati-brand fever dream. Extreme conspiracy theories were rare in Canberra. Locals think they give the government too much credit.

'Give the order!' screamed the man. 'Let them go!'

Andrew shook as he stared into the barrel of the gun. He

felt moisture run down his neck. He sincerely hoped he wasn't about to feel it anywhere else.

Before the man could yell at him again, a wooden protest sign crashed into the side of his face and sent him sprawling.

'Come on!' yelled Shanti, brandishing a sign that read 'Freedom now!'.

They sprinted up the hill towards DAS, skirting the crowd. Andrew risked a look over his shoulder at their assailant, who was getting to his knees, swaying as he dabbed at the fresh wound on the side of his head.

Andrew and Shanti bolted to the main gate. Waving their official ID like a winning ticket at the races, they slipped past the few police and through the main gate before it shut. It helped that it was being done manually by a single guard. He sweated and swore as the fence bucked and fought him on its shopping trolley wheels.

Andrew and Shanti headed inside to the dull roar of a thousand confused conversations. The hallways were full of people flowing into the main auditorium, directed by overhead alarms and calls to 'remain calm'.

'What's going on?' Shanti asked a passing China specialist.

'Cyber attack,' she said. 'Like, literally everything is failing.'

'Liam!' Andrew yelled. He'd spotted him in a doorway, letting the flow of humanity go past. Liam looked at him, white-faced.

Andrew dodged through the crowd.

'Is it really a cyber attack?' said Andrew. Liam's face was grey.

'The top-secret system was taken down,' said Liam. 'We've lost huge amounts of data. Entire networks.'

'What?' said Andrew.

'I hope you've got a good memory. Whatever you've been working on lately has probably been wiped.'

Liam then turned and shoved off into the crowd. Andrew

watched him go. Shanti had taken refuge in a separate doorway on the other side of the hall. She threw him a look. Another data-burst, but this one was of worry. He read it, no problem. Everything they had discovered, Roman's secret messages, Koil's activities, was all wiped. Without evidence, there was no help inside DAS from Internal Security. But what maniacs, or worse, waited for them outside?

TWENTY-EIGHT

HOURS LATER, THE SUN SET ON THE REMAINS OF THE protest outside DAS. Perimeter floodlights blazed into life as evening set in, illuminating dropped signs and rubbish. Police guarding the fence line became indistinguishable silhouettes. Others patrolled in groups of five or more, making sure no stragglers made trouble.

The last few hours had been a haze of megaphone speeches, flares, and discordant chants. But in the end, the protest short-circuited itself with its own fractious energy, disunited anger and aggression either driving the peaceful away, or creating further division to splinter the protest further. Opposing camps wound up staging their own separate events. Each shouted chants, sports stadium–style, to drown out the opposition, only uniting to banish a drum circle that tried forming in the middle.

The last straw was three busloads of police reinforcements that came screaming down the highway from Sydney. They swarmed out of the buses, making 'hut-hut' noises and setting up perimeters and observation points. However, it was almost dusk by then, and most of the peaceful protesters had, by that point, decided it was time to plot the revolution from the pub. Even those with a darker bent, the sort that bared their teeth and hissed at the police, called it a day.

Inside DAS they had power, but not computers. The building worked, even if the people didn't. Hundreds sat around in the main auditorium, waiting for airport-style updates that generally went 'All is well, just a little longer'. Absent facts, gossips rushed to fill the vacuum. Some were subtle, others gave lordly explanations, all sweeping gestures and 'Oh of course, but what you fail to realise …', etc. People would much rather be wrong than out of the loop. But being in the loop can be deceptive. You might think you're onto something when you're just going in circles.

During the wait, Andrew and Shanti tried to report what had just happened – to no avail. What security they had in the building was working on making sure no one got in. They didn't want to hear reports of shotgun-wielding maniacs outside. There was too much rumour and fearmongering going on.

Shanti was trying to get an update from the CSC on when the network would return, when Andrew saw James, his brawny interrogator, ploughing through the crowd. For the first time since joining DAS, he was glad to see him and moved to intercept.

'James!' he shouted.

James turned to him, but his expression darkened, and he turned away again.

'I've got to see Angela!' said Andrew, catching up with him. 'We were shot at!'

'I haven't got time for this,' James replied.

'But this guy had a gun, *and he knew our faces*!' yelled Andrew. Several nearby people started openly eavesdropping, but purely out of professional habit.

James wouldn't be slowed down. 'I've got people claiming to see grenade-wielding maniacs on the lawn,' he said. 'Some idiots were building barricades in the hallways, and I even caught one moron making a protest sign as camouflage in case they got in. Make your report another time.'

James ploughed ahead, and several cyber operators and one Russia analyst scattered in his wake.

Andrew ran after him. 'This is bullshit!' he yelled.

James stopped so suddenly that Andrew ran into him, ricocheted and landed square on his arse. The impact didn't shift James an inch. He turned like the deck guns on a battleship and leaned down. He was breathing fast and a vein in his temple looked ready to blow.

'This,' he growled, an inch away from Andrew's face, 'is a national security emergency we are trying to unfuck. Angela is busy and I'm thinking you're becoming a threat worth locking up as well.'

The warning lights in the ceiling abruptly switched from red to green. The three tones indicating an announcement chimed out from the PA. 'It is now safe to leave the building in an orderly fashion' announced the game show host voice. 'Normality is restored.'

'Just send me your precious report,' said James. 'Well? Off you fuck.'

* * *

With the all clear given, those not needed for IT repairs or briefing preparation streamed out of the DAS complex. They headed to their cars, bus stops, bikes and the occasional e-scooter as quickly as dignity would allow. However, anyone in a senior leadership position stayed at their post. This was a category five clusterfuck. A meeting had been called in Command Two, a fortified room deep in the bowels of the main building. A traditional meeting place when everything had gone to shit.

You can always tell the importance of an area by the speed of the executives going there. This was a corporate steeplechase and executives practically bolted down hallways, then were forced to awkwardly queue up at each security door and answer whatever biometric demand was made. Several doors later, the journey finished in a meeting room almost impossible to penetrate, either by listening device or conventional missile.

They filled up the seats furthest from the head chair first – no one wanted to be in the blast zone when the boss arrived. They didn't have long, people were still dropping into chairs when the DG walked in.

'I want a full report,' he growled as he headed in, 'I've got the PM in thirty minutes.'

Silence dropped and then everyone in the room stared at Angela to begin.

'The building is secure, and we cancelled Ministerial Adviser, Simon Fitcham's, pass,' she said, starting with the good news, plus the added cherry they wouldn't be getting the world's most annoying example of nepotism at the briefing. 'But we're still assessing damage to the computer networks.'

The DG reached the table and sat down. The executives shifted in their seats, swapping glances. If the DG were a James Bond villain, he'd be eyeing off the buttons that dropped poor-performing subordinates into the piranha tank below.

'So, we had a physical and cyber breach?'

'We weren't physically breached,' said Angela. 'Just … surprised. Some damaged cameras, fence reinforcements needed. That sort of thing.'

'What about the cyber breach?'

At the end of the table, the head of Cyber Division lightly cleared his throat for attention. His piercing eyes were fixed on some location miles away, beyond his interlaced fingers. He tended not to make eye contact, preferring to stare over your shoulder as he rummaged through files in his mind.

'We're still assessing the damage,' he said. 'We've regained limited functionality, but we have lost significant amounts of data.'

'Lost?' said Angela. 'As in stolen?'

'Exfiltrated,' he corrected. He was like a computer himself – if you used a technically incorrect term, he gave you an error message. 'But no,' he continued. 'Everything impacted was air-gapped. No outside connections, no downloads, and no physical hard drives missing. After the last … incident, we took additional precautions. However, it seems significant parts of the network were completely wiped.'

'How could you let this happen?' said Angela.

His interlaced fingers whitened. If a dressing down had to come, he didn't want it from her.

'Let it happen?' he said. 'This wasn't my fault. We only deal with *external* threats.'

'Enough,' said the DG, before Angela could respond. 'If this is in our house, I want those responsible found. *Now*. What about the protest?'

The room fell into babble as various department heads simultaneously tried to protect their patch. While everyone would agree there had been a problem, it most emphatically was not in *their* area.

As the DG opened his mouth to silence everyone, a single comment cut through the commotion.

'Russian tea party,' someone said.

The DG stared around the table.

'What was that?'

Peter leaned out of shadow in the corner. It wasn't his first crisis meeting. He was low in rank, but high in experience. Senior leaders usually need someone who knows what's really going on at the working level. He often got brought in, like the uncle at Halloween who had all the really good ghost stories.

'Russian tea party,' he repeated. 'Someone stirred up a lot of angry people online and pointed them at us.'

He stood up and walked around the table towards the DG. He had the measured pace of someone not trying to climb the greasy pole, and who knew there wasn't much that could be done to them at this point.

'You start a bunch of online groups angry about something like gun rights, climate change, vaccinations – whatever. The beauty is, all the people starting these groups are in a different country, but pretending they're not. Locals of different stripes join and get angry. In this case, the catalysing agent was NOA.'

'Noah?' said an executive. 'As in the ark?'

'No,' said Peter. 'As in the National Officer Act or NOA legislation proposed to make all DAS employees "Officers of the Nation", with the power to detain anyone at will.'

Peter let the expressions of confusion stew for a second before continuing.

'It's a lie,' he said. 'Completely fake, but convincingly told. Especially when backed up by very real-looking government media releases and even a few deepfakes of Minister Fitcham announcing it. The actual methodology is quite simple. First, they use these groups to spread the disinformation of choice. Then, once there's a triggering issue, the enemy announces a protest as a focus point. Says they'll be at X location and Y time, see you there. March on Canberra people! Everyone goes along, and even though the organisers don't show up, enough angry people do. Complexity and human nature ensues, and you set off a potentially violent protest from the comfort of the office.'

'How didn't we know about this?' said a senior director of Strategic Intelligence.

Peter shrugged. Specific technology wasn't his area of expertise, but he knew people very well.

'The internet is a big place,' he said. 'Plus, it moves fast. There was too much online noise to notice, or it was organised in spaces we're not covering. This tactic isn't common here. I saw it used against the Americans from 2016 onwards – a speciality of Russian military intel and a few others.'

'So, this was the Russians?' said the DG.

Peter shook his head.

'Unlikely,' he said. 'They invented it, but they mostly use it to poke US and Eastern European fringe groups into aggravation. From what I heard, this was much more complex and ran not one, but multiple groups. Anyway, the Russians have better targets than us right now.'

Everyone looked at the director for the Counter Foreign-Interference. She cleared her throat. 'Agreed. Nothing to indicate this was Russia. They're too busy with their proxy war with NATO and the US. Chinese info operations are focused on undermining Australian international efforts – that and controlling local expat and ethnic populations. And no one else cares enough about us to try something on this scale. These … incidents don't fit with what we normally see here.'

The DG straightened in his seat and addressed the room.

'The fact is, we were hit hard today, harder than we ever have been. In my experience, you're unlikely to be punched by two unrelated people at the same time. We were surprised, threatened from the outside and, while distracted, they hit us from the inside.'

He drummed his fingers on the table, each one striking the table like a firing pin. No one said anything.

'Finding out what happened and who did it is now our top priority. We can't fight someone who can send an army to our door and rip the seals off our most sensitive systems. Not if we don't know who they are.'

While he talked, James edged into the room. With quiet grace for such a large man, he sidled up to Angela and whispered in her ear. Her face hardened as she listened. If she'd been a hawk, this would be the moment her wings folded, and she plummeted towards the meal running below.

'Excuse me, sir,' she said. The DG gave her a 'Go on' wave.

'We have a lead.'

Twenty-Nine

THE NEXT MORNING, DAYLIGHT HAD ONLY JUST RETURNED as Andrew crossed the threshold into DAS. Guards stared unnervingly but, for once, didn't stop him. He made his way through the barriers and into the quiet building beyond. He made it to OSTRA without encountering another soul.

'Hello?' he called across the office.

Nothing. Just the background hum of the air conditioning. The computer gave a few clicks and an orchestral '*Gung!*' as it powered on.

Andrew spun on his chair like an office weathervane. He guessed a lot of people were calling in sick today. Or calling in not wanting to be locked in a complex surrounded by protesters again. But Peter's absence was unusual. He, like Intro-bot, was one of those ever-present entities. But whereas he'd imagined Intro-bot packed away at the end of the day, Andrew saw a lone Peter powering down around midnight, halfway through his precious reading. Perhaps the first morning janitor would notice his hunched form, stick a giant key in his back, and crank him back into life. Maybe that's why he was always cranky.

Andrew shook himself. That vision had come from fatigue. After a sleepless night of wild speculation and adrenaline-fuelled worry, he'd dived into a tired plateau somewhere around four AM. Lisa, Shanti, Peter, now psychos with shotguns and who knew what next? He'd come into the office because what else would he do?

Andrew rotated past the computer again. The screen was blacked-out, with a white message: *System Unavailable.*

So, they were still fixing that. Andrew wasn't sure what else he'd expected. He smiled to himself. At least there wouldn't be emails to deal with, no instant messages from one of the terrifying seniors who existed to torment him.

A noise no young person likes to hear crashed through his musing.

Riiiiiing! Riiiiiing!

Oh great. The phones still worked. Because of course they did.

It was his desk phone. No ignoring it. He grimaced and lifted it to his ear.

'Andrew!' barked James, before Andrew could speak.

'Yes?'

'Get to Angela's office right now!'

'I—'

'Don't keep talking!' James snapped. 'Drop the phone and run!'

Andrew did as he was told and sped out of the room. He made rapid, if stilted, progress through the building. It was a difficult building to run through. There were security doors, from glass to metal, interspersed at different points, each one needing a different form of biometric or other verification. Andrew ran down halls, skidded to a halt in front of the latest scanner and waited for it to accept his ID and shudder open.

He flew towards the vault door that marked Internal Security. James stood outside like a bouncer. Or more like a prison

250

guard, as it was his job to throw people inside. Andrew gave a breathless nod at James's scowl as he scurried inside.

The humid jungle atmosphere of Angela's office/bio-dome swept over him. She rose out of the greenery with praying mantis grace and fixed him with a stare.

'Andrew,' she said. 'Please take a seat.'

There was only one today, directly in front of the desk. Andrew sank into the groaning faux leather. Sank was the word. He slowly dropped, amidst leathery flatulent noises, until his eyes were almost level with his knees.

The door snapped shut. From near floor level, Andrew looked over his shoulder to see James inside, his meaty fist gripping the handle. At least Andrew now had a chance to tell them about the man with the shotgun, but he was derailed.

'Now, then,' said Angela. He looked back at her. She had settled down behind her desk.

'We're here to talk about some of your actions.'

'Alleged actions,' said another voice. Andrew looked over his other shoulder for the source.

'Peter!' he said, out of sheer relief. The old analyst nodded. He was leaning against the wall, his grey pants and white shirt and hair blending into the corporate tones behind him. Momentarily distracted, Andrew wondered how much of Peter's career had been spent blending into backgrounds and watching people go past unseen.

Angela waved an arm in Peter's direction.

'He is here as your immediate supervisor.'

Andrew's smile faded when Peter didn't return it. Then the situation he was in came crashing back into the foreground.

'We are here,' Angela continued, 'because we've had three serious attacks this year; insider, cyber and incited protests. You were present at the first. You've been accused of a role in the second.'

'What?' said Andrew. 'I was attacked myself in the protest,' he added. Unfortunately, he didn't get any further in his story as he was interrupted.

'Accused by who?' said Peter, his eyes narrowing at Angela.

Angela leaned back for a moment. Her gaze flicked to Peter. 'We received information from a co-worker. Liam Renovic.'

Andrew felt the bottom drop out of the world and his stomach. Sweat beaded on his forehead, or maybe it was the humidity from the plants. Being in there felt like a jungle, although Andrew knew the most dangerous creatures in here weren't hidden.

'Liam gave us information,' continued Angela, 'that you convinced him to escort you into Cyber Command. From there, through means unknown, you got on to our network and released whatever it was that took down the network.'

'He didn't—?' Andrew cut himself off in time. Had Liam told them about Koil?

'Hmmm?' said James behind him, sounding like a bandsaw warming up.

'He … he didn't say that,' managed Andrew. 'It's a lie.'

'I'm afraid he did say it,' said Angela. 'We don't fake videos here. That's a few floors up.'

James gave a boar-like snort. Andrew wasn't sure whether or not to pretend to laugh along.

Angela leaned in. 'So, what was it? What did you put in our system?'

'Before Andrew continues,' interrupted Peter, 'all you have now is an allegation. Any proof?'

Angela leaned out again, rustling a few leaves.

'Still gathering it', she said from the foliage.

'Well, then,' said Peter. 'This has been great and all, but none of it is a formal charge yet.'

'Yet,' echoed Angela. She turned her attention back to Andrew, sending a shiver down his spine.

'Peter,' she said, 'is, of course, quite right. We are still gathering evidence.' Andrew gulped as he peered out of the frying pan and into the flames below. 'But perhaps,' Angela continued, 'he can explain how important it is for you to cooperate with us as he escorts you back to your work area.'

Peter nodded at Andrew, who crawled out of the chair like a creature leaving the primordial ooze.

'You are on restricted duty while we investigate this,' continued Angela. 'For the moment, your access to top-secret information will be revoked and you will need to be escorted when in sensitive areas of the building.'

Andrew's eyes widened. His heart rattled against his rib cage.

'But you may continue administrative or other work classified as 'Protected' or lower. Perhaps do some training? That is all. And if we find something? Just remember what I said about angels.'

They left in silence. The creak of Peter's old leather shoes almost echoed as they left Internal Security.

Andrew winced as Peter slammed the door shut.

'Thanks,' said Andrew.

Peter didn't respond. He was too busy sticking his head into a nearby meeting room. He emerged and gestured for Andrew to follow.

They sat opposite each other, at a table meant for ten. The last meeting couldn't have been that long ago. The room smelt of coffee and clashes of cologne.

Andrew braced for another dressing down; Peter's stony face held no mercy.

'Ever heard of Kim Philby?' Peter asked casually, unballing his fists and placing them flat on the table. Andrew shook his head.

'English spook – MI6. Double agent, spent decades passing information to the Russians. Aldrich Ames, CIA, same thing.

Hundreds of human sources dead and millions of dollars wasted.'

Andrew's eyes flicked down to make sure Peter's hands were still empty.

'In hindsight, there were plenty of chances to discover and stop them,' said Peter. 'But no one thought it could happen on such a scale, which is exactly why it did.'

Ooo-kay, thought Andrew. His thoughts flicked back to the last thing Peter had said about their manipulation bet: *You should wonder if I've stopped*. Was he part of Roman's clique? He certainly didn't like Angela and Internal Security.

Andrew stared at his problems like a chimp at a chess board. Realistically, he didn't know anything useful and had only done the wrong thing again and again. Expendable to both sides.

'Angela is only letting you stay in here to find out if you're working with someone or whatever else you're up to,' said Peter. 'But if you're trying to deal with something yourself, stop it right now. Regardless of how bad you think it can get. Ask for help and you'll get it.'

Andrew nodded, tight-lipped. After a few seconds, Peter sighed and stood back up.

'All right,' he said. 'Let's head back. You'll need to gather your things. We need to find you a new workspace outside the top-secret area.'

They walked back to the office in silence.

* * *

Out in the dark, industrial edge of Melbourne, a squat warehouse sat on its own like a dropped brick. Back from the main road, it was fed by one lonely exit that peeled off the highway. All the major lighting for the highway pointed in, not out, leaving the warehouse in near darkness, except for a single light. It cast a weak jaundiced glow, enough to illuminate a set of three steps with a handrail leading to a door. The visibility trickled to nothingness further into the car park, with only the first row in the mishmash of parked vehicles vaguely lit. Most obvious were the motorbikes – big beefy machines with chrome reflecting the sickly glow. But beyond them were a mix of utes, sedans and trucks, some with anti-government protest signs or slogans painted or stuck to any flat surface.

Inside the warehouse, the vehicle's owners mixed under industrial lighting. Under the circumstances, being able to see clearly was unfortunate. Just a glance was enough to know you shouldn't look, lest you have to describe someone later and risk your safety. But this was mitigated, for now, by masks. Each person hid their face somehow, either through a full Halloween-style mask, or a bandanna, like bandits from an old western. There was a plastic folding table by the door with a few spare bandannas on it that had probably been used to clean engines. A crudely painted sign on the table said 'No Faces No Phones' in drippy black letters. Next to the table was an aluminium rubbish bin with its own label; 'Phones Here'.

There were several groups loitering in the cavernous space, eyeing each other off. They had more tattoos than a death metal concert. Nothing cute, like koi curling around a flower. The theme was mean. Threats, regrets, skeletons and sex curled out of raised sleeves, necklines and across one forehead.

The clothing was also to type – or rather, types. Each group had its own look. But Nazi memorabilia, gun motifs, camouflage and t-shirts with messages like 'No Gov and No Gays' or 'Rise and Resist' were in this season.

One group all had matching jackets embossed with 'Bush Boyz' over a comic-book shrub with menacing red eyes. The New Straya group proclaimed another set of tattoos such as skulls and stars, or quotes about brotherhood and power. Another lot called 'Hour Men' wore vests with military webbing and an image of crossed AR-15 machine guns on the back.

In short, the room was steeped in the negativity of an incel's chat history.

In the centre of the room, a giant of a man somewhat unnecessarily stood on a chair.

The muttering stopped. The only sound was the strained groans of a chair that couldn't last long.

'Welcome!' boomed the giant. 'Not long now, waiting on some others.'

'Why masks?' a Bush Boy called out.

'Security,' said the giant. 'For our protection and yours.'

'Sounds like a *mask mandate*,' said someone suspiciously.

'The sovereign nation of New Straya doesn't recognise UN mask authority!' someone else called out.

'Hold on,' called the giant, holding up his hands as muttering resumed. 'It's just until we're sure no one's recording. It's not a medicine thing.'

'We're definitely not doing this for health reasons?'

'No,' growled the giant.

'All right, then.'

The door shook as someone knocked from the outside. The giant nodded to an associate who rumbled over to open it. Several more men came in. All but one had white masks with neutral expressions. The last one, having sat on his original mask in the car, now had Pikachu the Pokemon instead, thanks to the kids' toys rack in the service station down the road. They had their phones taken and casually dropped in the bin. Pikachu put his phone in himself. No one noticed him hitting send before he dropped it.

* * *

At a far edge of the car park outside, an old Ford sat in near darkness. Inside were two police officers, both male, and of a comfortable, mid-life vintage. In the passenger seat, Senior Constable Phil Ballard's face lit up from his phone.

'Message received,' he said. 'Our guys are in, and targets are on-site.'

'Suspects,' said Sergeant John Hurst in the driver's seat.

'What?' said Phil.

'Suspects,' repeated John. 'They're not targets. You're not in the army anymore.'

'Old habits,' shrugged Phil.

John drummed an impatient beat on the steering wheel. They shared the surveillance detail well enough, in the forced intimacy of two men who've learned exactly how often the other farts. But it was far from fun.

'Can't see shit,' muttered John.

'Oh!' said Phil, this triggering a memory. 'Hang on, I'll get the night vision goggles!'

'What?' said John, as Phil rummaged under his own seat. 'No pay rises in three years, and I can't even get new notebooks, but you have night vision goggles!?'

'No one asked for 'em,' said Phil defensively. 'But all the shifts got them. The old deputy commissioner approved the contract. It was massive, all kinds of stuff from a major ex-military company.'

'Why would he do a contract with an ex-military company if we can't afford notebooks?' sighed John.

'Dunno,' replied Phil. 'You could ask him, he works there now.'

John didn't reply. He shook his fist at the car roof and silently cursed all upper management.

* * *

Back inside, Pikachu had problems of his own. While exploring the warehouse layout, he had been confronted by one of the Bush Boyz, a huge, swollen burrito of a man, with a sprawling beard that ran to his ample belly. Pikachu could see the masking bandanna, now slipping slightly, wasn't tied on. Instead, its corners had been tucked behind his ears to try to keep it on his massive face.

'You snooping about?' said the burrito. 'You better not be a cop.'

'Fuck you,' said Pikachu. 'I'm making sure there's no trap set by one of you bastards …' His voice trailed off.

'What?' said Burrito.

Pikachu leaned closer and hissed, 'I know you! You're a cop! You were in Northwest command. What the fuck?' Pretending to scratch his head, he flicked his mask up for a second.

The burrito's eyes widened in recognition and surprise.

'You? You transferred out last year! The fuck are you doing here? This belongs to my team! Counter Terrorism!'

'Bullshit!' hissed Pikachu. 'We've been working on this for months!'

'What team are you?' said Burrito.

'Counter *Extremism*.'

They both looked up as the door clanged open again. Three men in Guy Fawkes masks shuffled in, bumping into each other when stopped for their phones.

'All right!' shouted the giant from the centre of the room. 'That's everyone! Let's get started!'

The two undercover cops turned back to each other.

'Stay out of my way,' they both growled.

* * *

Out in the car, Senior Constable Phil had made a discovery of his own. As the junior partner, he had to do all the boring jobs, like checking licence plates.

'What do you mean, they're ours?' said John.

Phil stabbed away at the laptop.

'All the nearest plates have a Do Not Approach order. They're from different police commands! Plus, DAS High Threat Crime, Border Control ...'

Phil snapped the laptop shut and the car fell into darkness again. He pulled the night vision goggles on and powered them up. They beeped and the dark car park snapped into fuzzy green clarity.

'Well?' said John. 'Try to get some more plates. Can you see them?'

'Uh,' said Phil. 'There's a bunch of cars here with people still in them ...'

'Don't panic!' said John, breathing hard. 'They can't see us.'

'I think they can,' said Phil, slowly waving back at someone. 'They've all got night vision goggles.'

* * *

In the warehouse, things were getting unruly under what many considered an oppressive regime.

'No to masks!' chanted a group wearing Australian flags upside down.

'The people of New Straya don't recognise your authority!'

'Fine!' roared the giant, back on his unnecessary chair. 'We've made sure no one has a phone, so masks off!'

The effect was immediate. The crowd fell into noisy recognition and confusion as it became apparent there was more law enforcement representation than a policeman's ball.

'You?!'

'Me? What about you?'

Faces were recognised from years of inter-agency stoushes,

conferences and postings. They waved badges and threw law enforcement team and operation names about. The room filled with ironic anarchy as they all screamed at each other to submit.

'Down on the floor now!'

'New Straya, err, I mean the Counter Firearms Taskforce doesn't recognise your authority!'

'SHUT IT!' roared the giant. His chair finally gave way as steel legs bent and plastic components shattered, pelting the crowd. It was enough to silence everyone.

The giant, who'd been nimble enough to take the landing well and stay upright, looked across the mob of undercover police, holding up badges like concertgoers holding up phones.

'Now then,' he said, chair debris crunching under his feet, 'is there anyone here who isn't a cop?'

There were a few seconds of silence until someone muttered, 'Ah, fuck'.

Three men, the last three who'd entered in Guy Fawkes masks, shuffled closer together. They looked around the room with a mix of fear and feeble hope.

'Anyone else?' one asked.

* * *

John and Phil's police radio crackled into life.

'*GO GO GO!*' shouted a voice they didn't recognise. Undercover cars all revved into life, flicking on their high beams and driving to the warehouse entrance, but approaching simultaneously from different areas, they cut each other off and blinded each other.

John and Phil heard the shouts and swearing of police officers who hadn't taken off their night vision goggles before the high beams came on.

They watched three men burst out of the warehouse door.

Pursuing undercover cops jealously tripped and shoved each other aside until they all fell into an inter-agency scrum. John and Phil, sandwiched in-between two other police cars, watched the three men sprint off into the darkness.

'So much for the arrest,' said John, looking at the expanding police brawl and a lone Guy Fawkes mask left on the ground.

'Maybe not,' said Phil. 'I think I remember them from the army.'

* * *

The warehouse car park was bathed in light and chaos as police, DAS, and other departments yelled at each other to move *their* car first. Sirens whooped and torches, badges and guns were waved within a thunderous storm cloud of threats and insults. Luckily, there were no drones recording this mess. But if one had been present, and the operator wasn't laughing too hard, they might have thought to survey the wider scene. If they'd zoomed up and away, looking up the road a few hundred metres, just shy of the off-ramp, they'd have seen an old beaten-up car. From inside this sorry vehicle, Dave, the cancelled Neo-Nazi musician and wannabe revolutionary, sat and stared at the chaos. He'd pulled over as soon as he came off the highway almost an hour ago and had been there ever since. Just as well, as the warehouse, which was dark when he arrived, now looked like an alien mothership had landed.

You have got to be joking, he thought. He thumped his head back against the headrest and groaned. Dave had desperately wanted it to work this time, but caution and indecision paralysed him. Quite fortunately, as it turned out. He'd thought about going in straight away but had held back. Instead, spending the time arguing with himself as he watched distant people arrive and enter – until the whole site lit up under the confused spotlight of inter-agency rivalry and mistrust. However, Dave's good fortune and caution wasn't all his own idea.

He took out his phone and started typing in an encrypted chat.

U were right, he typed.

No shit, came the response. Three dots hovered at the bottom of the screen before more words flashed up. *Told you they were posers. All tyranny tools. Deep state killers.*

Lucky to escape, typed Dave.

Make your own luck, the message came back. *You just need a chance to show the world something. They would have killed you. I told you, I can help.*

As Dave pondered this, the highway lit up with fresh blues and reds. He frowned – more storm troopers on the way. Time to go before he wound up strapped to electrodes in some black site somewhere. He didn't need to think about the offer for long, this was someone he trusted and had been talking to for ages. Dave turned the engine on. As it idled, he typed a last hurried message and threw the phone on the seat next to him. He turned the wheel and drove back around onto the highway, returning to the city. With fresh air in the car and music on the stereo, Dave idly raised a middle finger to the police convoy barrelling past on the other side of the road divider and drove on.

On the front passenger seat, his phone shone with the last message sent:

Okay K0il, I'm in

THIRTY

COMPARED TO DAVE, ANDREW HAD FAR LESS ZEAL FOR HIS circumstances. For him, the days passed with swapping one set of walls for another. After the protest, he didn't dare go out socially and wore a face mask to and from work, just in case another psycho recognised him. At DAS, he sat in a small, ground floor meeting room. It was just beyond the first set of security gates and was reserved for visitors, job applicants and other untrustworthy folk. For now, it was his corporate equivalent of an oubliette.

He wasn't allowed any further into the building without an escort. The day after his meeting with Angela, Security took his gold pass, returning with a red visitor pass of shame. He couldn't even get into the cafe without an escort, as it was too far into the building. He'd walked to the cafe down the street instead. However, these walks didn't clear his head or make him feel any better. They reinforced his status as an outsider.

Peter visited from time to time, mostly to drop off work that was suitably dull and check-in. They'd reached a compromise on what to talk about.

'How am I supposed to do my job when I literally can't access secret stuff?' asked Andrew.

Peter shrugged in a complacent kind of way.

'Don't assume classified equals interesting, or even useful. Often, the reverse is true. You'd be surprised what's freely available. Just takes determination and imagination. At least have a look at these forum transcripts. Lots of potential gold in there.'

'How's Shanti?' said Andrew. 'Haven't seen her since ...' His voice trailed off. He'd felt terrible for getting her involved since the protest.

'She's fine,' said Peter brightly.

Fine, thought Andrew. She must be mad.

'It's good to have her back in OSTRA,' said Peter. 'Can't say she looked happy, but I won't take that personally.'

'She's back?' said Andrew.

'IOE said she was superfluous to current staffing requirements and operational directives,' said Peter. 'In other words, someone kicked her out. You wouldn't know anything about that, would you?'

Andrew shook his head like a five-year-old lying about eating a chocolate.

'Hmmm,' said Peter, staring at Andrew, who wouldn't make eye contact. 'That's what she said as well.'

With that, Peter dropped a thick folder on the desk, muttered a goodbye, and left, leaving Andrew to wonder what violence it would take to stop him printing everything out all the time.

Andrew's home life was no better. He became a phantom housemate, mostly hidden in his room with takeaway. Liam had moved somewhere else when no one was home. The first Andrew knew had been via a note on the fridge. Liam apologised for breaking the lease, but another opportunity had come up and they were welcome to use his deposit for the rent while they got someone else in. He wasn't even in DAS Headquarters anymore. Andrew, waiting in the line to enter DAS one morning, overheard that he'd moved to Parliament House as a Ministerial Liaison Officer. His dream role. Is that why he'd accused Andrew? A deal? Maybe the Minister really needed all the hands she could get in the lead-up to the Intelligence Futures Conference or something.

Whatever. He couldn't change it now. But that fucking rat was dead as far as he was concerned. Ministerial Liaison? Sure. At best, he'd be fetching coffee.

On the flip side, Andrew had embraced his daily searches with all the hallmarks of Stockholm Syndrome. For him, it was a fleeting chance for interaction. Jim, the old bouncer from security, had become his own personal Ghost of Bag Searches Past, Present and Yet to Come.

'Morning, Andrew,' said Jim as usual this morning. 'Random bag check. Could you please open all compartments for me?'

'Morning, Jim,' said Andrew. 'Anything exciting going on?'

'You should hope not,' said Jim, going through the backpack like a suspicious parent.

Having unzipped everything and turned it around a few times, he announced his satisfaction and judgement.

'All clear, Andrew, thanks. But your lunch could be better – try fruit sometime.'

A rhythmic jangling interrupted Andrew's response. Shanti, her ever-present bangles in full song, sauntered past.

Andrew swept his belongings back into his backpack and pounded down the corridor. He caught up with Shanti, ran in front of her, and raised one hand while he gulped for air.

'Hi,' said Andrew breathlessly. Shanti just stared. 'Can we talk?'

Shanti shook her head.

'No,' she said. 'I have a meeting and I'm late.'

'Me too,' said Andrew. 'On the third floor. Could you

escort me up there? Everyone else got called into something. I'm technically a security breach right now.'

Shanti glared at him and crossed her arms.

'C'mon!' said Andrew. 'You can't leave me alone,' he said, attempting humour. 'Don't want to let someone escape again.'

Shanti looked around and, now they were alone in the corridor, realised she was technically escorting him already.

'Fine,' she said in that tone women use to convey something is light-years from fine. 'My meeting's on the same floor. I'll drop you there, but someone else has to walk you back.'

The two of them headed up from the foyer to a stairwell. Shanti resolutely marched Andrew passed the elevator. Possibly, she didn't want to be seen with him.

'You know I'm innocent, right?' he said after a while. 'Everyone else has completely abandoned me. This is all part of Roman's game!'

'I don't know what's going on anymore,' said Shanti. 'Since first talking to you I've almost had my security clearance revoked, seen weird shit I can't explain, lost my transfer to the most exciting area in DAS, and, oh yeah, I've been fucking shot at!'

The following silence was so intense Andrew could hear the distant noise of people moving about outside the stairwell.

'I'm sorry,' he said at last. 'You're right, I'm making this about me, it's just—'

Shanti held up a warning finger. 'You say one thing about your so-called career …'

Andrew went quiet again.

'What we do is important!' snapped Shanti. 'Maybe not all the time – it can get pretty boring. But when it counts, it really counts. You've got to think bigger than yourself.'

Shanti's words echoed in Andrew's head, and he struggled to think of a response that conveyed how sorry and miserable he was. They didn't talk again until Shanti stopped in front of a door halfway along the third floor.

'Well,' she said, pointing at the steel name plate. 'This is me. Where do I need to take you?'

'Room C5?' said Andrew. 'That's where my meeting is as well.'

Shanti's face contorted in confusion, or possibly distaste that she'd be spending more time with him.

'Did you organise this?' she asked. Andrew shook his head.

'I just got the invite from some group inbox,' he replied.

'I organised it,' said another voice behind them.

They turned and saw Roman striding up the hallway. Talia, his executive officer, followed close behind. She was clearly not paid enough to smile.

Roman reached past and pushed the door open. Andrew moved aside so he didn't cop a shoulder in full flight.

'Shall we?' said Roman.

Without waiting for a response, he brushed past and headed into the room. Andrew raised his eyebrows at Shanti. She shrugged and went in. Andrew, not wanting to loiter in the corridor, followed her.

Inside, Roman sat at the far end of a conference table. Talia was off to one side, logging in to the computer that let you access the display screen near the entrance. The long meeting table was a sleek walnut brown, with enough space for the executives of a major company, terrorist group, or espionage agency.

Shanti and Andrew took two seats near the door. There were a few seconds of silence as they all stared from distant table ends, like a frosty WASP family dinner.

'I tried to play nice,' said Roman, sitting with his fingers interlaced on the table. 'I could have taken a harder line much sooner, but I didn't. I wanted to see if you'd speak with me, reach out as a friend, as I did. Instead, here we are.'

His US accent thickened and leaned on the 'are', making it a growled 'arrrr'.

'Okay?' quavered Andrew. 'What do you want?'

Roman broke his pose, apparently happy with something, and leaned in.

'Did you know rival gang members sometimes meet at airports because no one can bring a gun?' He waved a hand around the room, his Rolex shining in the light. '*I* like meeting in DAS because, ironically, no one can bring a listening device like a phone,' he said.

His waving hand slammed down onto the table so hard everything shook, including Andrew and Shanti.

'Now,' Roman growled in the following silence, 'drop the act.'

Despite the table distance, Andrew suddenly felt he and Shanti were far too close to this guy. The next country would have been preferable.

Roman continued, without waiting for a response. 'You two have been interfering with things beyond your understanding. It almost cost you a lot more than your jobs. It's time to stop.'

Despite the table slap still ringing in his ears, this rankled Andrew. 'We're messing with stuff?' he blurted as Roman's face turned to stone again. 'You're the one helping leakers into DAS. I bet you were behind the cyber attack as well.'

Shanti gave Andrew a warning look before turning back to Roman.

'Roman,' she said, stiff and formal. 'We don't know what you're talking about. If you continue with these threats and baseless accusations, we'll have to report your behaviour to Internal Security and the senior executive.'

Roman smiled, but there was a hardness in his eyes. 'Shanti, when Andrew told me you were at Lisa's escape as well, I thought you could know something. I was delighted to see you'd already applied to IOE, so it was easy to get you in.'

Roman chuckled darkly and his expression turned cynical.

'Your application had been paused because you were deemed a potential security threat. Hah! I should have listened, but we all make mistakes. Now all this recent unpleasantness is your faults.'

'Our fault?' said Shanti, 'but what about—'

'Did you know?' said Roman with sarcastic enthusiasm, 'that after you let me use your computer with my account, something strange happened? That afternoon, I got back to my office, logged in at my own terminal and I got a message! *You failed to log off your previous session. Would you like to restore?* It's like someone cancelled the logoff, did something, then turned it off in a panic.'

The colour drained from Shanti's face as Andrew squirmed, ever so slightly, in his seat.

Noting this, Roman continued.

'So, I restored the session and there it was. My email was open, even though I'd closed it when I thought I'd logged off before. When I checked it, there was nothing in sent, but something still in the deleted folder. You forgot that Shanti. That's where I found you forwarding my confidential messages to someone who famously associates with leakers. That was a line you two crossed. Shanti, I doubt this was all your idea, especially as you were so quick to send everything to Andrew. So, knowing that, we had to move some assets into play. Correct Talia?'

Talia looked up from the computer she'd logged into.

'Correct,' she said, as though they were in any other briefing. 'For the cohort mobilisation exercise, we prompted some conditioned assets with tailored messages, went full broadcast to increase the protest and, despite the schedule changes, performed quite well. As for the cyber aspect. It successfully exploited several known vulnerabilities and a zero day we've been holding. Don't worry about *your* operations, CMND also provides DAS a backup service that will restore most of what you lost. Two good outcomes. All in all, a lot of useful lessons learned.'

She spoke like she was delivering the last quarter's figures that were up overall.

'Useful?' said Shanti, shock all over her face. 'You engineered a riot and a cyber attack because of an email? We could have been killed! Wait… The gunman at the protest. How did he know Andrew and I? Was … was that you?'

Roman cracked a smile and several knuckles.

'I'll cut to the chase,' he said, ignoring Shanti. 'Go back to your day jobs and spreadsheets. That's your thing. My company's operation is none of your concern.'

'You mean Operation Polarize Dunk?' said Andrew. 'While we're dropping acts?'

There was a flicker, for just a moment, across Roman's carefully neutral face. Shanti stared at Andrew in disbelief.

'A sanctioned operation conducted under DAS authority within the Information Operations and Effects Division,' said Roman smoothly. 'CMND is a private company developing capabilities that will help national interests. That you know about it adds to your own security breaches.'

'There's no evidence we breached,' said Andrew pointedly. 'It was all wiped out in your cyber attack. I also know there's more to your operation than you're telling DAS.'

'And why are you looking for Lisa?' said Shanti. 'Are you after what she took?'

Roman looked back at the pair of them.

'You know, data is money,' he said. 'You can't have too much if you know how to make it work for you. Lisa was a smash and grab job. Sometimes, that's the only way to get what you want. But she proved unreliable.'

'Maybe she found more than you realise. Who'd have guessed that your home-grown traitor would betray you?' said Andrew.

For a second, Roman's face twisted into a snarl before it was pushed back behind a cold stare. He didn't take to sarcasm from juniors.

'I served for over twenty years,' said Roman, a dark cloud crossing his face. 'You know what I learned? Winners take risks. Look at the two of you, safe in here, or so you think. You've never taken a real risk in your life, have you?'

Andrew thought through events since he had come to DAS … but that wasn't conscious risk-taking so much as poor decision making.

'Perhaps you'll report me?' said Roman, more conversationally now. 'But as you said, where's the evidence?'

That was the thought front and centre for both Andrew and Shanti. Now officially, both sides didn't have anything on the other. Roman kept going in a seemingly carefree manner. He was impossible for them to read. Approachable entrepreneur one minute, threatening tyrant the next. Now that Andrew had seen his ugly side, talking to him was like expecting to be struck by lightning out of a clear blue sky.

'But as you brought up my op, next week I will be the main speaker at the biggest event of your year: Intelligence Futures,' said Roman. 'There, I'll brief the whole organisation on Polarize Dunk.'

'Why?' asked Andrew.

'Because I'm developing new capabilities that will be marketed to the world. I'm in this for the money. Australia was just where we developed and refined. Your little country, cute as it is, isn't the money maker. The real markets are out in the big wide world.'

'So, this is some kind of trial?' asked Shanti.

'Much more than that,' said Roman. 'This will be what

launches my company into billion-dollar operations.' His eyes brightened. 'The information wars have already begun, and war is where fortunes are made.'

He sat back, relaxed, with arms open wide like someone guaranteed their next round of venture capital. Both Shanti and Andrew jumped in their seats as he snapped forward and clapped his hands as though closing an auction.

'That's it,' he said. 'Now run along. You can't stop something approved by your own bosses.'

'We can still report what we've seen,' said Shanti. 'Maybe it'll be enough for others.'

'Yeah,' agreed Andrew. 'Don't rely on your cyber attack frame job sticking.'

Roman raised his eyebrows, looking at them with faux concern.

'Really?' he said. He theatrically muttered to himself – going 'oh gee whiz, guess I better give up,' then looked pointedly at Talia. Taking instruction from his look, she turned back to the computer screen for a moment.

'Project ran successfully,' she said. 'We have excellent footage.'

'Put it on the room's monitor,' said Roman.

Talia clicked the mouse and the monitor behind Andrew and Shanti blinked into life. They turned around, feeling uneasy about having their backs to Roman and Talia.

'This was posted thirty-two minutes ago,' said Talia. 'Multiple platforms and forums. Content moderation is reducing spread on major platforms, but they can't pull all of it. Early metrics show it's trending well on alternative platforms and anti-authority forums.'

She hit play and a shaky video began.

'I've done it!' a scratchy male voice said, their hand covering the camera. 'I've found another one!' The vision came back as the phone was put in a holder and a man sitting in a car came into view. His face had some bruising and a wild expression beneath the receding hairline. Shanti and Andrew both gasped as they recognised him. It was the shotgun-wielding man from the protest.

'I tried reasoning,' he said, tearing strips of heavy-duty duct tape off a large roll. 'But this is war. I failed the children once already and I'm sorry.'

Andrew stared at the screen in fascinated horror. There were actual tears in the man's eyes.

'I'm so, so sorry!' he said. 'I've been shown the terrible things that they do to you. But if we can't free you, we will avenge you! Thank you, those heroes who got me this information.'

The man looked off-screen, presumably out the car window.

'Now!' he said, 'it's time!'

The video jerked around as he pulled the phone out of the unseen holder and held it to his chest, facing out. Strips of duct tape came into view as he strapped the phone in place, being careful to leave the camera unobscured. As the man got out of the car, the video briefly turned white as the camera adjusted to different light conditions. As it cleared, the first view was white buildings sitting amongst green spaces. Shanti and Andrew recognised an area called the Parliamentary Triangle straight away. It was a space that held Parliament House, plus various important government buildings, scenic gardens and the permanent protest camp known as the Aboriginal Tent Embassy. Outside a few well-known pubs, it was the best place to find a high-profile political target.

The view turned and the man started hurrying up a wide series of steps. They could hear him breathing heavily as he went up. Andrew remembered he didn't look in good shape. The view was a blurring set of steps as he leaned forward to get up them.

The man halted and shouted, 'You! Stop!' He didn't say anything else for a few seconds, as he still needed to catch his breath. He was addressing someone standing on the same staircase, but several steps up and clearly on their way down. Confusingly, the only thing in view of the camera was the bottom two thirds of a man in a garish suit. In one hand he had his phone, in the other was a takeaway coffee tray. It held four coffees of varied sizes, you could almost make out the names and barista instructions written on the side in blue ink against white cardboard.

'Um, hello,' said the person on the steps. 'Can I help you?'

Andrew's ears pricked up as the formal tone was disturbingly familiar. Then the camera leaned back, bringing the top of the staircase and the man in question into view. Other people walked nearby, but it was clear this was his target.

'Liam!?' said Andrew. Shanti covered her mouth with her hand.

'You were warned!' the man spat, his voice cracking with emotion. 'Now all the dark servants will pay! Starting with you!'

The man lifted a large object into view. It was something horribly familiar and covered, this time, in a dull, grey blanket. Andrew flashed back to the protest, watching the material slide away to reveal the shotgun beneath. He remembered what it had felt like to stare down the barrels just seconds before the trigger was pulled – mercifully missing him. His stomach flipped and he froze, just as Liam did on the screen. He didn't run, scream or even drop the coffees. Within a few heartbeats, the man raised the shotgun just inches from Liam's face, the grey blanket sliding off and out of view.

Andrew saw Liam's hands shake, a tremor that spread to the rest of him in the space of a second. The coffees danced in their tray.

'Please–' he said just as both barrels roared, hurling propellant and metal shrapnel that, in an instant, punched through his face, pulverised his brain and sprayed the contents through an even larger exit wound across the cafe steps, glass frontage and cafegoers behind him.

People screamed and ran for cover, crashing into tables or down the steps. Others, standing stock still, cried out in shock, thinking they were hit, unaware the blood on their face and clothing wasn't theirs.

The shooter himself made a guttural sound – halfway between a laugh and a cry of anguish. It was like some throttled scream he'd been holding on to finally released.

He turned and took three steps back down, stopping as a police officer came running into view. She stopped at the bottom of the steps and drew her gun.

'Drop the weapon!' she shouted. The shooter twitched, the gun snapping up again as if he'd had an electric shock. The camera jerked about as the police officer fired several shots. The final one hadn't finished ringing out when the video stopped, presumably as a bullet went through the phone. The image reverted back to the first frame with a large white play triangle over it.

Silence filled the room, eventually broken by Roman.

'Did it get many views?' he asked. Talia shrugged and turned back to the keyboard. The screen blinked to blackness again as she closed the browser and logged out.

'There goes my cyber-witness,' said Roman. 'Yours too,' he added to Andrew. 'But that wasn't the point. Do you really think the frame up was important? Or that you two still are? Framing you was an act of mercy and patience, and now I am out of both. I hope you see that.'

Andrew and Shanti didn't move or respond. Both were trying not to be sick, trying not to jump out of the chairs and run. Shanti had been an analyst for a while, and this wasn't her first execution video. It was, however, the first one where she'd known the victim and then saw him die a few kilometres from her office. But suddenly, everything was far more real than anything she'd seen before. The instigators of the whole thing sat at the other end of the table, and it was clear they weren't finished yet.

'Don't be upset,' said Roman. 'Michael tells me he was more than willing to frame you in exchange for a transfer. He was mad at you for some reason, and, unlike him, we really do have contacts in the Minister's office. Always good to meet someone who knows what they want.'

Roman tutted to himself, as though raising some last point just when everyone thinks the meeting is finished. 'But honestly,' he said, 'I don't know why a young man would want to go there.' His eyes flicked to and from the black screen. 'Everyone knows all they do is fetch coffee.'

Andrew swallowed slowly, the sick feeling in his stomach slowly tumbling and rolling. His eyes felt hot and prickly, but he didn't want to cry. Not in front of Roman and Talia. Roman was enjoying this, like a man showing off his physical prowess at a medieval feast. Cracking walnuts in his fist and tearing the whole limbs off roasted animals with his hands.

Roman stared at them; his theatrical nonchalance pushed aside by the same dark cloud as before.

'I'd like to apologise for my earlier remark,' he said in a low, menacing tone. 'I was wrong. You have taken a real risk in your lives. You're doing it right now.'

Talia slid a piece of paper across the desk to him. He looked down and spoke, not bothering to talk directly to Andrew or Shanti.

'Be careful going home tonight,' he said. 'Lots of crazies about. You on the bus, Andrew? Fifty-five it says here. And you Shanti? Yellow Honda? Usually in the south-west car park? More trees there, good for shady spots. But a long, lonely walk from the office.'

Shanti paled, and Andrew's stomach churned. He remembered staring down those shotgun barrels.

Roman looked up from the paper with cold eyes. 'Now get out,' he said.

Both Shanti and Andrew took the opportunity to leave with haste. A chair tipped too far back and thumped to the floor as they scurried into the corridor.

Andrew stopped to look back at them. With two steps, Talia got to the door and slammed it in his face. Roman grinned as Andrew's shocked face vanished with the bang of the wood.

Now alone in the room together, Talia cleared her throat, making a sound like an outboard motor coming to life.

'Why not deal with them now?' she said, nodding in the direction of the corridor.

Roman snorted. 'As I thought, they're all talk and can't hurt us. Plus, you know the old saying: one's an incident, two's a pattern and three's a trend. No need to draw more attention before we're ready.'

Talia considered this and nodded.

'In any case,' Roman continued. 'They'll die with the others in the final phase before they figure it out. Make sure the failsafe is enabled. Set the date and cut comms.'

THIRTY-ONE

THE DOOR TO ANDREW'S TEMPORARY OFFICE BURST OPEN, hard enough for the doorknob to leave a mark on the wall.

Andrew and Shanti fell inside like they were escaping enemy fire. They'd rushed down from the meeting in silence. Each time Andrew tried to say something, Shanti shushed him and kept up the power walk that was one step down from a full-on sprint.

'Right!' snapped Shanti, sticking a finger in Andrew's face. 'You need to explain everything to me right now!'

At this distance, Shanti had the same intensity as Lisa. And perhaps Angela. Andrew wondered if he had a knack for aggravating everyone he met in the intelligence community.

'Just hold on,' he said, buying time. 'We can fix this.'

'Fix?' said Shanti, anger flaring in her face. 'People are dying! We are dealing with a traitor who could kill us too!'

Despite her valid point, Andrew felt an internal dam go somewhere inside. A torrent of rage and frustration, a lot of it at himself, burst.

'I know!' he yelled. Shanti flinched but didn't back down. Andrew's face turned red as he snapped back at her. 'It's my fault! Everything around me keeps going from worse to fucked!'

He raised his hands level with his face, fingers bent like claws.

'Everything I do backfires!' he said. 'I've been tricked, trapped and terrorised. I'm a fucking first-year grad and I'm caught up in some major conspiracy bullshit and I don't know what to do or who to trust.'

He took a step back from Shanti, panting, and leaned on a chair. His head swam from yelling what he'd been feeling for so long. He couldn't even mention Liam. The video was burned into his vision whenever he closed his eyes. It was Liam's expression he couldn't shake. The sudden fear and shaking, knowing there was nothing he could do. He died pleading, all because Andrew tricked him, and Roman wanted to make a point about loose ends.

Andrew and Shanti stayed in an awkward tableau, facing off like rival gunfighters who are both out of ammo.

Then a third, unexpected voice broke the silence.

'Do you know what I love about intelligence work?'

Both spun around to the figure seated in a chair in the corner.

'It's the honesty,' said Peter, an amused look on his face. On the chair next to him was a pile of printouts – no doubt more crap tasks on their way to Andrew. 'People think intelligence work is all lies and subterfuge, but they miss the analytical tradecraft.'

Shanti and Andrew just stood there agape, unsure if they were being told off or not.

'We're intelligence analysts,' said Peter. 'We say exactly what we think will or has happened, regardless of how terrible it is. We discuss brutal, illicit, and horrifying things that would make others panic. We do so to help people make decisions, in full knowledge of the cost. Name another white-collar industry that allows that kind of dangerously honest speech.'

Andrew considered the question rhetorical, because Peter walked over to the far side of the desk and sat down again. Shanti's face was grim, but calmer than before.

'So!' said Peter brightly, waving a hand at the seats on their side of the desk. 'What terrible things do you have to tell me?'

In the end, all three sat down at the table in Andrew's temporary penitentiary and exchanged information. For Andrew, any previous pride, self-interested justification, or selfish impulses had been washed away, replaced with visions of Liam saying 'please'.

So, he went first, laying out the broad strokes of what had happened since Lisa had escaped. He told them he'd been contacted and blackmailed by Lisa shortly after her escape. That he'd kept everything to himself and tried to fix it alone. He'd manipulated Liam – his throat briefly caught here – into researching Koil, as well as Shanti, convincing her to investigate too.

Shanti told Peter about the secret messages, plus the shotgun-wielding psycho at the protest and Roman's threats in their meeting.

'So, now our lives are in danger,' said Andrew.

'Shall we go to Angela now?' asked Shanti.

Peter shook his head.

'She's offsite,' he said. 'Moved to another secure facility, seeing as someone can just reach into our HQ computer systems. She's also spending a lot of time meeting with the government and our allies. A lot of them are concerned we can't be trusted with the information we share now if it's so easily destroyed. She has a lot on her plate right now.'

'We can still report it to James or someone else there,' said Andrew.

'What if they're involved?' said Peter drily. 'Perhaps Angela is as well?'

'Or you?' said Andrew. Peter casually responded with a 'could be' shrug.

Shanti shook her head. 'That's getting too paranoid,' she said. 'We should risk it. But only when we have something. So far, there's nothing we can report. No evidence, remember?' She pointed at Andrew. 'You should have reported it sooner. A lot of this could have been avoided.'

Andrew nodded gloomily.

'And you didn't report the secret messages from Roman,' said Peter to Shanti. 'Why's that?'

Shanti blinked several times and reddened. 'I …' She hesitated. 'I just wanted to know more before reporting officially. Andrew was on to something.'

'Sounds like he was,' agreed Peter. 'But perfect intelligence delivered late is useless.'

Shanti looked down and chewed a nail.

'So, you believe us, Peter?' asked Andrew.

'It's more of an assessment,' he said at last. 'You two are unlikely to make something like this up. It also tallies with a lot of what's been going on, so far as I know.'

'Thanks,' said Andrew. Shanti echoed him.

'But,' said Peter, 'Roman is a powerful man. He may not be DAS, but he's connected. He's a respected CEO with millions of dollars' worth of contracts, and therefore a lot of protective friends. To take someone like that down, you need to be surgical and have hard evidence. Otherwise, everyone just turns on each other.'

They were treated to a rare Peter smile.

'You've probably heard the rumours,' he said. 'I know what it's like when trust breaks down. I was part of a high-level counterintelligence team. I thought it was great work, spent years chasing some of the greatest threats to our national security.'

His smile faded.

'But then a defector tipped us off. We'd had a mole in the team for years.'

'What happened?' asked Andrew.

'A trap was set, and Internal Security caught him,' said Peter. 'It wrecked a lot of careers, mine included.'

'But you were innocent!' said Shanti.

Peter shook his head. 'Guilty by association. Everyone needed to be investigated,' he said. 'Particularly those of us who worked closely with him. The problem with moles is it can be hard to know if you got them all. After that, they dissolved the team and assigned those left to early retirement or gave them busy work in nothing areas. Just in case we were traitors ready to do more damage.'

'Sorry,' said Shanti.

Peter leaned back, folding his arms. 'The worst part,' he said, 'is finding out years of work never mattered. Everything you did was undone by the person sitting next to you ... But here we have a chance to do something.'

'Like what?' asked Andrew. 'We still don't really know what's happening.'

'What *do* we know?' asked Peter.

'I know what Operation Polarize Dunk is,' said Shanti.

They both stared at her.

'I read the summary,' she said. 'In the email? Roman was using a status update with a summary to send the hidden message, remember?'

'Well?' said Peter.

'Give me a sec.' Shanti closed her eyes to help her remember. 'It's a concept for new information warfare operations,' she said, eyes still closed. 'The summary was a bit … extra, you know? Sales pitch? But it talked about using bulk data and AI to track people who may be open to an approach from our agents. Or maybe opposition figures to a regime? Maybe even driving them to direct action, maybe even violence.' She opened her eyes. 'Roman's been on some kind of spending spree. He's bought psychologists, data scientists, people from social media companies. Lots of stuff about "psychographic profiling". Remember Cambridge Analytica?'

Peter nodded, but Andrew looked lost.

'Big political consulting company that helped sway elections,' said Shanti. 'They used data mining and strategic messaging to find and influence people to vote certain ways. That kind of thing was strongly involved in US and British elections, plus Brexit.'

'Hang on …' said Andrew. 'So, they want to find people who are open to approaches from spies?'

'More than that,' said Peter, frowning down at the table. 'Think about it. Not just information sources. In theory, you could find people with a propensity for violent or threatening action. Someone ready to take up a cause, or who needs one to fill a hole in their life.'

'So, this program can track radicals?' said Andrew.

'Think bigger,' said Peter. 'This program *creates* them. Maybe gives them the content and encouragement they need to tip them over the edge.'

He smiled again and looked at them. 'Imagine recruiting sources overseas, or convincing someone they need to strike a blow for freedom or whatever. All at the individual level. You already know who you're speaking to, what their drivers and desires are. Maybe all they need is a little push.' He shook his head in grudging professional respect. 'Got to hand it to them. Creating the next generation of extremist and espionage threats.'

'That was it!' said Shanti. 'There was something about "potential types".'

'Potentials?' said Andrew, remembering Roman's comment about the shotgun wielder.

Shanti waved her hands to shush him as she remembered. 'There was Thief, Saboteur, Protester and … one other one. Sorry.'

'It'll come to you,' said Peter.

'But it can't do those things,' Shanti went on. 'Not yet, anyway. It said it's only a proof of concept.'

'What?' said Andrew.

Shanti closed her eyes again. Peter took the opportunity to switch the fan on. It was getting stiflingly hot. It powered up with an off-kilter *whum-whum* from a badly balanced fan blade.

'It's only a trial,' she said. 'They're doing all the research, but not applying it. It's only to show the government it's theoretically possible. I guess they'll get funding once they show it's possible?'

Peter nodded as Andrew said, 'I mean, it sounds like a lot of things could go wrong. You'd want to be sure.'

Shanti closed her eyes again as she rummaged through her memories. The only noise was the fan whirring at increasing speeds.

'Stop interfering,' said Andrew suddenly.

'What?'

'Roman told us to *stop interfering*,' said Andrew. 'Not asking or poking around, but *interfering*. That means he's still got something planned. Something we can mess with. He's not done yet.'

'Agreed,' said Peter.

'Attacker!' said Shanti, her eyes flicking open.

'Huh?'

'That's the third type!' she said. 'I remembered because it was next to a picture of the Reserve Bank Shooter.'

Even Andrew had heard about him. It had been in the months before he joined DAS. A forty-year-old ex-accountant with a hunting rifle had attempted to storm the main Reserve Bank building. He had copies of his 300-page manifesto strapped all over his torso and legs as optimistic armour. The manifesto was a rambling condemnation of central financial authorities, state-backed cryptos and Jews, and detailed a UN plot to centralise all financial systems under Disney. 'The Truth Protects' was the title, but as it turned out, it doesn't when you're shot at close range. He'd researched his fantasies better than his targets and had failed to realise the Reserve Bank building backed onto a police station. He first wounded a parking inspector, due to his blue – therefore 'UN-affiliated' – uniform, before being shot by three police officers who had just turned the corner. He went down cursing police and the time it takes to work a bolt-action rifle.

'An active shooter in DAS?' said Andrew. 'Could you even get a gun in here?'

'Tricky,' said Peter. 'But not impossible. We'll start with that scenario.'

'So, we're working this?' said Shanti, a disbelieving grin on her face.

'Absolutely!' said Peter. 'Feels good to do something, doesn't it?'

Peter stood up and began walking back and forth in front of them.

'We have four days until Intelligence Futures,' he said. 'After that, Roman's outta here. His team will spend a couple of days packing up, and that's it. Something's going to happen in that window. Possibly a shooter, but I can't see Roman putting himself in harm's way.' He stopped pacing and faced them.

'We're working this as a live op,' he said. 'We'll divide up tasks and meet every day here at four to go through what we have. Oh, and we don't mention a single thing outside this room, and nothing on the network. Assume everything and everyone is compromised.'

* * *

Into the evening, the three of them worked on their new project: 'Operation Known Unknowns'. The purpose was to figure out what Roman and CMND were doing, how to stop it, and they only had a few days at most. Peter chose the name and grumpily stuck to it because he was the most senior person in the team. Particularly as he was covering for them and would tell anyone who asked they were needed for a 'special project'.

The plan was to work in the same isolated office Andrew had been initially banished to. With others to work with, his oubliette became more of a refuge. Albeit one that was slightly too small and smelled of spilled coffee that had seeped into the carpet.

Shanti's job was researching known extremist groups and individuals assessed as willing to shoot up a major intelligence headquarters. Who would target DAS? Although, in the deep sea of modern extremism, it was a pretty big list. She had to sort those who'd talk from those who'd act. She was also tasked with meeting with people she still knew in Information Operations and Effects. Anything to get hints as to what Roman was planning.

Andrew, meanwhile, was to scour social media and other public sources. The goal being to identify any other Lisa-style infiltrators who'd had a blank social media footprint until arrival. For all they knew, a wannabe active shooter was already on the premises with a smuggled weapon, just waiting to be activated.

'I get why,' said Andrew when told his role. 'But is that the only thing I get to do?'.

'I'll also need you for something else,' said Peter.

'What?'

'Liaison,' said Peter darkly. He turned back to his ever-present notebook, filled with his scrawled and unreadable handwriting that would baffle the most experience cryptologist.

Andrew felt his stomach churn at the risks they were taking. If they were wrong, they were definitely fired, and possibly dead. If they were right, they were possibly fired and probably dead. Shanti, although a little calmer on the outside, probably felt the same way. Peter, on the other hand, seemed to be enjoying himself for the first time in ages.

'You have your tasks,' said Peter. 'Go through them as quickly and thoroughly as you can. I'll be here each afternoon, but contact me if there's something urgent.'

'Like what?' asked Andrew.

'How about an attack?' said Peter.

Thirty-Two

The next morning, the door to Cafe Imontagu banged shut behind Andrew and he blinked in the sunshine. No longer security-cleared for the internal cafe, he had to get his fix from down the road. Even if it now had a lot of uncomfortable associations. He had his mocha in one hand and a paper bag with an egg and bacon roll in the other. The bag was already sagging with the heat and grease of the contents, releasing a wickedly promising smell of an indulgent and rebelliously unhealthy breakfast. It had been an impulse purchase. Something to enjoy, and Andrew wanted comfort if not the actual food.

He looked around, half delaying his departure and half checking for danger. The surrounding avenue, buildings and occasional green spaces seemed safe. No angry protesters, no shotgun-wielding maniacs. It was a halcyon Canberra scene. Just the apartments, cafes, a park and the occasional jogger or cafe goer.

Andrew sighed as he contemplated their efforts so far. The research to get a step ahead of Roman had so far found nothing useful. So, he took a moment to enjoy the sunshine before heading back. Behind him he heard the clamorous conversations of the cafe, muffled by double insulation and heavy door – like being outside a barn full of pigeons. The door flew open with a bang, making Andrew jump, and a woman carrying two coffees hurried past. As the door slowly swung back to close, internal babble poured out in an incoherent torrent. In Andrew's imagination, the serenity had been shattered and the protest was back with people chanting. He felt his heart race as he looked around, alone, but expecting a man with a gun to emerge at any second. He'd abandoned going everywhere masked, but now wondered if that was a good idea after all.

He started off for the office, walking past a beggar in a pale blue hoodie who sat hunched against the building with a crude cardboard sign that said 'hungry'. The absence of coins indicated they'd likely stay that way. Andrew felt wretched but had no cash.

'Hey Andrew,' said the beggar without looking up.

'What?' said Andrew, all automatic excuses short-circuited by the use of his name.

'It's me, Lisa,' said the beggar, without looking up. 'See that park? Go to the far edge by the trees. I'll be there in a minute. No contacting anyone, don't let go of the coffee or the bag, I'll be watching.'

Andrew stood in confusion for a second before going with the flow. So much for scanning for danger. Another thing he'd stuffed up.

He headed across the road to the park on the far side. As he walked, he heard Lisa get up and leave, presumably to get there another way. He got to the park and waited. Lisa, true to her word, appeared on the far edge of the park from another direction and headed over to him.

Not sure what to expect, he stayed silent as she approached. Lisa was wearing jeans, greying sneakers and had kept the hoodie up. Her hair was now a faded green, a few exploratory strands coming out of the hood that she tucked back in again as necessary.

She came close enough for conversation but stayed out of reach – keeping enough space to ensure a good gap if she had to break into a run. But the space went deeper than that and they both stared across a metaphorical chasm for several seconds.

'Good cafe, better than the one in headquarters,' she said, breaking the silence with unexpected small talk. 'I used to go in there all the time. Amazing egg and bacon on Turkish. Can't risk going in now of course, might get recognised.'

Andrew nodded, tight-lipped. Then, following her gaze, rolled his eyes and held the greasy and delicious smelling bag out.

Lisa hesitated, then stepped forward and snatched it. Just like the way she'd snatched the bag he'd handed back to her in DAS when they first met. It felt like an aeon ago in terms of experiences, if not time.

'Thanks for meeting,' said Andrew as Lisa ripped the paper open and started wolfing down the contents.

'Changing your game username to 'need2talk',' said Lisa while chewing, 'wasn't subtle.'

'Best way to get your attention,' said Andrew. 'Bunch of other players dropped me links to therapists.'

Lisa snorted at that before turning serious.

'I heard someone in DAS got shot,' she said. 'Wasn't sure if it was you.'

'Not me,' said Andrew, 'It was my housemate, Liam.'

'Oh,' said Lisa, apparently surprised. 'He was … um, yeah, sorry.'

She looked down and took advantage of the pause to take a large bite from the roll. Andrew didn't say anything as she chewed.

'So, what do you have on Koil?' she said eventually, changing the subject. 'I've got a lot to do on that front.'

Andrew thought about all he had to say as his eye fell on a nearby park bench. He wandered over and motioned Lisa to do the same. She followed and sat on the far edge.

'First,' said Andrew. 'I want to know what you're going to do with Central. Why'd do you even take it in the first place.'

Lisa considered his request. Andrew had no idea what she'd been up to, but it must be exhausting. She had bags under her eyes and was eating the roll like she'd skipped a few meals.

'Do you even know what it is?' she asked. Andrew shook his head, deciding honesty and silence were winning traits at this time.

'Central is the main database of all DAS's people,' she said.

'You mean all our undercover agents?' said Andrew, aghast.

Lisa shook her head. 'No, any field personnel in active operations aren't on there, too much of a risk. It's the central administrative database.'

Andrew's face scrunched up in confusion.

Lisa, seeing his confusion, faced him directly.

'It's an HR database for all the other people,' she said. 'The ones who aren't on secret undercover lists. DAS, or any intelligence agency for that matter, is a lot more than spies out in the field somewhere.'

She went on, and Andrew felt a chill of realisation as she told him. It wasn't just about people who play spy games, it was about all those who made it possible for them to do so. The reams of other professionals like human resources, building maintenance, executive assistants, janitors, IT support, cafe staff, payroll, technicians, archivists and even lawyers – DAS had floors of those to ensure what they did passed the legal bar, if not the pub test. There were thousands of people who came to work every day to ensure their part of the supporting bureaucracy worked as well as could be hoped and allow people like Andrew to exist. It had never even occurred to him. People who talk about being the pointy end of the spear sometimes forget how far back the shaft goes, and how much they depend on it.

'Yeah,' said Lisa, interrupting Andrew's thoughts. 'Didn't think about them, did you?'

While he didn't want to admit it, Andrew had to privately concede that she was right. Off in the distance, a kookaburra broke into guffawing birdsong.

'You're on there – graduate program administration,' Lisa casually added. 'All your details, it's how I managed to track you down. That, and the way others in the grad program really over-share online.'

Andrew grunted. He barely cared anymore and focused his attention on the towering eucalyptus trees that lined the park. Canberra was nicknamed the Bush Capital for a reason.

'So why do it? Why take Central?' he asked.

Lisa looked uncomfortable. It took a few seconds to dredge it up. 'It was a doxxing operation,' she said at last. 'We, I guess I, was going to dump it all on the net.'

'All the analysts and support staff?' said Andrew. 'All their details, who they are and where they work? Why?'

'Because they were collaborators!' snapped Lisa. She shoved the last of the roll in her mouth and scrunched up the bag like it was the one who got her into this mess.

'They're part of the problem too! We wanted the powerful to know that none of them were safe! We were going to blow all their secrecy away! See how they like their every movement being watched!'

Andrew counted to five in his head to make sure Lisa was finished.

'But,' he began, 'we don't watch everyone's every—'

'You know what I mean!' said Lisa. Despite her harsh tone,

she eased her grip on the scrunched-up bag and colour flowed back into her knuckles.

There was no telling what could be done with that information, or to those people, thought Andrew. He shivered as memories surfaced like whales; the angry crowd, the smell of fireworks, a shotgun aimed at him and a shaky voice saying 'please' to no avail.

'And it hasn't been released … yet,' said Lisa, emphasising the last word, 'because I was supposed to meet Koil after I escaped and then we'd take the next steps together. But seeing as he was connected on the inside, I'm guessing I was going to be immediately arrested if he was legit and killed if he wasn't. Who knows what he wants it for, but if you come through for me, I can find out.'

Andrew stopped examining the far trees. There was some warbled birdsong in the distance, but the kookaburra had gone elsewhere for amusement. He couldn't help Lisa and was surprised to realise he now actually wanted to. They both had the same enemy, but it was too late. The data around Koil was gone, and all of Roman's involvement wiped with it. Even if Andrew had the DG's access to DAS files, there was nothing to find. He could lie about that, string her along, but why bother? His career was over, his life –and others – were in danger, and those responsible for that enjoyed the unwitting full support of the intelligence establishment.

Andrew grimaced as this played through his head. He decided to come clean. What could she do?

'I can't get him for you,' he said flatly.

'You have to,' said Lisa. 'Find a way.'

'You don't understand,' said Andrew. 'No one can get him for you.' He looked at Lisa and explained everything that had happened. The protest, the cyber attack that wiped all evidence, and the confused human weapon who killed Liam – on Roman's orders. The same man who was pulling Koil's strings.

All things considered, Lisa took it fairly well. She didn't interrupt him, but her face tightened, and she blinked several times when he told her about the lost data. She understood that they were each on their own against a far more powerful and violent enemy than previously thought.

They were such an ashen-faced pair that a passing jogger momentarily slowed, then sped up again for fear of interrupting a breakup in full awkward flight.

After he finished, Lisa didn't say anything. She looked down and around, anywhere but at Andrew.

'So, go ahead and frame me,' said Andrew, irritated by the silence. 'Tell them we were in all this together, because what you're after doesn't exist. I can't get it.'

Lisa merely cleared her throat and kept looking away. She dropped the greasy paper bag that held the roll and wiped her hands on her jeans.

Andrew remembered he'd put a napkin in his pocket. He pulled it out, also extracting a cheap blue pen the napkin has wrapped itself around. He held out the napkin, raising it up in her peripheral vision. As she took it, Andrew found himself staring at the pen, triggering a memory.

'I get it,' he said. 'I mean, I don't know exactly what its been like, or what you've gone through, but I at least get what it's like to feel like you finally understand something, only to have it all switched and feel stupid again.'

'So, you think I'm stupid?' said Lisa, coming out of her funk with a vengeance.

'No!' said Andrew, wishing people would somehow hear the smart thing you meant, not the dumb thing you said.

'I was caught up in something,' she said, softly this time. 'With someone. I just wanted to make a difference.'

'I know,' said Andrew. 'But I think I can find you a way out of this. Maybe for both of us.'

'How?' she said.

'I don't know … yet,' he said, echoing her use of the word 'yet'. 'But I have some ideas.'

Lisa was silent for a few seconds, then she said: 'What makes you think I even want your help? Do you have any idea of the kind of injustice and bullshit going on in this country? I may have been doing things for the wrong reasons, but that doesn't make what I did wrong.'

'You're right that there's lots to be mad about,' agreed Andrew. 'But you don't really believe this action was the solution.'

'Why do you think that?' bristled Lisa.

'Because,' he replied, 'if you did, you would have released Central by now. Hell, you would have done it from the car park if you really didn't question anything. Why did you even look up Koil and your old group in the seconds before you left DAS? Something was nagging at you.'

'Don't patronise me,' snapped Lisa. 'You don't know me or why I did it.'

'Oh, I know why you did it,' said Andrew. 'Roman and CMND. I just don't know why you think you did it.'

Lisa shook her head. Andrew saw her knuckles whiten again and he wondered if he'd gone too far.

'You know what? Maybe I will release Central,' said Lisa defiantly. 'But my way! Maybe I'll just release samples to start with. The analysts like you.'

'The people like me?' Andrew murmured. 'Please don't release it.'

'And why shouldn't I?' said Lisa.

'Because,' Andrew replied, 'while you haven't, you still have something to bargain with. DAS will be desperate to stop Central getting out. The second it's out there, you haven't got anything but treason charges from DAS or a killer from CMND. Incidentally, your murderer has almost certainly already been programmed and sent on your trail. They just don't know where you are … yet.'

Lisa stood up, brushing off her dirty tracksuit and clearing her throat.

'Bye Andrew,' she said, looking at him with a hint of sadness in her eyes. 'Don't try and follow me. If I'm caught, Central gets released on a timer.'

With that, she turned and started walking away, hands in pockets and her head looking down.

'Lisa?' called out Andrew. To his relief, she stopped and turned around.

'I'll keep playing the game,' said Andrew. 'Maybe you could join me tonight? Or soon? Be good to go on a raid together?'

Lisa didn't say anything. She turned again and walked quickly away, vanishing behind a nearby apartment development.

Andrew looked up at the nearby tree as the kookaburra had returned to laugh at him again. He stood up and walked the opposite way to Lisa, back the long, winding path to DAS HQ.

He had work to do.

THIRTY-THREE

One day later

GROUPS LIKE 'US' AND 'THEM' ARE CREATED FOR THE
strangest reasons, and nothing divides Australians, both physically and socially, like rivers. In any major city bisected by one,
the enemy is typically any person on a different bank to you.
Everyone knows there are only losers or wankers on the other
side. Canberra is no different, but as they had no river, they
had to create an artificial lake. Just so they could observe the
traditional Australian value of water-based snobbery.

On the southern side of said lake – opposite to Andrew –
Lisa sat in an expansive, but tired-looking house, on a large
block of land. Typical of sprawling 1960s Canberra, it had
once been quite grand and surrounded by wide and verdant
lawns. It had since been repurposed – via inheritance – by a
far-left commune. The lawns had been replaced with vegetable
gardens, compost beds, and a chicken coop. Out the front, the
mailbox was always stuffed with 'free appraisal' offers from real
estate agents, some of whom dared knock on the peeling door.
However, they would only be refused, lectured on 'necro-capi-

talism', and sent on their way. Leaving them to weep in their BMWs at the lost commission on what could become a couple of million-dollar townhouses.

Inside, Lisa sat cross-legged on a cushion on the floor, as there were no chairs. She'd settled down in a corner of her 'room'. In this case, it was half of the living room that had been re-zoned with an old curtain strung through the middle to make a bedroom. Chaotic communal noise filtered through from the rest of the house. This being a place where people laughed, danced, ate, argued and fucked, sometimes within arms-reach of Lisa, only separated by cloth hanging off nails in opposing walls. As such, she'd had to learn to find focus in this choppy sea of noise. But after everything she'd been through, it was a perfect place to lay low before making her next move. She'd found the house after working her way into a network of leftist sympathisers and protest movements, both online and on campus. Still, you never knew who you were talking to, so they didn't know her real story. On the plus side, they were friendly and understanding of people on the run from something they weren't quite ready to talk about. They didn't care, only asking enough questions to ensure you were anti-war, but pro-revolution.

As normally hard as it was to block the noise out, Lisa was now barely aware of it. Her world was her laptop screen. This was where she was going to decide the rest of her life.

A wave of anxiety and adrenaline made her typing harsh – each keystroke a sharp *tak!* despite the keyboard's soft plastic. Across several tabs, her online selves leapt around on shifting ice flows of forums and encrypted chats, many about the infamous DAS leak that there were scant details on. There were millions online, but she needed the right people. The ones who'd be most interested in the information she had. What she was doing was her decision now, and she had to do it her way.

Her hands were clammy, and her stomach was rolling and

diving like it did when she first betrayed DAS. She thought about her conversations with Andrew. This course of action locked her in. She chewed on her lip as she typed:

Department of Australian Security Data from Feb-breach. First sample.

Her finger hovered over the keyboard as she paused and looked around. But she was still alone in her curtained-off den. The sounds of communal life drifted in from other rooms, giving the whole thing an unnerving normality. A part of her couldn't believe what she was about to do.

Lisa's fingers slid across the laptop's trackpad, dragging a file into place for upload. In the file preview screen, the logo of DAS alongside a classification banner of 'TOP-SECRET' was clearly visible.

The prompt lit up: *UPLOAD FILE?*

Lisa paused, finger hovering over the keyboard.

Your decision, she told herself. Your way.

She hit enter.

Thirty-Four

Two days later – Intelligence Futures Day

Dave stopped to breathe and adjust the bags on his back, one bulky and one long. Straps dug into his shoulders, and he pondered the wisdom of tying them together for easier carrying. Too late now. At least it was still cool this early, before the sun really started to climb. He continued up the hill, losing sight of the tiny path in the thick trees and scrub. There was a long way to go. He had to go all the way up and over to see the target.

Below him, a metallic twinkle was all he could see of his beloved Holden, now deep in some bushes. He'd planned to hide the car, but hadn't planned to do it quite so soon. That had been quite a corner.

It served him right. He'd driven all night from Melbourne to get here in time. The thrill got him most of the way, his eyes only getting heavy once he was in Canberra. Then that turn jumped out to meet him.

He looked back up the hill and stomped onwards. Adrenaline pushed him up the slope but was no replacement for oxygen. He stopped and took a few haggard breaths. He'd really lost a lot of condition since the riot. No performing, no gym, no fitness.

He checked his phone before moving on. The path was an old bush trail, meandering and barely wide enough for a person. The barely visible path was solid clay. Jagged rocks stuck up like broken teeth, ready to maul you if you fell, and there were plenty of trip hazards. Tree roots dived in and out of the ground like the tentacles of some ancient monster.

Geez, thought Dave. People hike through this? He coughed twice, then spat before starting off again.

The surrounding bush looked down on him. The plants were muscular natives, the sort that break boulders apart as they grow and refresh themselves with the occasional bushfire. Canberra people dig and tend their gardens with jackhammers, chainsaws, and a lot of swearing.

Dave joined them. He gave each and every obstacle a cursing threat until he ran out of breath. Once he was over the peak of the hill and heading down again, the path dwindled and the bushes ahead closed rank, clawing at him. His boot hit an arcing root, pitching him forward. Face raked by branches, he hit the ground.

This, thought Dave, is the fucking worst. Muttering imprecations against all plants, he got to his feet and stood up into a spider web.

He was still wildly clawing at his head as he stumbled into a tiny clearing that featured a granite boulder. It was big enough to lie on, with tree cover and perfect line of sight. Finally!

His bags thudded into the ground. One sagged slightly to the side as he grabbed one of the toggles and pulled it towards him. A sniper's ghillie suit poked out the top. It was a camouflage disguise, designed to make its wearer blend in by looking like the local foliage. Or Wookiee roadkill, if done poorly.

Haute couture for snipers and other soldiers who blend in and kill from afar. Dave had to stay undetected while he waited. He struggled into it, cursing and blinking sweat out of his eyes.

Settling down, Dave reached into his bag and pulled out a water bottle, two muesli bars, and a rifle scope. He peered through it, grimacing when he got an extreme close-up of a nearby tree. At the bottom of the hill, the buildings of DAS spread out. Roofs bristled with antennae and cars wound in and out at checkpoints, glinting in the sun. He adjusted the magnification and watched the people loitering around the entrance and the fence line. The crosshairs of the scope playfully bounced from person to person as Dave counted under his breath.

He put the rifle scope in a convenient groove in the boulder and checked his watch.

Not long now. Time to set up.

DAS's main foyer was packed for Intelligence Futures – a yearly festival of presentations, special guests, and enough snacks to sink a battleship faster than loose lips. Only in its fifth year, it had swelled into the kind of power circle hobnobbing that many business-people, academics and political brokers knifed each other for. It was originally small scale, intended as an event to give intelligence types a chance to relax. They could network without being recorded, swap stories without being arrested, and generally let their hair down without worrying about a national incident. However, defence contractors and other creatures of the politico-economic ecosystem soon got in and raised the showmanship. It was now the intelligence community's gala ball. A golden opportunity to see next year's ambitions and learn just who was worth watching.

Banners of various partner companies and intelligence

branches hung from every corner. The foyer was crammed with people in suits, uniforms, rich-casual, and the occasional cyber-related hoodie. Chatting merged into the busy roar of a water-fall. People exchanged greetings, caught up on gossip and ate volatile canapes that disintegrated or sprayed crumbs at first touch.

Roman and Michael were at the centre of the crowd, chat-ting with the DAS Director-General, with Talia at her usual bodyguard's remove. She was keeping opportunistic networkers away by glaring in a way that suggested she would unhinge her jaw and devour them if they approached. Michael broke off and darted through the crowd. He leaped up onto a temporary stage housing a lectern with microphone.

'Good morning, everyone!' he boomed through the PA, his used-car-selling smile shining through every word. The chatter dried up almost instantly.

'Thanks!' called Michael. 'Could all our guests from the CIA please identify yourselves? I kid, of course! My little joke.'

A light titter ran through the crowd. However, it had more than enough wattage to make Michael beam even brighter.

He launched into a painfully bright and cheerful welcome with all the traditional acknowledgements. But as he warbled on, Andrew and Shanti moved through the crowd, making their way to Peter.

'I've kept an eye on them,' said Peter, as they arrived. 'Nothing unexpected. You ready to go?'

Andrew swallowed. His Adam's apple felt like a wrecking ball in his throat.

'Yes.'

'Remember, this is our only chance. Lives depend on it.'

Andrew scowled like a teenager being told to do their best.

Peter smiled in response. He only ever seemed to do that when Andrew was just about to get out of his depth.

'Good enough. Let's go.'

Peter's timing was, as always, excellent. Michael finished his welcome and politely requested they all head into the auditorium for the keynote speech. The crowd dutifully poured into the auditorium's various doors, as slowly and noisily as water going down the plughole in a bath. Shanti placed her hand on Andrew's arm and gave him a smile.

* * *

Terrorism is scary – hence the name. But it isn't often acknowledged that it's scary for everyone, even the people doing it. Few people blow things up or kill without some apprehension or excitement. Israel made this an airport security concept. Unlike the rest of the world, who largely roll the dice on one excruciating search and stack all their potential victims in one place, Israel staggers minor checkpoints from the furthest edge of the airport in. They don't necessarily search you at each one – they look at you, initially checking for nervousness or unusual emotion. Someone about to commit a terrorist act is either excited or, more likely, absolutely shitting themselves. Nerves can be harder to hide than explosives.

Had there been an Israeli border guard back on the hill outside DAS, Dave would have been zip-tied or shot well before check-in. He kept whistling fragments of song, only for it to stop as his mouth dried up. Components shook and slipped from his sweaty hands as he worked. Finally, the last leg of the tripod clacked into place. Dave smiled at his handiwork. He rubbed a hand across his face, smearing the cheap camouflage paint. The emptied contents of his bags were now carefully arranged and mostly assembled.

This was it. Time to be a great man of history. He tried to think of all the great things that were going to happen. But the only thing that was in his mind was how badly he needed a piss. Again.

He'd read about how the snipers in the army would do that in situ. Just piss wherever they sat, so they didn't miss their shot.

Dave turned around and slid off the boulder to relieve himself against a tree.

'Almost there,' he said, doing up his fly. 'Almost there.'

He paused, leaned forward against the tree, and vomited.

* * *

Inside DAS the auditorium fell silent as the DG arrived at the lectern. He took control of the room, looking around in unembarrassed silence for a few seconds. The flags from Andrew's first day were still onstage, framing the DG as he regarded the audience. Abruptly, he broke with whatever game he was playing, smiled and began speaking. After the initial welcomes and acknowledgement of country, he got into the main event.

'We are here today,' he announced, 'to observe the amazing work done demonstrating the future of network-fused, information collection and disruption operations.'

People in the audience mentally playing 'bullshit bingo' tagged 'network-fused'.

'I welcome Roman Vorton, CEO of CMND and our partner for the last year in Information Operations and Effects. With his assistance, we have developed technologies in a public–private partnership that had the best of both worlds: the access and focus of government combined with the innovation and speed of the private sector.'

The audience took that line well, with only minor cynical snickering.

Roman took over the lectern, getting a handshake and a pat on the back from the DG. Smiling, he held up a hand to dim the applause.

'Thank you very much,' he said.

The white screen behind him lit up with the introductory slide. It was all shining computers, a suitably diverse groups of people working hard and blue beams connecting them.

'Before I begin, I would like to add that I welcome questions at any time. I'm not here to just talk at you. I'm not in the military anymore.'

A few minor laughs carried across the auditorium.

'We live in a challenging, complex and networked world,' he continued. The slide behind him changed, displaying social media, tech brands and infamous data leakers.

'Information operations, hacking, terrorist attacks, nation-state grey zone attacks – the list goes on. Trillions have been dedicated to detecting or preventing these activities – usually unsuccessfully.'

Roman paused and held up his index finger.

'But,' he said, 'this is an opportunity.'

Andrew shifted in his chair. He could hear the air conditioning rumbling away in the background. Despite that, he felt like he was in a sauna and his heartbeat was threatening to break his ribs.

From the next, seat Shanti gave him an encouraging smile. He gave a falsely cheerful grimace in response.

Back on stage, Roman became more animated.

'What if we adapted to all this data? What if we could, though a hybrid approach, shape self-directing threats against our adversaries?'

The presentation turned into a network map with the banner 'Operation Polarize Dunk'.

'This,' said Roman, 'is the future! With our algorithms and big data understanding, we can find potentials – people amongst our adversaries who can be uh, encouraged to commit actions against them. Our algorithms find people who meet the needed psychological profile. Thief? Saboteur? We understand a potential better than they understand themselves. With time, we can create and shape entire foreign protest movements or lone wolf threats.'

Roman took a moment to let this sink in. Low-level murmurs rolled through the crowd at a gentle boil.

'You give us the organisation or group you want to target, and we'll give you the potentials, perhaps already inside, and exactly how to motivate them.'

Roman snatched the microphone off the stand and walked around like a US television preacher.

'But how to motivate them?' he said. 'We developed a series of approaches that use both human and technical intelligence methods to recruit, retain and direct your potentials to the actions you want. We call them modules.'

Roman gestured and the slide behind him changed again. This time it was a series of pentagonal icons with different labels.

'Koil's missing!' someone in the crowd called out.

Roman paused for a second and scanned the crowd. When there was no follow-up, he ploughed on.

'These modules vary. Some rely on a mix of human interaction and cyber means. In our current concept, human intelligence experts would target them directly, or via intermediaries. But simultaneously, we make contact online and shrink their digital world to the content that reinforces the messages we want to send. We suggest chat rooms, create false online identities that pull them into other areas. They see the videos we want them to see. While all this is happening, they may meet new people online – people who reinforce this message as well.'

The crowd was now murmuring in low head-bent ways as people compared notes.

'In short,' said Roman, 'by targeting individuals, we can make the enemy attack itself.'

'What kind of enemies?' called out a voice in the crowd.

'All kinds,' responded Roman. 'We can target terrorist

groups, corporate companies, online networks, sects, ideological movements, political parties – you name it!'

'Intelligence agencies?'

Roman squinted under the stage lights as he peered into the crowd.

'Of course,' he said.

'Like this one?'

A murmur rumbled around the room. Chairs and necks creaked as people twisted around to look for the voice in the crowd.

There was a brief screech of tortured sound equipment as Intro-bot turned the Q&A mic on.

'Spontaneous questions are permitted,' said Intro-bot sourly. 'But please raise your hand, wait to be acknowledged, and state your name and title.'

'Andrew Stanton, intelligence analyst,' said Andrew, standing up. His arm stayed by his side.

DAS had lacked the dramatic foresight to invest in a roving spotlight, but a quick-thinking soul by the switch raised the house lights. Up on stage, Roman's expression stayed neutral as his body stiffened up.

'And?' said Roman, his eyes glittering with menace.

'What about intelligence agencies? Can you target them the same way?'

'But of course!' Roman said. 'We'd need to know who to target, but that would be a long-term goal of the program, but we still require the viability of live tests.'

'It's already been done once already,' said Andrew.

'Are there any other questions?' said Roman, looking away from Andrew.

'Lisa Chapman was recruited into DAS and directed to steal information through these methods,' said Andrew loudly.

The murmuring was much louder this time. It morphed into a muttering, just shy of a clamouring.

'Okay,' said Roman finally. 'What makes you think that?'

'We found her,' said Andrew. 'Her own testimony outlines how she was recruited and manipulated to attack DAS. She thought she was an idealist, but she was just a pawn. We'll release our investigation soon.'

Roman glared at Andrew. The murmuring boiled over into full-blown chatter. The auditorium buzzed like an audience at a magic show who'd been asked to look under their seat.

'I'm not going to comment on an ongoing matter,' said Roman. 'But if anything, it proves the need for CMND expertise to detect these threats.'

Andrew bent down and spoke to Shanti. They both got up and headed out of the auditorium.

'Now that concludes my part of the presentation,' said Roman, as he watched them hurry out of the room. A visibly confused Intro-bot, who knew this was not part of the schedule, hurried out to him. They had an urgent in-ear chat while Roman covered the microphone with his hand. Then Roman marched off-stage and Intro-bot took the microphone.

'Thank you, everyone,' he said. 'There are a few matters Roman has to attend to, but now we have a separate presentation from CMND on their successes in working with DAS.'

Intro-bot waved on the next speaker and clapped in perfect 4/4 time to get the crowd started. Michael, Roman's ever-reliable fill-in, sashayed up on stage like a salsa dancer on ice. Slicking back his hair to show how lush it was, he launched into the pitch script he always had ready.

'Good morning, everyone!' he said to the animated crowd. 'I hope you're as excited as I am!'

* * *

Outside in the corridor, Andrew and Shanti flinched as the

auditorium door flew open and slapped against the wall as Roman came out.

He stormed up to the pair with fire in his eyes. It was probably the last impression a number of his enemies got. His normally restrained fringe lost its footing and dangled in front of his face, giving him a deranged look.

'Just what the fuck do you think you're playing at?' he snarled.

Andrew cleared his throat to keep the squeak out of his voice.

'Took your advice,' said Andrew. 'We're taking a risk.'

'That's right,' said Shanti. 'We know you have something planned and we're here to stop it.'

Roman was no fool. Keeping his eyes on them, he stretched his neck, tilting his head, first one way, then the other. The crack it made seemed louder than the door impact had. The fire in his eyes focused to welding torch intensity.

He swept the area with his careful gaze. They were alone.

'You really don't know, do you?' he said, softly this time. 'Because you morons can't stop anything.'

'We know you have some of your terrorists – sorry, potentials – whipped up into a frenzy,' said Andrew.

'Just like the protest,' Shanti added icily.

Roman smiled at her, leaning in.

'Oh no,' he said. 'Nothing like that at all.'

Shanti leaned back. His expression chilled her to her core.

Roman's smile broadened. He knew they were alone and that recording devices were forbidden inside these walls. He reached over and patted Andrew on the shoulder, who took this like an awkward child at a family gathering. That is, until Roman's grip shifted, hooking his long fingers over the back of Andrew's shoulder and driving a .50 calibre thumb into the front.

Shanti gasped and covered her mouth as Andrew squealed with surprise and pain.

Roman moved in towithin a few centimetres of Andrew's face, studying his pained rictus with quiet interest.

'Even if,' he said with lawyerly composure, 'there were some idiots planning to attack DAS, they'd have a fail-safe.'

Andrew grimaced. The pain in his shoulder was excruciating. This reminded him of school, when bullies were pretending to be friends. The way they'd smile for distant teachers as their fingers ground into your bones, which was exactly what Roman was doing now.

'Any attempts to stop it, any overt attention, would only kick it into action,' said Roman.

'I know we can't,' gasped Andrew. 'We hoped you could. So, we changed the attack time.'

Roman's glare was replaced with shock as he released the Andrew's shoulder and stepped back.

'Changed? How? To when?' he growled.

Andrew rubbed some feeling back into his shoulder, but before he could reply the door burst open again.

This time, it was the DG who marched up. A guard pulled the door closed, staying on the other side.

The DG came down on them like a SWAT team. He was ex-Special Air Service and rumoured to have a past so heavily redacted with black-op that if you picked up his file you'd be washing black off your hands for days.

'What's going on here?' he said, pointing a trigger finger at Andrew.

'Sir,' said Andrew before Roman could stop him, 'this man and his company ran a long-term experiment on how to break our security and manipulate people into committing acts of theft, sabotage and murder. They're behind the insider threat Lisa Chapman, and engineered the cyber attack.'

Shanti, remembering the predictive element, added, 'And

we assess a violent attack on DAS is imminent. We don't know exactly what, but it will likely result in a large number of casualties. This is a proof of concept – how to home-grow threats in anyone's backyard.'

Roman whipped around to her with a snarl on his face. He was stopped by the DG's gnarled and immovable hand.

'Hold!' he said in a parade ground bark before saying more softly, 'What do you have to say to this?'

Roman's eye twitched, but years of training kicked in and he stayed put. 'Utter lies,' he growled. 'I don't know where they got the idea, but it's completely untrue. I'll be taking this up with the Minister.'

'What's this about an imminent attack?' said the DG, turning to Shanti and Andrew. 'Give me your information so we can stop it.'

'We can't stop it,' said Shanti. 'We don't know who they are.'

'But Roman does,' said Andrew. 'He can stop it. Or make contact and cancel it somehow. Code word, maybe? There'll be a way.'

Roman didn't flinch under the DG's gaze. His tight-lipped smile reminded Andrew of their last shoulder-grinding adventure together.

'Director-General,' said Roman, 'I don't know what they're talking about. I want these two sacked or arrested immediately.'

'This has gone far enough,' said the DG. 'I want you all—'

'Today,' said Andrew, uncharacteristically loud enough to drown everyone out.

'What?' snapped the DG.

'The attack is today. Any minute now.'

'What?' said Roman and the DG together.

'We got Lisa to reach out to a few activist groups,' said Andrew. 'With her credentials as the DAS leaker, they were only to happy to ask around. She couldn't find out who the attackers were, but she could warn them they were about to be arrested. People online passed on the message. Everyone knows someone who knows someone.'

Andrew looked directly at Roman.

'We couldn't stop the attack,' he said. 'But a fail-safe is just what someone like you would do. We thought any overt action to stop it would immediately trigger it. So, we triggered it for when you were in the building too. To motivate you to give the cancellation code. You were going to wait until CMND had packed up and left. Instead, you're risking your life with us now.'

There was silence for several seconds as everyone digested this disturbing bit of news.

'They're lying,' said Roman to the DG. 'Even if someone attacked, this place is a fortress. I have every confidence an attacker wouldn't make it inside alive.'

'He's right,' said Andrew.

'That's why we thought it had to be something different,' continued Shanti. 'His plan is to get everyone outside.

At that moment, a deafening whooping crackled out of the speaker system.

'Emergency! Emergency! The fire alarm has been activated! Please make your way to the nearest exit! Emergency!'

'Don't worry,' said Andrew amidst the alarms. 'There's nothing to fear out there. Just ask Roman. Should we all head out?'

* * *

Outside, the fire alarm wails carried across the tree-covered hills to Dave. He shifted and adjusted the tripod. Peering through the sight, he saw the building sparkle with exterior alarm lights. Just like Koil had said.

Not long now until they came out.

* * *

The door to the auditorium burst open again, only this time the whole crowd surged out. The wave of humanity dumped the guard previously on the door in front of them.

'Sir,' he said to the DG as people swarmed around them, 'we've got to evacuate.'

The DG leaned in and whispered something back. The guard nodded and barged his way back through the departing crowd. People parted as though the DG was Moses, then closed again for Andrew. Elbows, shoulders, cologne, perfume and BO assaulted him as they swarmed by.

The DG rounded on Roman. 'Well?' he said. 'Are my people in danger?'

Roman didn't flinch.

'We'll be fine,' he replied. 'These accusations are ridiculous.'

'Outside then,' said the DG. 'All of us, but you first Roman.'

'Where's Shanti?' said Andrew, looking around. She was nowhere to be found.

* * *

DAS HQ emptied like a kicked ant's nest. People streamed out to the marked-out assembly areas. Once outside, though, everyone lounged around in the sun and leaned on the chain-link fence that stopped them going any further. DAS had learned from its experience with Lisa. There was a green space between the building and the new fencing. If there was a serious threat to personnel, guards in the control room could hit the master release and open the main gates. Until then, evacuees, and any potential data thieves, would be kept inside the fence line, potentially safe from fire, until everything could be accounted for.

The DG marched off to corral and scare an update out of the senior executive. This left Andrew and Roman alone together.

The sun beat down from directly above. A line of sweat rolled down Andrew's neck. Roman was staring at him, looking like a cover shot from Corporate Psychopaths Monthly. Everything about him still seemed cool somehow. His suit probably came with air conditioning. But his stare was the coldest part overall. Andrew imagined the sweat freezing on his neck and the grass around him curling with frost. Having recovered from his initial temper tantrum, he had now gone as far as possible in the opposite direction.

'So,' said Andrew, trying to keep the shake out of his voice. 'Still prepared to sacrifice your life?'

'You little prick,' said Roman. 'You don't know what you're talking about.'

He waved an arm at the surrounding scene. A few people had even kicked off their shoes and were enjoying the sun.

'See? Nothing. Now let's go.'

'Just a moment,' someone interrupted.

It was Angela. She appeared out of nowhere with the DG and several guards. These weren't the jaded customer service sort Andrew was used to seeing at the front gate. Not by a long shot – which they'd no doubt hit with pinpoint accuracy. These guards didn't search bag – they put them over your head before you were bundled into a van and never seen again.

'Well?' said the DG.

'We're checking the area. No chatter we're aware of.'

Andrew's eyes bulged and guilt flooded his face. 'What are you doing here?' he asked.

'We all have our sources,' said Angela. 'Remember what I

said about angels? You better hope you're on the side of good here.'

* * *

Back on the hill, Dave focused all his attention through the sight. He could see the crowd now, down to their lanyards if he zoomed in enough. They were all milling about the fence, as if that offered any real protection from what was coming.

Any second now.

His heart hammered away, despite his attempts to breathe slowly. It was bloody hot in the ghillie suit, lying on the rock like a moss explosion. But at least he was concealed. Slowly, he reached out with his trigger finger.

And here we go …

His finger stopped moving. In the heat of the day, something cold and metallic pressed into his neck. Even if it's never happened to you before, there's something universally recognisable about a gun barrel.

'Don't move, you fucking camper,' whispered the soldier behind him.

* * *

Angela held her hand up to her earpiece and listened. After a few seconds, she nodded and turned to the DG.

'The attacker has been neutralised.'

Roman visibly relaxed. Andrew tensed up.

'Neutralised?' he said incredulously. 'The actual attack? Why say anything? This was my one chance to get Roman to confess!'

Roman smiled and walked a few steps away, roughly shouldering Andrew aside.

'It was our one chance to save lives,' said Angela. 'Your, ah, allegations will be discussed later.' She turned back to the DG. 'We've got the shooter. Single white male on the hill overlooking us.'

Roman's smile dropped. He glanced at the fence.

'Shooter?' he said, his voice full of confusion, not surprise.

* * *

'Say again, Bravo Team,' said the young corporal, running communications in the control room.

'Target secured, but no weaponry on-site,' the soldier repeated. Below him, Dave squirmed in his zip ties. He had a dusty size ten boot print on his face. This wasn't the action he'd been hoping for.

'Perving on everyone with a scope,' reported the solider, 'but no gun. Got some sort of video rig going.'

Dave 'mmmffd!' as hard as he could beneath the boot, but it was clear no one was going to turn the camera on for him.

* * *

'Hang on,' said Angela, handheld to the earpiece. 'The guy they got was unarmed. No weapons, but a bunch of camera equipment.'

Andrew's mind went into overdrive. A solitary guy. Up on a hill. With camera equipment. Why did they need to film something from far away? Like some YouTube 'best of' video, he saw a collage of violent imagery in his mind. Buildings ripped apart by sudden explosions to the background of stirring music. Or an armoured vehicle driving over a mine, unaware a camera was set up to capture the ambush. Terrorists and Hollywood both knew people love an explosion they're not part of. Recording was a vital part of any major attack; production values were as important as execution. That's modern terrorism.

It's not just about the kills. It's also about the views – the first thing Roman asked about after Liam died.

'It's a bombing!' Andrew cried out. Everyone around him went quiet. 'Don't you see? That isn't the attacker – just the camera guy! This isn't just a proof of concept – it's a promotional video.'

'I've had enough,' said Roman, starting to walk away. The DG held up a hand and two guards materialised in his way.

'You're not going anywhere,' he said.

'This is ridiculous!' Roman snarled.

'We still don't know what the threat is inside the building. The alarms are still on.'

Andrew pointed a finger through the fence to the roads outside.

'What's that?' he said.

The fence line they were standing at had one road that ran alongside. It led back down to an intersection that was quiet this time of morning. A dirty white, snub-nosed minivan came into view and stopped dead in the middle of the road, engine running. It triggered a memory from an extremist magazine. Photos of how to make and pack a tonne of ammonium nitrate–based explosives and roofing nails into a space normally filled with Amazon deliveries.

'Roman!' shouted Andrew. 'What's the cancel signal? How do we stop it?'

But Roman wasn't listening. He stared down the road like a dragon had appeared.

'No …' he murmured.

Andrew looked around. The DG, Angela ,and their guards had made a brisk withdrawal to the edge of the building, away from the fence.

'This fence is reinforced, right?' said Andrew. 'You can't drive a car through?'

Roman glared at Andrew.

'No,' he said. 'But you can blow up next to it, idiot! Does wire stop shock waves and shrapnel? You've killed us all, asshole!' He was shouting like a US drill sergeant cussing out a private who'd dropped a grenade.

'Then tell me how to cancel it!' Andrew yelled back, finding anger a useful analogue for bravery.

Down the road, the van's engine went from idling to full grunt, dropping into gear and leaping away as though stung. The engine roared as it struggled to raise speed. Either the van was underpowered or carrying something heavy.

'If I'm right,' said Andrew, 'this is a suicide bomber that you organised, come to attack a day early. Run inside and show them you know the alarm is fake or stay out here and face your real attackers. Some plan.'

'Lisa didn't go to plan and I'm still here,' said Roman. 'I'll survive this too.'

People were pointing and began backing away from the fence as it roared up the road. The sound of the engine got louder in Andrew's ears.

'Willing to risk your life?' asked Andrew.

Roman's bottom lip twitched as he made some internal calculation.

'I'm not sure—' began Andrew. But Roman grabbed him by the collar and shoulder and threw a knee into his leg. Andrew went to the ground as though gravity had tripled. Through the searing pain, he heard Roman above him.

'Stay here and die, you little prick,' he hissed. 'I've succeeded. I can raise an army remotely and that's a concept that sells. It will be my word against what's left of you.'

Andrew groaned and rolled over. He watched Roman power through the crowd and into the building. One of the guards took an elbow to the face trying to intercept him. Talia and Michael, waiting by the fire door, possibly out of self-preservation, smacked it open and ran in ahead of their boss. It happened so fast, Andrew was still crumpling to the ground as Roman slammed the fire door closed behind him.

Andrew gasped and rolled onto his back. Tears ran down his face. The smell of recently cut grass and soil filled his nose. He sat up with a partially suppressed wail.

'Not going for cover?' said Shanti, suddenly alongside him.

'Shanti?' said Andrew. She sat down in a characteristically careful way and smoothed out her skirt.

The van reached the end of the road and jumped the kerb in a crunch of protesting suspension. Tyres tore up the grass as it went into a turf-hurling power slide, stopping just short of the chain-link fence.

Andrew blinked and wiped his eyes, looking at the now inert vehicle. The engine cut off and Peter got out. He gave them all a wave.

Shanti nodded, as if this was the most normal thing in the world.

'Well?' called Peter.

'Congrats!' said Shanti. 'We got him.'

THIRTY-FIVE

PEOPLE FLOODED BACK INTO DAS WITH THE ALL CLEAR sounding over the PA. Excited chatter filled the hallways. Guards waved arms, directing people into the auditorium to be briefed on the 'attack drill' they just took part in.

Not all, though. Andrew and Shanti were scooped up and taken upstairs to the DG's office. Top level, home of the executive branch – where Andrew had once imagined a future office.

They passed through a waiting area, complete with flowering pot plants and safely abstract or landscape-style corporate art. The office itself also hinted at tasteful power – executive lush done right. There was a view of the lake, leather furniture and various paperweight-style gifts of appreciation and commemoration, etc. 'With gratitude from GCHQ', 'Greetings from the Central Intelligence Agency' and 'Warm regards from the Ministry of State Security – China'. That last one had been so extensively X-rayed, it almost glowed.

The DG sat behind a desk you could have a war on. He pressed some unseen button, there was a creaking mechanical noise, and the lake view slowly receded behind descending metal shutters. Andrew cocked his head slightly as he felt something in his ears. A sensation, perhaps a noise just beyond human hearing. Probably one of many electronic countermeasures to prevent someone listening to these conversations.

The DG waited in pointed silence until the shutters finished lowering before beginning.

'There will be enquiries out of all this,' he said. 'Questions will be asked.'

Angela held up a hand.

'Excuse me, sir,' she said. 'Before we continue, I have to deal with some leftover tech from the operation.'

She turned to Andrew and held out her hand.

He gasped as he remembered and reached into his top pocket, producing a mobile phone.

The DG stared at the forbidden device as if it was pornography laid out before the pope. Andrew started to wonder if carrying forbidden tech into the DG's office was a bigger faux pas than helping Lisa out of the building.

Angela snatched it out of his hand and dropped it into a carry bag lined with signal-blocking mesh. She then put *that* in another lockbox.

Andrew gave a cartoonish gulp and Shanti paled.

'Any other recording devices?' asked the DG icily.

'No, sir,' said Angela. 'This ... violation was necessary. Our target had a weak spot. He believed he could speak freely within DAS because of the recording device ban. This is our evidence.'

'Of what?' said the DG. 'I need an immediate debrief.'

Angela cleared her throat. 'DAS was attacked by Roman Vorton and his company CMND, a US business we partnered with in Information Operations. They used their position and expertise to conduct insider operations against us – including data theft, network sabotage and a planned suicide bomber assault on DAS HQ. They were also conducting influence and recruitment operations of DAS staff.'

The DG's eyes narrowed, but he gave nothing away.

'CMND came to DAS to develop new information warfare capabilities. They have extensive expertise in data science, AI, and psychological profiling, with previous successes in identifying radicalised threats online. They requested access to DAS HQ, and our data, in order to conduct a trial that would help develop next-generation tools and AI. The Minister agreed, as DAS was to be the first to benefit from any discoveries, plus CMND were doing it at no cost to the government.'

Andrew stirred as he struggled to remember something. He must have looked lost because Peter gave him a warning nudge.

'This trial,' said Angela,' was dubbed Operation Polarize Dunk, in line with standard non-referential naming protocols.'

Now Peter was the one who stirred, but Andrew knew better than to nudge him back.

'This operation,' said Angela, 'had two stages. First was finding people, ordinary people, through big data manipulation, who could be … easily influenced to infiltrate or commit disruptive acts against chosen organisations. This included complex AI-powered data analysis and profiling to build a complete psychological profile of likely candidates.'

'They used government data for this?' the DG asked.

'Not much,' said Angela. 'Mostly they bought it elsewhere.'

The DG raised an eyebrow.

'Governments have extensive data on who people are as part of a group,' Angela explained, 'but not as an individual. Someone's political views, food preferences, socio-economic status and other drivers are found in their online footprint. As Roman himself said, most browsers know more about the populace than DAS does. His company bought and scraped this data, then weaponised it.'

In Andrew's mind, he visualised Roman as a Rumpelstilt-skin figure, only this one spun the straw of data into uranium, not gold.

Satisfied there were no further questions, Angela continued. 'The second part was … influencing these individuals. Guiding them by shaping their online content, befriending them and communicating with them. Running them as agents, basically, until they achieved the desired end.'

The DG held up a hand. 'I know the pitch. We partnered with them for a proof of concept to identify individuals with access to foreign or domestic threats that could be convinced to work with us. How does this relate?'

Po-tay-to, po-tah-to, thought Andrew.

'The op was a lie,' he said, unthinkingly. 'Roman manipu-lated us.'

Andrew's stomach knotted up as he found himself the subject of the room's combined stare. The vacuum of silence dragged more words out of him.

'The proof of concept was a smokescreen. The data Roman was after was *us*. He was profiling and analysing a whole intelli-gence agency, watching threats unfold in real time and seeing the reactions. Learning how we think and act. You can't buy that data. He already knew how to radicalise or manipulate people in theory, but needed a live test with a real target if it was ever to be profitable and repeatable. After he proved it with DAS, he could sell it in the big markets. Maybe even Russia? China? He told us what he was doing the whole time. We just didn't see he was doing it to us.' A memory flared as he remem-bered what had eluded him before. 'No cost to the govern-ment, right? When the service is free, you are the product. That's how the online world works.'

The DG stared fixedly at Andrew, deploying one of his famed aggressive silences. Through whatever non-verbal command, Angela stayed silent too.

'It was an experiment, like he claimed,' said Andrew, hurling words into the void. 'Only we were a guinea pig who thought it was a scientist.'

Angela winced, and Peter quietly cleared his throat as the DG stiffened.

'Roman triggered the cyber attack when we got close,' said Shanti, attempting to break the tension. 'To destroy the evidence I found, then frame Andrew, because they didn't have another potential ready to take the blame. He was probably waiting to pass that weapon to the next Lisa he smuggled into the building.'

Andrew reddened at Lisa's name. Shanti was the friend bringing up the humiliating ex you were desperately trying to forget.

'What of the bomb threat?' asked the DG, unexpectedly coming to Andrew's aid.

Angela stepped in again, over Andrew and Shanti's Scooby-Doo explanations.

'Our investigation discovered three individuals who'd been kept off the DAS radar by Roman. While active in multiple forums, they were chiefly communicating in a small chat room run by Roman's people. They were highly agitated, anti-government, and believed they were going to be found and violently executed, along with their families, as part of a DAS-led coup within the week. They had a grand and suicidal plan thanks to the explosives expertise of the fourth member.'

'Fourth?' said the DG.

Angela shook her head. 'No such person,' she said. 'CMND was passing them the weapons needed.'

'Purpose,' murmured Peter.

'The attack was a proof of concept and an advertisement,' said Shanti. 'If they achieved all that here, perfected the research algorithms, psychological profiles and whatever else they have, they could sell it anywhere. Insider threats, external attackers, all made to order.'

The DG looked up for a moment, deep in thought. His frown was so deep it probably went to the bone. The clock on the wall boomed out the passing seconds.

'Angela,' said the DG, refocusing, 'how did you find them?'

'Lisa Chapman,' she said. 'She fell out with her handlers when she realised her group was a fake. From there, we developed leads in our internal investigation.'

The DG raised a questioning eyebrow.

'She made contact with me, sir,' piped up Andrew, taking the hint. 'She remembered me from, uh … Anyway, she contacted me with this information and tried to blackmail me to help her.'

'Did you report this?' asked the DG. Andrew squirmed in his seat and scratched the back of his head.

'Eventually,' said Angela, 'within enough time to act and get Lisa's help.'

'Help?' said the DG.

Angela looked uneasy. 'With Andrew facilitating contact, we came to a mutual arrangement. I'll brief you later.'

The DG nodded his assent.

'Her knowledge and position meant she got access that would have taken us months to cultivate,' said Angela. 'This was helped by releasing data samples of what she stole – not the real thing, obviously. We supplied her with convincing but fake intelligence reports to gain interest. Nothing that would embarrass us or betray a vital capability. She reached out to a few anti-government networks we selected and was eventually passed to one of the real members, who bent their own rules for her. People love celebrity. Lisa was warned to be ready in a few days, told it would be big, but that's all she could get.'

The DG pointed a warning finger. 'Do we have the attackers?'

Angela nodded. 'Lisa's communications left enough digital breadcrumbs to find the main players. IT took some time, but special operations groups did hard entry on two locations during the fake DAS attack. We got all three alive, but they're fanatics. It may be a while before anyone talks. In any case, we probably know more than they do.'

Andrew felt a shiver run down his spine. It had been bad enough in the fake attack. He was glad someone else had to go charging into these people's houses.

'If I may,' said Peter, chiming in. 'Back in DAS, we identified the most likely avenue of attack, targets, and methodology. CMND were pulling out more than their people. Computers, servers, back-ups – everything was being moved to another location. That indicated they expected either severe damage or being unable to access the building for some time. Biological agents are too unreliable, same with chemical. You're more likely to make harmless smoke than anything else. Plus, the final factor made a car bomb most likely.'

'Final factor?' said the DG.

'If this was a trial *and* advertisement,' said Peter, 'it had to be bold, dramatic and able to capture global attention.'

'So, how did you know?' said the DG.

'We didn't,' said Andrew. 'It was an assessment.'

Angela glared at Andrew, who obediently shut up.

'We developed a scenario based on all the information we had to hand,' she said smoothly. 'This was a highly unconventional situation and team, but they performed well for an excellent result.'

The DG considered this and stared at the ceiling. After a brief communion, he looked down again.

'Except for our official enquiries, none of you are to mention any of this. To anyone,' he emphasised. 'Andrew, pending review of your involvement with Lisa Chapman, consider yourself on leave. We'll make a decision about you shortly.'

Andrew felt his stomach bottom out, but said nothing.

'Come on,' said Shanti, taking the hint to leave.

'Yeah,' chimed in Peter, 'we'll have to escort you out.'

* * *

Three days later

Shanti paced back and forth in the hallway. Working in a high-security building with no personal phone made the addiction bite hard. Especially when you were trying to kill time and take your mind off something. The only thing worse was when you thought you really did have your phone on you. That made you panic because it was an immediate black mark on your record. Plus, losing your phone for who knows how long while security takes it away and electronically strip searches it to make sure you didn't steal or record anything – the whole experience is an anxiety-inducing loop around a phone that may or may not be present.

Shanti sat down on a leather couch but stood up again seconds later and continue pacing. She stopped and stared at the frosted glass door. From inside, she heard the clang of the metal door that was just inside Internal Security's waiting area, beyond the glass.

Andrew emerged from the door like the world's saddest game show contestant. However, he managed a smile for Shanti.

She smiled back. 'Hi,' she said. 'Still got a job?'

Andrew shrugged. 'They're not firing me,' he said at last.

'That's great!' said Shanti.

'But I'm not going to be doing anything on your level,' said Andrew. 'Not for a bit, anyway.'

'Where are you going?' she asked.

'Vetting,' replied Andrew. As Shanti's expression registered shock and confusion, he added, 'Yeah, I think it's someone's idea of a joke too. Angela said at least this time I'd know what to look for.'

Shanti stayed quiet at that. Vetting was where careers went to die. Or at least endure a lengthy hibernation. Nothing cool or attention-grabbing there. The only thing duller than filling out forms was reading them.

'At least I'm still an analyst,' said Andrew. 'I'm okay with that. I'll be back up at your level in no time.'

They walked in silence for a while.

'You know,' said Andrew, 'in some ways, this was worth it. Getting to see how people get manipulated, what it's like to be under attack, not knowing who to trust – all that stuff. Good to remember when we're doing things from the safety of this building.'

Shanti nodded. 'That's a good attitude,' she said.

'Thanks,' he replied. 'But what about you?'

'I'm being moved into a new team,' she said. 'It looks really exciting. Can't go into it much, they're still setting it up. But Angela requested me.'

'Congratulations,' said Andrew, surprised he meant it.

'Thanks,' Shanti, 'Now how about a coffee? I don't have to head straight back.'

'Sure thing,' said Andrew.

The pair peeled off towards the cafe. The reassuring background chatter and clinking plates grew louder as they got away from the quiet of Internal Security. They walked with the silence of two people preparing their own awkward news.

'So ...' said Andrew eventually. 'How long were you spying on me?'

Shanti stood in front of Andrew to stop him, hands raised.

'Wow,' she said. 'Drama much?'

Andrew looked back at her with tired resignation, but not anger.

'You seemed to know a lot about Lisa. Especially for someone who doesn't get involved with Internal Security,' said Andrew. 'Also, it was something Angela said: we all have our sources.'

Shanti lowered her hands.

'Angela said you'd find out now,' she said. 'But it wasn't like that. When you let Lisa go, I was in trouble with security, like I told you. Angela wanted to make sure nothing else happened. She told me to keep an eye on you and let her know what was going on. She didn't know how far it would go.'

Andrew paused. In the context of betrayal, it seemed minor compared to what he'd done.

'Come on,' said Shanti. 'It worked out in the end. Without me having a direct line to Angela, she never would have helped us. It was the only way to get her back from whatever secure site they had her in. James would have stopped you or Peter passing anything on – he was in Roman's pocket. Our maniac with the shotgun? That story never reached Angela, despite your report. James buried it. It's how she knew she had a leak in her office. Heard he's on "administrative leave" as well.'

Andrew's surprise was written all over his face, making Shanti smile again.

'Fair enough,' he managed. 'But it still would have been nice of you and Peter to tell me the van was fake.'

'We had to sell it to Roman,' said Shanti. 'We didn't actually expect you to stand there. That was very brave.'

Andrew cleared his throat, feeling his cheeks flush. In the distance he could hear the watery chortles and hissing of the coffee machine. It smelled like they were still doing hot food too.

'Come on,' he stammered. 'Let's get that coffee.'

They walked in silence the rest of the way. Once seated, though, Shanti couldn't hold it in any longer.

'Where's Lisa?' she whispered, leaning in.

Andrew shrugged. 'No one will say. She made a deal, I know that much. I spoke to Lisa a few times in the game, convinced her to help out and passed her the fake intel reports. After that, Angela wanted to deal with her directly. I guess the rest is up to them.'

'Do you think you'll see her again?' asked Shanti.

Andrew grinned.

'If I do, I won't point out the exit.'

* * *

Meanwhile, inside Angela's office, Peter brushed a hibiscus branch aside and tapped a large box on the table that was encased with wire mesh.

'So that's it?' he asked.

'That's Operation Polarize Dunk,' said Angela. 'All the core data. Roman gave it up.'

'We all make our moves,' said Peter. 'He couldn't resist an anagram, could he? Polarize Dunk? From *polezni durak* – Russian spy phrase for "useful idiot". Typically, someone easily manipulated or useful for blindly supporting your plans. I only just got that. We intel folk can't help ourselves. Always have to give a hint.'

Angela waved this off.

'In the short term, we can use this to make sure our house is in order. All his moles and potentials are being purged.' she said.

'And in the long run?' asked Peter.

'Are you ready to play with the big boys again?' said Angela. 'We've got lots on. Not to mention working up a few trial runs of these methods against some long-running targets overseas.

Think of what you could do with more than a junior analyst and a grad behind you.'

Peter nodded thoughtfully, leaning back in his chair.

'This was an attack right under our noses,' he said, after a moment's pause. 'It dodged all our security measures, turned us against ourselves and almost cost hundreds of lives.'

'Yes,' said Angela brusquely. 'That's why we're making sure it won't go to waste.'

Thirty-Six

A few days later, in the Parliamentary Triangle, Canberra's sanitised space for Parliament House and other rogues of state, there was a memorial for Liam outside the cafe where he died. It had rained that morning but cleared up just in time for the VIPs to arrive. Something that, no doubt, some adviser somewhere was currently taking the credit for. But as the clouds wandered off over the mountains, an insolent wind stayed behind to ruffle hair and howl during speeches. The organisers had erected a speaker's podium, complete with a bouquet of microphones, next to a tactfully refreshed pile of flower wreaths marking the spot. Not that anyone had really known Liam well, but it was what you did. The assembled media pack took the front row as various journalists looked solemnly to camera. Scattered around the place, other journalists and some wannabes did the same thing with selfie sticks or just by hand for that genuine look.

All in all, it was an over-orchestrated and slightly pompous affair. Something Liam may have appreciated. The Prime Minister was there, along with the Director-General of DAS – who didn't speak – and scores of lesser political and journalistic guests – due to the proximity to Parliament House. It was like someone had kicked a very formal hive. One where the bees poured out and instead of stinging, explained how with proper funding and vigilance, such attacks would be defended against in future. Steely eyed police carrying machine guns and enough equipment to open a camping and restraints store wandered the edge of the crowd, occasionally muttering into radios.

The Prime Minister spoke at length about not caving into extremism, the brave work of the local police and the sad example of the shooter. The mainstream media were doing their best not to name him, lest they inflame his legend. Although they had little sway in the circles where he'd be praised. Publicly, he had been written off as a self-radicalised loner. Just a hate-filled extremist who'd snapped at the government and took it out on a young man with a bright future.

Some in the crowd knew better, like Andrew and Shanti. They weren't there in any official capacity but felt they should attend. Andrew was secretly grateful and guilty he didn't have to go to Liam's funeral, which had been designated family only. He couldn't face them, but still felt obliged to honour what the job cost sometimes.

Further out, wandering along the edge of the crowd, was another person who knew more – Lisa. She wore jeans, a black Hello Kitty t-shirt and an official press ID that someone had been careless enough to leave on the edge of their bag.

She left the memorial during the speeches and walked further down the road to a rose garden off to the side. There were several gardens in the Parliamentary Triangle, empty today, like most weekdays, but full of wedding ceremonies on weekends. Lisa sat down on a bench and tried to steady her breathing. No matter what internal exercise she tried, her heart kept buzzing. A beat that only increased as approaching footsteps crunched on the garden's gravel path. Lisa tried to ignore them and stared ahead until someone joined her on the other end of the bench.

'Good morning,' said Angela, 'nice to meet you at last. After our correspondence via Andrew.'

Lisa took Angela in for a moment, studying the person next to her as though racking her memory.

'Yeah,' said Lisa, 'Wasn't sure you'd show up.'

'Me? I'm nothing if not reliable. Threats and promises, I keep them all,' said Lisa.

Despite being nervous to the bone, Lisa thought this was funny and felt the hint of a smile form.

'Let's do it then,' said Lisa, pulling the USB stick out of her pocket.

Angela took it gently and waved her spare hand in the air. From another entrance, a burly-looking man entered the garden. He wore jeans and a large, loose-fitting jacket that could hide anything up to a shoulder-mounted missile launcher. Without a word, he came up and took the USB out Angela's hand.

Once he was safely out of earshot, Angela turned to Lisa with a worryingly bright expression.

'While they verify no copies were made, let me ask – what are you going to do now?' she said.

'Honestly? I'm still expecting to be in handcuffs or dead any second. Hard to plan past that,' said Lisa.

Angela smiled in a knowing way that often concerned her political rivals in DAS. 'Don't worry,' she said. 'Like I told you, both my threats and promises are kept. I promised you amnesty for your cooperation, plus return of Central with no copies made. If all conditions are met, you'll get what you want. And in all honesty, we don't want this in the courts.'

Lisa didn't like that last line. Killing her was just as effective as keeping it out of the courts. Never the less, she steeled herself.

'You promised amnesty *and* payment,' said Lisa pointedly. 'I've got to eat and you're probably not going to give me a reference.'

'Oh, you never know,' said Angela. 'Depends on the job.'

She reached into her handbag and produced a small phone, holding it out to Lisa.

'So, we can talk sometime,' she added.

After a moment's hesitation, Lisa took the phone from Angela and held it in her hand. Then, having made some internal decision, looked up and sent it spinning into a nearby rose bush. Bees took off in alarm and petals gently fell to the ground as the stalks bounced back and forth from the impact.

Lisa stared at Angela in defiance, but annoyingly, Angela smiled. Even worse, this time she looked genuinely amused.

'Fair enough,' she said and dug about in her handbag again.

'Take this,' she said, holding out a folded piece of paper. Her sunny expression briefly flashed something that warned a storm remained possible. 'It's another method of communicating that doesn't involve location tracking.'

Lisa took it, resisting the urge for any more gestures.

The burly man that was potentially concealing an armoury walked back in. He held an old backpack with both straps in one hand. Given his size, it was hard to guess if anything heavy was inside. A man like that would carry a bag of feathers or gold bars with the same ease.

'Good news,' said Angela, watching him approach. 'It looks like you've been honest with me as well. That's how you build trust.'

'You don't trust me,' said Lisa defiantly. 'You hate me like the rest of them, but you know what? I don't regret what I did.'

The man placed the backpack on the ground next to Angela, retrieved the phone from the rose bush, and left again in silence.

'Hate? Oh, come on,' said Angela like a playful aunt. 'We

assess in intelligence, we don't judge. You're practical, adaptive, and you appreciate life's complexities. That includes the importance of alliances.'

'Alliances?' said Lisa, all nervousness forgotten. 'I did this to fight the powerful, the ones who think they get away with everything.'

'Well, you've certainly come a long way from smoke bombs and corporate dinners,' said Angela.

Lisa's stomach did fresh somersaults as Angela's point hit home. Did she really know who she was and her past? Or was that a lucky guess?

But before she could ask, Angela stood up.

'It was good to meet you. Feel free to get in contact,' she said – as though Lisa was an old friend she'd run into and invited to brunch. 'You helped stop people who were prepared to kill hundreds. Not to mention their puppet masters, who were also so cruel to you. We're glad you decided to help us out.'

'Andrew was convincing,' she said. 'And a surprisingly sneaky person to work with. Tell him no hard feelings.'

Angela stood up and turned to Lisa.

'One last thing,' she said. 'We're still wrapping up Roman's networks. It's difficult, even though CMND has declared bankruptcy. In particular, I'm on the lookout for one of the koils – a man also known as Blake.'

Lisa stared at her, wide-eyed.

'I have a few leads,' continued Angela, 'but not enough people.'

She let the offer hang in the air. 'Well then,' Angela said at last, 'All the best in your future endeavours and I hope to hear from you.'

She smiled again, in a way that was vaguely unnerving, and walked away up the path. As she left the entrance with hedges on either side, the one-man army emerged and blocked the view of Angela, looking directly at Lisa. She stared back at him, feeling stuck to the bench with fresh fear as he put a hand in his jacket pocket. Lisa wondered what weapon would emerge before everything went black.

Instead, he put his other hand in the corresponding jacket pocket as well. After a couple of seconds, he gave her a professional nod and headed off in the same direction as Angela.

Once they were definitely out of sight, Lisa gently unzipped the bag and opened it away from her. After nothing detonated, she had a quick look inside, while being careful not to touch anything.

She smiled, deeply and broadly, for the first time in a long time. Shouldering the bag on her right side, she headed off to the garden exit on the opposite side of the garden. As she walked, she carefully slid the piece of paper into her pocket.

The End.

Acknowledgments

Firstly, I'd like to thank my family and friends for their support. I'm lucky in so many ways. I'd also like to thank all the industry professionals who contributed to this work. From a manuscript assessment that steered me to finishing, to the edits, structure and even the cover. I'm so glad I paid excellent people who know what they're doing to deliver a superior result. For all the emerging, self-published authors out there, please pay a professional where you can. You're investing in the industry you're a part of and they will do an amazing job.

Most of all, I'd like to thank you, the reader. I sincerely hope you enjoyed this book. A more organised author would have a website ready, but I'm not that prepared. However, I'd love to hear from you. Writing is an isolating business and any decent analyst knows the power of networks. If you'd like to reach out, I can be found at samuelollie.substack.com.